hacks and headlines

Rashme Sehgal started her career in the 1970s as a poet and short-story writer. She moved to journalism and went on to work for several leading newspapers, including *The Independent, The Telegraph* and *The Times of India.* Some landmark events she has covered during her journalistic career, spanning fifteen years, have been the exodus of the Kashmiri Pandits from the Valley, the destruction of the Babri Masjid in Ayodhya, the Kargil war, and more recently, the Taj corridor scam, thereby helping to save India's best-known monument.

She has published a book of poems, titled *A Home for Bhadrakali and Other Poems*. She has also translated a collection of short stories by Premchand.

Rashme Sehgal is married to film critic Anil Saari. She has three children and lives in New Delhi. *Hacks and Headlines* is her first novel.

OTHER INDIAINK TITLES :

Anjana Appachana	*Listening Now*
I. Allan Sealy	*The Everest Hotel*
I. Allan Sealy	*Trotternama*
Indrajit Hazra	*The Garden of Earthly Delights*
Manju Kapur	*A Married Woman*
Marina Budhos	*The Professor of Light*
Pankaj Mishra	*The Romantics*
Paro Anand	*I'm Not Butter Chicken*
Paro Anand	*Wingless*
Paro Anand	*No Guns at My Son's Funeral*
Ramchandra Gandhi	*Muniya's Light: A Narrative of Truth and Myth*
Ranjit Lal	*The Life & Times of Altu-Faltu*
Susan Visvanathan	*Something Barely Remembered*
Susan Visvanathan	*The Visiting Moon*

FORTHCOMING TITLES :

Kalpana Swaminathan	*The Page 3 Murders*
Boman Desai	*Servant, Master, Mistress*
Sharmistha Mohanty	*New Life*
C. P. Surendran	*An Iron Harvest*
Tom Alter	*The Longest Race*
Ranjit Lal	*The Small Tigers of Shergarh*

hacks and headlines

a novel

rashme sehgal

IN LOVING MEMORY OF MY FATHER
LT. COL MANGAL SEN SEHGAL AND MY
MOTHER PADMA SEHGAL

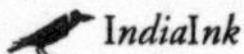

First published in 2005
I*ndia*I*nk*
An imprint of
Roli Books Pvt. Ltd.
M-75, G.K. II Market
New Delhi 110 048
Phones: ++91 (011) 2921 2271, 2921 2782
2921 0886, Fax: ++91 (011) 2921 7185
E-mail: roli@vsnl.com; Website: rolibooks.com
Also at
Varanasi, Bangalore, Jaipur

Cover design: Sneha Pamneja
Layout design: Narendra Shahi

ISBN: 81-86939-20-2

Typeset by AGaramound Roli Books Pvt. Ltd. and printed at Syndicate Binders, Noida - 201 305

one

It was four o'clock in the afternoon. Paro and Jano extricated themselves from the crowded tempo with growing trepidation. The tempo stand overlooked the Shamli police thana. From here, it was a brisk half-hour walk to their village. In the distance, spilling over a hillock, they could see the densely crowded hutments consisting largely of mud and brick houses. Smoke curled upwards from the rooftops, merging with the black kites making concentric circles in the sky.

Paro, her long hair pulled back in a tight braid, was dressed in a bright-green salwar kameez with a red, gota-lined dupatta thrown over her shoulders. Her red and green glass bangles came up to her elbows. The red sindoor stretching across the centre parting of her hair indicated her married status.

Unlike her partner, whose deep brown eyes and creased forehead signalled a growing anxiety, one look at the fields around her had transformed Paro's nervousness into a feeling of unconcealed joy. The air smelt pure, almost luxuriant. The trees, with their wide overturned skirts, were a blaze of green. As a child, she had spent long summer afternoons under the shade of these very mango trees as she and her brother, Jagdamba, took their motley assortment of goats, cows and buffaloes to graze along these grass-lined embankments of the swift-flowing Yamuna canal.

It was the month of June. The mangoes were back on the trees, swinging gaily against the background of a crystal-clear sky spread like a shining dome on all sides. It provided the perfect backdrop for noisy birds flitting through the trees with an exaggerated sense of importance. Heads of sugarcane grew in straight lines along the road. Paro had to restrain herself from dashing across the road and sinking her teeth into a ripe stalk.

Their decision to return to their village was a hasty one. Only the day before, Jano had spoken to his uncle, Sukhram, from a phone booth in Ambala. Sukhram had urged them to return, insisting that Jano's younger sister, an invalid for several years, had been clamouring to see her brother. The furore over their elopement, he assured them, was a thing of the past and even the gram panchayat no longer spoke of taking punitive action against them. Paro's uncle, Pappu Yadav, who had sworn revenge against Jano's family appeared to have cooled down and reconciled himself to their marriage.

Paro remained unconvinced by these urgings. She knew her uncle too well. True to his status as a family patriach, he neither forgave nor forgot. To reassure her, Jano insisted Paro talk directly to Sukhram. She had never used the instrument before in her life and held it upside down with the earpiece placed before her mouth. The phone booth owner, a shifty-eyed Sardar, spat out a blob of phlegm into the corner of his tiny cubicle and muttered, 'Bloody villagers! Don't even know how to hold a telephone properly!'

Taken aback by his rudeness, Paro handed the instrument back to Jano. Sukhram was bellowing at the top of his voice. She overheard him tell Jano. 'I swear on your father's head that not a hair on your heads will be harmed. Your chacha has also written a letter to you at your uncle's address in Ambala assuring you of a safe passage. How long can you keep moving around from one place to another? Tell Paro from all of us that her mother-in-law is keenly awaiting her return.'

Sukhram's words were enticing for the eighteen-year-old. Within a week of their running away, Jano's money had run out. He had first thought of pressing ahead to Delhi but then decided to stop at Ambala where his uncle ran a tailor shop. Not that he proved of great help though he did help them in locating a tiny flat on the town's outskirts for a rent of Rs 250 per month. Jano went through a succession of jobs till he finally landed one as an odd-job fellow at the local bania's shop for a salary of Rs 1000.

He had not bothered to contact anyone back home in Shamli. His family members were ostensibly in touch with his uncle, who came one evening and informed them about his sister's deteriorating health. Jano had nursed her from childhood, returning from school to carry her around the house, her polio-ridden legs hanging down his sides like a pair of limp branches. It was the memory of his sister that sealed the couple's decision to board the tempo to Shamli.

'I suppose everything will be all right?' Jano muttered as they finally reached the village. As they walked up the slight incline leading up to the primary school located in the middle of the village, Paro began to feel afraid. She covered her face with her dupatta in order not to draw attention to herself. Jano quickened his footsteps. He, too, would feel safe only once he was inside his father's house.

Suddenly a hand swooped down from behind to clutch his shirt and yanked Jano off his feet. Dangling like a marionette in the air, Jano tried to break free but found himself caught in an iron grip. He looked around and saw Kishan, Ramesh and Satvir holding on to him while Pappu Yadav rushed forward and caught hold of Paro dragging her to the centre of the village chaupal.

Her loud screams drew the attention of the menfolk in the village. They came running to see what the commotion was all about. Their wives and daughters, faces covered by multicoloured sari pallus, and spindly, ill-clad children followed on their heels. Soon a huge crowd formed a semicircle around them.

Paro lunged around, trying desperately to break free of her uncle's hold. Her terrified eyes looked pleadingly around for help. In the scuffle, her kameez tore down the front, and her left breast, with its taut brown nipple was partially exposed.

Jano could not bear to see her humiliation. 'Leave Paro alone – what harm has she done!' he cried.

A blow from a lathi hit him on his legs. A second hit him on his head. Blood spurted over his forehead and nose. 'We Yadavs are all governed by one set of rules – a lower-caste Jatav cannot marry an upper-caste girl. How did you think you could escape these laws?' Livid with anger, Pappu spat on his face. Picking up some dirt, he hurled it into Jano's eyes.

Jano tried to wipe the dirt away. He could feel the blood mix with the dirt as it ran down his face and shirt. But his hands were held tightly behind his back by Kishan and Ramesh.

'The world has changed – the caste system is a relic of the past. You say one thing, the Delhi Sarkar another,' Jano cried.

'Then get those bastards in Delhi to come and save you!'

Jano struggled to free himself from his captors. For a brief moment, he managed to extricate himself and tried to force his way through the circle of villagers in the direction of the school, but they stood tightly to the man, bodies pressed one to the other to create an impenetrable wall.

'Kaka Babu! Forgive us! We are your children!' Paro cried, falling at her uncle's feet.

Pappu's face contorted with rage. Short and stocky, he wore a tehmat tied tightly around his waist over which hung a brown-coloured loose kurta. His eyes stared at her with a cold fury. Her appearance with her bridal dupatta and the sindoor splashed over her forehead only served to infuriate him further.

'The moment you entered Shamli dressed in all your bridal finery, you signed your death warrant! How did you have the temerity to run away with a chamar? I could never have dreamt a daughter of our village could have brought us so much shame.'

Clutching her uncle's feet, Paro wept, 'Kaka Babu! I made a mistake! Forgive me!'

Jano searched the crowd desperately for a familiar face. He saw Sukhram standing at one side with a dazed expression on his face. How had he managed to reach Shamli so quickly? He was in league with Paro's uncle. He had helped lay this trap.

'Call Pitaji! Fetch my brother Kapil immediately!' Jano yelled.

Sukhram did not move.

Pappu's eyes followed Jano's. Sukhram's presence was not lost on him. He signalled to Kishan to get on with the job. Kishan belonged to his caste. He shared Pappu's belief that no upper-caste girl could marry outside the biradiri. Raising the axe, he swung it down. The blade cut through Jano's neck. He repeated the action, and the dismembered head fell to the ground.

'Kaka Babu! Kaka Babu! You have been both a mother and father to me!' Paro screamed.

Pappu's face convulsed in a fresh paroxysm of rage. 'This is the way you rewarded my efforts. I thought my blood flowed through your veins. I was wrong.'

Paro clutched at her uncles's feet. Yadav had to restrain himself from trampling over her body.

'You whore! By wearing a bridal dress, did you think you could become a bride? When the biradiri has not accepted you, what meaning can your marriage have for us? Even the kothawalis are better off than you. At least they have their pimps to take care of them.'

There was mud in Paro's eyes and hair. Her torn clothes were streaked with blood. She looked around like a cornered animal. For one fleeting second she saw her grandmother's face. She was sitting on the rooftop of the primary school staring intently at the goings on. Before her mouth could articulate a cry for help, Kishan dismembered her head from her body with one swing of the axe. The arms and legs thrashed violently for some time as the blood spurted from her torso onto the dry earth.

Kishan and Satvir dragged Jano's body and dumped it at the base of the peepal tree. Paro's body was drawn by the legs and dumped next to his. Her blood-spattered dupatta lay in tatters near her feet.

Pappu Yadav turned in disgust to the villagers. 'What are you standing around for, like halfwits at a nautanki? Haven't you had enough tamasha for the day?'

No one dared to speak. The crowd began to disperse slowly. Sukhram continued to stand rooted to the spot. It was obvious that he was in a state of shock. Yadav picked up a stone and threw it at him. It hit him on his leg. Wincing in pain, he bolted like a street dog with his tail between his legs.

'You better warn your family members not to collect here, or they will meet the same fate as these two,' Pappu screamed after him.

Ramesh, Satvir and Kishan looked apprehensively around. Now that the killings were over, they sensed trouble. 'I think we should disappear from here before the police arrive. What should we do with the bodies? Dump them into the canal?'

Pappu shook his head. 'Let them lie here. Let it be a warning to the lower castes not to dare cast their eyes at our daughters again.'

Kishan, a tall lumbering man with coal-black eyes, glanced around unhappily.

'Ustaad, you may have good police contacts, but common sense tells me it is better to lie low for the next few days. Otherwise we will all end up in the lockup. Not a happy prospect.'

The others nodded. Pappu saw the logic of their argument.

They could not afford to be caught napping. Picking up the axe and lathis, all four men disappeared in the direction of the mango orchard which lay to the east of the village stretching out for several acres before it melted into a series of tiny agricultural plots.

The bodies lay out in the open for over three hours before a police jeep arrived. The two beat constables, Bhim Singh and Ram Nath Pande, got out of the jeep and walked up to the corpses.

'Bloody hell!' shouted Bhim. Bhim's short and squat body seemed to be balanced carefully over a pair of powerful legs. His dark eyes seldom remained expressionless at the time of a crisis but even he was taken aback to see the bodies of these two teenagers. 'More killings!' he yelled. 'First, those bloody Uttarkhandis decide to get themselves shot in this very village, and we had the entire place swarming with Garhwalis. That problem had barely subsided when nine Jatav boys were massacred by a couple of Jats. And now this killing! This village is jinxed!'

The second constable, Pande, now spoke up. He was round and fat like a pear. A thinning pate gave him an old-fashioned air. He was even more nervous than Bhim. He had five young daughters to marry off. Experience had taught him that killings always meant trouble. Someone was going to have to take the rap for these killings. It was not going to be him. Twenty years in the police force had deepened his philosophical disposition and taught him to become ultra-cautious. Killings, rapes, extortions, thuggery and the like must always be dealt with in a low-key, routine fashion.

'Keep quiet, you big talking oaf! Let's find out from those schoolteachers what has been going on.'

The two primary schoolteachers, Balram Prakash and Mohan Ram, were sitting outside their classroom discussing the morning's developments. Prakash, the more senior teacher had in view of the morning's developments, given the students the day off.

Pande approached Prakash. 'What is this – more killings in this area?'

Taking out a packet of paan masala, Prakash passed it around to the constables who happily emptied the contents into their mouths. Having majored in history at a nearby college in Muzzaffarnagar, he loved to flaunt his academic credentials before his hapless students. The entire medieval history of the country was neatly summed up in a couple of anecdotes. His most favoured stories revolved around the adventures of Akbar and Birbal. His students had by now tired of hearing the same jokes over and over again.

Reciting historical anecdotes was one thing, seeing Jano, one of his most conscientious students executed before his own eyes was another. Paro had never attended school. Given the unfortunate circumstances of her childhood, Prakash had regarded Paro kindly.

He felt it was best to underplay the morning's events. Caste killings were a common enough occurrence and these incidents were best ignored.

'Arre, Panditji, thorre bahut dange to hote rahte him. Ek aur ho gaya! (Arre, Panditji, spats break out here and there, all the time. This is just one more.) A lower-caste Jatav boy had the temerity to run away with one of our daughters. He added insult to injury by bringing her back to the village. The situation could not be taken lying down. It became a matter of honour for the village. Poor Pappu Yadav was forced to take the law into his hands. If he had not done so, what face would he have been left with before his biradiri?'

Pande shuddered, acknowledging the wisdom of his argument. If one of his five daughters had done the same, he would not have hesitated to kill her with his bare hands.

Mohan Ram heard his colleague with an air of solemnity. It was obvious he did not want the policemen to make any arrests since this might ferment more trouble.

'Yadav is not a troublemaker. Let him and his associates lie low for a few weeks. We will have the bodies cremated in the village cremation ground. The matter will be soon forgotten,' said Pande.

Prakash handed Pande another pouch of paan masala.

'Did the entire village witness the killing?'

'Yes, they were all there. Everything was over in a couple of minutes. Kishan wielded the axe. A few thwacks and they were bleeding like a pair of headless chickens.'

'Did the school children witness the killing?'

'It was a free circus. Everyone had a good time,' added Mohan Ram with seeming relish. 'In the movies, everything takes place on a screen. Here everything took place before our own eyes.'

'Jano's parents can create trouble. Let the bhangis come and pick up these bodies from here. The job should be over in a couple of minutes,' said Pande.

The two constables looked around appraisingly. It was late in the evening. Two killings had occurred in a village that fell under their jurisdiction but they were returning to the police station empty-handed. Under the present circumstances, they could scarcely expect these poorly paid teachers to fork out a couple of rupees for their evening drink.

Pande gratefully accepted another packet of paan masala from Prakash and slid it into his shirt pocket. Jumping into the driver's seat of the Maruti matador, he dexterously adjusted his fat buttocks on to the small seat and then revved up the engine. Bhim jumped in beside him. With an exaggerated flourish of hands, they drove away.

The bodies lay in a heap in the chaupal. Only a few village dogs came sniffing around to nose into the blood and gore.

**

It had been late the previous evening when Bhuja realized something was seriously amiss. All day, a tense Pappu Yadav had kept rushing in and out of the house in what appeared to be an attempt to complete urgent chores. He returned home after sunset carrying a bagful of flour and potatoes. Throwing the stuff outside their makeshift kitchen, he shouted, 'Make sure there's food for five or six more people tonight. I will be joined by friends later this evening.'

It was a hot June evening. A thick pall of dust hung over the horizon, blurring the stars. A wafer-thin moon hung inconsequentially from a diminished sky. The village was already in a state of semi-slumber. The menfolk were sprawled on their charpais while their wives kept moistening their foreheads with wet towels. A long electricity breakdown had ensured that people not play their usually blaring radio and occasional TV sets, making for a ghostlike silence to descend upon what was generally a garrulous village community.

Bhuja sat on one side of the small courtyard that had been partially enclosed with thatch to form a small kitchen. A tiny woman, she had drawn the torn pallu of her sari over her head to hide the web of uncombed white hair tied in a loose bun at the nape of her neck. Ever since Paro's abrupt departure, the daily grind of work had shifted entirely on to her frail shoulders. Too old to cope with the responsibility of taking the animals out to graze, preparing their fodder and attending to a succession of household tasks, she had repeatedly pleaded with Pappu to find some additional help.

Short-tempered and irritable, her son seldom complied with her demands. A petty cattle thief, Pappu had the habit of disappearing for weeks on end and then reappearing out of the blue, a wad of notes bulging out of his torn kurta pocket. The money never lasted long, and soon he vanished once again on his next surreptitious mission.

Ever since she could remember, he had hardly given her any money. She had survived by selling milk to a few regular customers. Since there was no one to provide fodder on a regular basis to the buffaloes, their milk had begun to dry up. With no other source of income, she searched around frantically for a little work.

She complained to no one. Life had taught her never to argue with anyone, least of all her son. She simply wandered over to the nearby fields and scrounged around for a handful of potatoes or some edible grass which she mixed with rice to prepare a thin gruel cooked over dry twigs. She subsisted on this till Pappu returned with some money.

Paro and she had gone through this routine many times in the past. Paro had never once complained about having to eat this thin gruel for days on end. She had never groused over wearing torn rags which scarcely covered her body. Quiet and docile, as a young child she used to follow Bhuja around like a shadow.

Her neighbours, with their large double-storied house towering over her run-down hut had never extended a helping hand. And why would they? Some months ago, when two buffaloes of their neighbour, Lal Singh, had mysteriously disappeared, he had warned Bhuja he would file a case against Pappu. He did not do so because lately Pappu had been hobnobbing with members of the Tyagi gang notorious for extortion, kidnapping-for-ransom and car robberies. Cowed down by her son's reputation, Bhuja felt it was best to keep to herself and go on with her daily grind as long as her frail body permitted. Bhuja lifted herself slowly and dragged the bag of flour to her kitchen, which was no more than a clay stove with dry stalks serving as fuel. The potatoes were put to boil in a black, soot-scarred saucepan. The flour she emptied into a plate. She began kneading it into thick dough. Two hours later she had finished making thirty big chapattis along with a potato curry floating in a mash of red chillies. With the meal out of the way, she brought out two broken-down string beds and placed them in the courtyard.

Pappu arrived a few minutes later carrying two bottles of country-made liquor. He had barely settled down on a charpai when he was joined by his friends, Kishan, Satvir and Ramesh. Sitting in a huddle, smoking beedis and taking large swigs from the bottle, they talked in loud whispers about what Bhuja presumed was yet another robbery. She realized something more was afoot when she saw Kishan take an axe out of the cloth bag he was carrying over his shoulder. Running his hand over the blade, Kishan remarked, 'Sharp enough to fell a peepal tree in one blow!' The blade caught the light of the lantern and glinted ominously.

Bhuja lay in one corner listening to snatches of their conversation. She heard Pappu swear. 'Women, land, money and chamars – they are a curse on mankind!' Ramesh occasionally broke into a low song interrupted by a bout of loud coughing. 'Jai Kali Ma!' he would keep muttering. When the coughing got too loud, Pappu, whose nerves were clearly on edge, let loose a round of abuses. No one slept. Early in the morning, all four slipped silently out of the house clutching their lathis in their right hands. Kishan carried the axe slung over his right shoulder.

Bhuja, who had drifted into a light sleep, paid no attention to their going. She was sweeping the courtyard later in the morning when she heard a loud commotion outside. Her neighbours were running in the direction of the primary school. Thinking they were going to attend an early morning prayer meet, she continued with her chores. She was shaken out of her stupor when the neighbour's eight-year old son, Lallu, stuck his neck into the courtyard and yelled. 'Amma! Paro has come back!'

Her heart sank. What could this mean? Why had that girl chosen to come back? Barefoot, she hurried out of the house, forgetting to put on her torn slippers. A dirt track used by tractors and carts, meandered in front of the house, going past a maze of brick houses, past the village temple, straight up to the primary school. Diagonally opposite the school was the double-storied home of the village sarpanch, Chowdhury Ram Lal, who had used a criss-cross of parrot green and brick red hues to embellish his front façade. The empty space between the two buildings was used as a chaupal where the panchayat met.

It was presently overflowing with villagers standing shoulder to shoulder. Many had clambered up on to the rooftops of the two buildings; others were spilling out of windows and open doors. Even the peepal tree that grew in the centre of the chaupal had chattering young school children jumping from one branch to the other like monkeys, anxious to get a better view.

Bhuja hurried up the staircase that wound its way to Ram Lal's rooftop, pushing past young and old alike, to find out what was happening. Paro's screams were resounding in her ears.

'Kaka Babu! Forgive us this one last time! You will not set eyes on even our shadows again!'

She reached the rooftop to find Kishan dragging Paro by her hair and throwing her at her uncle's feet. Pappu spat on her face. For a brief moment, Jano freed himself and ran in the direction of the school. The villagers seemed to instinctively regroup and come closer to one other to ensure he could not run away. It was almost as though they collectively believed he deserved the punishment being meted out to him. She saw him being pinned down and his head being chopped off in a hatchet-like motion by Kishan's fast moving axe.

Paro's turn came next. Scuttling from one to another, her body caked with mud, her torn kameez exposing her left breast, her screams rose to a crescendo over the silence of the mob. Trembling like a leaf, she saw the brief hesitation in Kishan's eyes as he held the axe over his head. Then it came down with a thud. Bhuja saw Paro's dismembered head roll to the ground, the blood spurt out of her body. It continued to gush for some time almost like a sacrificial offering received by the dry earth. Her long hair was matted with blood. Even her clothes seemed transformed into a shield of blood. For some strange reason, Bhuja felt as if Paro's open eyes were staring at her. They had always been sharp and watchful. She could not escape them.

Paro had lost her mother at childbirth. Her father, a proud farmer who tilled his 12-acre plot with passion, died of tuberculosis when she was just six. Paro grew up a quiet child who spoke little. Her eyes silently watched everything around her. Nothing escaped her gaze even as she grew into a slim, attractive adolescent.

Terrified of Pappu Yadav, she would cower behind Bhuja every time he entered the house. Her elder brother Jagdamba, two years her elder, was quite the opposite. He made no attempt to hide his hatred for his uncle. After a particularly stiff beating, one day, he packed up his few belongings and disappeared. Paro was so shaken by his departure that she did not speak to anyone for months. She continued to do all the work that was expected of her: working as a labourer in the fields, collecting firewood, fetching water from the well and taking care of the animals. Occasionally, Jano also brought his animals to graze along the canal bank. He seemed a kind-hearted boy who did not scorn her obvious poverty. Although from a lower caste, he had been to school. His father, Ram Pal, owned a cycle repair shop on the Delhi-Muzzaffarnagar highway and Jano told her that one of his uncles ran a tailor shop in Ambala.

As Paro grew older, Bhuja had hinted to Pappu to find her a suitable match. Her uncle had no interest in finding her a groom, simply because he did not wish to spend any money on her marriage. Bhuja had suggested the names of one or two boys. Pappu dismissed them as good-for-nothings.

With no escape in sight, Paro began to encourage the attentions of Jano who seemed well-disposed towards her. Few villagers brought their cattle to graze along the canal bank. The tall sarkanda grass and sheesham trees provided protection from the prying eyes of her uncle.

Paro began to feel reassured in Jano's presence. She confided her fears about her uncle and his cruel ways. She told him how she wanted to run away to Delhi to find her brother Jagdamba. Jano sympathized with her and told her he would take her there. He could not bear to see her cry. It made him feel soft, the way he did every time he played with his polio-stricken sister.

'I will take you to Delhi. I have friends there. They will help me find your brother,' he told her

'How can I go with you? It will not be accepted in our village.'

'We can get married. No one will say anything then.'

Paro's heart leapt with joy. She stared into his light brown eyes to see if he was serious. They were warm and effusive. A tall, strapping youth, he had a kind expression on his face. Anything was preferable to living in this miserable situation. They continued to meet secretly and decided to leave the village on a day when Pappu was not around. Late one April evening, when the mango trees were awash in a mist of flowers and a pair of lovelorn peacocks screamed loudly from the parapet of the village temple, Pappu Yadav announced his departure on a week-long visit to Hardwar.

The young lovers decided to take advantage of his absence to get away. Early next morning, Paro slipped out of the house. Jano was waiting for her along the canal bank. Moving under the shadow of trees, terrified the sound of the cracking twigs under their feet might attract attention, they fled towards the main road to tumble into an overcrowded bus leaving for Ambala. Jano's tailor uncle might be willing to finance their trip to Delhi.

On reaching Ambala, Jano hustled her to a roadside temple where, after some quick whisperings, followed by the slipping of Rs 101 into the pandit's palm, the two were married in a brief ceremony. The uncle in Ambala did not take kindly to their request for shelter in his house.

'I am a family person. You will have to make your own arrangements,' he said, unwilling to allow them to enter his house.

Finding work proved to be a daunting task. It took a month of running around before Jano finally managed to get a job as an errand boy with a local baniya.

Bhuja had no inkling of Paro's plans. On learning about her elopement, she had felt relieved. Pappu and she were now spared the expense of having to find a groom for her. When Paro and Jagdamba were children, their grandmother had often sweet-talked them into believing that Pappu had done his best for them. 'He may have fed you dry roti but at least he did not allow you to starve!' Bhuja used to insist. Both children gave her disbelieving looks. They knew better than to argue with her.

She too had done her best for them. How much could an old woman do anyway? The land left by their father had been gambled away by Pappu. His own three-bigha stretch had turned alkaline and could not be used for growing crops.

For many years Bhuja had worked as a farmhand. Paro had done the same. They'd had no other choice. Women had always been treated badly by their menfolk. Bhuja had suffered abuse at her husband's hands. Why should she expect something different from her son?

Pappu had repeatedly assured Paro he would find a suitable groom for her. The girl should have trusted her uncle. Instead, she had chosen to run away with a Jatav. Which uncle could accept such a deed? How did Paro remain blind to the consequences of her deed? Had she failed to recognize that the village biradiri was governed by immutable laws that had withstood the test of centuries? The caste system formed its bedrock. No one dared question this. It was for this reason that the entire village had stood by and approved of the killing.

Who was she, an old hag, to believe things could be different? After the killing, she had walked back to her house telling herself that everything happened for the best. It was a blessing that Jagdamba had run away. He had not been witness to his sister's lynching.

She knew she did not have long to live. Would Pappu be around to help her during this rite of passage? She did not think so.

two

Dalip Jha, special correspondent of the Calcutta-based *Morning Chronicle,* knew it was a deadbeat story the minute he moved his large frame out of the rickety DLY taxi and walked on to the parade ground, where the organizers were putting last-minute finishing touches to a hastily erected podium. In the centre of the podium a bust of Ambedkar, with his trademark black coat, black tie and round spectacles, had been placed to show the public of Meerut what a substantial contribution this lesser-known hero had made to the cause of Dalits and the freedom struggle.

Leelawati, on becoming chief minister for the second time, was clearly a woman in a hurry, having already dotted UP's landscape with shoddily made statues of Ambedkar, now popping up in practically every provincial town. The shock therapy being administered to the entrenched political establishment through the Ambedkar brand was also reinforced through Leelawati's own carefully cultivated image of a political upstart. Only a few months ago, she had thrown down the gauntlet to her political opponents through her no-holds-barred, 'Kunwarin hoon, chamarin hoon' speech that was lustily cheered by large crowds consisting mainly of unemployed youth. This was followed by a string of Gandhi-bashing statements, where the Father of the Nation was described as 'manuvadi', 'anti-Dalit', 'status quoist' in opposition to Ambedkar, who was the true upholder and messiah of the Bahujan Samaj Party.

These attacks on Gandhi – coming on top of his being called a 'baniya bastard' by a Delhi-based bohemian gay activist – had generated sufficient interest for making good news copy. It was with this in view that Dalip Jha had decided to cover Leelawati's present rally in Meerut. Dalip had accepted the one-day trip gratefully. For some time now, he had been wanting to get away from Delhi, even if it was only for a couple of hours.

A group of policemen drifted in listlessly and stood looking around the parade ground venue, lathis in hand. A few moved towards the podium, where last-minute work was still going on, even as a still-swelling crowd of a lakh or so had already assembled awaiting their beloved Leelawati behenji. And keeping the restless crowd occupied was Chandanbhan Singh, convenor of the Dalit Udhdhaar Front, one of the several Bahujan Samaj-focussed smaller advocacy groups that had sprouted up in the last few months.

Leelawati arrived two hours late. Dressed in a pink, designer salwar kameez suit, she walked briskly to the podium. Her new hairstyle, (some celebrity magazines had reported that she had dispensed with her mouse-like plait and opted for a short, boyish look), was hidden behind a bright pink dupatta. Huge diamond earrings hung from her ears and a large diamond pendant adorned her thick neck. With one quick motion, she pulled aside the red cloth over the bust and amidst a wave of loud applause, garlanded the statue with a marigold necklace. Other illustrious party members followed suit, each garlanding the bust and shouting slogans of 'Jai Bhim'. The formalities over, she walked up to the waiting microphone and launched a frontal attack on all political parties except her own.

'Our Dalit samaj has been marginalized for thousands of years. But now the reality has changed. We are poised to sweep the polls in every state of this country. We will become the rulers of this nation. Look at all that I have done for you the people. In a matter of three months, I have put one-and-a-half lakh bahujan-virodhi elements behind bars and have installed 850 statues of Baba Ambedkar and set up thirty Ambedkar parks in different cities. My enemies have tried to silence me many a time, but with your support the day is not far off when we shall rule from the gaddi of Hindustan.'

The crowd listened in appreciative silence. Dalip took down a few desultory notes. There was no mention this time of Gandhi. There was no meat in the story. A local journalist, Pramod Tripathi, from the *Amar Jagaran* walked up to him unnoticed.

'You know, she is charging ten lakh rupees for each transfer, and she has already had two hundred officers transferred. Do you have a calculator on you? I'll tell you how much she has earned from these transfers. This transfer industry has become very lucrative. It provides for ready cash. Let me give you the most recent example of her doings. The superintendent of police here is her own man. He must have paid her an advance of five lakh rupees to get himself transferred to Meerut. Now he's busy extracting money from local businessmen to recover the investment. The police are hand in glove with the local mafia,' Tripathi whispered into Dalip's ear.

Leelawati's speech ended as abruptly as it had started. She had spoken to the gathering for barely fifteen minutes and was obviously keen to move on. One or two close confidants came up to her and whispered something in her ear. She nodded in agreement. Waving to the crowd in her brusque manner, she walked briskly with fast, firm strides towards her Contessa.

Dalip watched in amazement. Why was she hurrying out in this fashion? Her meetings generally lasted longer. She could be a fiery demagogue when she wanted to be.

Leelawati had barely stepped out of the maidan, when the

organizers found that all the special invitees, including the journalists, had rushed across to the three tables spread over with an assortment of snacks and begun wolfing them down. At the corner of the podium stood Chandanbhan Singh, distributing sealed envelopes to select local reporters.

'We have been reduced to accepting our salaries from the local politicians and businessmen. Our proprietors no longer pay us. They have given us carte blanche in the use of their newspaper space but we have to get our salaries from the people we write about,' Tripathi told the astonished Dalip. He had heard about this practice but to hear it straight from the mouth of a small town journalist took him by surprise.

The government PRO, Sunil Malhotra, hurried over to Dalip. 'Bhai Saheb! You are our honoured guest from Delhi. Be quick. Otherwise, there will be no food left.' As he had predicted, five minutes later, the tables had been emptied, with paper plates and pink napkins strewn all over the ground.

Dalip turned away. It was past eleven o'clock and it had become hot. Having left Delhi early in the morning, he was feeling hungry. He needed to find himself a cool air-conditioned restaurant and unwind with a glass of chilled beer.

Tripathi must have read his thoughts. 'Let's go and have a chat at Cozy Comfort restaurant. It's just down the road. You will find it interesting. I can give you a lowdown on all the local gossip.'

Dalip heard him out with a look of bored acquiescence. What could possibly happen in this pedestrian town that could merit anyone's attention? Another 1857 mutiny? He almost guffawed at his own joke. He had withdrawn Rs 1000 from his office and so far had spent only twenty rupees from it. Even if they both ate a couple of hundred rupees worth of food, it would make little difference to his company.

Cozy Comfort turned out to be a typical small-town restaurant with rexine-coated chairs and minimal lighting. Guests had to stumble in the darkness to find their way around. The place was deserted. Fortunately the AC was functioning. Dalip sank into a chair with a sigh.

'This place is famous for its tandoori chicken,' Tripathi announced.

'I thought you were a vegetarian – you're a Brahmin, aren't you? I'm also a Mythil Brahmin from Bihar,' Dalip remarked caustically.

'My forefathers did not eat meat. I make up for them by eating everything. I eat meat, vegetables, potatoes, garlic and onion … I've even eaten cow's meat. Nothing was forbidden by our scriptures. Good food, pretty women, chilled beer … these are all the prerequisites for a good life.' He smacked his lips to stress the point.

Dalip decided to humour him. He ordered three bottles of chilled Kingfisher beer, tandoori chicken, paneer tikka, meat korma and a plate of seekh kebabs.

'Enough to feed an entire community of Brahmins,' Tripathi giggled.

'Now let's hear the local gossip!' Dalip gave a low chuckle.

'You know there was a double murder on the outskirts of the city last evening.'

'No big deal. In Delhi, we average seven to eight murders a day. Give me the lowdown on the political gossip.'

'Sir, this murder is rooted in caste conflict. The girl was upper caste and poor, the boy was lower caste but well off. Their heads were chopped off yesterday evening. The story has still to break in the dailies. With Leelawati at the helm, she may choose to exploit it.'

Dalip mulled over what he had been told. There was nothing earthshaking about a young couple being hacked to death. These caste conundrums were getting more complex by the day. His own state of Bihar had become a pioneer in this.

'Where did the murder take place?'

'Near Shamli.'

'I thought there's a Ruskin Bond story by this name.'

Tripathi gave him a blank look. He had just finished wolfing down the tandoori chicken, and, even though his plate was overflowing with food, he was already deliberating over the list of sweet dishes printed at the end of the menu card. 'I don't understand why the name Tutti Frutti has been given to an ice cream. 'Tutti' in Hindi means broken; 'Frutti' is a drink. It is one of the surprises of the English language that broken and drink have combined to become an ice cream. I will end my meal with a broken-drink-ice cream.'

Dalip was trying to choose between a peach melba and a cassatta. A slight detour via this Shamli place might just help inflate accounts a little further.

'How far is Shamli from here?'

'You chaps sitting in Delhi are so lucky with your expense-paid travel accounts. Our owners do not permit us to travel anywhere. If somehow we were granted permission to go on a tour, they would expect us to meet all the expenses from our own pockets. I may be a journalist, but I have not stepped out of this town for the last three years.'

It was only after Tripathi had finished eating his tutti frutti that he supplied him with all the information on the murder. 'Shamli is fifty miles from here on the Delhi-Muzzaffarnagar road. The village where it happened is about ten minutes from the police chowki. Ask anyone there, and they will tell you where it is. One of our freelancers happened to be visiting the place, when this fracas occurred. If you leave right away, you will get there by late afternoon. I think the killing took place near their primary school.'

Dalip noted the information down on a piece of paper. The bill came to the preposterous sum of Rs 389. Deciding against tipping the waiter, he walked out into the hot sun and asked the Sardar taxi driver to take him to Shamli. Two hours later he drove into the village which appeared to be quiet with the villagers going about their tasks in their usual desultory manner. The driver stopped the cab outside the primary school. It was closed. Dalip got out of the taxi and approached an elderly man dragging his cycle along the muddy track.

'Did any untoward incident take place here last evening?'

'How would I know? I just got into the village a few seconds before you did,' the old man replied.

A young boy walked past him dragging a buffalo. The same question was put to him. The boy turned pale. 'I don't know about these things.'

Dalip walked up to the dilapidated primary school building Tripathi had spoken about, with its broken window panes and missing front doors.

Walking past the peepal tree, he noticed that fresh dirt had been sprinkled all around its roots and in the open space in front of it. He stopped to take a closer look. There were no signs of blood or any scuffle but fresh tyre marks criss-crossed the freely strewn earth.

He walked towards Chowdhury Ram Lal's jazzy red-and-yellow brick house. A long nosed, unshaven elderly gentleman was sitting on a charpai enjoying his hookah. The old man beckoned to him to sit down and share his hookah.

'Looking for someone? What brings you here today?'

Dalip showed him his press card.

'I heard there was a killing here in the morning. What has been done with the bodies?'

'Sahib, I have no idea. I was tilling my fields and returned home late in the evening. You should talk to the sarpanch.'

'But I was told the entire village had witnessed the killing.'

'How would I know, sahib? I was not present.'

Wily bastards, Dalip muttered. These villagers are the same everywhere. Feign collective amnesia whenever it suits them. He was reminded of his own village in Bihar, where the villagers conveniently forgot to pay half their produce to his grandfather till they were prodded and beaten into doing so.

'I am told both the victims have their families here?'

The old man took a few hard puffs on his hookah. It was obvious he was not keen to part with even the tiniest bit of information.

'I think the girl's grandmother lives somewhere around here. Ask anyone for Pappu Yadav's house. It's close enough,' he finally muttered in an irritable tone.

The old man was right. Finding Pappu Yadav's house did not prove difficult. A scantily dressed, spindly youngster playing marbles with his friends volunteered to show him the way.

From across the primary school, the boy headed left. Dalip followed him panting loudly. Every few yards, he passed groups of men sitting outside their homes on string cots, playing cards and smoking hookahs. A few heads of cattle, tied close by, were digging their noses into finely chopped greens and munching in a slow, cogitative manner. As they walked along, the young boy recounted all that had happened the day before.

The duo walked nearly half a kilometre before the young kid pointed to Yadav's house. Dalip was taken aback at its dilapidated state. The roof made from dry straw seemed to have caved in at the centre. The mud walls were crumbling. It was difficult to believe anybody could live in something so rundown.

A decrepit old woman was sitting with her back to the main entrance. She appeared deep in thought, for she did not hear him opening the small wooden gate to step inside.

'Namaste Amma! I need to talk to Pappu Yadav.'

She turned round, but made no reply.

'Where is he? Can I see him?' Dalip repeated.

There was still no answer.

He looked around helplessly. On an impulse, he took off his shoes, left them outside and sat down next to her.

'Would you mind if I took a photograph of you?'

She did not look up as he clicked her picture. Pulling the sari pallu over her head, she sat as before in sphinx-like silence.

'Amma, I am like your son. I would be very happy if you could trust me.'

Seeing her miserable plight, he took out a fifty-rupee note and placed it discreetly in her hands. 'I have come from Delhi and am trying to understand this whole problem. Do you think what your son did was right?'

Bhuja took the fifty-rupee note and tucked it away into her blouse. Her expression remained cold and unflinching.

'Of course he did the right thing. Our laws are made by our biradiri and everyone must follow them. When our elders decree something, it must be obeyed. We lead different lives from you people out there in cities.' Her tone was firm.

'But Amma, she was your grandchild, your own son's daughter. How could you support her killing?'

'If I had possessed the strength, I would have hacked her to death myself. To run away with a low-caste boy and then to dare return to our village! She came back to drag us through the mud. Hamara naak katwane ke liye aai thi. She made a mockery of us all.'

Dalip had got his story. This was the quote he had wanted to hear. He gave one more glance at this crumbling house and the old crone who expressed no anguish at seeing her grandchild's public execution.

'Did you witness the killings?'

'Of course! The entire village saw it. No one was willing to spare her or that useless chamar who had plotted this entire mischief!'

'What were their names?'

Looking at him with intense hatred, she exploded. 'You city folk are all meddlers. It is you lot who have ruined our lives. What will you do with their names – they are dead now.' Pulling her dupatta over her shoulders, she retreated into her cocoon of silence.

It was obvious she was not going to say anything more. He folded his notepad and slipped it back into his pocket. Time to get home, he decided. The detour back would be just enough to inflate his TA/DA bill. He walked to the taxi. The Sardar driver was only too happy to drive away from this wretched village that seemed stuck in a time warp.

**

Dalip ran up the flight of steps, two at a time, to enter a tiny windowless room on the first floor that made do as the Delhi bureau office of the *Morning Chronicle*. The room was cluttered with tables on which lay computers, newspaper files, ashtrays overflowing with cigarette stubs, tea-stained cups and saucers and dirty glasses.

He had to manoeuvre past a series of tables to reach a small cubicle, in which in deference to his position as special correspondent, a separate computer had been kept which no one else was allowed to use. The office peon, Hare Krishna, wearing an expression of stoic calm, brought him a glass of water.

The Shamli killings, Dalip had decided, were not deserving of more than a couple of paras. It took him fifteen minutes to knock out the story. Stepping out of the claustrophobic office, he debated whether he should return home and decided against it. A double rum at the Press Club seemed a better option. Married for the third time, he was already beginning to find life with his wife Simi tiresome. A journalist like himself, she had strong opinions on practically every subject under the sun and did not hesitate to express them. She seemed to know everything there was to know in politics, economics, literature, alternative systems of healing and even his own relatives, though they had been married less than two months. Nor did she hesitate, every time the opportunity arose, to launch into fresh diatribes against all his friends and acquaintances.

Wednesday being open for guests, the club was overflowing with people. He saw several friends swirling around lost in a cacophony of loud exclamations and the reek of cheap booze that was the hallmark of the place. Making a beeline for the bar, he caught the bartender's eye. The bartender gave him a smile of recognition.

'Sirji, a Bloody Mary?'

'No yaar – rum and soda will do very well.'

'On the double, sir ji.'

Within seconds, the bartender had placed a cool glass of rum tinkling with ice in front of him. Dalip took a grateful sip. Looking around to see whose table he should join, he saw Raveena Bedi from *The Indian Sentinel* beckoning to him from one corner of the room. Moon-faced and buxom, Raveena was one helluva heavyweight. She was known to have started her career as a door-to-door salesgirl selling lurid coloured bras and panties to unsuspecting housewives. She had then graduated to being a telephone operator who had struck up a relationship with an editor who gave her a major break as a local municipal reporter. Her sweet, suggestive smile was invariably accompanied by a hard-hitting riposte.

'Dalip! What a surprise! Come and join me!'

Picking up his glass, Dalip went across to sit by her side.

'My handsome Romeo – how come you are here all by yourself? Where is your beautiful wife? Like all good husbands, I can see you've left her alone in the house.'

Dalip grinned. 'Arre yaar, why are you nagging me! You are sounding just like my mother! I've just returned from Meerut. I had gone there to cover a rally.'

Raveena giggled. She understood men, and if Dalip had

come alone to the Press Club, it meant he was on the lookout for another woman. It was her evening out. She too was in the mood to enjoy herself.

'How unchivalrous of you to be drinking all by yourself. You have not even bothered to offer me a glass of wine.'

'I am so sorry. What would you like to drink?'

'Red wine will do very well. Now let me look into your handsome brown eyes and try and fathom what you are thinking.'

Dalip's eyes lit up. He could see Raveena was in the mood to flirt. 'I am dead tired. I've been out in this heat and dust from the morning,' he said.

'We all have to sing for our supper. Your face tells me you are happily married to the wonderful Simi.'

Dalip grimaced. 'Why are you bringing my wife into this conversation? Let us just talk about you and me.'

'We can't talk about you and me in the middle of a crowded bar. Let's go and sit in the family room, if you want a meaningful conversation.'

Dalip hesitated for a brief moment. He took a quick look around. There was no one from his office to carry tales to Simi. Picking up his drink, he followed Raveena into the family room which turned out to be completely deserted. A television set, perched precariously just below the wooden roof, was spewing some political garbage on the achievements of the prime minister.

Raveena, carrying her bulk with great aplomb, pulled up a chair and sat down on his right. Her warm thighs were soon pressing against his and every time she lifted her wine glass she would move it provocatively over his arm. Dalip, always happy with the attentions of a woman, quickly finished his third glass of rum. 'What's happening in your great empire? Who is going up? Who is coming down?'

'Baby, I've told you so many times in the past to move over to my paper. Your stories are getting wasted in Calcutta. Who cares for the Bengali bhadralok anyway? No one reads the *Morning Chronicle* in Delhi. You have to move to *The Indian Sentinel* to get noticed. The only problem is, our owner will not hire you unless some Cabinet minister recommends your case. Let's go over to my flat and I will make a few phone calls on your behalf to my political well-wishers.'

Dalip heard her out with not a little interest. Moving might be a good idea especially if *The Indian Sentinel*'s editor Vikram Aggarwal, offered him the vacant slot of chief of bureau. 'Let's have one more round of drinks and then I'll drive you back to your flat. I've heard you've got a cushy place,' Dalip said.

Raveena pouted. 'Yes, it's just like me – soft and cute.'

His eyes went over her chubby cheeks, thick arms, and well-padded shoulders. He was pretty well-padded himself but if she ever mounted him, he would be flattened out like a squashed tomato. Still, she was being generous in offering to help him change organizations.

It was past eleven p.m. as the two of them made their way to the waiting cabbie. The Sardar taxi driver had only to see Dalip leading the fat woman towards his taxi to understand what was going on. Picking up the hand towel placed behind his seat, he wiped his brow angrily. It had been a hot, exhausting day and he was not willing to hang around any longer.

'Sir, I am having a problem with the car engine. It's not starting. Kindly settle the accounts so I can go home,' he growled.

Dalip took out a hundred rupee note from his wallet. 'I'll give you two more of these notes if you agree to drop this lady at her house. I have to stop for a couple of minutes in her house.'

The engine started instantly and the taxi lurched forward with a roar. The combination of beer and rum had taken its toll and by the time the taxi tore across the newly constructed Yamuna bridge, Dalip had dozed off. When he woke up at a red light, he found

Raveena, arm locked inside his, giving directions to the driver on how to reach her barsati flat. He wondered what Simi was doing. She would not mind his staying out so late if she knew he was striving to improve his career prospects.

They were both panting heavily by the time they reached Raveena's two-room flat located on the third floor of what seemed like a particularly dilapidated building. Dalip collapsed on the divan placed in the main living room and tried to get his breath back. Raveena went into the kitchen and poured out two stiff whiskies. Handing one glass to Dalip, she picked up the phone and began dialling some numbers.

'It's a little late to be calling up people at this hour.'

'Arre yaar, all our politicians wake up only after midnight. They are typical Sardars.'

Raveena dialled the homes of Sharad Pawar, Pramod Mahajan and Chandrashekhar. Speaking to them in a mixture of Hindi and English, she told them how they must take time off from their busy schedules to meet this promising star of Indian journalism. Each time Raveena put down the phone, she smiled to herself. Just dialling their phone numbers served to bring her into the charmed circle of the political elite. It was this handful of people who ran the country. It was important to be on good terms with them.

Putting the phone down, she came and sat down next to Dalip. 'They have all promised to help. Mahajan wants to see your bio-data. He's a good fellow!'

He could feel her proximity. Her breath was coming swift and heavy. It smelt of elaichi and paan masala. Her breasts looked large and tempting. She smiled provocatively at him, her eyes hard and calculating. With all her tantrums, Simi had never given him such a rapacious look. It frightened him. Looking at his wristwatch he exclaimed, 'It's past one o'clock! I didn't realize it was so late. I was so mesmerized by your beauty, it simply slipped my mind.'

Raveena was in no mood to let him escape. 'Stay a few minutes. I'm an expert masseur. I'll give you a quick massage. It will take the tiredness out of you.'

Her thick hands moved skilfully over his legs kneading the muscles of his thighs and legs in a soft, slow motion. Dalip knew he was being ensnared into a trap. The motion of her hands was so enticing. A dark heat emanated from her body. She snatched his hand and drew it over her large bulbous breasts. He must flee!

'We'll make it together some other time! I promise! You're really wonderful! I must get back or else Simi will throw me out of the house!'

'If she does that you can always come back here!' Raveena pouted in frustration.

Before she could stop him, Dalip had jumped up from the divan and lunged out of the door. Rushing down the steps two at a time, he clutched onto the wobbly banister to prevent himself from slipping. He breathed a sigh of relief when he saw the Sardar cabbie.

'Shit! I've been drinking too much,' he muttered tucking his shirt into his trousers and slipping into the back seat of the cab. Better look presentable when he showed up before Simi.

Lighting a cigarette, Raveena poured herself another large whisky. Dalip was not the first man to have rushed out of her apartment in this fashion. She knew she had been snubbed. She also knew how to settle scores. She would bide her time and hit back at him when the time came.

three

Dalip felt guilt stricken when he saw Simi pacing up and down the front verandah waiting for him. It was past two a.m. He knew she was going to blow her top.

'How come you're returning home so late? The Leelawati rally finished pretty early in the morning!' Simi fumed. Her dark, brown eyes were bright with anger; her thin, lithe frame was tense and febrile, like an angry cat.

'I took a slight detour from Meerut to a village called Shamli because of a caste killing.'

Simi looked at her watch. 'It's ten past two. Surely the Shamli murder did not take place at midnight?' As she spoke, she came close to him and began sniffing him, as would a young puppy. 'You're smelling of perfume! Who have you been out with this time?'

'I went to the Press Club for a drink and that Raveena woman came and plonked herself next to me.'

'I see. So this time round, it's that fat cow Raveena who is to blame!'

'She just latched on to me. I swear! She promised to introduce me to Vikram Aggarwal, the proprietor of the *Sentinel*.'

'From where has that fatso managed to acquire so much clout?'

'She's well connected. She spends all her time cultivating the movers and shakers of this city.'

Simi guffawed loudly. 'Journalists are not altruisitic by nature. What is she getting out of helping you? Don't try and pull a fast one on me!' she screamed.

Dalip tried to mollify her by putting his arms round her. If she continued to shriek out loud in this manner, his mother and sisters would be standing on his head wanting to know what the commotion was all about. 'Let's not make a public spectacle of ourselves. The neighbours will hear. We can go into the bedroom and thrash it out there,' said Dalip.

Simi spurned the offer of his hand and marched into their bedroom. Her temper once roused was not easily assuaged. Some of her colleagues had warned her about Dalip's reputation as a womanizer. He had got rid of his first wife Kanti without batting an eyelid. His second marriage was also short-lived and most journalists knew little about the second wife's whereabouts. No one could say what this smart alec Bihari would be up to next. Dalip must have got an inkling of her thoughts. He staggered up to her and kissed her on her cheek, 'My sweetie baba! My sweetie baba! How can I live without you!'

Simi tried pushing him aside. He would not let her go. Too drunk to bother about changing his clothes, Dalip collapsed on the bed. Wrapping his arms around Simi, he kissed her on her forehead. Reassured, Simi snuggled up beside him and within seconds was snoring like a baby.

Dalip liked to wake up early in the mornings and spend an hour or two reading the papers. Simi's only interest in the morning news lay in seeing whether her story had been well displayed. If it was front page and unedited, she was in a good mood; if it was buried inside and slashed down to a couple of paras, she remained in a sulk till such time as she geared up to work on another story.

The rustling of the morning newspapers woke her. Picking up

her nail polish remover, she busied herself wiping her toenails clean in order to apply a fresh coat of polish over them.

'Mummy is quite miserly. Last evening she shouted at the maid for wanting to eat a third chapatti.'

Dalip ignored the remark. They were sitting face to face on their double bed which filled up the entire length of the tiny room. Last night's clothes and the morning papers were strewn all over the bed. A small dressing table had been placed on the right side on which Dalip had kept his much loved Sony music system. A music aficionado, he allowed no one to touch it.

Sitting on the bed, Simi chucked a few dirty pieces of cotton wool at the waste-paper basket kept on the right of the dressing table. Missing the basket, they landed on the music system.

Dalip watched angrily at the way the cotton buds were landing on the music system. Some of the wet nail polish could have rubbed off onto the system.

'Are you mad! Do you want to ruin my system?'

Simi grimaced at his words. She continued to chuck the cotton pieces into the waste-paper basket.

Upset that his words were not having the slightest impact, Dalip began shouting even louder. 'How many times have I told you not to get into an argument with my mother? Let her do as she pleases. The maid has just come fresh from the village. When they see so much food in their lives, they tend to go berserk. Their food intake has to be regulated,' he said.

Simi ignored his remark. Pulling up her nightie so that her blue lace panties were visible, Simi began applying a fresh coat of paint over her long toenails. Her long hair fell over her shoulders and there was a soft, sensuous expression in her expressive, brown eyes.

'You look so sexy,' Dalip murmured putting the papers aside.

Simi pouted. 'Mummy serves her such small portions. She's slaving for us night and day. Dammit, she should be allowed to eat.'

'Why are you getting into the politics of the house? You concentrate on your office work and let Mummy handle the kitchen department.'

'It seems a little strange to be writing day and night about poverty and starvation and then seeing your own maid being forced to survive on a subsistence diet.'

There was a knock at the door. Dalip's mother entered carrying a tea tray with a plate of biscuits. She was wearing a maroon housecoat. A bright red scarf was tied over her head like a turban.

'Good morning, children. Have some hot tea.'

'Mummy! How sweet of you!'

Dalip tumbled out of bed and took the tray from her outstretched hands. Simi, flinching inwardly at the grotesque sight of her mother-in-law's turban, worn to hide a concoction of egg yolk, mehendi, coffee and black hair dye layered all over her head, continued polishing her nails.

'Would you like to come in?' Simi asked in a cool, business-like tone.

Aruna Jha, unable to take her gaze away from her daughter-in-law's transparent nightie, replied in an equally cold voice, 'No. I have to make tea for Papaji. He doesn't like to be kept waiting.'

She turned abruptly and marched out.

'That was hardly the way to talk to Amma,' said Dalip.

'What did I say? I merely asked her to come inside.'

'You sounded cold.'

'I couldn't take her get-up. She looked so odd with all that hair dye plastered over her skull.'

Her words upset Dalip. He did not want to hear his mother being ridiculed. He began to pace the length of the small room. Each time he reached the writing table, he took an abrupt U-turn and marched to the other end of the room where he had to jerk his head abruptly to the right side to avoid hitting the wooden ledge overflowing with an assortment of creams and shampoos.

Simi burst into laughter. 'You look like a clockwork soldier marching up and down in that funny fashion.'

Red with anger, Dalip chucked the pillow at her. 'You're always criticizing someone or the other in my family. Do you imagine yourself to be some superior sort of a bitch?'

'How dare you speak to me like that? I have never spoken a word against you. I find it a little odd that your mother is constantly trying to sneak into our bedroom under one pretext or the other. Sometimes it's to bring in the newspapers, sometimes it's to bring us tea, and sometimes it is to get a cheque signed. Why is she always hovering around? Why doesn't she simply leave us alone? Papaji is no better. Like every good politician, he is always delivering lectures to me on how to speak the English language … considering his own English is so appalling. To be honest I'm disgusted at the way your parents treat their servants. Bihar maybe a hellhole, but we don't have to transplant it in our own house.'

Picking up a towel and change of clothes, Simi stormed out of the room to the bathroom located at the other end of the house. The lack of an attached bathroom was only one of the many grouses she held against the Jha family. She wished she had heeded her father, Rakesh Taneja, a prosperous factory owner, who had warned her not to rush into marriage. Rakesh had from the start been sceptical about Dalip's claim that his domineering father had coerced him into marrying an illiterate woman from his village in order to uphold their family honour. The breaking up of the second marriage was a matter of greater concern because this time round, Dalip had conceded to Simi in one of his drunken moments, that his second wife was a 'high flying corporate bird' from Mumbai.

From early January that year, Dalip had been paying special attention to Simi. He had helped rewrite her stories and ensured they were displayed well. He also encouraged her to start doing political reporting in order to gain more clout within the organization. Occasionally, he asked her to collaborate with him on a story, which would appear the next day with a joint byline.

Soon they were going out, and one evening, after a couple of drinks at the Press Club, he had proposed to her. Simi quickly agreed. As he drove her home, they had exchanged their first kiss. It turned out to be a tepid affair. She seemed shy and inhibited. He sensed her bashfulness and hoped she would prove a quick learner.

Marriage had put an end to all that bashfulness. From the very first day, Simi made it clear that she had a mind of her own. She kept a distance from his parents and sisters and refused to exchange even perfunctory greetings with them.

All kinds of thoughts flashed through Simi's mind as she came out of her bath. Should she go and spend the next few days at her parents' house? Should she escape to her teacher friend, Anita? But she would return home from school only after three p.m.

Simi decided to first go to office and see what assignments had been scheduled for her. Slipping into a pair of blue jeans and a white top, she rang for a cab. Dalip did not try to stop her. If she was going to behave in this over aggressive manner, she would end up digging her own grave.

Simi was busy keying a story into the computer by the time Dalip arrived at the *Morning Chronicle* office. It was past one p.m. His mother must have spent the morning brainwashing him against her. Close on his heels came the tall, benevolent looking, Inder sahib, who was both chief of bureau and senior editor at the *Chronicle*.

Inder sahib enjoyed playing the role of a Hugh Hefner clone before his women correspondents. Under the pretext of reading their stories, he enjoyed patting them on their backs and, if they chanced to be alone in the room, squeeze their breasts for good measure.

He stopped to read what Simi was writing. 'Marriage has improved your writing skills!' Inder sahib exclaimed.

Simi stood up before him in a show of deference. He immediately put his arm around her and began stroking her back.

'Inder sahib, you're always so encouraging. I'm feeling lousy. I could break this computer – I'm not getting the story right,' Simi cried.

'Arre baba, don't break the computer. Adhikari will send the bill to me and then I will have to get it repaired at my own expense. You know, I purchased all these chairs in this office. Adhikari reimbursed the money to me several months later. Poor fellow! In those days he was going through a bad patch financially. You should consider yourself lucky that the *Morning Chronicle* has finally broken even in Calcutta.'

Inder sahib loved to boast about his contributions in building up the paper. Most journalists saw through his tall talk. The paper's owner Adhikari continued to trust him and ultimately that was all that mattered.

Inder sahib looked at his watch. 'I say, Dalip, that *Swadesh* girl was supposed to be joining our office yesterday. There are no signs of her. Did she call you up to let you know she was not coming?'

Dalip shook his head. 'This is the first I'm hearing about a new recruit. What will she be doing here?'

'City reporting. We have nobody to cover the main city beats! Adhikari wanted coverage of these beats to be strengthened.'

Just then a tall, athletic girl in blue jeans and a clinging black top walked into the office. She announced her presence with a brilliant smile. 'Hi folks! I'm Kiki!'

'Not Kiki the parrot,' muttered high-strung Rita Sawhney, who covered the railway and civil aviation beats. She was possessive about them with rare ferocity and saw all newcomers as possible threats to her domain.

Inder sahib greeted the attractive newcomer enthusiastically, putting his arms around her and giving her a warm embrace.

'Welcome aboard! I gather you have been working with the *Swadesh* group for the last three years. You were to have joined us yesterday.'

'Some urgent work cropped up and I was forced to play truant.'

'Dalip will brief you on your beats and also tell you about our distinct approach to tackling stories. We prefer to do hardcore investigative reports. We also pay a great deal of attention to the way each story is written.

'I can assure you, young lady, Dalip will take good care of you. Don't go by the look of this overcrowded and untidy room. We have a crack team of reporters with tremendous expertise in covering national events,' Inder sahib told her.

'Without any offence to my male colleagues – when we first opened a bureau here, I had an all-women team working under me. Beautiful, high-strung women all of them! I used to boast I ran a harem. One day, one of them lost her temper and threw an ashtray at me. Thank God I was not hit. Another time, one of them threw a typewriter at my face. Aah! Such fiery creatures! They don't make them like that anymore,' Inder sahib muttered smacking his lips, his hand still around Kiki's shoulder.

Kiki tittered loudly. 'I'm surprised you didn't fire the woman who threw an ashtray at you.'

'Tauba tauba! Fire my star reporter? I put up with all their tantrums because they were hardcore professionals.'

Dalip gave Kiki a close look. Within minutes of her arrival, she was chatting and laughing with everyone. She went up to him and introduced herself. He offered her a cigarette, which she accepted. Soon they were cracking bawdy jokes and dissolving into loud laughter.

Simi watched the duo with growing unease. It was obvious to everyone present in the office that they were getting along like a house on fire. Rita Sawhney walked up to Simi's table.

'What's cooking?' she whispered. 'Do they know each other from before?'

'I don't know.'

'It's very strange – she's behaving as though they're long-lost buddies.'

Inder sahib must have also sensed that something was amiss. He came up to Dalip and said, 'What was the need for you to do a story on the caste killings in Shamli? Since when have caste killings become important? Why don't you and Simi focus on doing some good investigative reports on the defence ministry? It's reeking with scandals.'

'I think that is an excellent suggestion. I could do a few stories with Kiki also. Teach her the ropes as it were ...'

Kiki was delighted. 'I would love that. I've always wanted to work under someone dynamic, like you,' she said.

Rita gave Simi a knowing look. 'You better watch out or you're going to be in big trouble!' she whispered.

Simi was completely out of her depth. The arrival of this new woman seemed to have changed the equations in the office. At a loss for words she said, 'My God! I had to reach Shastri Bhavan by two p.m. I'm already late.'

Dalip said nothing as Simi walked out of the office. He was in no mood to forgive her for her morning's behaviour. Kiki was providing him with a convenient distraction. He was tired of all the mood swings that seemed to symbolize relationships these days.

Turning to the crime reporter, Sandeep Ahuja, he ordered him to go and attend a press conference called by the police commissioner. He would spend the afternoon chatting with this new recruit.

'Have you had lunch? We've got a nice dosa joint just across the street.'

Kiki could not believe her luck. The famous Dalip Jha was inviting her for a meal on the first day of her joining the group.

Lunch was a slow, relaxed affair. Dalip downed a couple of beers and boasted of all the ministers he had exposed during his last ten years in journalism. They were still chatting when Simi returned to the office two hours later.

She gave them a wary look but said nothing. Settling down before a computer, Simi decided to complete her story and then head for her parents' home across the Yamuna. Dalip must have sensed her unease. He came up to her table and began reading what she had written.

'Very good! Very good!' he murmured in encouragement and returned to his seat only to resume talking to Kiki again.

By now, her husband's behaviour was driving Simi insane. He had humiliated her before all her colleagues. As soon as she completed her story, Dalip got up from his table and said, 'Let's go home.'

They drove in silence for a few minutes. Then Simi exploded. 'Last night it was Raveena, today it is Kiki! What kind of a fellow are you?'

Dalip feigned innocence. 'What are you talking about?'

'I'm talking about YOU! You just went overboard with that woman.'

'I was just being friendly. Trying to make her feel at home.'

'The only two men so inclined to make that poor waif feel at home was an old lech called Inder sahib and a young lech called Dalip Jha! How come no one else in the office felt so generously inclined?'

Dalip controlled himself. 'Don't read motives where none exist,' he said.

'Everyone was shocked at the way you latched on to her. If you don't behave yourself, I'm going to complain to Adhikari, I swear,' Simi said belligerently.

Dalip brought the car to an abrupt halt. 'Don't you dare try and threaten me! If you do that again, I'll kill you. I swear it!'

Simi was beside herself with rage. 'You raise your hands against me and I'll charge you with assault.'

Dalip cooled down at once. 'I was just joking, baby! You know I didn't mean it.'

'Nor did I.'

They drove the rest of the way home in silence. Dalip tried to make light of Simi's jealousy. She was always screaming and shouting.

His mind kept going over to his conversation with Kiki. She seemed radiant with energy with her provocative smile and loud laughter. Each time she spoke, her large black eyes shone with a rare intensity. The only way he coud get to know Kiki better would be to send Simi out of town for a few days. There were a couple of out-of-station assignments coming up. If Simi fell for the bait, he would be a free bird, at least for a while.

four

Vikram drummed his fingers on his study table and hummed to himself as he gazed out of the bay windows of his office. They provided a panoramic view of the concrete jungle ahead – a vast stretch of buildings extending right up to the Delhi police headquarters. These massive rectangular structures almost hugged each other, their lofty towers only broken by black lines of cable TV antenna and water tanks standing like bulbous erections against the Delhi sky.

Bahadur Shah Zafar Marg was the nerve centre of the Indian newspaper industry. Indulgently referred to as India's Fleet Street, it consisted of a series of multi-storey office buildings housing Hindi and English newspapers, magazines and business complexes, all situated haphazardly along this main arterial road that linked the old, rundown Delhi of imperial Mughal grandeur with Lutyen's New Delhi. This maze of offices opened into a bylane connecting Bahadur Shah Zafar Marg from two ends that had been built primarily to take some of the load off the heavy traffic that poured down the main arterial road. Not that it made much difference. The area remained chock-full with vehicular traffic of every size and dimension, so much so that it had come to be described as Delhi's gas chamber. Hundreds of

Blueline buses and black-and-white auto rickshaws rattled past this road, their lines lost in the billows of smoke let out by their exhausts.

The sky stretched out like a lustrous pearl bathed in a sheen of blue. A pair of turtledoves were doing an intricate tap dance, tilting away and towards each other in a perfectly synchronized manner. Vikram could see a slim peepal sapling arching out of his rooftop. The sapling had shot up in the last two years and now imposed its tall shadow across a large part of his roof.

Vikram had made several requests to the upkeep department to hack it down. Rakesh Shukla, General Manager, Maintenance, laughingly put the matter off saying this was not an auspicious act. Everyone in the department seemed to agree. The tree remained where it was.

This was the whole problem with running a newspaper organization. No one took orders any more, though they were always the first to offer unsolicited advice. Journalists, in particular, were the biggest windbags he had met – more facetious and crafty than lawyers, politicians and teachers put together. Shukla was not a journalist, but he had been around long enough to learn the tricks of the trade. When specifically asked why the tree had not been chopped down, he came up with a long rigmarole about how a peepal sapling, even when it grew from the rooftop, provided immunity from evil spirits and wily enemies. Its leaves possessed unique medicinal value and the sheer aesthetics of seeing a sapling with its heart-shaped leaves against the sky was, to use a Keatsian phrase, a joy to behold.

The bit about 'wily enemies' had particularly unnerved Vikram Aggarwal. *The Indian Sentinel*, for one, certainly had too many enemies and too few friends. His biggest worry was his own father's health which had deteriorated in the last two years. The spreading cancer had left him so debilitated that Papaji had left the day-to-day running of the paper to Vikram.

Managing a newspaper empire had proved an awesome undertaking especially for someone who in his adolescence had dreamt of becoming a wildlife photographer. Just as he was beginning to learn the ropes, three cases under the dreaded Foreign Exchange Regulation Act (FERA) were slapped on Papaji. Rival newspapers went to town disclosing details of the vast sums of money Papaji had apparently stashed into secret Swiss accounts. Other incriminating stories about the management resorting to regular harassment of its workforce also began to surface.

The hate campaign against him left Papaji even more vulnerable. He soon started accepting counsel from all and sundry. Everyone seemed to have a suggestion or two on how the company should be run and how the senior Aggarwal should handle the FERA cases. The government's ham-handed attempts to arrest him led to a fresh blaze of adverse publicity and an increased frequency of his visits to his favourite ashram. Vikram knew who was instigating the government against Papaji. Leading the smear campaign was a caucus of rival newspaper barons, some of whom were neighbours along this very street. They had definitely succeeded in whipping up a media frenzy against his family.

Relatives and friends had rallied around insisting that Vikram should mount an effective counter-attack. All kinds of suggestions began doing the rounds. An elderly uncle suggested a spectacular fashion show; the tantalizing display of tits and bums by pleasure women specially flown in from Hong Kong would keep the investigative officials so preoccupied that they would lose interest in the case. A maternal aunt proposed a special tantrik puja costing upwards of thirty lakh rupees. A distant relative, also a director in the company, suggested that their legal advisers address a press conference to present their point of view before the public.

The last idea seemed sensible at first. But it backfired. Apart from saddling the establishment with a five-lakh rupee hotel bill spent on satiating the appetites of the hordes of scribes, and another thirty-lakh rupees coughed up as fees to their legal team, the briefing turned out to be an unmitigated disaster. Instead of highlighting the vicious witch-hunt against his father, it provided the right platform for the press to go to town revealing all kinds of salacious details about the family and its involvement in other underhanded deals. To have forked out so much money, only to get egg thrown on one's face, was hardly the best way to do business.

Vikram was convinced that there was no point in pushing things further. It was better instead to adopt a low-key approach. One could very well keep the pressure on the government by running a series of hard-hitting stories and entering into a settlement of sorts once the right appeasement noises started emanating from the other side. After all, no government, leave alone this ragtag coalition, could ignore a thirteen-lakh circulation daily.

Aggarwal Junior next drew up his impeccable plan of action. At a specially convened closed-door meeting at the Oberoi, the bureau chiefs and resident editors of the major centres were told to plan for a daily front-page item focussing on human rights violations by the state. Custodial deaths, unprovoked police firing, harassment of businessmen, Draconian laws conferring powers to the State to make arrests without any trial or right of appeal ... the idea was to churn out a sustained campaign showing how arbitrary the government was.

Above all, there would also be a daily column educating the public on various legislations and how they were being misused by the bureaucracy to hinder legitimate business activity. The problem in this otherwise brilliant, well-laid out strategy lay in the sort of people manning the positions of senior editors and bureau chiefs. Most of them behaved like over-fed poodles. Too many perks had left them a pampered and spoilt lot. They lacked the killer instinct.

Vikram nervously drummed his fingers on the table. These people needed to be shown what they were really worth. The paper wasn't selling because of them. Rather, they owed their bloody existence to this damn paper. Vikram always resented his father for giving far too much attention to these editorial wallahs. Useless fellows! They didn't even know how to sell soap, leave alone newspapers! Anyway, how many people read what they wrote? Even if some did, what sense could they make out of all their pontificatory prose?

Picking up the bell, Vikram pressed it impatiently. Laxman, a chaprasi employed with the company for the last thirty years, tottered into the room. 'Ask Rajan to come and see me right away.'

Rajan, a senior manager who had wormed his way into Vikram's confidence by helping increase advertising revenues, was sitting in a cabin located just below Vikram's office on the sixth floor. When he saw Laxman at his door, he knew it was a call from the big boss. Hurrying up the staircase, he almost collided into Ajay Singh, the editor-in-chief of their Hindi daily, *Amar Prakash* and a trusted confidant of Vikram. Ajay, he noticed, was wearing a suit and tie instead of his usual grubby jeans. Could he be going out for a television interview? This man was always cocking a snook at the management and needed to be cut to size. So far Rajan had steered clear of him because he was considered one of Vikram's confidants. The situation could always be made to change. Vikram was never known to hold on to his favourites for long.

As Rajan walked down the long corridor that led to Vikram's office, his mind kept returning to the expectant look on Ajay's face. A rumour had been doing the rounds that the owner might offer Ajay the post of a director if he succeeded in soliciting the prime minister's help in removing the FERA cases against Aggarwal senior. Ajay was known to have visited the PM's office twice during the last fortnight. Little was known of what had transpired between the two men. Rajan had himself been coveting the post of director. He was not going to allow it to be handed over to a man who subscribed to the old value-based school of journalism with its outmoded notion of fair play and minimum interference from the sixth floor. If this interference increased beyond legitimate proportions, Ajay would not hesitate to take the brand managers to task. This would not do. Rajan strode into Vikram's room and without further ado informed Vikram, 'I've just got word that the CBI plan to reopen File 213 in a fresh attempt to harass you.'

Vikram knew that File No 213 dealt with Papaji's case. Their opponents were always putting pressure to get his father re-arrested. Three such attempts had been made during the last twelve months. All three times they had succeeded in aborting such a bid. Still, no one knew what the directorate would come up with next. The next man there, M.K. Hazarika, a 1967 Assam cadre IAS officer seemed a specially tough nut to crack.

Vikram turned pale. 'Why would the directorate take such a step? I thought we had taken care of the minister,' he blurted.

'Yes, of course. We paid him a big sum of money. We still need to be careful. He's only a minister of state.'

'Why are you making such a noise about their wanting to reopen the file? It could be just a routine enquiry.'

Rajan was at his authoritative best. 'This business has to stop. If the case is reopened, all kinds of genies will pop out of the bottle. Why should we allow ourselves to be placed in the dock at a time when we have almost succeeded in brushing this entire episode under the carpet?'

Vikram mulled over his words. There was some truth in what he said. 'Shall I ask Gupta to phone the minister again? Maybe we need to send another instalment of cash to him.'

Gupta was the main fixer of their organization and operated from a separate office in Greater Kailash.

'Sir, that will not do at all. Ministers only know how to shoot orders. It is the foot soldiers who fight their battles. Gupta is overwhelmed with handling work for the entire organization. We need a separate troubleshooter to interface with the bureaucrats. Someone who can meet them day in and day out and then slam their faces hard if required. We need to fix that Hazarika fellow.'

Vikram exploded. 'I'm sick of hiring people! I am not running a charitable institution! This is an overstaffed organization. We need to get rid of people.'

'Sir, forgive me for doing some plain speaking. The reopening of a file could be a precursor to the issuing of fresh charges. We are surrounded by enemies. I had warned you to be prepared for a long fight.'

Vikram sat back in his chair and stared out at the peepal tree. 'What do you suggest I do?'

'We need a troubleshooter to interface with the government. He must also handle the unions on our behalf and keep us informed about what is happening in that snake-pit downstairs.'

Vikram nodded. The man spoke sense. 'All right. I'll get back to you on this.'

Rajan had barely stepped out when Ajay Singh knocked and entered the room, expectancy written large all over his eager face. Vikram had seen the expression many times in the past on the faces of prospective job seekers. The look irritated him. Not that Ajay Singh was by any standards a job-seeker. He was an exceptional journalist with a sharp news sense and a command over both Hindi and English. He had built up the *Amar Prakash* daily from scratch.

Since Ajay had a close working relationship with the prime minister, Vikram had asked him to put in a word at 7 Race Course to get the FERA cases withdrawn. Both times the PM had promised to stop the witch-hunt. Unfortunately, little had emerged from these meetings.

Vikram indicated to Ajay Singh to sit down. Then in a seemingly deliberate, almost rude manner, he turned his gaze to the vast sky which by now had turned to a dark, menacing grey. A dust storm was beginning to pick up, and the leaves of the peepal tree were flapping wildly in the air. There was pindrop silence in the room.

Ajay looked uneasily at Vikram, who continued to stare out of the window,

'I have repeatedly told people in this organization that I mean the best for them. They deliberately misunderstand my words because they have no stake in their profession. Journalists are concerned only with self-promotion. Today we are in a situation where no one has any stake left in this organization – not even the editor.'

Ajay Singh looked curiously at Vikram. Whenever he spoke in riddles, it meant he was trying to evade the key issue at hand. Behind that pleasant exterior lay a shifty, cunning personality with eyes that never focussed on any person or object for long.

'It is because of this lack of involvement that we are seeing an overall decline in both the quality and content of newspapers. I believe that if such a situation continues, there will be no newspapers left in the country.'

Jumping out of the chair with studied anguish, Vikram started thumping the table. 'There are forty million unemployed graduates registered in our employment exchange. Has the government helped one of them get a job? At the same time, the government thinks nothing of harassing a hundred-year-old institution that provides employment to five lakh people. It is because of this government indifference that youngsters are turning to crime. There has been a dramatic increase in cases of murder, rape and extortion. Where all this will end, no one knows. I shudder to think of what the future holds for all of us.'

Ajay Singh crossed and uncrossed his legs uncomfortably. Why was he spewing this shit at him? Whenever he had told Vikram to adopt a hard-hitting line against the government, he had insisted they take a more restrained approach.

'If newspapers shut down, it will be the man on the street who will be the loser. The rich and powerful will get their news through Internet and cable. It is the poor people who sit in dhabas and share one common newspaper who will be the sufferers.

'Do not presume I am less socially committed than anyone else. Some editors may claim they are more powerful than others, but they are all dispensable. My institution has provided a forum for every changing nuance in this nation. I wear the mantle of history on my shoulders.

'I know my enemies want to destroy me. They will leave no stone unturned to sabotage my organization. They have subverted the entire government machinery for their ends. I will not cave in so easily. I am biding my time and will retaliate when the iron is hot.'

Ajay Singh could no longer hide his restlessness. He crossed and uncrossed his legs and snatched a glance through the huge windows. The storm continued to rage outside. Dust-laden winds were circling outside like whirling dervishes. A self-effacing sun resurfaced in the sky for a few moments and then retreated behind an armada of dark clouds. It was obvious Vikram was no longer interested in offering him the directorship.

By now Vikram was pacing the room, his feet moving as rapidly as the tempest outside. 'I need trusted assistants. I need reliable friends. I am carrying the weight of the nation on my shoulders.'

Walking up to Ajay, he impulsively stretched his right hand out in a handshake. Taken aback, Ajay Singh clasped it with both his hands. The meeting was over. The proprietor had demonstrated his affection for his employee by shaking hands with him. He had offered him little else. Ajay had entered the room with high hopes. He was walking out empty-handed.

To Ajay's surprise, Rajan was standing outside, file in hand. One look at Ajay's dejected face was sufficient indication of what had transpired inside. Rubbing his face with obvious satisfaction, Rajan strode into Vikram's room.

'I thought I'd provide you with a quick update on the case. I think I've found the operative clause we can use to demolish the opposition.'

'Do we need to make a fresh representation before the damn minister?'

'Not at all! This time round we will concentrate on the babus. It is they who will do our work. I've just singled out someone in the Enforcement Directorate who will bend in our favour. Everything rests on the terms of our offer. Once that is worked out, he can start his stonewalling tactics.'

Vikram tugged at the corners of his greying moustache. Middle age was setting in. Soon he too would begin to feel like an old man. 'How many people do I have to keep bribing? Dammit, I have already told you this is not a charitable institution.'

'Sir, we cannot allow our files to be scrutinized repeatedly. We must launch a counterattack against the other newspaper barons many of whom have got away scot-free for worse crimes.'

Vikram mulled over Rajan's suggestions. There was a grain of truth in what he spoke. 'Leave the files here. I'll go through them again.'

Rajan left the room rejoicing to see his boss's nose stuck once again in a mound of files. It would keep him occupied for some time. On entering his room, he picked up the phone. It was celebration time. He would host a party for some office colleagues. Ajay's wings were now clipped. He dialled his residence number.

'H-e-l-l-o!,' cooed Arati.

Kala Muthu had his hands cupped round her breast and was playing with her nipples.

'Oouch!' She screamed.

'Arati, what is the matter? Are you all right?'

Arati shoved her elbow into Kala Muthu's stomach.

'I'm fine. For a second, I thought I was going to have a blackout.'

'I need to call a few people over in the evening. Will you be able to organize dinner at such short notice?' asked Rajan.

'How many people?'

'Twenty-thirty.'

'Are you joking? You want thirty hulks fed at such short notice?'

Kala Muthu had started stroking her thighs. She gave a loud tinkle of laughter and sighed with satisfaction.

'Baba, you give me no choice. Everything will be ready by seven p.m. Come soon. I'm missing you.'

She slammed the phone down. Kala Muthu hurriedly removed her remaining clothes and bit her breasts and neck till she was screaming with delight. It was obvious he fancied her body. She found him a little uncouth, but he satisfied her and that was all she wanted. He was ready to give her one orgasm after another. She glanced at her watch. It was nearing four p.m. Soon it would be time to call the servants. He must leave the house before they arrived. He could join her at the party. She would invite him and introduce him to her husband. Rajan was a hospitable host and always liked to entertain fellow Tamilians. Kala Muthu may not belong to their caste; he was nonetheless a good Tamilian boy.

**

Attar Singh had been a peon with *The Indian Sentinel* for thirty-five years. He had joined the company as a lad of sixteen, fresh from his village in Unnao near Kanpur. For several months after joining work, he used to arrive at the office looking every inch the country yokel with a freshly ironed dhoti tied round his legs and a red safa placed rakishly on his head.

One morning, Aggarwal senior saw him enter the office dressed in this manner.

'Who is this joker? Get him a proper uniform!' he thundered.

The head of the personnel division hurriedly passed these instructions to another underling and within the next two hours, Attar Singh was strutting around in a grey safari suit. He had worn the grey flannel uniform ever since.

When the uniform had been handed to him, a member of the personnel staff had warned him. 'You will not enter the office with unironed clothes! Is that clear?'

Attar Singh followed his advice. He arrived every morning on the dot of nine, wearing an immaculately ironed uniform. He left office at eight sharp, and this remained his routine all through the next 35-odd years. As a peon, he earned a salary of three hundred rupees per month, barely enough to make ends meet. To augment his income, and on the advice of friends, he had started lending out small amounts of money on interest to both friends and colleagues. It was a small, low-key affair. The interest money helped in paying for the education of his only child. Attar Singh wanted the best for his daughter Shanti and had insisted on admitting her into a private school.

During the summer months, on his way back from work to his one-room tenement in Gautam Nagar, he invariably stopped at Shiv Rabriwallah to buy two hundred grams of rabri for Shanti, who had just completed her tenth class board exams.

Shiv Rabriwallah always parked his cart outside the *Daily Tej* newspaper office, a tall building located to the left of the *Sentinel* building. The routine was no different today. It was a hot, sultry summer evening. Stepping out of the cool air-conditioned office, Attar Singh grumbled to himself, 'Always the same! Flies and mosquitoes! Flies and mosquitoes! Take one step and you could well be stepping into dog shit! Take another, and you might break your ankle in a pothole.'

He was mumbling to himself when he reached Shiv Rabriwallah who gave him a welcoming smile.

'Barre bhai, I've kept aside the best portion for you. How did your betiya like the rabri yesterday?'

'Arre baba, Shanti refuses to sleep at night till she has eaten this stuff. I've never missed buying it for twenty years now.'

'Yes, barre bhai, it's been a lifetime. You were buying it from my father before me.'

He measured the amount and packed it carefully into a plastic packet. Attar Singh put the packet into a small cloth bag dangling from his arm.

Even though it was quite late in the evening, the narrow lane that swept by the front of the newspaper offices was still overflowing with people. Headlights from the cars flashed straight into his eyes dazzling him for a moment. Pedestrians had to weave their way in and out of this incessant traffic, terrified of being knocked down at any moment.

Attar Singh continued to mumble to himself. 'Flies and mosquitoes!' There were no street lights on the road. A usual phenomenon, he told himself, clutching his bag as he began to make his way through the traffic. He passed the juice-wallahs, the paratha-wallahs, the chaat-wallahs, the ice cream wallahs, all of whom manned their regular positions on both sides of the road.

The smell of the food intermixed with the traffic fumes depressed him. He hurried along as he did not want to miss his bus, which left ITO sharp at eight-fifteen p.m.The incessant roar of the traffic on the Bahadur Shah Zafar Marg deafened the sounds emanating from the presses working overtime in the adjoining buildings. Going past Link House, he crossed the makeshift jhuggi housing Chowdhury's Taxi Service stand, which derived much of its business from the newspaper officers in Fleet Street.

As he walked past the taxi stand, the shadow of a man crossed the road and reached out behind him. In a flash, a sharp narrow blade was taken out of its scabbard and thrust into his abdomen. Attar Singh was still conscious when a deep-throated voice hissed, 'Be warned! I've let you off this time. But the second time this knife sinks into your flesh, you will be a dead man.'

The man disappeared, leaving him to lie bleeding on the roadside.

**

Attar Singh sat on his string bed. Bandaged around the abdomen, he was glancing through the pages of some crude cash account books trying to make sense of a jumble of numbers. During the last two days, confined to a hospital bed, his mind had been constantly at work. A good Samaritan had rushed him to the nearby Lok Nayak hospital, but recovery was slow. The office had granted him one month's medical leave. The office union had taken up his case insisting that he be given leave with full pay till he recovered completely.

Even after being shifted home, his colleagues continued to pour in and enquire about his condition.

'Hell and damnation! Who could have done it? Why would anyone want to bump you off?' This was the first question his colleague, Jodh Singh, also a peon at his office, asked him as he pulled up a chair and sat down next to him at his house. 'Do you think one of the fellows who did not pay you back was taking his revenge on you?'

Attar shook his head sadly. 'I don't know. Mine was a small business. I never lent too much money to anyone. I just did it to earn a little extra money. I never thought I had a single enemy in this world.'

Jodh Singh nodded his head. There was some truth in what Attar said. Why would anyone want to kill this harmless old buffoon?

Jodh Singh glanced at Attar's pleasant-looking daughter, Shanti, who had brought him a cup of tea. She had nursed her father right through the period he had spent in hospital. His wife, Radha had been of no help at all. She had gone into acute depression and was under medication. Even after Attar Singh was brought home, she lay in one corner of the house unable to reconcile herself to the stabbing of her husband.

Shanti remained in full control of the situation. She dressed his wound daily and made sure he took his medicines on time. Once he was able to sit up, the first thing Attar demanded was that Shanti bring all his registers and lay them out in front of him. He now spent all his time studying these books, which he had so meticulously maintained for the last thirty-five years.

Occasionally, loans had been extended to people working in other offices as well, but these were exceptions. The principal loan sum never exceeded thirty thousand rupees, and though he charged interest at two per cent per month, his recovery levels were pretty good. There had been to date only a couple of defaulters. Jodh Singh was amongst them. He had borrowed twelve thousand rupees. Attar had warned him many times to return the money. Every time Jodh Singh had promised to pay up, but one calamity or the other hit his personal life and nothing came out of these warnings.

Even though they were friends, Attar Singh had reported the matter of his default to Shankar Sen, president of *The Indian Sentinel* union for the last thirty-eight years. Sen had reassured Attar Singh that if Jodh Singh, an active member of the union, failed to pay the amount by the end of this year, they would collect the money from the other union members and pay it back on his behalf.

The second person he had lent money to was Billa, a small-time pickpocket who worked outside the Red Fort area. Attar would never have lent him the money had his old-time friend Gulabo Khan Pathan not stood as guarantor. Gulabo Khan Pathan knew everyone who mattered in and around Chandni Chowk. Billa needed ten thousand rupees for his sister's wedding and promised to return it over a period of two years.

Attar Singh had actually attended the ceremony and was confident the money would be returned as promised. Unfortunately Billa was knocked down by a speeding DTC bus, leaving him a cripple who could only walk around with the help of a stick. Once he recovered, he started doing odd jobs, but he could no longer return to his old business. He was hardly in a position to put a knife into anyone.

The more he thought about the stabbing, the more confused he became. He was a man with few enemies and yet someone wanted him out of the way. Who could this person be? He had a vague suspicion that the person was someone belonging to his office. Otherwise why would the stabbing have taken place on Fleet Street? Attar Singh was determined to get to the bottom of this mystery.

five

Raveena Bedi hurried up the flight of steps leading into the *Sentinel* office. She had not slept well last night after Dalip's abrupt departure. She must find herself an apartment in a more upmarket area. She needed to lay her hands on some extra money. *The Indian Sentinel* was the richest media house in the country. She must find herself a godfather inside the organization who would help her earn the big bucks. Rajan may be an opportune choice. He drew a salary which was larger than the entire pay package being doled out to the journalists working in the *Amar Prakash* stable. Work on him, or better still, on the owner?

Just then, Kala Muthu, dressed in tight black jeans, an orange shirt and knee-high cowboy boots, hurried into the office only to find himself stopped by a smartly dressed receptionist.

Raveena eyed him with interest. What was this peculiar-looking character doing inside her office? Raveena stopped at the entrance to overhear the receptionist ask him, 'Who have you come to meet?'

'Mr Rajan! He is expecting me,' Kala Muthu replied in his curiously accented English.

'Yes, of course,' the receptionist said and began typing out his particulars onto a computer. Raveena looked at her watch. It was five past twelve. Ajit Jolly, newly appointed acting bureau chief of the *Sentinel*, had allowed her, a city reporter, to sit in in the bureau meeting and she did not want to be late for it.

Entering the bureau, Raveena found only three out of the twelve special correspondents attending the meeting. They listened to Jolly's rambling discourse on the virtues of breaking exclusive stories with an air of obvious boredom. The morning edition looked dreadfully dull with two major items front-paged by their rivals not even figuring in the paper. Not that there was anything new in this. As was often the case, the concerned correspondent had filed the story, only to find it axed at the last moment to make space for a management plug.

Lighting a cigarette, Raveena inhaled deeply. A master at smooth talk, an art she had perfected over time to selectively deploy with her amorous bosses, Raveena exhaled a cloud of smoke. Determined to become the centre of attention, she pounded her thick fist on the Burmese teak table and yelled, 'Sir! You must read your report to us. It will serve as an objective lesson on how news is to be reported.'

Jolly blushed. Removing his spectacles, he began wiping them, surveying the scene with a grim expression on his face. Nattily dressed in a grey suit and maroon silk tie, he epitomized the growing tribe of journalists, who spent more time currying favours with the managerial establishment on the fifth floor, than discussing the intricacies of news-gathering with their demoralized bureau colleagues.

'No no! I'm too old to be giving sermons from the pulpit. I'll read it sitting from this chair.'

'OK. If that suits you, it's fine with us too.'

Jolly needed no further encouragement. Without further ado, he picked up that morning's edition and began reading out the lead story in his characteristically loud American-Punjabi twang.

'Speaking from the ramparts of the Red Fort, Prime Minister Ananda Krishnan today announced a far-reaching package of programmes to address the needs of the girl child. Every girl, on attaining the age of five, would be compulsorily registered in a primary school. The local schoolteacher would open a Nirman Patra account in her name in a bank with an initial sum of five hundred rupees. The money will be kept there as a fixed deposit till she reached the age of eighteen or completed Class 12. This money would then have multiplied to the sum of Rs 21,000 and could be used to cover her marriage expenses.'

Still to recover from their previous night's hangover, the other reporters watched the goings-on in disbelief. Jolly was actually reading out this puerile rubbish as though it were a Pulitzer Prize winning dispatch.

'Wah! Wah!' muttered Keith D'Souza, an erstwhile firebrand hack and union activist, much-chastened now after a recent two-year stint in the insurgency-ridden north-east. 'If only you had read this out from the ramparts of the Red Fort. At least, it would have carried more conviction.'

Picking up his notebook, Keith strode out of the room. As always, the joke had not registered. If this was the calibre of our bureau chiefs, God help this profession, he told himself.

**

Kala Muthu had never seen such a plush newspaper office in his life. He was expecting a claustrophobic, overcrowded hole littered with broken-down chairs and tables, overused typewriters and pieces of yellow paper thrown all over the floor. At least that was what newspaper offices looked like back home in Chennai. *The Indian Sentinel* office turned out to have the ambience of a five-star hotel with sparkling granite floors and expensive artefacts lining the walls. The marble portico at the entrance had a glistening fountain in the centre. Gilded statues of gods and goddesses lined the entrance, and the walls had murals from the *Ramayana* and *Mahabharata* embossed on them.

The décor reminded him of Rajan's own house – all glitter and shine. Arati had been effusive in the way she had introduced him to Rajan at last night's party.

'He's looking for a job. He comes from our village – a good Tamilian. Innocent and pure at heart.'

'Where did you meet him?' Rajan asked. He was always happy to meet a fellow Tamilian.

'I met him some months ago at my friend Appachana's house. He has been helping Appachana in the running of his factory. Appachana told me he was good at handling people. He is a tough guy!'

Rajan had invited him to visit his office the very next day. Realizing this was a golden opportunity to gain a foothold into a high profile organization, Kala Muthu had arrived there looking his best.

Rajan was astonished to see his clothes. 'Do you know Hindi?' he asked.

'No problem, saar, I speak well both Hindi and English,' Kala Muthu shot back, breaking into a distinctly Madrasi Hindi. 'What work will I be expected to do?'

Confident chap, Rajan said to himself. He was reminded of his own Mylapore days, when the only impressive thing he possessed, apart from his 32-inch bell bottoms, was abundant cockiness and an ability to adapt to any situation.

'Keep an eye on what is happening. Keep me informed and updated about any union plans. I'll explain in the next few days how you will be expected to get the information across.'

'Under what designation will I work?'

'Don't worry about that – you will get a good salary. Technically we are hiring you as an administrative trainee. But your main job will be to keep an eye on what is happening here. You will follow instructions closely. It will be a low profile but lucrative designation if you do it seriously, OK?'

Rajan rang the bell a couple of times. Jodh Singh, the peon, dawdled inside. 'Take him to meet Nangiaji, so he can get his ID card made Then shift him to Cabin 65.'

'Cabin 65?' Jodh Singh looked surprised.

'Why are you looking at me like that? Can't understand Hindi or what?'

'No sahib ... I will take him there right away.'

Jodh Singh, small and cunning, cocked his face at Kala Muthu in a deliberately insolent manner. Leading him down a corridor that opened into a large hall where groups of workers were sitting on the floor slipping supplements into the main paper, he said cheekily, 'One more Madrasi fellow has joined our paper.'

'If you make that statement again I'll beat you up.'

Jodh Singh was not one to get intimidated easily.

'Arre, the owner has not been able to beat me up for the last thirty-six years. Who are you?'

Kala Muthu swore under his breath.

'Take me to the ID card wallah and get on with your job.'

Jodh Singh led him down a flight of steps to a large basement. At the end of this room, he could see two cabins opening into the main hall. Jodh Singh led him to the first room, where slumped on a chair stamping envelopes was a white-haired, broad-shouldered fellow with sharp black eyes. An assortment of workers sat around him slurping tea from tiny mugs.

'Nangia Sahib, there is a new arrival here. He's come to get a collar put around his neck,' announced Jodh Singh.

Nangia looked at Kala Muthu in surprise. 'He must be a new recruit for the security section. Why have you brought him here?'

'Arre sir-ji, he's the new recruit for Cabin 65. At least give him a decent chair to sit on.'

'We are all the illegitimate progeny of this mighty organization. From where can I produce an extra chair?' Picking up the phone, Nangia dialled the photo section. 'Mahender, we have a new fellow here. Come over and take his picture. He needs an ID card.'

Mahender sauntered in a couple of minutes later, camera in hand.

'He's going to be sitting in Cabin 65,' Nangia informed him with a tight grimace on his face.

Mahender's face contorted in disgust. 'One more management flunkey has joined our company. He looks like a cowboy from the deep south,' he said.

Nangia tried hard to keep a straight face. The others in the room howled with laughter. 'Our office is unique. Every day they get hold of a new character.'

Mahender got Kala Muthu to stand at one end of the room. Settling his hair and shirt, he focussed the camera on his face and clicked.

'Jodh Singh, you're right about unique characters. Have the pix collected from the photo section in the next two hours,' said Mahender and walked off.

Kala Muthu was beginning to feel uncomfortable. Why were these people making all these snide remarks about him considering he had scarcely stepped into the office? More than that, he couldn't understand their Hindi, though he could make out that they were pretty liberal with expletives obviously targeted at him. Turning to Jodh Singh he said, 'What d'you mean by calling me a management flunkey? I've joined as a management trainee! You open your big mouth again and I'll break your front teeth.'

Jodh Singh caught him by the shirt and hit him hard on the head. The other workers joined in, and the blows reined on his back and head. Kala Muthu tried hitting back but was outnumbered.

'Stop fighting in my cabin!' Nangia screamed ostensibly concerned but making no effort to end the quarrel.

'Traitor! How much are they paying you to ensure our families and children starve?' asked one bearded worker.

'Motherfucker! Sneaked in here to snatch our livelihood away,' said another.

A security guard who happened to be passing by pressed the alarm bell. Within minutes, a posse of security men rescued Kala Muthu. He was led outside the building to the first-aid room where the doctor on duty began attending to his wounds.

A few minutes later, an agitated Rajan hurried into the room. 'What is this? This is your first day at work, and you've already succeeded in creating a scene,' shouted Rajan.

'Sahib, I had gone to get my photo taken when these people attacked me.'

'I suggest you return to your cabin and keep the door locked for the time being. You lay off these guys. Is that clear?'

Kala Muthu was not willing to let Rajan off that easily.

'Do workers here go around beating up administrative trainees without any provocation? What have I done?' he asked defiantly.

Offended at his tone, Rajan rebuked him sternly. 'I have not hired you so that you could pick a quarrel with anyone. Learn to take things in your stride. And kindly remember one more detail for the future. Please do not come to office wearing these flamboyant clothes. This is a newspaper office, not a film studio.'

Rajan strode out of the room without another word.

Kala Muthu was feeling shaky as he walked back to his cabin. He cursed Arati for allowing him to get trapped in this situation. Bitch! Sleeping around with all kinds of men when she had a perfectly decent husband taking care of her. These high-flying Delhi women were all the same. Determined to derive pleasure, even if it meant exploiting a poor country bumpkin like himself.

Sitting down quietly on a chair, Kala Muthu went over the

morning's events. There was something about this cabin which spelt trouble. The minute the peon came to know that he was being placed in Cabin 65, he had turned belligerent. He must get to the bottom of this mystery or else his own head would be on the chopping block.

Rajan had insisted a security guard be posted outside his cabin. His presence seemed to have made no difference as two workers burst into his room without any resistance. 'Bloody black Madrasi!' they shouted raising their fists threateningly at him.

Frightened they might attack him, Kala Muthu hid under the table. Just then the phone rang. He picked it up diffidently. 'You motherfucker! We'll kill you yet!' a husky voice said from the other end.

He slammed the phone down. These guys really hated him but he couldn't fathom why.

He decided to seek out Shankar Sen, president of the *Sentinel* union. Sen might provide him with an explanation to why he was being treated in this manner. Sen's cabin was actually a tinier version of his own. Four plastic chairs were placed in a semicircle opposite his small desk.

'Come in! Come in!' Sen said with a flourish. A genial, middle-aged man with a sizeable girth, there was a certain dignity about his bearing. 'You are the famous Kala Muthu. I heard my workers roughed you up this morning.'

Kala Muthu nodded.

'You poor fellow! What a welcome to receive in a new office. Did you try acting funny with them?'

'No saar. I have come to ask you exactly this question. I had barely stepped inside the office when these men started abusing me and beating me up.'

Sen shook his head indulgently.

'Youngsters today have become very hot-headed. I keep warning them to mend their ways, but they will not listen to me.

They cannot be blamed entirely. If you are working in an organization where the company has not paid their dues for the last eight-nine months, you too will end up becoming belligerent. No one wants to lose his job.'

'But why hit out at me? I am just a management trainee.'

Kala Muthu's eyes kept wandering about the room as they talked. The walls were paan stained and filthy. A heap of files was stacked away in one corner. He presumed these had something to do with the union's activities. He would come back and go through them when no one was around.

Sen must have understood what was going on in his mind. In his quiet and understated style he said, 'Actually the management here has the keys to all our rooms. Nothing is hidden from them.'

Kala Muthu flushed. 'I am here to seek your guidance. I want to cooperate with you and all the workers. Let me know if I can be of any service to the union.'

Just then two workers barged into the room.

A bearded fellow whose name turned out to be Krishna Mohan Singh thumped the table and shouted, 'Sen sahib, we are being forcibly shifted from Daryaganj to Sahibabad. We will be forced to spend two extra hours commuting back and forth every day. This will cost us at least three hundred rupees more in bus fares. Who will reimburse us for these additional transportation costs?'

Sen heard them out patiently, 'Comrades, let me first find out the details, then I will get back to you on this matter.'

Krishna Mohan was not reassured.

'We can't be expected to take everything lying down. We insist that details of our transfers be made known to us. We are planning to go from one department to another and hold meetings to highlight our grievances.'

'Does the management know of your plans?'

Shakeel, the second worker, spat on the floor scornfully.

'Do we need to take the management's permission every time we fart? We will take a procession out this very evening.'

Kala Muthu got up hastily. He had managed to get some juicy bit of information. Hurrying back to his cabin, he picked up the phone and rang Rajan.

'I have some important news to give you. The union members are planning to lead a procession and distribute pamphlets this evening.'

'You bloody fool! Every phone in this office is tapped. The unions have their men everywhere. My secretary will give you a pager number. Leave all your messages there. You will be contacted at the appropriate time,' Rajan bellowed back.

'Don't you want to hear what I was going to tell you?' Kala Muthu remonstrated.

'The workers will be holding a demonstration to express their grievances. I already know about this,' Rajan shouted and slammed the phone down.

Kala Muthu dialled Arati's number.

'I need to see you urgently.'

Arati tittered, 'No, you can't see me today. I have a date with my hairdresser. I have to attend a party this evening. Call me tomorrow morning and we'll fix a date.'

Just three rooms away, Krishan Mohan Singh and Shakeel were holding a meeting with some workers to finalize the strategy for the evening's demonstration. Both had worked as typesetters in *The Indian Sentinel* for twenty years. The advent of new technology including PC servers and automatic pagination had made their jobs redundant. Being graduates with fluency in both English and Hindi, they believed that the management could have helped upgrade their skills, but they had been deliberately bypassed because of their union activities.

A few minutes after five p.m., Krishna Mohan and Shakeel led a group of workers up a flight of steps to the second floor office from where *Amar Prakash* was published. As they entered, two members of the security staff forcibly gripped Krishna Mohan by his shoulders and warned him to stop. Mohan resisted. A scuffle ensued. Losing his balance, Mohan went tumbling down the steps hitting his forehead against a corner.

Bleeding profusely, Krishna Mohan Singh screamed. 'You bunch of Mir Jaffars! Aren't you ashamed of licking your master's arses? You have become like the East India Company – squeezing the Indians of their last drop of blood, so that your filthy rich masters get even richer. Get out of my way or we will fight you through.'

Hearing his shouts, more workers poured in from the basement. The security men were forced to beat a hasty retreat. A triumphant Krishna Mohan, handkerchief tied around his bleeding head, led his team of workers from floor to floor shouting 'Inquilab Zindabad!' Soon a large crowd of over one hundred workers had assembled in the foyer leading into the second floor offices.

Striking a heroic pose, Krishna Mohan Singh made an impassioned speech. 'Brothers, I have come to warn you. Today, the security staff stopped me from entering your offices. Tomorrow they will treat you all in the same manner. The management wants everyone to keep their eyes shut, so that they can continue to play their cunning games with us.'

'They are continuing their devious strategy of getting rid of the majority of our workers. Today, they are doing it with me – tomorrow they will do the same with all of you. This year their profits have quadrupled to Rs 120 crore. How has this come about? By sacking six hundred staffers from around the country. We are now being forced to move to Sahibabad. I am warning you all. Unless we join hands, you will all meet the same fate. They are not even sparing reporters, let alone people like us. The entire bureau has been told to use only one phone. Reporters are being told to buy their own notebooks and pens. Tomorrow they will grudge your entering this office and will demand a toll from you because you are trespassing into their private office space. We have lost all vestiges of our dignity and are in the process of becoming slaves.'

By this time, the entire editorial staff had gathered to listen to Krishna Mohan's polemics. No one dared utter a word in support. Most of them had been hired on contracts and did not want to be seen publicly associating with these union wallahs. Many of them knew they had been reduced to nothing more than glorified stenos. The overall economic situation in the country was so dismal, they had no choice but to cling desperately to their present jobs.

The only journalists doing well in these times were those who had forged direct links with the managerial types in the company. These super hacks, nicknamed the Bhishma Pitamaahs of *The Indian Sentinel*, strode into the office with supercilious smirks on their faces, confidence oozing out of every pore. Vikram Aggarwal provided them loans to buy all the latest gizmos from cars to even roll-on deodorants. And since they were the ones who were seen to be calling the shots – whether in selecting which story was to be chosen and where it was to be displayed, or in deciding who was to be promoted and to what level – the ordinary hacks had no option but to bend over backwards to curry favour with them.

Krishna Mohan Singh knew his words were falling on deaf ears. He soldiered on, allowing his oratorial blast to last a good thirty minutes. The group then trudged up to the sixth floor. It was completely deserted.

Raveena Bedi had also got wind of the union's plans. Realizing she could use this opportunity to win points with Vikram Aggarwal, she had rushed up to the top floor and informed his stenographer, Banerjee, that she needed to see the proprietor on an urgent matter. Banerjee stared at her with disbelief. No correspondent had ever come up to him with such a strange request. The momentary confusion provided her with the chance to barge into his room.

'The union people are planning to create trouble for you. You must leave at once.'

Vikram Aggarwal stared at Raveena. How did this fat woman have the gumption to enter his office in this manner? Rajan had warned him to expect some trouble from these union ruffians but he had presumed the demonstration would turn out to be little more than a pinprick. The large security contingent in his office should have been able to take care of it.

'Hurry up sir! The situation can become explosive!' Raveena said. She opened the door briefly and he could hear the shouts of the union workers expressing solidarity for their cause.

Picking up his briefcase, he hurried to the emergency exit that opened into a special car park where his steel grey Mercedes Benz was parked. Raveena followed him up to the exit. The security staff, led by Major Anupam Sood, trailed haplessly behind.

As soon as Vikram had driven off, Raveena decided to go back to office and find out what the union wallahs were up to. She took a lift up to the sixth floor where the union leaders were moving from one executive's room to another.

Kala Muthu was following Krishna Mohan, listening in to what the union leaders were saying to one another.

Raveena walked up to Kala Muthu. This was a good opportunity to find out a little bit about this stranger.

'You must be a management trainee? Is this your first day at work?' Raveena flashed one of her most coaxing smiles.

'Yaas,' Kala Muthu replied. She was the first person in the *Sentinel* to have spoken to him in a normal manner.

'What is your name?'

'Kala Muthu.'

Raveena shuddered. What a peculiar name. Something was seriously amiss. She forced herself to whisper, 'What an interesting name!'

Just then Major Sood, a retired security personnel, came and stood next to Raveena. With a sarcastic smirk he said, 'These union guys are all barking up the wrong tree. They have no locus standi any more; they should simply shut shop and return home.'

A journalist trainee, who happened to overhear him, interjected angrily, 'You're being too harsh. Some of the things he's saying make sense. I've heard that one or two of the union leaders – Sen and Kautaliya – wield a great deal of power and credibility. If they give a call for a strike, the entire organization will come to a halt.'

'I agree with the views of this young fellow,' Raveena echoed. 'Both Sen and Kautaliya have impeccable reputations. They are a source of inspiration for all of us.'

Raveena clutched Kala Muthu's arm. 'We can't talk in a place like this. Let's meet this evening at the Press Club for a drink. We'll get a chance to chat,' she said.

Kala Muthu grinned. He liked this girl. She was a spunky go-getter.

The Press Club turned out to be exactly the kind of place Kala Muthu liked. Full of smoke, boisterous talk and drink flowing like water. He quickly downed two drinks before replying to Raveena's question, 'I was working with a Chennai-based consultancy company before joining here'

'What kind of work were you doing there?'

'Er, advisory work.'

Raveena gave him a quizzical look. 'Oh I see. But the newspaper line has little scope for advisory work.'

'I'm here as an administrative trainee. Once I complete my training, I will see where I can get deputed. I may try to go abroad.'

Kala Muthu wanted this questioning to end. He lifted his right foot and began to stroke her leg.

Raveena smiled and ordered another round of drinks.

'What kind of work do you do in this office?'

Raveena smiled. 'I expect to be made special correspondent within the next few days. I do not see myself in that position for very long. I see myself becoming an editor within the next six months. Eventually, I intend to become editor-in-chief.'

Kala Muthu was impressed. She spoke like a real Englishwoman. These Tamil girls were useless. They could never speak English with the correct accent. She held the cigarette so immaculately at the end of her manicured fingers.

'How do you know Rajan?'

'We come from the same village, from back home.'

Raveena smiled indulgently. It was the Tamil connection at work. He wasn't telling her very much. It was all right. He knew how to stroke her thighs and that was more important than ferreting useless information out of him.

Finishing his fourth drink, Kala Muthu knew seducing this woman was not going to prove a difficult task.

six

Vikram Aggarwal stormed into the *Sentinel* office the next morning in a very bad mood. Every daily newspaper had gone to town about yesterday's incident and how he had been forced to flee the office. What was the point of spending lakhs of rupees on security personnel every month, when not one of them was around to save him from the clutches of those union braggarts. If it were not for that fat cow of a girl, he may have even ended up being roughed up by those characters.

The union must be crushed ruthlessly. Rajan's latest recruit must swing into action and collectively lynch all those despicable worms.

Opening his brief case he took out File 213 which dealt with his father's case. Rajan had been egging him on to pay a bribe to that Assamese bureaucrat. Vikram was not prepared to pay some lowly joint secretary. Paying bribes to ministers had become a necessary evil. They had huge coteries to feed. To have to pay bureaucrats was insufferable. With their huge line-up of perks and lifelong pensions, Foreign Exchange Regulation Act or no Foreign Exchange Regulation Act, this was one set of palms he was not willing to grease.

Rajan made it a point to come in early to work. A tip-off from the security staff that the 'barre sahib' had arrived saw him rush up to Vikram's office. Hurrying into Vikram's room, Rajan said, 'Two security officers have been suspended. This kind of insurrection will not be tolerated any more.'

Vikram wiped his spectacles and stared out at the peepal tree. The bell-shaped leaves glittered seductively in the morning sunshine. It was going to be another warm day.

'The union has to be finished off. Not even a nail must remind us of their presence. These bankrupt hooligans have the gall to hold me to ransom. Drown these rats in the Yamuna!'

'What decision have you taken over File 213? Hazarika needs to be tackled right away,' Rajan said turning the tables on him.

Vikram's irritation mounted. He knew this tribe of journalists and managers, They must all be making fun of him for having turned tail and run away last evening. No wonder this upstart was now trying to push him around. He needed to put them all in their proper place. He must hold an edit meeting right away.

'Tell all the senior editors of *The Indian Sentinel*, *Financial Sentinel* and *Amar Prakash* that I want them to be in the conference room by ten o'clock in the morning. I need to discuss some important matters with them. It's already nine o'clock. You better pick up a phone and start ringing them up.'

Rajan knew he was being ordered out. 'Sir, I shall send for them right away.'

'Make sure that fat girl is also present at the meeting.'

Rajan's eyebrows cocked up. He must be talking about Raveena Bedi. My God, I hope he isn't planning to have an affair with her. These proprietors were a whimsical lot, he thought to himself as he walked out.

Twenty stoney-eyed journalists shuffled into the conference room at the prescribed hour, each wondering what new tongue-lashing their boss would subject them to. A delighted Raveena, notebook in hand, scampered into the room and took up a prominent position facing Vikram. Opening her notebook, she began scribbling down every word he spoke. Each time he stopped to take a deep breath, Raveena Bedi would flash him one of her most bewitching smiles.

Vikram, never one to waste time, got to the point immediately. 'The Hindi newspapers are no longer in a position to compete for a slice of the ad pie. The majority of ads have moved to the English newspapers. Actually, to put the issue in perspective, the ads have moved to the television industry.'

Ajay Singh's eyebrows shot up. Was he planning to shut down all the Hindi newspapers and magazines being brought out of his stable? Vikram's grandiose statements would not be allowed to go unchallenged. 'Sir, I do not agree with your assessment. All our rival competitors in the Hindi universe have repackaged their local editions in such a manner as to become more reader-friendly. They have obviously succeeded in their efforts because they are getting plenty of ads.'

Vikram hated being interrupted. Flapping his hands, he indicated to Ajay to be quiet. 'Four newspapers are being printed out of this one building. All four have separate reporters to cover the same events. For every press conference being held in the city, four of my staffers, representing the different papers, go and report on this event. Do we need so many people to do what could well be done by one individual?

'I propose that we have a single central pool of reporters feeding all these four editions. What this means is that we have one reporter providing the input for all four newspapers. And since the English dailies are forking in better revenues, let the Hindi newspapers translate these stories and use them for their editions,' Vikram said.

There was complete silence. The four editors, the four resident editors, the four chiefs of bureau and the four brand managers shifted uncomfortably in their seats. Vikram had always shown a propensity for coming up with the most hare-brained schemes. But this one was simply outrageous.

'Will the editorials of the Hindi newspapers also be a translation of what is being published in the English papers? So far all four publications have enjoyed the freedom to pursue four different editorial positions on the same subject,' Ajay asked.

Vikram looked nonplussed. It was obvious he had not given a thought to this point.

'What I am trying to stress is that we do not need four people to work on the same story. We could build up a central pool of information which could be accessed by our entire staff. To explain my point of view, why can't the financial news that appears in the *Financial Sentinel* be incorporated into *The Indian Sentinel* or for that matter into *Amar Prakash*.'

Satyajit Ghosh, the whiz kid of the *Financial Sentinel* heaved a sigh of relief. His paper was not going to be affected by these changes. He could not care less what happened to the others.

Ajay Singh found himself trembling with anger. He had spent the last four years building up this paper brick by brick. The owner was now proceeding to tear it apart.

'Vikramji, I need you to understand one simple point. So far, if one paper chose to be left-of-centre, another felt free to pursue a rightist tilt. In the same way, some papers are openly pro-reform while others advocate conservatism and caution in economic policy. Am I to understand that in future, the Hindi newspapers will be made to follow one central diktat flowing from the English dailies?' Ajay asked.

Vikram drummed his fingers uncertainly. Looking around at the row of faces watching him in silence, he wondered how he should reply to such a direct query.

Rajan came to his rescue. 'Our English papers have been trend-setters. Once the Hindi papers start carrying the same content as their English counterparts, the Indian readership will also start enjoying whatever they are provided to read. After all, even Hindi readers want to know about Tom Cruise and Madonna.'

'What happens in homes which subscribe to both our Hindi and English newspapers? If one paper is a duplicate copy of the other, our readers will immediately switch over to a rival Hindi daily.'

'Our readership surveys indicate a miniscule section of subscribers buy both *The Indian Sentinel* and *Amar Prakash*. These numbers would run to only a few thousand. We can forego such small numbers. Compare this to the savings I will be able to initiate if I have a central pool of news providers,' Vikram retorted.

Ajay gave a scorching look to all his colleagues. Not one of them was willing to stick his neck out. 'Vikramji, I can understand your point about cutting costs but I must emphasize that reporting for a Hindi newspaper is very different from the reportage being done for an English daily. Our readers belong to a different socio-economic background, their concerns and interests are different. If you open the pages of the *Sentinel* and *Amar Prakash,* you will find that page for page, story for story, we operate along different standards. If the *Sentinel* focusses on stories on the usage of cars, our emphasis will be on public transport because that is what is being used by our readers. In the same way, when the *Sentinel* pitches in for the privatization of our health services, we continue to do investigative reporting on the status and performance of government services.'

Vikram turned away in disgust. 'All these are lost causes anyway. Everything needs to be privatized, and it is going to happen sooner than later.'

This comment did not deter Ajay Singh from continuing to speak out in his blunt manner. 'Sir, under your stewardship, *Amar Prakash* has built up a crack team of correspondents who are rated amongst the best in the profession. I feel it would do our publications great credit if you continued to follow the pluralistic approach that you initiated ever since you took over the reins of this organization.'

Vikram Aggarwal nodded his head. There was some truth in what Ajay had said. But before he could respond, Rajan cut this discussion short.

'Sir, if I may interrupt. We are not in the business of charity; we are here to make money. No paper can afford to be subsidized indefinitely. *Amar Prakash,* despite Ajay's crack team of correspondents, has not been getting ads. This year, the paper had to be subsidized to the tune of two crore rupees.'

'Are you trying to tell me that my editorial team and I have been doing a substandard job? Have your brand managers ever tried to project the paper in any of the smaller towns that have mushroomed around the metro cities?' Ajay retorted. He was not afraid to hit back at Rajan.

Vikram at once went on the defensive. He hated direct confrontations, preferring the cloak-and-dagger approach to resolve issues. 'Ajay, why are you taking all this so personally? We are simply wanting to try out a new marketing strategy. If it does not succeed, we will go back to our old method of operations.'

Ajay felt he could not put up with this diabolic conversation any more. 'Sir, as editor, I too have some responsibility towards my staff, many of whom have won their spurs in covering difficult assignments. They gave up well-paid jobs to join this paper. If you go ahead with such a scheme, I offer my resignation here and now.'

With these words Ajay Singh got up and walked out of the conference room.

Vikram gave a thin smile. This man had just lost his job. He was not going to find a replacement for him in a hurry. Pushing his chair back, he stood up and looked at the leaders of his outfit. 'I have always been a believer in dialogue. Nothing should be taken in a personal light. During our brainstorming sessions, there are bound to be differences of opinion. These need to be respected,' he said and strode out of the room.

Rajan rushed to his side. 'Some of these fellows are getting too big for their boots,' he said.

Vikram nodded perfunctorily. There was a gnawing doubt in his head. Ajay Singh's proximity to the prime minister should not be allowed to adversely influence his father's case. It would also not bode well for the paper if he was picked up by one of their adversaries.

Rajan understood his apprehensions. 'We are facing a delicate situation. We need to put the government on the mat. We need to kickstart a human rights campaign in order to put pressure on them.'

'What kind of campaign do you have in mind? Kindly be clearer with the details,' Vikram snapped.

For a moment Rajan was flummoxed. He had not thought about what kind of campaign the paper should undertake. He glanced at random at a couple of newspapers lying on Vikram's table. His eyes fell on the *Morning Chronicle* which had a front page report on some caste killings. Jabbing a finger at Dalip Jha's story he said, 'We need to take up an issue like this and whip up an entire media campaign around it. Young people are being summarily executed simply because they have chosen to marry outside their caste. An exposé like this can prove to be political and social dynamite.'

Vikram realized that he should never underestimate this wily Brahmin from Mylapore. A human rights campaign at this juncture would put tremendous pressure on the government. Once they were in the dock, he could extract all manner of concessions from them.

Vikram chuckled. Picking up the paper, he read Dalip's story word for word. 'This is a brilliant idea. Get a special team cracking on the job right away.'

'Yes sir,' Rajan said.

Raveena Bedi was standing outside Vikram's room waiting to thank him for inviting her to the meeting. He brushed past her without acknowledging her presence. She turned to give Rajan an effusive smile. Rajan nodded his head in acknowledgement but her standing in that courtier-like fashion outside the boss's room was not lost upon him.

Rajan saw Vikram into his room and then climbed down the staircase to make his way into his own study. Picking up the phone he asked Ajit Jolly to come and see him right away.

Within minutes, Jolly was standing opposite Rajan looking a trifle nervous. 'There's been a caste killing in Shamli. It's a matter of grave significance. I want it covered in great depth.'

Jolly looked relieved. 'Do you want the bureau to cover it or do you want a reporter to do the job?'

'These are technicalities. Send someone today itself.'

'Yes sir.'

Surprises never ceased in an organization of this size. Till only a few days ago, the management had scorned stories dealing with human rights. Today, they had shifted gear and decided to move in a completely different direction. They could do as they pleased. It made no sense for a special to be sent to this Shamli place. The story could well be done by a mere reporter.

He would speak to the metro editor Mahesh Prasad and have him depute a reporter for the job. Why should his specials have to go and jostle around in the heat and dust? Most of Prasad's reporters were a lazy lot. They needed to be pushed around just to do even the most routine reporting.

**

News about Ajay's resignation had spread like wildfire in the office. Two of his colleagues, the news editor and the chief of bureau, arrived in his room to find out what had happened.

Ajay gave them a brief update. 'The management has other plans up their sleeve. Let us hope none of you is forced to give up his job,' he said.

Ajay Singh was not in the mood to give greater details. He was worried one of his colleagues might ring up his wife Sheena and break the news to her. She was expecting him to become a company director. This development would come as a shock to her. It was best to get home and tell her what had transpired.

A red light at the busy ITO intersection forced Ajay to switch off the engine. Two small pairs of grimy hands were stuck against the car window. Rolling the window down, he told the younger kid, 'How many times have I told you not to beg?'

'Dada! I'm hungry. Give me money, I want to eat,' the child bawled.

Patting the kid on his head Ajay said, 'Tell your mother to send you to school.'

The light turned green and the traffic surged forward in a rush. Ajay restarted the car looking all the while through the mirror to see that both the kids had managed to reach the safety of the kerb. Despite running a six-month long campaign in *Amar Prakash* and getting repeated assurances from the government that they would put an end to begging, little had changed at these traffic intersections where groups of young kids continued to be forced into begging by greedy parents or gangs of extortionists.

Turning left, he drove along Mathura Road past Pragati Maidan and the large Delhi Public School building to turn his car into Jangpura Extension where he had rented a small one-bedroom flat. He was surprised to find Meenakshi Raja's car parked outside his house. A loud-mouthed, trouble maker. Every time Ajay had run into her, it had meant trouble.

The last time she had come to his house, Ajay, normally a docile person had lost his temper and given her a tongue-lashing. The argument had been over her insistence that Sheena help her with a craft project in Baramullah in Kashmir.

'It's too dangerous!' Ajay had exploded.

'Mind your own business,' Meenakshi had retorted. 'Sheena is old enough to make up her own mind.'

'If you don't know how to speak to me, don't come to my house,' Ajay had shot back.

Meenakshi got up and left the house in a huff and had not set foot in it since. What was she doing here this evening, he wondered. He walked into the living room. Sheena and Meenakshi were not there. They must be in the bedroom he thought. He switched on the television. Meenakshi marched into the room, arms akimbo, and switched it off.

'Sheena is very ill. You have to keep the television set off today. She cannot take the noise.'

'What's happened to her? She was fine in the morning,' said Ajay and switched it on again.

'Will you switch that bloody thing off? Haven't I told you that your wife is very ill?'

'What is the problem?'

'She's just had an abortion.'

'Abortion? What are you talking about – why wasn't I informed?'

'Apparently she was three months pregnant. She went to the Marie Stopes clinic and had herself cleaned out.'

Ajay rushed into the bedroom to find a heavily sedated Sheena lying asleep in one corner of the bed. A white sheet was spread over her making her look like a corpse. The only thing visible about her was her long tousled hair coiling all over the pillow.

Ajay paled. Shaking her arm he said, 'Sheena! Are you all right?'

She opened her brown eyes for one fleeting moment and then closed them again.

'You went ahead and had an abortion without even consulting me? You know I love children.'

'I'm not feeling well. We'll talk later,' she whispered.

'No! You have to tell me now. How many months pregnant

were you? Why didn't you think it appropriate to discuss this with me before taking such a step?'

Sheena turned her face away from him.

Meenakshi caught Ajay by the shoulder and edged him out of the room.

'Don't trouble her now. She has lost a lot of blood. Sheena rang me up this morning and said that she wasn't feeling well. Would I be willing to accompany her to the nursing home? I did so without really knowing what was going on. She would have gone through this whole thing herself had it not been for the gynae's insistence that a relative or friend be present at the nursing home in order to help her get back home.'

'Why didn't you call me up at my office right away? Why was this whole thing kept a secret from me?'

'Where was the time to think? I reached the clinic when she was literally being wheeled into the operation theatre. After she was cleaned out, I just brought her home.'

Ajay broke into loud sobs. 'She aborted my child without even informing me.'

'Oh come on Ajay! If you're so fond of kids, you can always adopt a child.'

Ajay could not stop crying. 'It was my child, my son! She has killed my son! To do this to me after being my wife for the last eleven years.'

Vidya, the old ayah, waddled into the room carrying two cups of tea. 'Beta, everything will be all right. Leave everything in the hands of fate.'

'Take it like a man,' Meenakshi urged him and marched out of the room. A little later, he heard a car engine rev up and he knew she had left.

The tears did not stop. Ever since he had married Sheena, she had made fun of both him and his parents. She used to refer to his parents as VV, short for 'vile villagers' and often mimicked their

Bhojpuri accent before her friends. Ajay had made light of her dislike. City bred and convent educated, she could hardly be expected to understand the ways of poor village folk, who had eked out their livelihood by the sweat of their brow. In the initial days of his marriage, he had believed she would change. He was proved wrong. She made no attempt to be civil towards any friend or relative who visited him from his hometown of Ghazipur. On his insistence, his parents had visited him once. She had refused to even speak to them. They left the next day never to return.

Now she had destroyed his child without so much as informing him.

Vidya entered the room. 'Beta, I have served dinner. Why don't you eat a little food? You will feel better.'

He could not bring himself to get up. It was past midnight when Vidya entered the room again, 'Beta, I am an old woman. I need to rest. You must also go to sleep, beta. You have a long day ahead of you tomorrow.'

Tears welled into his eyes. The only person from whom he had received a little sympathy was this old maid. To expect someone in this city to offer even one word of kindness was to expect too much. Sheena would never bear him a child. His only hope of happiness had evaporated into thin air.

**

Ever since Attar Singh was discharged from hospital, he spent all his spare time pouring through his ledgers. For the last twenty-four hours, he had done virtually nothing, apart from going through with a fine comb, all the records he had meticulously maintained for the past twenty years. Too weak to walk around, he waited for Shanti to hand him one ledger at a time, and ponder over every tiny notation he had made in each page. Each entry was written out in his neat and distinctive hand and contained the name of every single loanee along with the amount loaned and the date on which it was lent. Below each name were separate notings on the interest and repayment schedules.

He had not been able to fathom why anyone would want to kill him. He was after all not the only one doing this side business in the office. Many of his colleagues were also engaged in the business of lending money. But after what Laxman had told him, he too had veered down to the view that a loan defaulter could have been behind his stabbing.

Late that night, there was a loud knock at the door. Shanti peered through the peephole recently drilled into the main door.

'It's Billa,' she told Attar Singh.

'Let your mother open the door. Go and sit in the back room and don't come out till I call.'

She did as she was told. The dupatta hung low over her face to make sure no stranger could see her face.

A tall, rugged brown-haired man entered the room walking with a distinct limp. Dressed in a grey pathan suit with a brown turban tied tightly over his head, Billa's green eyes shone with a fierce intensity. 'You had sent for me?' Billa asked in his loud voice.

'Yes, Billa I've been trying to meet you for some weeks now.'

'What is it about?'

'I'm trying to get to the bottom of a small problem.'

'I know. Hell and damnation – you are trying to understand who was behind this knifing. I can understand your being suspicious of me but let me tell you I may be a petty thief – a little stealing here and there – but I'm no murderer. There are too many weapons floating around in the business today. You kill one guy, you make an enemy of all his relatives and friends. I can't afford to have enemies in my dhanda. You stick a knife in one guy, ten guys end up sticking knives into you. No murders sir – that's not my scene,' Billa said in a loud, indignant tone.

'Billa, you are not as simple as you pretend to be. Two years ago you borrowed twenty thousand rupees from me; since then you have never shown your face again at my doorstep. Your case was recommended by Gulabo Pathan otherwise there was no way that I would have loaned you so much cash. You're not worth half-a-paisa but I cannot turn down the Pathan.'

'Mere mai baap, forgive me. Ever since a Blue Line bus ran me down, I have been surrounded by problems. My dhanda is chaupat. With my limp, I can no longer slide my hand into anyone's pocket.'

Lifting his pyjama he pointed to a huge scar running across the entire span of his left leg. 'That's sixty-five stitches and two broken bones for you. I was in hospital for two months. It's God's punishment for my sins. I cannot escape my karma. You helped me get my sister married – I am indebted to you for life. I am trying to start a small grocery shop. Once I do that, I will start repaying your loan.'

'Flies and mosquitoes! That is all we are left with! Your accident is now one year old. Every time I ask you to repay the money, you stall the issue,' Attar Singh said irascibly.

'Why are you singling me out? What about Jodh Singh? He too has not repaid your money.'

'He is part of the office union. The union is willing to pay up in case he fails to do so.'

Billa became contemplative. 'No one can escape his destiny. When I was active, on a good day, I could earn a couple of thousand rupees. Now I consider myself lucky if I have even five rupees in my pocket.'

Attar Singh also gave a deep sigh. 'You are right. Situations change overnight. Look at me! I did not think I possessed a single enemy in the world. Now I have suddenly realized that someone wants me out of his way. This stabbing has taught me one lesson. Life is uncertain. I may not live very long and I am left with one liability. I must get my daughter married off at the earliest. But even as I make plans in that direction, I also need to know who is behind this killing. You have good contacts with the underworld. You can snoop around and get to the bottom of this mystery.'

By now Billa was beginning to look uncomfortable. Attar Singh, he realized, was in a position to arm-twist him.

Attar continued, 'We both come from the same village. I can create a lot of trouble for you. I have your signature on all my documents. All the witnesses who testified on your behalf are still alive. The interest on the loan alone would work out to over forty thousand rupees. I can easily take over the village land owned by your family. Nobody will object to that. I just want you to do me a small favour. Use your contacts in the underworld to find out who was behind this. I will write off the entire loan and the interest if you can find out the name of the party who wants to have me bumped off.'

Billa scratched his head. 'Maybe there are other loanees who you have been harassing. They might want to have you out of the way.'

'I've been lending money for over twenty-five years. I have had only two defaulters. One Jodh Singh, the other you. Are you interested in getting me out of the way?'

Billa's green eyes looked around the room with catlike speed. It was as though he were taking down every detail. He swore under his breath 'What do you want me to do?'

'I want you to find out who was behind this. On the face of it, I have no enemies. Yet someone wants to stop my croaking.'

Billa gave Attar Singh a contemptuous look. A feeble-looking character like him could be brought down by one blow of the neck. The guy who stabbed him must have been an untrained idiot to push the knife into his abdomen instead of his gullet.

'You need to give me some leads … the names of three or four people who hate your face!'

'I can't think of even one. I have no possessions, or big money. I have nothing that anyone would want.' Attar Singh sounded completely confused.

There was some logic in his words. This man was a completely nondescript character with no political affiliations. The stabbing was not the handiwork of a small-time thief because in that case he could have broken into his house and extracted the money from his wife or daughter. If they had wanted to knock him out cold, they would have done so. The stabbing had been done to issue a warning. This added a chilling dimension to the mystery. Someone ruthless was behind this act.

Billa lit a beedi. 'There is something seriously amiss about your case. I'll need some time to get to the bottom of this mystery. You have to give me a couple of days.'

'I don't have much time. You need to act fast. Don't forget, if you come up with good leads, I'll write off your entire loan amount.'

Billa smiled, his face contorted into an expression of relief. 'May the gods protect you with long life,' he said giving Attar Singh a low salaam.

Attar Singh felt more confident after his meeting with Billa. He was a reliable fellow. Once he set out to do something, he usually succeeded.

seven

Mahesh Prasad, the oversized chief reporter with sharp eyes and a biting tongue, sent for Rajneesh Mishra, the crime reporter, and insisted he go down to the village of Shamli to do a story on a caste killing of a young couple. Being a crime story, he would be able to do all the background investigation and come up with a lot of juicy details.

'It will make a good, strong story,' Prasad told him.

'Sir, nothing happens in our villages. People just wallow around there like cows and buffaloes,' retorted Mishra.

'You fool! Are you a journalist or a company clerk! You don't know what you are talking about. Anyone in the bureau would jump at such an opportunity, but I think you will do a good job. That is why I am recommending that you go,' Prasad bellowed back.

'Boss, you know I have no interest in small-town stories – why don't you send somebody else to Shamli?'

'Arre you Brahmin fool! Anyone else would give their right arm to go there. What are you babbling on about!'

Just then Raveena Bedi, with her newly acquired clout and dressed in an expensive designer salwar kameez walked by, cigarette in hand. Ever since she had barged into the proprietor's room, she had gone around boasting to both the staff and the brand managers that she was responsible for saving Vikram Aggarwal's life. Since Banerjee made no attempt to deny her story, everyone had begun to believe that she did indeed enjoy a special proximity with the boss. The fact that she had been singled out and invited for a board meeting comprising editors and brand managers only served to increase her clout.

'Where does this young man not wish to go?' she asked with her supercilious smile.

'Arre, it's nothing. We're just having a small argument,' Prasad muttered, not wanting to involve her in the matter.

Raveena turned to Mishra. 'Mishra, I heard you complain about not going some place. Where was it?'

'Shamli!' replied Mishra turning red in the face. Soon the entire office would be in the know about his refusal.

Raveena gave them a placatory smile and walked away. This inexperienced idiot was being bundled off to do a woman-related issue, which so obviously fell under the jurisdiction of the bureau. She would take up this matter with Ajit Jolly

Entering the bureau, Raveena pulled up a chair and sat down across from Jolly's desk.

'You're a great bureau chief – one of the best that we've ever had.'

Jolly blushed. 'Get to the point Raveena. What's on your mind?'

'Why am I not being sent to cover the Shamli killing – why is this blundering Rajneesh Mishra being sent off there?'

Jolly did not want to antagonize one of the rising stars in the establishment. 'I have no idea why he has been selected. If you really want to go, then I will tell Prasad to forget about sending that nitwit and have you go instead.'

Raveena thought hard. She was meeting Kala Muthu for lunch today. He might be able to provide her with far more juicy titbits than she could hope to pick up from the boondocks of India. 'I don't have the time to go today but in future, my name had better be on top of your list. Remember that, sweetheart, or you'll be in serious trouble.'

Looking sheepishly around, Jolly muttered, 'Who would want to be in the bad books of a princess like you?'

Scarcely had Raveena left, than Mahesh Prasad gave a hard shove to Rajneesh. 'You fool! Better get out of here fast before that lady runs away with your story.'

'Sir, but it's nightmarish to have to visit these places,' Mishra wailed.

'Just go!' shrieked Prasad. 'The taxi will be waiting for you downstairs.'

'This idiot is only good at doing health stories and needs to be taken off the crime beat,' Prasad told himself collapsing back into his chair.

Rajneesh Misra cursed his luck. There was no fate worse than being a city reporter for the *Sentinel*. He had started his career here by covering the health beat under the Municipal Corporation's jurisdiction. In less than a year's time, he had emerged as an authority of sorts on Delhi's diseased underbelly. He knew all the ways in which TB, malaria, cholera, diphtheria, dropsy and influenza had infiltrated practically every home in the city. He knew how government hospitals had to constantly fudge statistics to present an overall not-so-dismal picture.

No one wanted to acknowledge trouble even when it was knocking at their door. Through his interactions with prostitutes in GB Road and with drug addicts huddled in the vicinity of the Hanuman Mandir in the old city, Rajneesh had extensively documented the dimensions of the new generation scourges including AIDS and Hepatitis B. In the process, he had also uncovered the nexus between the administration and a select group of favoured NGOs on whom were bestowed massive grants in the name of spreading awareness on safe sex. Many of these NGOs were actually paper organizations set up by wives of top bureaucrats.

Ever since his colleague Vineet Sagar went on leave, Rajneesh had been asked to take temporary charge of the crime beat. It was in this connection that Jolly had asked him to travel down to this godforsaken Shamli village to investigate a killing.

The assignment, he knew, would turn out to be a fate worse than death.

Nothing ever happened in these villages. People lived there with their cows and buffaloes and generally revelled in their backwardness. The whole world had moved forward but these goddamn villages with their outdated ideologies continued to live in the Stone Age.

He should know. One had only to open the newspaper to read how a father had sacrificed his four children to appease Kali; a pregnant woman was raped and killed by a neighbour because her husband's cattle had strayed into his fields. Punishment magnified out of all proportion to the crimes of the dead. That summed up what was going on in our villages. If this was not bad enough, visiting these places with their overflowing population, lack of drinking water and women hiding behind their huge ghungats invariably proved to be a nightmarish experience. Muzzaffarnagar boasted huge, oversized flies. Its mosquitoes were the size of small bats.

These villagers were always rambling on about the same puerile rubbish, especially the inequalities between them and their urban brothers. Who wanted to hear the same old rubbish? If they were stuck in their ghetto-like existence, too bad for them. Of course, since they were breeding like rabbits, they could hardly be ignored. All they did was pour into the cities and convert them into slums.

Not that being a crime reporter in a city was much fun either. People were getting more barbaric by the day. Some of the crimes these Delhiwallahs committed were really lurid:

A girl of six raped twelve times by her uncle.

Husband poisons wife and six children and throws their bodies and himself in a well.

Lover strangles paramour, then takes cyanide.

A judge in a music competition is strangled to death by a losing competitor.

Father cuts off son's head; he was seen talking to a neighbour's daughter.

Neighbour throws acid on neighbour's wife. Reason: petty quarrel.

Paramour kills lover and throws her body into the Yamuna. Reason: she was wearing the wrong coloured dupatta.

Every day some bloody fucker in this city figured out a new way to die.

Most guys liked to treat life like one big fart anyway. Why then was such a hue and cry being raised over this damn Shamli murder? Two people died. Let their souls rest in peace.

Every time he filed a report, he stuck to the bare facts. No frills, no unnecessary trappings for him. His job was to produce a strictly factual copy and let the reader arrive at his own conclusions. Most times, even the listing of these facts turned out to be a pretty gruesome exercise. Three days into this beat had taught him that people enjoyed quarrelling. They could fight over any petty little issue. What was the point of overplaying these everyday occurrences? Sensationalizing crime only served to build up a greater appetite for it.

Mahesh Prasad, the chief reporter, often complained that his writing was too drab. The first time he used this phrase, Rajneesh returned to his desk and opened a dictionary to find out what the word meant. It meant plain, very dull. Better to be dull than factually incorrect. Look at the kind of political reporting going on in the media. Most of them were pieces of fiction attributed to some anonymous source. Or look at the kind of gimmicks politicians resorted to during elections. During the last general election, the prime minister had inaugurated thirty projects in his constituency alone. Not one was likely to see the light of day.

Running down the steps, Rajneesh ran into Keith D'Souza ambling into the office, a black bag hanging from his shoulder.

'Where are you off to, young man?' Keith asked.

Rajneesh had always admired Keith and hoped to become a special correspondent like him. 'I'm being sent to Shamli to do a special story. Some caste killing, I've been told.'

'Do a good job and make sure you collect all the facts.'

Rajneesh nodded his head in agreement. Keith was always so encouraging, he inevitably had a kind word for young reporters.

The taxi was soon out of the congested cityscape and rolling past a blaze of green. He could see young, freshly planted paddy saplings raising their earnest heads in field after field. Sugarcane grew in abundance, as did tiny mangoes, dangling on slender twigs from the shadows of the vast trees.

The taxi had rolled along the main Delhi-Muzzaffarnagar highway for almost three hours before the taxi driver swerved off the main road onto a narrow metalled track.

'Hey, is this the road going to Shamli? You better find out before taking me in the wrong direction,' Rajneesh ordered.

The ever-compliant driver muttered, 'Yes sir' and lurched to a halt right in the middle of the road. 'Is this the way to Shamli?' the driver asked a middle-aged man walking leisurely down on the opposite side.

'Go down half a kilometre and then turn left. It's a straight road from there. Won't take you more than another half-hour,' the stranger replied.

His instructions proved to be correct. Once they reached Shamli, it was only a short drive to the village.

The village sarpanch, Chowdhury Ram Lal, was sitting outside his house feeding some freshly cut grass to two tethered buffaloes when the white Ambassador stopped at his doorstep. Rajneesh peered out of the window. 'I want to meet Chowdhury Ram Lal. Do you know where I could find him?'

'What difference would it make to the world if you did find him,' Ram Lal said with a loud cackle.

'I need to talk to him.'

'Shriman, I am the selfsame man.'

Rajneesh decided it was better to approach the subject in a roundabout manner. 'I am a journalist with *The Indian Sentinel* published from Delhi. I am doing a feature on the problems farmers are facing these days. I have heard you are not getting water for your fields? Is that the case?'

The elderly sarpanch had interacted many times with journalists. He gave Rajneesh a puzzled look. 'You mean you have come all the way from Delhi to find out if my fields are not getting enough water?'

'Yes, I want to speak to a whole cross-section of farmers.'

'Shriman, it is a hot day. Why don't you come inside and first refresh yourself. Then we will discuss the water problem in a more relaxed manner.'

Rajneesh was led to a long rectangular room in the centre of which two charpais were placed. A broken-down table next to one charpai had a small rickety fan placed on it. Ram Lal pressed the fan switch. The blades did not rotate. 'No light I'm afraid,' he muttered and settled down on a charpai facing Rajneesh. Ram Lal's wife, face hidden behind a dupatta, soon brought two cups of piping hot tea brewed in gur. As they sipped the tea, Ram Lal began a convoluted story on how the average farmer was caught in a debt trap with the price of seeds, fertilizers and pesticides constantly going up.

'In Punjab, farmers have been given free electricity, but we UP wallahs have been left to the dogs. We do not get electricity, that is why we are not able to use our pumps to draw water.'

Rajneesh wiped the sweat off his brow. How was he going to broach the topic of the murder? Clearing his throat he said, 'Your village has become notorious for violent incidents!'

'No sahib – we are like any other village in this Muzzaffarnagar belt. This is a crime prone area in general. The police openly shelter criminals. We are at their mercy.'

'But what happens when the villagers and the panchayat decide to take the law into their own hands?'

'What are you referring to?'

'The recent incident involving a married couple. Your panchayat sanctioned the execution.'

'Now you have come to the point. You are referring to the killing of Pappu Yadav's niece. These things keep happening – there is nothing new about it.'

'What do you mean?'

'You people sitting in Delhi keep making laws. You pass one law after another. But you have never cared to understand whether these laws are useful for us or not. We villagers have functioned as a cohesive unit for thousands of years. This stupid girl from our biradiri ran away with a low-caste boy. Her uncle was left with no standing in his community. He had no choice but to kill both of them. I am not speaking for myself; this is the unanimous opinion of every member of the panch. I'll call them here. You can hear their side of the story.'

'Arre Kallu! Come here!' he yelled.

A young black-faced boy came up to the door.

'Tell all the panch members to come to my house right away. Tell them a big journalist from Delhi is here to meet them.'

Kallu disappeared with a saucy grin. In less than half an hour the entire panchayat had assembled in the room. The two teachers, Balram Prakash and Mohan Ram had also hurried along to participate in the discussion.

Ram Lal's wife placed two more string cots but the men

preferred to huddle together on one charpai. Ram Lal passed the hookah around. The eldest in the group, 76-year-old Chattur Lal owning twenty acres of land, patted Rajneesh genially on his back.

'Only last week we had some other gentleman from Delhi here. Why are you beating your head over the same old story?' Chattur Lal, with his glowing red cheeks and large bulbous nose, asked. 'This killing is over and done with. So many other things are happening in our country. Why don't you focus on them?'

'Give me an idea about what happened.'

Balram Prakash interrupted him. He preferred to see himself as the spokesperson for the village. Emptying a packet of paan masala in his mouth, he said, 'Arre, nothing much happened. The couple who eloped came back. Pappu Yadav and his gang had them executed. The gang lay low for a few days, now they are back to their old tricks. The other day I ran into Kishan. He was trying to steal someone's goat.'

'You all supported the killing?' Rajneesh asked.

'Yes,' they all said in unison. 'We are simply following the example of our forefathers. Marriages are arranged by the family elders – it's not some gulli-danda ka khel that children can indulge in according to their whims and fancies.'

The hookah was being passed from one panch member to the other. Each panch member inhaled, letting out a cloud of smoke.

'If any other young couple should repeat this practice, would you resort to a similar execution?'

Ram Lal decided to play it safe. 'Who can tell about the future? But one thing we will say – our village does not accept inter-caste marriage.'

'Have the police filed a First Information Report against the killers?'

Upset at his persistent cross-questioning, Balram Prakash turned red with anger. 'Why should they file a First Information Report when no crime was committed in the first place?' he asked.

'Two murders have taken place and you insist no crime took place,' Rajneesh shot back.

'Pose that question to the police. We do not consider these as murders but rather as warnings to our youngsters not to go astray,' Ram Lal said getting up from the charpai.

Rajneesh stared into the bewildering array of faces, conviction written large across them. 'The execution took place in public. How come not one person in your village intervened to stop the killing?' Rajneesh asked.

'Look, we agree what took place was unfortunate, but at that moment, tempers were running high. If anyone had dared intervene, he too would have been killed,' replied Balram Prakash. For a moment, Rajneesh wondered where he had heard that spiel before. This man sounded like Advani or Vajpayee, post the Babri Masjid demolition. Unfortunate that it happened, but it was a spontaneous outburst of righteous anger, you see!

Mishra realized it was pointless arguing with them any further. 'Where does this Yadav fellow live? Can I have a word with him or any other member of his family,' he asked.

'We do not know Pappu Yadav's whereabouts. He keeps moving around. You can try your luck by going down to his hut. His mother lives there. Kallu will show you the way.'

Now that the journalist was going away, Chowdhury Ram Lal picked up the hookah and inhaled deeply, letting out a stream of smoke. Then coming up close to Rajneesh he said, 'We Yadavs are a notorious lot. A few years ago, you could not have gone past us wearing that gold chain dangling around your neck.'

In one quick movement, he unlocked the chain from around Rajneesh's neck and dangled it triumphantly on his forefinger. The whole exercise had been conducted so smoothly, Rajneesh could not believe his eyes.

'We were famous for our skills of pickpocketing and thieving.

Nobody dared enter our village wearing gold. What are a few chains here and there, we thought nothing about breaking into safes and bank lockers. Now we have all mellowed down. We do not want to bring disrepute to our leader Amir Singh Yadav. For the present no more robberies and burglaries, but who can tell about the future?'

The panch members screamed with laughter.

Rajneesh snatched the chain from Ram Lal's hand. Eyeing it carefully he said 'I hope you haven't duplicated it?'

Kallu led him along an uneven winding track along which grew a few scraggy neem trees. Reaching a decrepit-looking thatch structure clearly on its last legs, he saw an elderly woman in a torn grey sari sweeping the courtyard with a broom made of a few twigs.

'Amma – you have a visitor from Delhi!' shouted Kallu.

There was no response from the other end.

'He is a reporter from Delhi. He wants to ask you a few questions.'

Bhuja continued with her sweeping. Giving Rajneesh a sheepish smile, Kallu turned tail and disappeared.

Rajneesh concluded he had not seen a more miserable-looking person before. Forcing himself to be polite he said, 'Amma, I need to speak to you.'

There was no reply.

By now, Rajneesh was running out of patience. Taking out a twenty-rupee note from his breast pocket, he threw it at her feet.

'Come on old woman, pick it up. I have to get on with my work,' he muttered between his teeth.

Bhuja picked it up and tied it in her sari fold.

'I have come to ask you a few questions about your grandchild.'

Bhuja's eyes became cloudy. In an impassive tone she said, 'Paro was a dutiful child . She never disobeyed anybody. As a young girl, any untoward noise or quarrel saw her go scuttling under the charpai,' she said pointing to a broken-down cot lying in the verandah. 'But that chamar boy did some jadu-tona on her. He made her go against her own will. She never was what she became.'

'If she was so timid, why did you allow her to get killed in this fashion?'

'It is all one's destiny. She was destined to die in this manner and she did,' and Bhuja, picking up the broom, resumed her sweeping.

Rajneesh decided to leave her alone. What could this old woman tell him anyway? He walked slowly to the taxi parked at the entrance of the village. His hand kept going back to the chain around his neck. He must visit the goldsmith tomorrow to make sure he had not been returned a fake.

The drive back to Delhi was uneventful. Rajneesh decided to go straight to the office to file the story. Hurrying into the reporter's section, he sat down before his venerable Modi Olivetti 286 PC and started keying in the facts:

> Shamli (Muzzaffarnagar) June 2: The axing to death of a young couple who dared marry outside their caste has sent shock waves in the already crime-prone wild west territory adjoining the eastern Yamuna canal.
>
> Paro Tyagi (age 16) had eloped with Jano Ram (age 18) a boy from the Jatav community, a few weeks ago. Following their untimely return, the couple was publicly executed in the village courtyard by Paro's uncle, Pappu Yadav and his accomplices.
>
> The killing was done in broad daylight last Friday afternoon, with the entire village community witnessing the event. Surprisingly not one villager intervened to stop Yadav and his cohorts. Nor are they willing to speak out against it. Even the police seem indifferent and have not registered any FIR against the killers so far.
>
> The sarpanch of the village, Chowdhury Ram Lal along with other members of the panchayat told this reporter that

> what took place was 'unfortunate'. At the same time he said that Yadav was 'forced' to take this extreme step to defend the honour of his community and safeguard traditional value systems that had stood the test of time.
>
> Ram Lal expressed outrage at how the 'cityfolk' were hell-bent on presenting a distorted picture and not focussing on the real day-to-day problems being faced by the community. 'Young people cannot flout our traditional, age old customs and practices, and if they dare transgress our laws, they will be punished for it,' Ram Lal added.

Rajneesh handed over the five-paragraph story to Mahesh Prasad. Prasad read the printout and exploded. 'What the hell is this? You were at Shamli for practically the entire day and this is all the information you were able to cull?'

'What more do you want? Did you expect me to write a *Ramayana* on this one killing?' Rajneesh shot back.

Prasad backed down at once. Although he revelled in throwing his weight around, he was always the first to retreat at the slightest hint of assertion from the other side. 'When I send a reporter to do a first-hand report, I expect some background details, a little colour, maybe some quotes from other family members,' he said.

Before he could complete his sentence Rajneesh thundered, 'What can you expect in a bloody poverty-stricken village anyway? Some Madhuri Dixit style gyrations?'

'Listen, get a bit serious. I've been told to play up this murder story – obviously the sixth floor finds it important. Yours is a very stereotype report.'

'Why didn't you tell me all this earlier? I would have done some more running around.'

Prasad gave him a contemptuous look. 'I'll have to find a way out. Give me the broad details and then let me see what we can string together,' he said.

Rajneesh took out his notebook and rattled out all the notes he had taken down. Prasad then sent for George Thomas, a sub known to be an expert rewrite man – one who could turn around even the most opaque copy into an exciting event.

'I'll take you to the Press Club. You can have an Old Monk on me,' Prasad told the 52-year old Syrian Christian.

A bottle of Old Monk was incentive enough. Within half an hour, Thomas had revised the entire copy.

> Shamli (Muzzaffarnagar) June 2: The heinous murder of sixteen-year old Paro Tyagi and her husband, eighteen-year old Jano Ram, has sent shock waves through the sleepy town of Muzzaffarnagar. What is even more alarming is that the public execution enjoyed the tacit approval of the newly-elected panchayat who were witness to this gruesome act.
>
> This premeditated murder is alleged to be the handiwork of Paro's uncle Pappu Yadav and his four accomplices. Unhappy that his niece had eloped with a lower-caste youth belonging to the Jatav community, her uncle had sworn revenge.
>
> He is reported to have hatched a plot to get them back to the village. The newlyweds had barely entered the village, when Yadav's henchmen reportedly went into action and killed them outside the primary school building. The three hundred schoolchildren, all below the age of ten, also witnessed this horrendous deed.
>
> Members of the panchayat led by the sarpanch, Chowdhury Ram Lal, justified the killings, insisting that the villagers continue to be bound by traditions which are immutable. 'One thing is clear, our village does not accept inter-caste marriage,' Ram Lal said.
>
> Killings between the upper caste and lower castes are on the rise and seem, in most cases, to enjoy the tacit support of the

parents. Paro's aged grandmother justified the killings saying, 'My son Yadav did the right thing by killing her.'

Women's organizations have strongly protested against this heinous crime. The Mahila Dakshata Samiti has pointed out that the killing of a sixteen-year-old only because she married a boy of her choice is a slap in the face of the pro-women and pro-girl policies that this government claims it is committed to.

Hundreds of women across the country are being raped, molested, battered and burned for lack of adequate dowries, and yet the government has prepared no action plan to end this systematic brutalization. The failure of the police to even lodge an FIR against the murderers in the Jano-Paro case is indication enough of how little importance is bestowed on such flagrant acts.

The story was okayed by the sixth floor and appeared as the lead story with banner headlines the following morning. All the *Sentinel* editions picked it up.

eight

Vikram was feeling triumphant. The screaming banner headlines of the morning newspaper 'Public Execution Becomes the Order of the Day' would give a real kick in the arse to all his rivals. It would also help put this fumbling government in its place.

Fooling around with Papaji was going to prove an expensive business for them. His rivals could go to any length to humiliate him, but Vikram was determined to ensure *The Indian Sentinel* went down as the greatest success story of post-independent India.

Unlike these cowards who were trying to fire their shots from behind someone else's shoulder, he was game to step out into the open and face the consequences of his hard-hitting campaign. He possessed several weapons in his armoury. Sensationalizing a caste-based killing in a village not very distant from Delhi and attributing it to the indifference of the Central Government was only the first step. His gameplan would unfold step by step to ensure this bunch of knaves was smashed to smithereens. The present coalition government lacked cohesion. It was only a matter of time before it fell apart under the weight of its own inner contradictions.

Vikram never forgot how two days after the swearing in, he

had approached Prime Minister Ananda Krishnan to look into his father's case. The PM's reply was terse. 'Let the law take its own course.' It was obvious he did not want to get involved. If the law could follow its own course, so could his paper.

Vikram scanned the other headlines. Bomb blasts in Kashmir, two MIG planes crash, Safdarjung doctors on strike for higher pay. The usual rubbish. He flung the newspaper on the ground and walked into his bedroom. The old antique watch showed the time as seven forty-five a.m.

Kavita had gone off on a European sojourn, taking both the children with her. She should have stayed back to provide some emotional support to Papaji reeling under attacks from so many fronts. They were so many details to be sorted out. His top priority was to keep up the pressure on the government. Once they were in the doghouse, they would immediately agree to repeal the Foreign Exchange Regulation Act and come up with a more diluted legislation.

He hated being alone in this huge house. A servant brought him a glass of fresh orange juice. He drank it down in one gulp, dressed and left for office in his Mercedes. It was five past nine when he entered the *Sentinel* building. The auxiliary staff was still engaged in cleaning the premises. He took the stairs all the way up to the top floor. Settling down on his desk, he pressed the dome-shapped bell to send for his chaprasi.

'Haan mai-baap sarkar,' muttered old Laxman. He slept on the premises and was known to start cleaning Vikram's room a little after eight in the morning.

'Get me some hot tea. And tell Banerjee to come and take some notes,' he ordered.

Minutes later, Laxman arrived carrying a cup of piping hot tea, followed by Banerjee, notebook in hand.

Vikram took a sip of the tea. 'Laxman, tell Rajan to be here in ten minutes' time. I want to finish with some paperwork.'

Vikram dictated three letters in quick succession, grimacing all the while at the sight of the grubby notebook being used by his lanky, white-haired secretary. These people possessed no finesse. Outside the window, the peepal tree was still standing tall as before, the leaves doing a series of rapid gymnastics in the breeze.

Rajan arrived to find a glum-looking boss making doodles on a sheet of blotting paper. Vikram's flared nostrils and glinting eyes told him that the boss was not in a happy frame of mind.

'What did you think of the lead story?' Rajan asked in his obsequious manner.

'We'll fix them now. I want a sequel to be carried every day till next week – banner headlines, gory details and all.'

Rajan looked perplexed. What was he trying to prove? A caste killing was hardly ammunition enough to attack a new government. He knew better than to argue with him. Experience had taught Rajan that Vikram always operated on the basis of a well-calculated strategy. Something must be ticking away at the back of his mind.

Seeing the momentary confusion on Rajan's face, Vikram was back to his sermonizing. 'Future crises will no longer be political in nature. The public, and here I include the politicians and bureaucrats, have reconciled themselves to the inevitability of corruption. Everyone is dipping their hands into this sinking ship called India and till such time as it is completely ripped apart, people will continue to tear out its entrails and suck its blood.

'I believe a social issue, if mounted and directed in an appropriate manner, will go a long way in escalating social tensions. This must form the crux of our strategy. Look at it from another point of view. Shamli is close to the capital. A caste killing of a young couple can have far-reaching repercussions. By putting both Leelawati and Amir Singh Yadav on the defensive, we can persuade them to step up their criticism of the Central Government.'

'Sir, what kind of momentum can a story like this create? In the past also, we have carried several crusades around social issues. The majority sank without a whimper. And moreover, how can it help us! Surely, we are not into reforming society?'

'We have taught the public to love celebrities – we'll teach them now to get involved with social issues.'

It was obvious Vikram was not going to be deterred. 'Mark my words – this government is running out of steam. A couple of hard pushes and it will come tumbling down. I want all these Shamli stories to be personally monitored by you. They must carry the right amount of punch. Is that clear? Oh yes and before you leave – what is the latest on that trade union wallah? Has he joined the office? I am not going to be jostled around in this manner again.' He thumped the table for effect. 'I'll sack the entire damn office. I'll close this damn newspaper down. I don't care. I'll take sanyas. I'll be very happy doing it.'

'We know that very well sir.'

'What did you say that trade union fellow's name was?'

'Kala Muthu. It means Black Pearl in English'

'What an absurd name – have him rechristened at once. Call him Ghanshyam or Krishan Murari – anything but that ridiculous name.'

'Sir, his real name is Gajamukham which means elephant head. He looks more like a bull if you ask me.'

'I don't care what he looks like. I hope he knows his job. He will need to do some tightrope walking. I want him to destroy these bloody unions. I want these characters booted out of here lock, stock and barrel. Do they think they own this office that they can do a nautanki here whenever they choose?'

'Keep a tab on that blackie character's movements. Make sure he is not bought over by our enemies both inside and outside this organization,' Vikram added as Rajan made to leave the room.

'Of course sir. He has already started interacting with our union members.'

Vikram returned to reading the papers.

Rajan knew he had been dismissed and made his exit.

**

Billa lit a beedi and went over his conversation with Attar Singh. That man had dangled a carrot in front of him. It would be foolish of him not to bite it.

The stabbing of Attar Singh had left him baffled. Who would want to kill a nondescript character like Attar? There was nothing even vaguely attractive about him. Under the guise of helping friends and acquaintances, he had started a moneylending business. He charged the same interest rates as did the bigger sharks in the market but this was to be expected. Who lent money free of charge these days?

But why would anyone want to bump him off? Who could be behind this dastardly act? Billa was clueless. His own accident had left him a cripple. His pickpocket friends had disowned him. They did not want him around any more.

Attar Singh had agreed to loan him the money only because Gulabo Pathan, with his legendary underworld connections, had agreed to become his guarantor. By not returning the money, Billa had let the Pathan down. It was not that he had wanted to. But the accident with the DTC bus had reduced his left leg to a pulp, forcing him to doing odd jobs that never brought in much money.

It was to Gulabo Pathan's credit that he had not put pressure on him to return the loan. The days had turned into weeks, the months into years. Fate had intervened and provided him with an opportunity to put the loan money behind him altogether. He must find out who the murderer was.

But before he sought Gulabo Pathan out, he must trace out Ram Bharose, known to be the Pathan's eyes and ears. A raconteur and great gossip, he would take him along to soften up the Pathan.

Ram Bharose spent all his time loafing around Bahadur Shah Zafar Marg, moving from one shop to another. His large circle of friends kept him informed about the goings-on and he was known to have his finger in several pies. His most popular haunt was Benarasi Lal paanwallah's, and it was here that Billa found him this warm June afternoon, locked in a loud discussion with two peons from Tej publications, a rival to the *Sentinel* group.

'Poor man! I've heard Attar Singh is still not able to get up from his charpai!' remarked the paanwallah, deftly spreading some brown katha over a wet, light green, heart-shaped paan leaf.

Folding it into a neat triangle, Bharose popped the paan into his mouth and then started to chew it in a slow, meditative manner. 'I've heard a lot of strange developments are taking place in the *Sentinel* these days. They have hired a new fellow with a funny name. The unionwallahs call him Kala Nag. He has stopped here a couple of times to buy cigarettes.'

'Where did they get hold of such a character?'

Ram Bharose giggled in a self-deprecatory manner. 'The *Sentinel* is famous for such things. New people keep popping in and old people keep being booted out at regular intervals. It's all very cyclical. Everyone on the paper has been taken aback by stabbing of Attar. He's such a low-key guy.'

The paanwallah heard them out intently. Wiping his mouth with a rag kept on the counter, he turned to Bharose. 'No one has been able to fathom why anyone would want to bump off a character like Attar.'

Pointing to a wooden shack located just adajcent to his shop and serving as a makeshift restaurant specializing in parathas, Benarasi continued with an exaggerated flourish, 'Arre yaar, the stabbing took place a couple of yards away from this paratha shop. He always stopped there to buy rabri for his daughter.'

Billa followed their conversation with keen interest. 'We are living in strange times. Do you think the unionwallahs could be behind this?'

'No!' the paanwallah guffawed. 'Attar is a harmless type. Home to office and office to home. He has never participated in any extra-curricular activity like boozing or visiting the kothas. It's all very strange.'

Bharose looked uncomfortable. For a moment Billa thought he spotted a look of intense embarrassment on Bharose's face. This soon changed to hatred and anger. Catching Bharose by the wrist he said, 'I want you to come with me to Chitli Kabbar.'

'Why do you want to visit that den of vice?'

'Arre yaar, I need to go and visit Gulabo Pathan. After that, we'll both sit down and share a bottle of tharra. That will be on me.'

Bharose gave him an appraising look. 'Why do you want to take me along? You can find your way there easily enough.'

'I want to discuss something along the way. Now come along,' Billa replied.

Hailing a rickshaw, they scrambled aboard with some difficulty. The rexine seat hardly provided space enough for these two big-built characters. Driving through the crowded Daryaganj marketplace, Billa found it difficult to strike a conversation with Bharose, so the two men proceeded in silence.

The rickshawwallah drove them straight to the Pathan's house situated in the middle of a bustling street in the heart of Chitli Kabbar. Traders and shopkeepers selling an assortment of goods could be seen jostling on both sides of the narrow street above which ran a tangle of electric wires. Hundreds of pigeons, perched on the wires, cooed incessantly. Their sound seemed to form a backdrop to the screams and shouts emanating from the street. Above the pigeons, tiny paper kites were painting the sky with a myriad strokes of colour.

Gulabo was found lying on a takht, wearing a langotia and

smoking a hookah. An elderly mallishwallah sat on the floor massaging his long, stick-like legs with warm mustard oil. Gulabo's mehndi-coloured beard had been cropped close to the cheek and his plumed, flowing turban was kept carefully on a table close to his bed.

Billa touched his feet reverentially.

'Ustaadji. I have come to take your blessings.'

Gulabo eyed him suspiciously. 'Whenever someone comes here to ask me for my blessings, it means they are up to no good,' he replied.

Billa looked chastened with this rebuke. Pathan, for him, symbolized the noblest qualities that could be found in any human being. He was always tongue-tied in his presence. He turned his gaze to the narrow window which opened onto the street. Any number of sabziwallahs, fruitwallahs, banglewallahs, mithaiwallahs, chaiwallahs, chappal sellers and sellers of cheap toys were lined on both sides of the road selling their wares. Looking at the rush of people on the road, Billa was sure this single street would be generating business worth millions of rupees every month. His fingers curled in anticipation – if only he could return to his pickpocketing, he could become a rich man.

Gulabo gave him an impatient stare. 'What has brought you here today?'

Billa cleared his throat. 'Ustaadji, you must have heard about the Attar Singh stabbing. Singh called me to his house the other day. He says he will write off my loan, and even the interest, if I can help him find the man behind this evil deed. But as you can well see, I have become lame; I can barely walk. All my energy goes into taking care of my ailing mother. My kind badshah, you know everyone who matters in this city, I thought you might help me unravel this mystery.'

The mallishwallah arrived with three glasses of steaming tea.

The Pathan took a loud slurp and indicated to the mallishwallah to continue rubbing oil on his feet. 'I do not keep well myself. Ever since my stroke, I don't move around much. Ram Bharose helps me with my business and does all the running around for me. What do you think about this case, Ram Bharose?'

Bharose was not comfortable with this question. The squint in his right eye flickered. 'I can't think of anyone even wanting to slap that wimp, leave alone putting a knife into him …' he put his hands up in frustration. There was something false about the way he spoke. Billa could sense it. But he could not put his finger on what it was that didn't ring true.

Gulabo stared out of the window deep in thought. 'I have known Attar for many years. When I had my stroke, he used to come around and see me every day. I regret I have not been able to go and enquire about his health. He has been lending money for over twenty years; the amounts are inconsequential – nothing that people would want to murder him over. If I remember correctly, he lent you twenty thousand rupees. Some years ago.'

The Pathan spoke softly but his voice had a sharp, dangerous edge to it. Billa nodded his head. 'Honourable one, before you I cannot tell a lie. When I took the money, I swore I would return it...'

'Kindly desist from philosophizing. Everyone who borrows does so with the intention of returning what they have taken. You are no exception. You came to me and begged that I should be your guarantor. I had warned you even then that I do not stand guarantor for pickpockets. Tomorrow, if word of this spreads around, every pimp and murderer in Old Delhi would seek me out and demand the same favour from me. I did not turn you down because you have done me many favours in the past. I agreed against my better judgement. You were not able to return the money. That has weighed heavily on my conscience. Attar Singh did complain a few times to me. Fortunately, he is a patient man.

When I heard about the stabbing, I tried to make some sense out of it. I failed. What do you say, Bharose?'

Ram Bharose smiled. 'Maybe some village enmity was behind the killing. After all, we have no idea what has been going on in his village.'

Gulabo was not convinced.

Putting down his glass of tea, the Pathan said, 'The answer does not lie in his village. He does not belong to a landed family. The answer lies somewhere else.'

Billa looked up in surprise.

'I believe the answer to this puzzle lies in his figures.'

'F-figures?' mumbled Billa. He could neither read nor write.

'Have you ever given thought to what Attar Singh does day in and day out? I have visited his home on many occasions. His young daughter only reinforced my impression that all her father did after returning home from office was sit on his charpai and fill out pages and pages with numbers. He maintains several ledger books all overflowing with numbers.'

'Numbers?' repeated Billa.

'Those jumbled up figures contain many mysteries.'

'Every grocer and merchant maintains account books. They don't go around getting stabbed,' observed Bharose.

'You fool! This is not the handiwork of some petty thief. A knifing takes place outside the *Sentinel* office. What can you understand from this? Someone is trying to send out a message and that someone is a powerful man. Of course, this is only speculation. There could be any number of reasons.' Gulabo Pathan turned to the right. The mallishwallah immediately began rubbing his right leg.

Billa could not understand head or tail of what the Pathan was trying to say. Gulabo Pathan read the expression on his face. 'Arre bewakoof! Figures are dangerous especially when they have been written out in black and white. Look at the chaiwallah sitting outside my house. All the figures of his daily transactions are kept inside his head. Nothing is written down. Attar is a different kettle of fish. He just goes on copying pages and pages of god knows what. Maybe, he has copied down something from somewhere which someone may not have liked.'

Billa shook his head. What did Gulabo Pathan mean? It made no sense to him at all. His accident had left him empty-headed. The Pathan was wise and knew the ways of the world. He must know what he was talking about.

'You are a wise man. You know many things. I cannot even sign my own name. I need time to sit down and try and comprehend what you have said,' Billa said getting to his feet with difficulty.

He indicated to Bharose that he was leaving. Bharose declined to follow him out. 'There is something I want to discuss with Pathan sahib. You carry on,' he murmured.

Barely had Billa left the room when Bharose turned on Gulabo. 'What do you mean by doing so much talking in front of this idiot. You want me to get into trouble eh?'

Gulabo smiled. 'No one will get into trouble. Do you think he can make sense out of all these happenings? Rubbish! On the contrary, I wanted to confuse him and to that extent I have succeeded.'

Bharose was not convinced. 'Let us be very clear about this – I am no fool. I know how to hit back and when I do, no one, not even my old associates will be spared,' he said.

Gulabo sighed. 'The problem with all you youngsters is that you have become very impatient. You trust nobody at all.'

Bharose spat at the doorway and walked out of the room in disgust. His father had always told him not to trust a Muslim and definitely not a Pathan. If he got too big for his boots, Gulabo Pathan would also be fixed at the appropriate time.

**

Billa entered Attar Singh's house apprehensively. He had found no clues so far and was certain Attar Singh would accuse him of making no effort.

Attar Singh's office colleagues, Jodh Singh and Krishna Mohan Singh were sitting around him involved in a heated discussion on the very subject that he had gone to discuss at Gulabo's house. The Pathan had not been able to solve the riddle, he informed the trio. He had however provided him with some useful tips. These were faithfully repeated to them.

All three heard Billa out. When he had finished, Krishna was the first to speak. 'I always suspected our maliks were up to no good. They all have black money accounts and Swiss banks accounts – god knows what gol maal these people indulge in,' he said.

Attar's face had turned white as chalk. He was not happy with this news. All these years, he had, on the advice of his mentor, chief accountant Purshottam Lal, done some accountancy work in his spare time in order to earn some extra money. He had always known the company had maintained one set of expense books for their white money expenditures and another for their black money. All these ledgers were kept temporarily in the basement before being dispatched to some unknown destination. Attar had confined himself to doing whatever, Purshottam Lal had ordered him to do but since supervision was slack and since his own financial situation was poor, he had occasionally helped himself to one of the empty ledger books. These were used to keep a record of his own financial dealings.

Occasionally, when he had opened one of these stolen ledgers, he had come across a few pages with some strange notations inside. He had not thought it worthwhile to return the ledger for the sake of a couple of pages, and carried on using the book.

'Are you trying to say some of these books contain some kind of listings of their underhand dealings?' Attar asked Krishna.

'Who can say? I am only making a guess.'

Jodh Singh scratched his light brown hair. 'I cannot make head or tail of what is going on. Do you think it could be a case of office politics? Maybe, the attacker mistook you for somebody else.'

Attar shook his head. 'Mine is not a case of mistaken identity. Somebody wanted to send out a signal – and I'm afraid he has succeeded in what he had set out to achieve. Billa's information has left me more frightened than ever before.'

Jodh Singh took both of Attar Singh's hands and kissed them gently. 'We are there for you, my friend; you have no need to worry. My land in my village is being sold next week. The money you have loaned will be given back to you.'

Krishna Mohan Singh was still trying to unravel the mystery. 'If people had a problem with the ledgers, they could have broken into your house and taken them away. I cannot understand it,' he said.

'Yes – that is exactly what I have also been thinking all along. If someone was suspicious about the books that were in my possession, they could have entered my house and taken them away. Why would they want to kill me? I will speak to Purshottam Lal. He will help me resolve matters,' said Attar.

'Were they after the ledger books or were they after you?' Billa wondered lighting a beedi.

Krishna Mohan Singh looked at his watch. A union meeting had been scheduled in the office an hour from now. 'I think we need to spend more time trying to understand what is going on inside these ledgers. But for the moment, you need to recover your strength and get back to your old office routine,' said Krishna.

And with these words the two peons got up to leave. They were standing at the door when Attar Singh stopped them.

'Today I have come to realize one thing. Some powerful people want me out of the way. In case they succeed, I want you to make a promise to me. You must get Shanti married to a good boy. I have a small provident fund account. Use that money for her marriage.

As for my wife, once the marriage is over, Jodh Singh, you can leave her at my brother's house in Unnao. He will take care of her.'

Turning to Billa he said grimly, 'You have got me no new information. If you want the debt written off, get me the name of the person who stabbed me. Now scoot.'

Shanti had been listening to the conversation from the kitchen. She had never heard her father speak with so much despair. She started sobbing. Not wanting to upset him, she ran to the kitchen sink and splashed water on her face.

After the three men had departed, Attar Singh got Shanti to fetch him all his ledgers. He would check them all out again. He took out a ledger dated 1996-97. The first six pages were filled with notations made by a company official. On the fifth page, he noticed the numbers were written in what appeared to be a coded message. He underlined them with a red ball point.

There was something mysterious about the way the numbers had been noted. Could these be a Swiss bank account number? Most unlikely, he thought. If they were indeed such secretive numbers, why would the company allow them to find their way into a register which was going to be dumped inside a basement?

Could one of those mighty brand managers located on the sixth floor have erred and ended up making a notation in the wrong place? The room in the basement always remained locked and no one had access to the keys except Purshottam Lal. Attar Singh had been allowed access by the security staff only because he was close to Purshottam Lal.

He opened another ledger. This time on page seven, he came across lists of numbers which seemed similar to the ones he had noticed on the fifth page of the earlier ledger. Eventually, Attar Singh found three ledgers in all with the strange notations.

Attar Singh wrote them down on a slip of paper and slipped them into his pocket. Krishna Mohan Singh's words rang in his ears. He must talk to someone else who was more knowledgeable about these matters.

If they did indeed turn out to be Swiss bank account numbers, he could sell this top secret information to a rival newspaper owner and use the money to finance his daughter's wedding. That would seal the fate of Aggarwal Senior. He did not care less. The stabbing had left him shaken. The feeling of gratitude and lifelong indebtedness that a poor villager invariably feels for the owners of the organization that had given him a job had given way to a feeling of hatred and revenge.

Someone in *The Indian Sentinel* was involved with this stabbing. They had never been known to treat their employees well but he could never have imagined they would go to these lengths. He was prepared to go down fighting.

nine

Dalip Jha swore angrily as he leapt across the bed and ran to the passage to pick up the phone. Which blighter had got it into his head to ring up at six a.m. in the morning?

It was Inder sahib. Apu Antony, a reporter in *The Chronicle*, was supposed to be covering the prime minister's visit to Guwahati. His mother had slipped and sprained her ankle. Would he like to go instead?

'I'll send Simi. She's already covered one or two of his important speeches. It will help build up her confidence,' said Dalip.

Inder sahib had no objection. 'Anyone can go as long as the speech is covered. She can always fall back on the PTI report for a back up. Tell her to be at Palam airport in the next forty minutes,' Inder sahib barked, slamming down the phone.

Picking up the newspapers, Dalip gazed at the headlines. His eyes nearly fell out of his head when he saw the way the *Sentinel* had sensationalized the Paro-Jano murder.

'Hey! What's up! That was my fucking story!' Dalip spluttered.

'That old geezer must be up to something!' Dalip muttered to himself. Vikram was hardly the kind of person to give one centimetre of space to someone unless he hoped to make some money out of him. Something was cooking in the *Sentinel* stew. He would find that out later. He must first wake Simi up to make sure she caught the flight out with the prime minister.

Simi hated his mutterings. She half-opened one eye and snapped, 'Stop making so much noise! I worked till midnight but you and your family won't let anyone sleep in peace.'

'Are you out of your mind? I've been awake for the last ten minutes. Inder sahib just called.'

Simi was suddenly wide awake. 'Why did he call?'

'He wants you to go with Ananda Krishnan to Guwahati.'

Simi jumped out of bed. 'I can't believe it. M-e-e!'

'Yes. Absolutely. Only you.'

'When is he going?'

'You have to be at the airport in the next thirty minutes.'

Simi shrieked. 'That is impossible. I haven't even brushed my teeth.'

'You can do that on the plane. They have superb loos.'

'You must be joking.' She slid a pair of black jeans over her slim, long thighs and slipped on a yellow, flowery top. Stuffing her notebooks into her bag, she searched around for her tape recorder.

'I hope your sister hasn't borrowed it again.'

Dalip was trying hard to keep cool. 'Hurry up. Should I drive you to the airport?'

'No. I think I'll take a cab. It's too early and I know you haven't done your jobs yet.'

'That's OK.'

She picked up her large black leather bag, then put it down again. Sitting on the edge of the bed, she gazed indulgently at her own reflection in the mirror.

'What has happened now ?'

'I don't want to go.'

'You don't want to go?'

'No!'

'Then don't go.'

'You're right. We don't spend any time together. I'll really miss you like crazy the whole day.'

'You're going to be back late evening.'

'We fight so much. I'm scared. Where is our relationship going? Your family is so mean. They are of no help at all.'

'Forget them. Forget everyone. Just get on with your own life.'

Simi applied some lipstick and slipped on a pair of green, dangling earrings. They were both heading towards the front verandah when Dalip's mother emerged from her bedroom wearing her trademark maroon housecoat over a pink nightdress.

'Is she leaving us already? You've been married such a short time!' Aruna Jha gasped in a mixture of consternation and relief.

'I'm not leaving, much as you would like me to. I'm going on an assignment with the Prime Minister of India,' replied Simi sarcastically.

'Mother, please!' Dalip shouted in between giving directions over the phone to the neighbourhood cabbie to get over to their house at the earliest. He could not cope with another early morning confrontation.

'I haven't said anything. I was just going to make some tea,' said Aruna, walking briskly towards the kitchen.

The taxi arrived within minutes. Simi clutched Dalip's left arm, then scrambled into the Omni van. The driver revved up the engine and the taxi fishtailed wildly before lurching forward and vanishing into the pale morning light.

Dalip walked into the living room and dialled Kiki's number. 'There's an important press conference at eleven a.m. Make sure you are in office by ten o'clock.'

'Yes boss. I thought you were going to take me to see a movie.' She wasn't sounding sleepy at all.

Dalip laughed. 'We'll discuss it when I get to office.'

His mother was standing in front of him balancing four cups of tea on a tiny, black tray. 'Where has she gone?'

'Guwahati.'

'She talks too much.'

'Mother, you are much older. If she behaves foolishly, what stops you from at least trying to be civilized?'

Aruna's eyebrows rose imperiously. 'Baba, all that high falutin' English does not impress me. A daughter-in-law should behave like a daughter-in-law. That's what we learnt back home in Bihar.'

'I'm not denying that. I can't argue with you women. Just give me a mug of tea.'

Dalip was finding it increasingly difficult to cope with his domineering mother and his three strong-willed sisters. He had been attracted to Simi because he thought she was soft-natured and sweet – unlike the general run of women journalists. Two days into their marriage and she was as loud-mouthed and pugnacious as the brood in his own house. All three of his sisters hated her and Simi made no effort to adjust to them.

Despite his entire salary being pumped into meeting the household expenses, the women were never satisfied. Dalip had taken to doing a lot of travelling in order to earn some extra cash to meet his own mounting expenses. He loved buying books and CDs. His other major expense was his Press Club bills. Mother kept warning him about the need for putting aside some money to meet his sisters' marriage expenses. The thought of having to raise so much money unnerved him.

Dalip's spirits lifted by the time he stepped into the overcrowded *Chronicle* office. No one had reached so early except for the peon, Hare Krishna, who was tinkering with a broken-down electric stove used for making tea.

'Make some tea for me,' Dalip said picking up *The Indian Sentinel* and reading Mishra's story out loud.

Inder sahib sauntered in a few minutes later. 'I'm surprised at why the *Sentinel* has picked up our story. Have you spoken to someone in their office to find out what is happening?' he said

'I was just going to ring up Jolly,' Dalip replied.

'A minimum of fifteen-twenty caste killings take place in this Delhi-Muzzafarpur belt every year. How come they have not bothered to highlight any of these stories in the past? My hunch is they are trying to put pressure on the government. It must have something to do with their FERA case,' Inder sahib continued.

'Oh come on Inder sahib! They're such a rich and powerful group. They can buy out whoever they want.'

'It's not that easy. Even the rich have their enemies. Try speaking to that Jolly character. Let's see what he has to say.'

Dalip dialled Ajit Jolly's number. Ajit sounded as pompous as ever. 'Vikramji is a very committed person. He comes from a Marwari background and you know how Marwaris, more than any other community in India, believe in the sanctity of life.'

Dalip could not suppress a guffaw. 'Arre bhai, what has the sancticty of life got to do with his decision to highlight a caste killing.'

Speaking in his American-Indian twang, Ajit drawled, 'To understand Vikramji's desire to highlight this killing, you need to go back in history and understand their whole tradition of ahimsa and peaceful living. He has obviously got upset with this whole caste conundrum and the way it is affecting the future of our nation.'

'Spare me all this big talk, yaar. What have the Marwaris ever done to prevent violence in our society? We have more people meeting violent ends here than in any other part of the globe,' Dalip said.

Ajit was not interested. When he became home minister he would worry about people dying. 'We are the second-largest selling paper in the world. Every word that is published here is treated as gospel truth by the Government of India.'

Dalip snorted. 'You're a great guy! You work for a great paper! You seem to forget that we journos are scavengers, man. I happen to collect my news from all the slush that flows along the roadside. That's the kind of profession we are in, man,' and he slammed down the phone.

Next, he rang up Raveena Bedi. She was in a deep post-coital slumber, Kala Muthu's arm resting on her breasts.

'Who is it?' she asked.

'Dalip.'

Never one to forget a slight, she was at her coldest, 'My dear Dalip, what service can I render you this morning?'

'Have you read the papers? *The Indian Sentinel* has played up my story. I'm just trying to understand why.'

Raveena was rising rapidly in the *Sentinel* hierarchy. She was not going to utter a word that would compromise her newly-acquired status.

'Are you unhappy about your scoop being picked up by a rival paper? You seem to have forgotten my words of warning – no one reads your paper anyway.' Kala Muthu was playing with her nipples.

'I'm not disputing that. I'm just curious to know why so much space is being given to a non-issue.'

Raveena laughed her soft, tinkling laugh. 'How would I know, yaar. I've just been promoted to the special correspondent grade. I'm in the same slot as you are. We'll be covering the same beats. I'll see you around sometime,' she said and put the phone down.

'None of them seem to have any idea of what is going on. If there is one organization which can turn you insane it's the *Sentinel,'* Dalip informed Inder sahib.

Kiki sauntered into the office at one o'clock. By this time, most of the correspondents had arrived for the afternoon meeting. A shortage of chairs forced two of the reporters to sit on the computer tables right through the half-hour meeting.

'What story am I supposed to be doing today?' Kiki asked, pouting provocatively at Dalip.

'Ask Inder sahib. Why are you asking me?'

'A nice-looking girl like you doesn't have to start working on her second day. Let me take you out to lunch at the Press Club,' said Inder sahib.

'If you have to take her out to lunch then you may as well take her to the Taj Man Singh or some fancy place like that. Why should you opt for such a third-rate joint?' Dalip muttered under his breath, stepping out into the verandah for a smoke.

Kiki followed him out as did Inder sahib.

Inder sahib had made up his mind to take her out for a meal. Dalip could read his intentions and was determined to try and stop him.

'I think you should encourage Kiki to work. She's been here two days already and hasn't filed anything yet. If she's not careful, Calcutta will start raising eyebrows very soon,' Dalip said.

Inder sahib stretched his arms out and, for one brief second, Kiki thought he was going to place his hand on her breast. She hurriedly stepped back. Losing her footing, she grabbed Dalip's shoulder for support. Taking the cigarette from his hand, she inhaled deeply.

Inder sahib was horrified at this familiarity. 'Kiki, you shouldn't smoke. It's bad for your health.'

'You sound just like my dad. OK. I promise this will be my last cigarette for the day.'

'Don't listen to all that bullshit! Here, take a cigarette from me,' said Dalip and took out a packet of cigarettes from his shirt pocket. She accepted one and used Dalip's cigarette to light her own.

Inder sahib shrugged in disgust. Pushing the door open, he stepped back into the *Chronicle* office.

'I thought you were going to take me to see a matinee show,' Kiki whispered mischievously into Dalip's ear.

'Let's go and see the evening show instead.'

'I'm game.'

'Good! Let's meet outside Rivoli at six p.m. sharp. We'll both reach separately. I don't want everyone in the office to start gossiping.'

They steered clear of each other for the rest of the day. Dalip sat in his cubicle the entire afternoon trying to complete a feature story meant for the Sunday magazine section. He was much too distracted to be able to concentrate. Kiki seemed interesting and friendly. He wanted to get to know her better. But if that happened where would it leave Simi? His wife was hardly the understanding kind.

Not wanting the others to become suspicious, he left the office an hour before Kiki. Parking his battered white Fiat at Hanuman Mandir, Dalip looked round cautiously before making a dash for the Rivoli theatre. Kiki was already waiting in the foyer smoking a cigarette. Stupid girl! Smoking in a public place was the surest way of attracting attention. He must warn her against indulging in such brazen behaviour in the future.

They climbed up the steps leading to the balcony. The hall was full and their seats were in the last row. They had barely sat down when Dalip felt her elbow press against his arm. Her shoulder was touching his and he could feel the warmth of her body against his. He made no attempt to reach out and hold her hand though he knew this was what she would have liked. He refused to leave the auditorium during the interval insisting they remain seated right through the show.

It was only when the film was over and they had walked back to the Hanuman Mandir parking lot that he allowed her to light another cigarette.

'Why don't you come to my barsati in Kalkaji Extension for a drink? I have a bottle of Napoleon brandy – we can share it!'

Dalip looked hurriedly at his watch. He had another two hours to go. Simi's flight was expected to land at eleven p.m. 'I think I might just be able to have a quick drink.'

Kiki drove her blue Maruti 800 out of the Hanuman Mandir parking lot first. Dalip followed in his Fiat. Her two-room apartment was tastefully decorated with attractive furniture and knick-knacks. He settled down on a low divan. Kiki poured out two brandies with expert ease. As they sipped their drinks, he could see her long, smooth legs emerging from below her blue dress. Her body was tanned a ripe, dark brown. She was any day more desirable than that fat cow of a Raveena woman or even Simi for that matter.

Looking around her flat, Dalip's eye fell on a set of photographs. A young Kiki was being carried in the sturdy arms of a tall, good-looking uniformed officer. 'I've just realized, I know very little about you.'

'What would you like to know?' she asked coquettishly.

'Where did you spend your childhood?'

'I was like a gypsy. With my father in the army, I spent my childhood wandering from one place to another.'

'Sounds adventurous. I never moved out of my village in Bihar. I was sixteen years old when I got my first train ride.'

'No wonder you're a country bumpkin.'

Kiki took out a notebook from a drawer. She came and sat next to him. 'I want you to read some of my poems. Your English is much better than mine. I'd be delighted if you would edit them for me.'

Dalip flicked through some pages.

Love is a meeting of glances
Of locking the eyes into an intimacy
That subsumes the senses
Stretching the heart from one end to another,
Menstruation, an unwelcome guest,
Carrying a brandmark ...

She hardly looked the kind of person who could write poetry. When it came to filing stories, he doubted she would be capable of writing two sentences of correct English. He decided to keep these thoughts to himself and keep up with the flattery.

'Why should a young girl like you be writing such serious stuff? You remind me of Slyvia Plath,' said Dalip, his head swimming with the brandy.

'Keeps me amused. But seriously, what do you think about my poems?'

She was sitting much too close for comfort. He leaned against her and touched her breasts. Her lips grazed against his mouth. Dalip switched off the light and hurriedly took off her blouse. She unhooked her brassiere. Two tiny nipples, like two round eyes, rose against her chest. His hand pressed hard against them. Her mouth was soft, like whipped cream. He mounted her easily. They rocked in unison and he realized he had never experienced so much pleasure.

'I think you are a very good poet. I believe you are an even better lover,' Dalip muttered.

'You teach me English and I'll teach you about other things,' she whispered and they proceeded to make love all over again.

**

Prime Minister Ananda Krishnan's plane landed at Palam airport at eleven-thirty p.m. Dalip, at the airport to receive Simi, hurried up to Ananda Krishnan and gave him a low salute. 'What an excellent speech you made at Guwahati.'

Ananda Krishnan smiled. 'Fortunately, I did not have to speak in Hindi.'

'Your Hindi is very good,' said Simi.

'It is but I'm still nervous about speaking before the pucca Hindiwallahs. They say my pronunciation is very bad,' said Ananda Krishnan breaking into a loud giggle. He always enjoyed his own jokes. By then several ministers and journalists had crowded around him providing Dalip and Simi with an opportunity to slip away.

Simi slipped her arm into Dalip's as they walked towards the car park.

'Did you miss me?'

Dalip gave no reply.

'Guwahati was beautiful. The hills, the temple, the people. Ananda made a rotten speech. The whole place is overflowing with ULFA elements. It's sad what we're doing to our country.'

'Have you filed your story?'

'Of course. I sent it out at five p.m. I've been loafing around since. What story did you do today?'

'Routine.The CBI has caught hold of three AIIMS professors selling examination papers to students. Nothing new – the professors are denying the charge totally. One of them treats the President of India so I guess one had better be careful collecting dope on him.'

It was a hot, muggy night without a trace of breeze. Dalip wiped the sweat from his forehead and started the car. It was pushing past midnight. 'Have you had dinner?'

'No. Actually there was a goof up and they didn't serve us any food on the plane.'

'You want to go to a restaurant?'

'Let's just go home and eat something. It's quite late and we're both tired.'

'I don't know what has been cooked in the house. Everyone must be asleep.'

'Not your mother. She watches serials till one at night.'

The front door was not locked. The light in his mother's bedroom was still on. Not wishing to disturb her, both of them tiptoed into the kitchen to get something to eat. Switching on the light, Simi's hand hit a steel glass which clanged to the floor. Within seconds, Dalip's mother wearing her maroon nightgown, was standing at the door wanting to know what had happened.

'We were just trying to get a bite, mother. We'll manage,' said Dalip taking out a bowl of dal from the fridge.

'There isn't very much food in the fridge. I had kept that dal for the maid's breakfast. You didn't inform me that you both were planning to have dinner in the house,' said his mother in her loud monotone.

Dalip put the bowl back into the fridge. 'We can eat bread and eggs,' he murmured.

As soon as his mother's back turned, Simi collapsed on a chair near the kitchen door. 'I can't believe this. First she makes a huge hue and cry about how the maid is eating her out of house and hearth. Then, when her famished son and daughter-in-law arrive home after a long day's work, she takes objection to our eating a bowl of dal and chapattis. I think we should seriously think of moving out of here. I'm insulted, to say the least.'

Simi was shaking with anger. She wanted to control herself but once she grew upset, there was no stopping her. Bitter words poured out of her mouth like a torrent.

Dalip slammed the glass of water he was drinking on the table and stalked out of the room. 'Just stop it now. Your bickering has begun to get on my nerves,' he said.

Simi followed him into the bedroom still screaming. 'How is it my fault? What have I done? Can't you see how abnormally your mother behaves? Why don't you say something to her? You and your family are just driving me nuts!'

Dalip lit a cigarette. 'Listen, babe! Stop shouting! The neighbours will hear!'

'To hell with the neighbours! Your entire salary goes to support your family! Why should they be allowed to treat us like shit?'

'They don't. They are all right. You have to learn to accept their little faults without becoming hysterical.'

Simi collapsed on the bed sobbing loudly. 'It's all my fault. I can never do anything right. This is not the way I had thought my marriage would turn out to be.'

Dalip turned his face away. He was sick of the whole lot of them. He was going to find himself another place to stay. Simi would not be allowed to enter it. Nor would his mother. Let the two of them fight each other out. They were welcome to kill each other, if they wanted. If they succeeded in doing so, he for one would hoot with delight. He would go to the Hanuman Mandir and give thanks to God. He would offer Him a Rs 101 prasad as thanksgiving for having rid him of these two viragos from his life.

ten

Tim Robertson's dislike of Delhi began minutes after he had stepped out of a British Airways flight on a hot, humid June morning. Tim got an inkling of what to expect from a nation with a one billion population when he was made to join a serpentine queue of passengers waiting in the disembarkation line to get their passports stamped.

A woman balancing one child against her left shoulder and leading another toddler with her right hand protested against the delay. She had already waited thirty minutes and the line was hardly moving. The middle-aged clerk with his shifty eyes saw this as a sign of dissidence. How dare she question his authority? She was ordered to step outside the queue. Her turn would now come last.

Robertson moved forward and protested on her behalf. 'It's a little unfair to have a mother of two kids waiting out as though she were a petty criminal.'

The clerk glowered back.

'You are welcome to join her if you so so wish,' he retorted in a thin, whiny voice.

Tim decided to avoid a scene. There were hundreds of

passengers waiting to get out of this overheated hall. No one bothered to speak up. It was better to allow the lady to weep her heart out than to start a confrontation with this fat-arsed imbecile.

Collecting his luggage turned out to be an equally arduous task, with hundreds of people pushing their trollies right up to the luggage conveyor belt. Once the belt started moving, he found himself having to peer over the shoulders of two hefty Sardars to try and spot his luggage. The belt had completed two rounds. One overstuffed bag chased another. There were no signs of his bag.

Suddenly a sinister-looking bearded character sidled up to him and told him he would help locate his stuff if he gave him five dollars. Exasperated at the delay, Tim took out a new five dollar note and handed it to the man who led him to the other end of the hall where several suitcases were strewn around haphazardly, one on top of the other. Within a couple of minutes he had located both his bags. They were lying at the bottom of the pile. He felt cheated. He had given him the money in good faith. It seemed like a deliberate ploy by the airport staff to make an extra buck.

He made his way out to the main exit to find a veritable sea of humanity pushing and shoving in front of a steel barricade, obviously erected to keep these very people out. Like vultures waiting to tear into human carrion, they were greedily eyeing every passenger coming out of the terminal. He had never seen such a disreputable and foul-smelling lot. The heat along with their sweaty odour made him nauseous.

'Dear God!' he sighed, reconciling himself to his fate. Ron William from the *International Herald Tribune* had warned him that Delhi was a punishment posting. With night temperatures hovering at 36 degrees Celsius, he could look forward to a blistering time.

The drive from the airport was equally depressing. The old cabbie drove his ramshackle Ambassador at a snail's pace. The taxi was not air-conditioned. It smelt of putrid water and incense. Tim was feeling even more nauseous by the time he checked into Claridges, one of Delhi's oldest hotels.

He had just settled down in his room and poured himself a large peg of Black Label whiskey when the bellboy rang the bell. There were some fax messages from Tim's London office.

David Knight, the news editor was trying to be funny 'You can get to work straight away. The High Commission blokes have fixed a meeting for you with Mr R.K. Nagendra, Principal Information Officer of the Government of India at two-thirty p.m. (Indian time). He works at Shastri Bhawan located on Rajendra Prasad Road. They got the dates mixed up and the meeting is scheduled for today.'

Tim looked at his watch. It was showing seven-thirty a.m. London time. The hotel watch showed eleven a.m. He had time enough to unpack and have a quick nap.

Shastri Bhawan turned out to be a dense, unimposing structure with plaster peeling off the walls. The narrow, dank corridor on the first floor led him to the door on which Nagendra's nameplate was prominently displayed.

Two minutes later he was inside a room, which in contrast to the smelly corridor was a showpiece of elegance with a beige silk carpet spread in the middle of the floor and matching silk curtains drawn across the entire length of the sprawling room.

'Hello! I'm Nagendra. You must be Tim Robertson from *The London Times*. I'm very pleased to have you in India,' a short, nondescript man with a Clark Gable moustache said in a squeaky, high-pitched tone. Barely had the coffee and biscuits been served and initial pleasantries exchanged, when Nagendra launched into a sudden tirade.

'We are not like China. This is a democratic country where you are free to travel anywhere. The problem with you gentlemen is that you seldom recognize this fact. Have you ever wondered how, in spite of all our multi-ethnicity, different religions and languages, we have survived as a nation?'

'What is this guy driving at?' Tim thought.

'We are a vibrant, functional democracy. We are not a theocratic state with weak democratic underpinnings like our immediate neighbour. We are also a fundamentally peace-loving nation. But yet you people try to project a different picture of what we are.'

Tim pushed back his chair and stared at the carpet. He had not come here to listen to this man's lecture. Nagendra was in no mood to stop his broadside.

'I must say with a great sense of regret that the Western press has not presented us in a fair light. We are being shown as a nation that does not tolerate its minorities and is engaged in repression against Kashmiris. A few months ago, the BBC showed Indian army tanks mowing down the local population in the so-called "Indian-administered Kashmir".'

Nagendra flipped open the latest edition of *The Economist*, which carried a story on the Kashmir problem. 'Look at the map shown here. Look how a part of the land of my country has been knocked off and is being shown as part of Pakistan. It is the British who first hacked our nation into pieces fifty years back. And now what do they do? Divide Kashmir into an Indian-administered and Pakistan-administered state. How would you feel if we had taken the same position on Ulster or on Ireland? Let's be clear. The so-called Pakistan-administered Kashmir is an integral part of our territory that has been illegally occupied by our neighbour.'

Nagendra continued his attack. 'Oh! By the way, let me complete what I was saying earlier on that great BBC story. On checking out the veracity of the footage, you know what? We figured out the shots actually pertained to a Central Asian country.' Nagendra burst into a chuckle.

Tim wondered what would come next.

'I am sorry for being so frank. I am only expressing my personal opinions. You shouldn't think otherwise. Sometimes one is left with a genuine sense of regret at how the foreign press has simply failed to come to grips with the world's largest democracy and a five thousand-year-old civilization. Why don't you write something positive about this country? About the changes taking place in our villages, how we have recently introduced thirty-three per cent reservations for women to enable them to be elected to local decision-making bodies ...'

Nagendra's voiced appeared to falter, but his razor-sharp eyes did not leave Tim's face for even a moment. Suddenly he changed tack.

'I was generally trying to inform you about the many initiatives we have launched in our country. Now let me ask you a few questions about yourself. Is this your first trip to India?'

'That's right. Never been here before.'

'Then you must visit the Taj Mahal.'

Tim had to restrain himself from smiling,

'Er, yes, yes, of course. I have heard a lot about it. I wouldn't dream of missing it.'

'You will need an accreditation, a special phone and fax connection. There are a few formalities that need to be completed. We will get them over with within the next few days. But you are always welcome to contact me for any help.'

A few more pleasantries were exchanged. Tim shook hands and walked out, his head heavy with that entire verbal lashing. Walking down, he felt the hot midday sun hit him like a ton of bricks. His legs felt like jelly. He staggered and gripped a chair placed near the entrance for support. Harpreet, the young Sardar taxi driver, seemed to realize what had happened, for he rushed across the road and gripped him by his right shoulder.

Leading him to the cab he said, 'It's the heat. It must have got you.'

'Let's get back to the hotel fast,' gasped Tim,

The Sardar revved up the engine and turned on the air-conditioner. As soon as the car cooled down, Tim began to feel better.

'Englishmen find this country very hot. Is that not the case?'

'I felt I was being roasted alive.'

'Sir, you need to cool off with some chilled beer and some hot women. I can arrange.'

Tim had never felt so astonished in his life.

'From where will you be able to arrange this interesting combination?'

'Don't worry sir. I have my contacts. I'm only doing this for you and no one else. I hate the Indian men who come and stay in these hotels. They want everything free.'

'Thanks for the offer. I will definitely consider it. But for the moment I think it is best that you simply drive me back to my hotel.'

He wondered how his ex-wife Mary, now living with a computer nerd, would react to such a proposition. He stared at the driver with his distinctive flowing black beard, long nose and sharp, brown eyes. He seemed like a resourceful bloke.

'Is this supplying of women part of your regular business?'

'No sir. I do no such thing. Mine is a straight business. My father was a taxi driver. I am following his dhanda. I only offer this to a few exceptional customers, otherwise none of this hanky panky. You look like a good man, for you I will do it. No one else.'

'What is your name, if I may ask?'

'Harpreet Singh. I come from Bhatinda in Punjab. I have been in this taxi business now for five years. I know all the ins and outs of this trade.'

'Very good.'

They had arrived at the hotel and Tim decided to leave it at that. Hurrying back into his room, he scanned through the pile of Indian newspapers. The lead story of *The Indian Sentinel* related to a caste killing involving a young boy and girl that took place in Shamli. Star-crossed lovers, he told himself. That seemed like an interesting lead on which he could do a follow up. Would cause quite a sensation back home. He'd ring up this Nagendra fellow and find out just how far Shamli was from Delhi.

eleven

Nagendra had given Tim Robertson very precise directions on how to reach Shamli. The village was less than a hundred kilometres from the capital. Nagendra had been intrigued by the way *The Indian Sentinel* was playing up the story. He did not mention this detail to Tim, who having no understanding of the caste conundrums that plagued India, nevertheless felt it was a good story with which to make a debut.

Harpreet Singh was delighted to take him to Shamli and so, one day after his arrival, Tim found himself being driven in a ridiculously unelegant car called the Contessa, over a smooth, black tarmac road.

Tim took extensive notes of all that he saw, Harpreet, with his pidgin English, providing the background details. During a quick tea break, Harpreet seized the chance to pump him with intimate details of his childhood spent in Bhatinda in the Punjab.

As the taxi entered Shamli, a crowd of people gathered round the car. A bunch of kids with unkempt bleached hair and yellow teeth pressed their faces against the windows of the car. Being a foreigner, Tim realized, meant attracting more attention than he had bargained for.

He pushed down the window. Two teenaged boys, without even being asked, offered to take him to Chowdhury Ram Lal's house.

'Why him?' Tim enquired.

'He is the village sarpanch and these days all the strangers who come to our village make a beeline for his house,' the elder of the boys informed him.

Robertson followed them to Ram Lal's house to find him lying on a charpai. A fellow villager squatting on the floor was massaging his legs. The village teacher, Balram Prakash, was sitting near him on a sturdy looking unpolished chair. Ram Lal's son was his student. The sarpanch went out of his way to humour him giving him free seeds and pesticides. The result was that Ram Lal's son invariably stood first in his class.

Taken aback at seeing a foreigner entering his house, Ram Lal jumped up from the charpai and welcomed him with a low namaste. Balram Prakash, equally surprised, got up from his chair and insisted Tim sit on it.

'You are from the World Bank?' asked Prakash, taking out a packet of paan masala from his shirt pocket and stuffing its contents into his mouth.

'No. I'm a journalist with *The London Times*,' Tim replied eyeing the packet of paan masala in Prakash's hand. He'd seen packets of this stuff dangling outside several chai and paan shops. It was obviously popular with the locals.

Prakash could not hide his astonishment. 'We had a couple of journalists here just two days ago. But of course they were from Indian papers. What brings you here? At one time I used to listen to the news regularly over BBC radio, now of course, with TV, one does not listen to radio much,' said Prakash, determined to use this opportunity to display his mastery over English not only before the visiting gentlemen but also for the benefit of his village colleagues.

Tim decided to come straight to the point. 'You had a mishap here recently – there was a caste-based killing?' he asked.

'A minor accident! So much is being made of such a small incident,' Ram Lal murmured. He spoke with an obvious sense of discomfort. Better to make money under the table and allow his other panchayat brothers to do the same than get embroiled in needless controversy.

Prakash interceded, 'The incident is making us famous. Everybody in Delhi is talking about it.'

Tim could see Ram Lal's discomfort written large over his face. He decided to change tack. Turning to the sarpanch he asked, 'Do you have any children?'

'Yes. Four sons and six daughters. My youngest son is studying in school, but my eldest son is the father of two children,' Ram Lal replied in Hindi. Prakash translated for him.

'Would you have responded in a similar fashion if your own daughter had run away with a boy?'

Ram Lal's reply was prompt. 'I would have done worse. I would have killed the boy's parents and burnt down their house as well.'

Prakash added his bit. 'Sir, we continue to follow rules laid down by our elders many hundreds of years ago. These have not changed. It is for this reason that our villages, unlike our cities, have remained cohesive units.'

'You are the local schoolteacher here – I understand the killing took place right in front of your school?' Tim asked.

'You cannot compare what is going on in our villages with the kind of life people are leading in the cities. Those have become dens of sin,' Prakash said.

'From what I understand, your government has been actively promoting inter-caste marriages. It wants to remove the evil of casteism from your society. Isn't that so?'

Prakash guffawed. 'The government says a lot of things. It says there should be no poverty. Has it ended? It says there should be no corruption but there is more corruption today than at any time in our history. They say no man should have two wives but our Cabinet ministers are known to have three and four wives each. In the cities, everyone does as he pleases. If we repeated that pattern in our villages, there would be chaos.'

Tim heard him out with interest. 'There will always be a difference between customary practice and the law but let me rephrase my question. The younger people in your village must want to live life differently from the older generation.'

Ram Lal took a drag at the chillum. The hookah bubbled merrily as he drew into it, its small flames darting out like a serpent's tongue. 'They can look at it any way they want but they cannot transgress traditional customs and practices,' he retorted.

Prakash did some quick translation for Tim's benefit.

'Do the women in the village accept what you are saying? Does your wife accept what you say?' Tim asked.

'Let her speak for herself. Arre Rani, come out here for a second. A foreign patrakar wants to take your interview,' Ram Lal shouted.

There was no reply.

'Our village women feel shy to talk before strangers. Let me go inside and fetch her myself.'

The sarpanch emerged a few minutes later followed by a fat woman with a sari pallu covering her face and draped over her bosom right down to her waist.

'Shoot your questions. She will speak for herself.'

Robertson looked at the woman. She was wrapped from head to toe in reams of cloth. Her head was covered by the end of her sari which she had raised to create a small opening for her voice to come through. How was he expected to hold a conversation with her?

'Do you believe young people should be executed in this

manner? If your own daughter had run away with a young man, would you have supported her execution?'

She bent towards her husband and muttered something into his ear. Ram Lal repeated what she had said to Prakash who in turn translated it into English for Tim's benefit.

'She is saying that young children must follow the tried and tested customs of their elders. You ask young people this question and they will give the same reply.'

She bent down and whispered again in Ram Lal's ear.

Prakash spat out a stream of red, and emptied more paan masala into his mouth. Then translating the sarpanch's words he said, 'His wife is saying that the government is to blame for this mess. Earlier, villagers could marry their daughters by spending one or two thousand rupees. Now, with menfolk demanding huge dowries, families are not finding grooms. How can poor families be expected to pay so much? A girl from a poor family has no choice but to run away with a boy. That is exactly what Paro did. But that does not make her behaviour justifiable.'

Everyone heard her out in silence. Embarrassed at the attention she was receiving, Rani fled inside the house only to reappear a few minutes later carrying six small glasses of tea on a large plate.

Tim accepted the tea a little gingerly. Not wanting to appear rude, he forced himself to take a few sips of the sweet liquid syrup. He felt he was trapped inside a furnace. The sun was blazing down and there was not a breath of air. He wished they had offered him a cold drink instead. The others slurped down their chai with great relish.

'The girl's relatives live in this village?' Tim enquired.

'Of course! You must go down to meet them. I would have taken you there myself but I have to go and attend a sarkari meeting,' said Ram Lal who was beginning to feel more and more uncomfortable with this foreigner. He was tired of all these journalists. They were a bunch of busybodies, given to snooping about and asking awkward questions. He muttered to Prakash to take him across to meet Pappu Yadav.

Balram Prakash was delighted to do so. He wanted to make this foreigner realize how well-read and well-informed a village schoolteacher could be. 'I will just take him in a few minutes. I do wish that like his forefathers, he had brought a sola topee to cover his head. If he has a sunstroke, her Majesty's government will accuse us poor villagers of having harmed one of her subjects.'

Tim grinned, wiping his brow. 'I've made a dreadful mistake. I should have worn a topee or else brought an umbrella along.'

He was perspiring heavily as he followed Prakash along the makeshift village path. They walked in single file. Harpreet followed a few steps behind them. A bunch of kids who giggled and chattered incessantly trailed behind the trio.

'Sir, in Delhi you must be living in a big air-conditioned house?'

'No. I'm living in a hotel. I just arrived a couple of days ago and I have to still find a place for myself. I was under the impression that it would be less hot in the villages. Less concrete, you know?'

'Do you know that the British architect Lutyens built the Rashtrapati Bhavan on top of a Siva temple?' Balram asked

'No. I'm afraid I had no idea about this –'

'The Rashtrapati Bhavan should be broken down and make way for a temple which is bigger than even the Somnath temple.'

'Of course,' muttered Tim wiping his brow.

Prakash stopped outside a dilapidated house. Peering over a makeshift fence made from thorn bushes he said, 'You are in luck, sir. Pappu Yadav, the girl's uncle is here. Arre Pappu bhai, you have become a celebrity – you have a visitor from London.'

Pappu was lying on a charpai smoking a beedi. He stared at Robertson with a mixture of suspicion and pride.

'You mean he has crossed the seven seas to come all the way to Shamli?' Yadav asked getting up from his charpai.

Tim had seldom seen such an ugly-looking fellow. Pappu Yadav's eyes were bloodshot, and his face was covered with dark stubble that had not yet become a beard. Tim forced himself to sound friendly.

'Yes, in a sense what you say is right – but let me make a slight correction. No one crosses the seven seas anymore. We fly over them, navigating the friendly skies in an aeroplane.'

Pappu grinned, 'I've seen these planes fly over our village a couple of times – they vanish in a few seconds.'

'This sahib is a journalist. He has come here to find out what happened to your niece,' Balram interjected.

Pappu's face registered no expression, but Bhuja, sitting in one corner, looked up with interest. 'Well what about her?' he asked dryly.

'Arre bhai, he is trying to understand our Indian customs. He wants to know about Paro and Jano,' Prakash interjected.

Yadav spat out a ball of spittle and lit another beedi. 'What could have happened? She was killed. That is all.'

Tim stared at him. 'Why did you allow this to happen? Don't you want to give young people some freedom?'

Prakash was only too happy to continue with his role as translator.

'What kind of hypothetical question are you asking me? Paro was not a child. She knew I was in the process of negotiating a marriage for her with another boy in a neighbouring village. She could have waited and chosen to be married off in a respectable manner. But no! She decided to run off with a bloody chamar.'

'Excuse me, I have not been in India for long but I have not heard of any rule which forbids a woman to marry a man of her choice,' Tim interrupted.

Balram Prakash nodded his head indignantly. 'You have been completely misinformed. Marriages are invariably arranged by family elders.'

'Even if I accept the argument that she disobeyed your customary laws, why didn't you hand her over to the police?' Tim interjected.

Pappu grimaced. 'There is something called village pride that stands over and above the rules made by our bloody government. The whole village was witness to this execution.'

Tim wiped his brows and turned to Bhuja who was following the conversation closely. 'I presume she is Paro's grandmother. I heard the girl was orphaned at a young age and it was you who brought her up. Do you support this collective decision?'

Bhuja remained quiet.

Prakash went up to her and egged her on. 'Mataji, speak your mind. What you say will be printed in London.'

Bhuja continued to look away.

Pappu lost his temper. 'Our womenfolk are a useless lot. The whole day they nag their menfolk about one thing or another but when asked to speak their minds, they pretend to turn dumb.'

Bhuja gave him a frightened look. It was obvious she was scared of her son.

Tim turned once again to Pappu.

'What is your profession, sir?'

'I am a farmer. I own a small patch of land.'

'Very good. Is there some other way in which you earn your living?'

'I do all kinds of odd jobs. Everyone knows me around here. No one tries fooling around with me.'

'Can I take a photograph of you?' Tim asked, taking out his camera.

Throwing his beedi down, Pappu caught hold of Prakash's arm. 'Get him out of here – is that clear? Why did you bring him here in the first place? He must have given you a fat commission. Is he a foreign agent or on the payroll of some government agency? I didn't invite him.'

For a brief second Tim thought Pappu was going to hit Prakash. Prakash extricated himself from his grip and half-walked, half-ran out of the house. Nasty fellow! He could have broken his arm or done something worse. It was best to get out of here fast.

Tim hurried out behind Prakash. Harpreet followed at their heels. As they reached the village primary school, Tim asked Balram Prakash if he could take him to meet Jano's family.

'I can take you there but I do not know whether I want to enter the house. They are being boycotted by the village community.'

Jano's house was located on the western edge of the village. For Tim, it meant another long walk past an ancient looking village temple located at the edge of a pond in whose muddy waters children were squealing and splashing water on buffaloes. Taking a curve around what must have been a makeshift village bazaar consisting of a few shops, Tim found several villagers stopping Prakash to make enquiries about him.

Prakash continued to badger Tim about England. His constant questioning and the heat had begun to get on Tim's nerves.

'Does your Queen Elizabeth continue to sit on the Peacock Throne forcibly taken away from us by the marauder Nadir Shah? Is the British government going to return the throne to us?'

'I don't think there is too much of a Peacock Throne left you know. Some of those diamonds and emeralds are now adorning the Queen's crown. Personally, I think she should return all that stuff. At the end of the day, she's a pretty rich lady,' Tim said.

Prakash nudged Harpreet by his shoulder. 'Your sahib is a very generous Englishman. He wants the Peacock Throne to be returned to India.'

'Let it stay where it is. If it comes back to India, it will only get stolen by one of our ministers,' Harpreet said.

They crossed several houses before stopping outside a double-storied building. Prakash banged the front door hard with his fist. He had to knock several times before a young teenage boy with light brown eyes and long unkempt hair finally opened the door. He did not ask them to come inside.

Seeing the boy, Balram seemed to forget his earlier intention of not entering the house 'Kapil beta, how come you are at home today? I thought you were studying in a college in Delhi?' he enquired and forced his way inside.

'I am here for a few days,' the boy replied looking nervously at Tim and Harpreet who followed Balram into the house.

Plonking himself on a chair, Balram pulled out yet another packet of paan masala. A clothesline with clothes hanging on it stretched across the entire length of the room. The walls on all four sides were covered with pictures of different gods and goddesses. A photograph of a youthful looking boy hung in the centre of the room. A garland of stale marigold flowers adorned it.

'Beta, we have a senior journalist from a big paper in the UK.' Turning to Tim he said, 'This is Kapil, Jano's brother. He studies in a college in Delhi and can speak English. Where are your parents?'

'They have gone to Delhi.'

'Are you alone in the house?' Balram asked.

'No, my bhabi is here with me, but she does not come out before strangers.'

Tim decided to come straight to the point.

'Why did your brother Jano decide to return to Shamli especially when he knew everyone was against him?'

Kapil looked uncomfortable. His eyes wore a trapped look.

Balram egged him on. 'Don't be afraid, son. Tell him what happened.'

Kapil flushed. For a moment it seemed he would burst into

tears. Then in a faltering voice he said, 'Pappu Yadav had set a trap for him. He must have put pressure on my uncle Sukhram because he lied to Jano and told him that our younger sister was ill and wanted to meet him. Jano adored her. My uncle gave an assurance to Jano that Chowdhury Ram Lal and the other panchayat members no longer had any objections to their marriage. Jano was fool enough to believe him. He and Paro returned to Shamli only to meet their death.'

'Beta, where is your sister? I do not see her?' asked the ever-inquisitive Prakash.

'She is inside with my bhabi,' Kapil replied.

'Why should your uncle, Sukhram deliberately distort facts? Why should he have lied to his own nephew?' Tim asked.

The boy's eyes remained stoney. It was obvious he had still not come to terms with the tragedy. 'Everyone can be purchased. He must have been offered a sizeable sum of money to tell a lie.'

'Who would have offered him money? Pappu Yadav looks completely penniless!'

'He is penniless. But he manages to raise money whenever he is in need of it.'

'You think he could have bribed your uncle to lie to Jano?'

'Yes, I believe so. Since we belong to a backward caste, we have been pushed around all our lives. My father worked hard and has done well. He owns a good business. Do you imagine a good-for-nothing murderer like Pappu Yadav being able to digest that?

'My parents wanted the whole situation to calm down before asking Jano to return. Pappu somehow came to know that Jano was in touch with us and planned out this whole operation with Sukhram's help.' Kapil's voice was flat and expressionless.

'You believe there was a conspiracy?'

'Of course.'

Balram flushed with anger. 'Don't talk like that before a stranger. You know the village follows certain norms very strictly. No one can go against them.'

Kapil gave him an angry look. 'Tau, there is no point in indulging in lecture-baazi with me. The truth of the matter is that all you upper castes hate us for doing well. You want us to keep grovelling at your feet. You cannot tolerate the fact that my father has built his own house. Because of our job reservations, you all keep grumbling about how the government is discriminating against upper castes. It's all jealousy and nothing else.'

Kapil's words were pouring out like a torrent. He was obviously charged up. 'No one defended Jano. They were killed before the whole village. Chowdhury Ram Lal saw the killings. What use is this panchayat if they cannot defend us? All these upper-class bastards are hand in glove. My father visits the police station everyday but the police have not even bothered to file a First Information Report. He has travelled down to Muzzaffarnagar to meet the senior police officials including the DCP. No one has raised his finger. Now my father has gone to Delhi to meet some minister who has promised to help us. If an upper-caste boy had been killed, these people would have burnt down our homes in retaliation. We continue to suffer while the murderers are roaming about freely,' Kapil said.

'Did the entire village witness the killing?' Tim asked.

'Yes. Even Balram was there. He did not raise his hand to help. Everything was over in a matter of seconds.'

'What does your family feel about this whole episode?'

By now Kapil was shaking with rage. 'What is there to say? Have you been to that petty thief Pappu Yadav's house? He has not done a day's work in his life. First, his nephew ran away because he could not take his beatings. Pappu Yadav would not feed Paro for days on end. She was terrified of him. Each time she saw him, she would run in the opposite direction. That old grandmother of hers is also terrified of her son. My brother made the mistake of feeling sorry for Paro. He paid for this sympathy with his life,' he said.

Tim shut his notebook. Phew! What a story. It had all the ingredients of a blockbuster movie. Elopement, caste violence, intrigue, murder, political repercussions ... This rural India seemed very different from the saintly picture that Nagendra had projected. He was sure his first dispatch from India would make a big splash.

twelve

Home Minister L.K. Puri had always considered himself a person with an exalted dispositon. Exempted by his long career in the IAS from any personal contact with the public, he had succeeded in ingratiating himself with Ananda Krishnan's family by sheer accident. Serving as joint secretary in the Ministry of Culture, Puri had obliged Krishnan's wife, Vasundhra by helping her to establish a Bharatnatyam school in the capital for which land and start-up funds were generously made available.

Krishnan was just an MP then, but Puri believed he understood the way the government functioned. An MP today could well become a prime minister tomorrow. His hunch proved correct. Not only did Krishnan go on to become chief minister of Karnataka, he surpassed his own wildest expectations, by finding himself selected as the compromise candidate of the United Janata Dal in the race for prime ministership. As a provincial leader with apparently little at stake in the politics of the Hindi heartland, he was acceptable to the other members of this ragtag coalition, each of whom considered himself a leader in his own right in the vast cow belt.

Puri was even more surprised to find Krishnan taking him aside immediately after he was sworn in as prime minister and informing him that he was being considered for the post of home minister.

'I-I-I can hardly be described as being in politics,' Puri managed to stutter.

'That is exactly why I want to bring you to join my government; I want an apolitical man,' came the prime ministerial reply.

Having accepted the offer, Puri realized in no time at all, that the government would not last. The built-in frailties of the coalition were becoming apparent, with infighting steadily taking its toll. The home ministry, Puri concluded, had been assigned to him by Krishnan mainly so he could keep a tight control over the Intelligence Bureau and other agencies and prevent this flow of information from reaching the ear of a rival who might create trouble for him. What made his job even more complex was his inablility to protect his ministry's flank against the rapid encroachments being made by the all-powerful PMO and RAW. His interest now was basically centred round arranging a fifteen crore rupee bank loan for his son to set up a shoe factory in Agra. Once that sanction came through, he did not care if he remained home minister any longer.

Puri stood before the mirror and stared at his face which, he had to admit, had lost its youthfulness. It had begun to look old and frayed like the government he was in command of. There were lines going down from his nose and along the corners of his mouth and eyes. How haggard and tired he looked. He had always promised himself that post-retirement, he would settle down in his cottage tucked away in Kasauli to write half-a-dozen books on the arts. The way this government was performing, there was every likelihood his dream would come true sooner than later.

Puri had no ambition to set the country right. All he hoped was that history would take a charitable view of him. This was the only objective of governance he had carried into his new office located in the stately-looking, red sandstone office complex comprising spacious rooms and large, rambling verandahs that was known as North Block.

When one of his aides showed him the report of the Paro-Jano killing in *The London Times*, he was not particularly perturbed. The western press had always been hostile to India. Most of their stories concentrated on Kashmir. Writing about Dalit atrocities seemed to be a new craze thereby adding a new dimension to human rights violation by the Indian state.

T.J. George, his PS from the Kerala cadre, entered the room carrying a newspaper clipping. 'Sir, three reports on this killing have already appeared in our local papers. Now *The London Times* has carried a largish report. We cannot allow this to snowball into a major controversy. After all, it is an inter-caste killing.'

Puri hated the word caste. His family had been forced to migrate from Lahore during Partition carrying little with them except the clothes on their backs. Having been forced to sever all ties with the past, he, like thousands of fellow Punjabis, no longer subscribed to the old theories of casteism and the division of Indian society into millions of sects and sub-sects. People must learn to seize and to hold the initiative in their own hands to solve their problems.

Nevertheless, the years spent in the bureaucracy had taught him restraint and discretion. India was a complex nation. Its governance was no easy task and he must not be caught napping. Picking up the phone, he dialled the police commissioner of Delhi.

Lalji Tandon instinctively straightened his back when he heard the home minister's voice at the other end.

'What is this killing in Shamli all about?' Puri drawled in his Westernized accent.

Tandon drew a blank. He had not been following this case.

'Sir, I did read some details in the press but I will need to find out the particulars from Lucknow.'

‘Get back to me at the earliest with all the details.’

Tandon looked perplexed as he slammed the phone down. Due for retirement in May, he was surprised and excited when the present prime minister chose to give him a last-minute extension and promote him to the job of police commissioner. The excitement over his promotion was short-lived. Two days after putting on his pips, the Delhi police shot down a prominent businessman in the heart of Connaught Place. They had mistaken him for a UP mafia don! This goof-up was followed by the mysterious death of three teenage boys in police custody. The press began to snipe at him and he began to be described as a bumbling, heartless cop whose fat stomach and bulbous nose were being caricatured in all the national dailies coming out of Fleet Street.

Picking up the phone, Tandon asked the operator to put through a lightning call to the Director-General of Police, Rameshwar Prasad, in Lucknow. Prasad also belonged to the ’65 batch and their friendship spanned three decades.

Within a few seconds of this request, the phone was ringing in Prasad’s house in Lucknow. Sitting in his spacious lawns enjoying a cup of hot tea, he took the receiver a flunkey handed over to him.

Tandon got to the point right away.

‘Arre bhai, what are these fireworks taking place near Muzzaffarnagar? LP rang me up this morning sounding very agitated.’

Prasad broke into loud laughter. ‘A few killings here and there help to keep this country going – otherwise how are we going to justify an annual expenditure of Rs 7000 crore spent on our police force? Gangs of terrorists with RDX and AK 47s are roaming freely in Mumbai, J&K, Assam, Andhra and Tamil Nadu. The mafia is ruling Bihar and UP. No one is bothered about all these developments. Why should anyone lose their sleep over a goddamn caste killing in Shamli?’

'No, the problem is these human rights wallahs are breathing down the PM's neck. The western media is also playing up this story.'

'That is the whole problem with these bleeding liberals. Everybody needs human rights protection including the mafia. The only people who don't need it are the police. Now tell me, Tandon, in this case the couple were lynched and killed before the entire village. What are we supposed to do? If we nab the killers, there will be a phone from some Yadav or Dalit politician. These are powerful communities and the last thing this government wants is to be called anti-farmer or anti-Dalit.

'The police have been around for five thousand years but now every time we arrest a criminal, we are expected to furnish an explanation to these bloody human rights wallahs. Considering they are getting millions of dollars to make this noise, why don't they run the country for us? They can use their sweet-smelling dollars to administer justice while we sit back with our feet on the table.'

Once Prasad got started there was no stopping him. Shouting on top of his voice, Prasad continued, 'Arre baba, the Mafia dons have all the human rights, you and I can be shot down in cold blood like goddamn cockroaches. When our leader tells us produce thirty lakhs for a transfer, that is not a human rights violation. No sir! It is not a gross violation of our rules of conduct either. Our leaders stink to high heaven. This whole human rights brigade stinks to high heaven.'

Tandon chuckled loudly. Prasad had learnt little in the twenty-six years he had spent in service. Always one to speak his mind freely before his bosses, he had paid a high price for this folly. Constantly being transferred around like a shuttlecock, his first year in service saw him being transferred three times in a span of six months.

Leelawati had taken a complete dislike to Prasad and after one sitting with him, where he had differed with her on her policy to freely grant licenses for guns and revolvers to be used in self-defence by Dalits, she had him banished to Srinagar in the Tehri so he could spend his time cooling himself in the ice cold waters of the Mandakini river.

'Arre Prasad bhai – get those damn Shamli killers tracked down and arrested or the National Commission for Women will start a dharna outside my office,' Tandon ordered in his loudest policeman voice.

'I already have six super idiots holding a dharna in this burning sun outside my office. If a couple of pretty women join you outside yours, then good luck to you. But jokes apart, I'll have to find out what we can really do about this case. I'll call you back in a couple of minutes,' Prasad replied.

Yelling into the intercom, he asked to be connected to SSP Varun Kataria in Muzzaffarnagar.

Within seconds, the phone rang.

'Kataria, crime in your area is showing a dramatic increase. You don't seem concerned about rising crime statistics. Do I have to inform you about this caste murder in Shamli near Muzzaffarnagar?' he bellowed.

Kataria was not one to get intimidated easily. 'No sir – nothing extraordinary. The usual robberies, dacoities, kidnappings and rapes. Sir, statistics collated by my office during the last three months show we are witnessing a decline in all major crime. I can have the report faxed to you within the next hour.'

'You idiot! I am not preparing an annual stocktaking report. The home minister has personally queried about the killing of this couple in Shamli. You know how image-conscious he is, especially in the international arena. I already have ninety-two ministers in this jumbo state cabinet to deal with, I can't afford to have the home minister sitting on my head now.'

'Sir, I read a news report in one of the local dailies about this killing. It's one of those usual cases of inter-caste conflict. Nothing new! Last month, we reported six such cases.'

'I don't care. Go over to Shamli and check out the facts. What exactly happened and what follow-up action has been taken so far. Get back to me with all the facts. I want a report from the police and not from the press.'

'Yes, sir.'

'Do it right away. I don't want any central government minister breathing down my neck.'

'Sir, I'll go there right away.'

Putting down the phone, Kataria did some quick calculations. The Central Government was not going to last long. Once Lalji Tandon was kicked out, Prasad's neck would be next on the chopping block. Why bother with instructions from someone who was on his way out. He decided to ask a local ACP to do the follow-up.

Picking up the phone he asked the operator to connect him to ACP Rajesh Verma. 'Go to Shamli and collect all the facts of the case. L.K. Puri is shitting bricks on this case. Get me all the details by the evening,' he shouted to his subordinate.

Slamming down the phone, he settled back on his comfortable armchair to enjoy a large breakfast of alloo parathas and sweet lassi.

thirteen

UP's chief minister Leelawati got her information officer Babu Ram to read out Rajneesh Mishra's report with interest. The coverage on this killing had gained momentum. It was also being written about in the vernacular press which wielded considerable clout amongst her votebank.

Sitting in the sprawling library of the chief ministerial residence in Lucknow, her large working table faced a full-length mirror that had been placed there, she had been informed, by none other than Warren Hastings. God knows who he was. For the present, she was the Vicerine of UP. On both sides of the room were narrow, rectangular windows opening onto a rose garden.

While Babu Ram read out the various newspaper reports in his loud, monotonous voice, Leelawati's eyes kept wandering to the mirror. Gone was the thin, ugly little plait tied tightly at the nape of her neck. Her mop of newly cut hair gave a boyish touch to her round face which opened into a broad neck and an even heavier body. The hairstyle, she thought gave her more class. Her hairdresser had told her that she thought Leelawati now resembled Indira Gandhi. Poor thing! She may have been Jawaharlal Nehru's daughter but she had never enjoyed the distinction of becoming chief minister of UP.

None of these dumb-looking bureaucrats had dared comment on her looks. No one opened their mouths before her. She couldn't care less about what they said about her behind her back. What a pity, her long-time friend and confidant Abhijit Nath was not around to shower her with compliments. Bedridden after heart surgery, he spent most of his time resting in New Delhi, leaving her to single-handedly orchestrate one political campaign after another. Political expediency forced her to move in the interiors comprising poverty-stricken villages whose dust tracks were filled with the faces of hungry children leaping around like baboons. Grown men and women prostrated themselves at her feet as did bureaucrats and businessmen. She returned from every trip rejuvenated with the awareness that she wielded enormous power. With every passing election, her vote bank increased.

Journalists never had a kind word to say about her. They were a scurrilous bunch of scoundrels anyway. The only people they had nice things to say about were those who paid them to get stuff written. The trouble with male journalists was that they bonded well only with male politicians. Women politicians were treated as cheesecake. So, Sonia Gandhi was written about as a dumb Italian housewife. Uma Bharati was an eccentric sanyasin, and Mamta Banerjee, the less said about her the better. Didi had run out of steam after resigning from the railway ministry. If a male politician had been criticized in this way, one of his chelas would have contrived to beat up the journalist black and blue. Or better still, arrange to have him pushed off a running train.

The last few months had seen several newspapers questioning how a small-time schoolteacher like her could have acquired so much property. How had her brothers become industrialists? The Utopian fools! If they had their way, political parties would be run on empty words. Nath had warned her never to buy property in her own name. He did not come from a Dalit background but he realized what she was up against. A Dalit woman in politics was an opportune target for all these crafty Brahmins. They hated her guts! They hated her style! She would fix the lot of them yet.

Her interventions seldom saw poverty alleviation taking place on the ground. The bureaucracy did not want to execute any change. She knew how spineless they were. It was for this reason that she had no qualms in extracting large sums of money from them. They were all making money hand over fist.

Just then the phone rang. It was Abhijit Nath. His voice sounded faint. He could barely speak. 'What is this I am hearing? Amir Singh is planning to hold a rally in Shamli?

Leelawati was taken aback. 'I just read the statement he has issued in favour of that Yadav boy but Chandanbhan Singh has not informed me about any rally. When are they planning to hold it?'

'Some time this week.'

'I can always outwit them by holding an impromptu rally tomorrow or the day after.'

'Dekh lo! You've just returned from Muzzaffarnagar.'

His voice was already faltering. Before Leelawati could reply, he had put the phone down.

Babu Ram continued to read Mishra's report. His voice droned on but her thoughts had moved on to Abhijit's warning. She had read the statement Amir Singh Yadav had issued in support of Pappu Yadav and his niece, Paro. *Amar Ujjala* newspaper had given it a great deal of prominence.

Leelawati adjusted her solitaire nose pin. Its weight was beginning to press down her nose. She had pleaded with the Shah brothers who owned several showrooms in South Delhi, not to present her with such a big diamond. They refused to heed her. What could she do? Wherever she went people showered her with gifts. She looked at her watch. It was past eleven a.m. The chief secretary and the two other secretaries must have been cooling their heels for her for over an hour.

Adjusting her dupatta, she marched into the anteroom where the state's three senior bureaucrats were awaiting her arrival. They got up as soon as she entered the room. Leelawati beckoned the chief secretary M.S. Duggal to sit down opposite her.

'Why is this farmers' agitation in Saharanpur being allowed to continue in this fashion? If it picks up greater momentum, it will mean adverse publicity for my government.' Leelawati's question was addressed to Duggal.

Duggal must have come prepared for this query. His reply was prompter than usual. 'Madam, I have spoken three times to the district commissioner. Three PAC battalions have been sent there to ensure the farmers do not turn violent,' he said in a cautious manner.

'Aren't you putting too much faith in one DC? What can he do? The entire region is simmering with discontent and you are trying to reassure me that the presence of three PAC battalions will make a great difference,' she retorted.

'Ring up that Mittal character and tell him to start purchasing more sugarcane from the factories otherwise some of his factories will get raided for excise evasion.'

'I spoke to Mittal yesterday. He claims he has already picked up an extra hundred wagon loads of sugarcane for his ten sugarcane factories. He insists he does not have the capacity to buy more,' Duggal protested.

'He can burn it for all I care. How dare he tell me what to do? He will follow my instructions – it will not be the other way around.'

'Yes, madam.'

'Has the UP Electricity Board finished providing electricity to those three Dalit villages in Azamgarh?' Leelawati asked in her authoritarian manner.

'I think they will complete their job by the end of the week.'

Turning to Duggal she said, 'Why is the press making so much noise about this Shamli killing?'

There was complete silence. Duggal's eyes were pointed in the direction of his shoes. The other two looked around equally shifty eyed. Fat roosters, the whole lot of them!

'I asked you a question!'

'Madam, these days the press can pick up any issue and blow it out of proportion. This is a terrible trend. I feel nervous every time I pick up the newspaper in the morning, trembling. God knows what new scandal will explode under my nose,' Duggal stuttered.

R.S. Srivastava, Secretary, Agriculture, agreed. 'The opposition parties have only one mantra. No government is allowed to function normally. The result is that the administration stands completely paralysed,' he said.

Leelawati picked up her phone and dialled Abhijit Nath. She deliberately chose to make this phone call in the presence of these bureaucrats. Srivastava was known to be close to Amir Singh. The first thing he would do on leaving this room would be to get one of his courtiers to repeat her words to Amir Singh.

'If Amir Singh holds a rally in Shamli, I can easily get him arrested under TADA. He's a threat to civil society,' Leelawati told Abhijit.

'Don't be foolish. Today you are in power, tomorrow you may fall out of power and he will do the same to you. We have to learn our political tactics from Mohandas Gandhi. That is why it has always been said that though Ambedkar was a brilliant lawyer, no one could beat Gandhi in tactical warfare,' Nath replied.

'Do you want me to organize a salt march to Shamli!'

'No! But you can organize a Dalit march and get Dalits from all over the country to reach there and express solidarity with you.'

Leelawati laughed. What a brilliant suggestion! A Dalit march would propel her into the limelight again.

'How soon should I hold the rally?' she wondered.

'As soon as possible,' he replied and put down the phone.

Leelawati put the handset on the receiver. All three bureaucrats continued to stare at their shoes. She waved her hand indicating that they leave. They picked their files, and like obedient soldiers, marched out.

Picking up the phone again, she asked Babu Ram to put her through to Chandanbhan Singh. Within seconds, he had connected her to Muzzaffarnagar. Leelawati let out a string of choice abuses.

'You worm! I picked you from the gutter and gave you a national identity. Today, all you do is faff around like a fat duck doing absolutely no work.'

'Behenji!' the voice squeaked from the other end.

'You allow snakes to bloom in your garden and then have the temeiity to call me a sister.'

'Snakes!' Chandanbhan exclaimed from the other end.

'Amir Singh is holding a rally in Shamli and I am not informed about it.'

Chandanbhan was out of his depth completely. 'I had no idea. It must be something that was planned out in the last few hours,' he fumbled.

'You are paid to keep abreast with the developments of your political opponents! Now listen with your ears open wide. I will reach Muzzaffarnagar tomorrow morning by nine o'clock. Duggal will intimate you about the timings. I plan to drive down to Shamli. Tell the DC there to make all necessary arrangements. Make sure there is a large enough crowd to follow me around. Also, alert the local agencies about my arrival. My show must receive the best media coverage possible.'

Slamming the phone down, she glared at the solitaire sticking like a white egg on the forefinger of her left hand. One more roadshow to be enacted in the dust-rimmed interiors of Uttar Pradesh. Each of these journeys meant being followed by a multitude of smelly, sweaty villagers who openly leered at her oversize buttocks and breasts. Not that those fossilized bureaucrats were any better. No wonder, some women politicians preferred to be swathed in capes. But UP was her fiefdom.

She had spent the last decade travelling through every nook and corner of the state in order to understand its complex political realities. If she failed to capitalize on this opportunity, one of her rivals would capture her Dalit vote bank.

She must speak to Abhijit and inform him of her plans.

'I'm going to Shamli village tomorrow. I'll take a padyatra through the village.'

There was no answer from the other end.

'I was thinking, if I don't undertake it, Tikait might step in and try and take advantage of the present unrest. He is also trying to restrengthen his position as a leader of the farmers' community.'

'Tikait is a spent force. He possesses only a nuisance value. You must never lose sight of your real enemies – these remain both the BJP and the Congress.'

'He maybe a spent force – but how is he always so flushed with funds?'

'He's getting his money from the sugar lobby. He has persuaded the farmers to sell sugar under the table to some of the factory owners. The factory owners are giving Tikait a cut which I am told is running into several crores,' Abhijit said.

Leelawati's face contorted in a paroxysm of rage. 'How dare any bastard be allowed to make money in my state? This will not be permitted.'

'Arre bhai, don't take a panga with Tikait. He's a troublesome character. We will handle him at some other opportune moment. Leela, don't push your luck too hard. Things aren't looking very good out here.'

The phone had gone dead again. Trust Abhijit to fall ill when she needed him the most.

She rang him once again. 'Are you telling me the Central Government might topple my government? I have not even completed two months in office.'

Abhijit was sounding tired. 'The government at the centre is weak. If the centre is not strong, why will it want to be surrounded by strong state governments? The way the press is going hammer and tongs on this killing, it is obvious one of the owners has a vested interest in ousting the Central Government. If there is a casualty at the centre, it might affect you also. Better protect yourself and not do anything to rock the boat.'

Leelawati heard him out in admiration. How beautifully he had summed up the whole situation. She pressed the bell for the attendant. Babu Ram rushed into the room.

Leelawati barked. 'Get hold of the SSP in Muzzaffarnagar and tell him I will be arriving there tomorrow morning by helicopter. Tell Duggal that all arrangements must be made for my stay there. I will be driving down to Shamli and then returning to Muzzaffarnagar by late afternoon. All my meetings fixed for tomorrow can be rescheduled. Also, inform the press secretary to issue a press release giving full details of my itinerary to all the local and national newspapers.'

Looking at her watch she continued, 'It's already twelve p.m. If you hurry up, you can catch the one p.m. news announcement. The announcements of my visit must be continued right through the day. Tell Chandanbhan Singh to be waiting at the helipad with a decent crowd. I want no slip-up in the arrangements.'

Leelawati's no-nonsense manner had created the necessary impact. A frightened-looking Chandanbhan Singh, leading a sea of blue flag-carrying, slogan-shouting BSP followers, was waiting at the helipad when the chief minister's helicopter touched base at Muzzaffarnagar. A huge police contingent led by DCP Kataria was also present.

A triumphant looking Leelawati, waving briskly, and taking

large, manly steps, walked towards the white air-conditioned Ambassador that would take her straight to Shamli. Her followers and the police jumped into a line of waiting Ambassador cars. The cavalcade drove out amidst a great deal of dust and confusion.

Her car was brought to a halt at the primary school in Shamli where the entire panchayat led by a nervous Chowdhury Ram Lal was waiting, at the base of a hastily erected podium, to greet her. Both the schoolteachers, Balram Prakash and Mohan Ram were prominently positioned next to the panchayat members.

Calling Chandanbhan Singh aside, she whispered, 'The gathering today does not seem to be large enough. I have to emerge from today's meeting as the undisputed queen of UP. I want all my rivals to be squirming in garbage once I finish with this meeting.'

'Madam, once you start your padyatra, hordes of people will follow you,' Chandanbhan reassured her.

Leelawati nodded. She was a street fighter. She knew her strengths. If the crowds did not come to her, she would go to them. She decided to send for Jano's family members.

'Where are the family members of the boy who was killed?' Leelawati asked the panchayat members.

Balram Prakash decided this was a godsent opportunity to create a good impression on Behenji. He replied, 'Ever since Jano's execution, his family members are scared to come out into the open. They are scared someone in the village may attack them. Behenji, I am a teacher in the government school here. I taught Jano up to the eighth class. I am the only villager to have gone to Jano's house to express condolences for his death. I will be happy to take you to their home.'

This was the opportunity she was looking for. Leelawati shouted, 'Jano's family may be scared to come here, I am not scared to go to them. I will take a padyatra right through this village. You villagers must follow me.'

A large number of journalists jostled around her to ask her questions. Dalip Jha and Tim Robertson had also joined in the melee.

Dalip Jha, Tim and a couple of other journalists from English dailies had driven down from New Delhi to cover Leelawati's padyatra. The Hindi journalists from the local Hindi dailies had hopped into local buses to make their way to Shamli.

Leelawati stopped to reply to their queries before setting off for Jano's house.

'Ask your questions one at a time!' Leelawati ordered.

Pramod Tripathi of *Amar Jagaran* was the first journalist to fire off a salvo. 'The killing took place some time ago. Why are you reacting so late?'

'My sympathies have always been with the bereaved family. I took some time coming here because of the sensitivity of the subject. Our local administration is already overstrained; I did not want to add to their difficulties,' she replied.

'How come the local administration does not feel this same concern? Why has no FIR been lodged so far?' asked Dalip Jha who always believed in adopting a frontal attack approach. He was standing next to Tripathi.

Leelawati feigned innocence. Turning to Kataria she asked, 'Is it true that no FIR been lodged? Why is the investigation proceeding so slowly?'

The crowds were impressed. It was the first time a senior police officer had received a public dressing down in this manner.

'According to the information I have received, an FIR has been lodged. I need to doublecheck with the local SHO about the exact date,' Kataria replied. He looked ill at ease and was waiting for this roadshow to end.

Dalip Jha persisted, 'Dalits in our society are a marginalized lot. What steps are you taking to improve their state?'

'I am a Dalit. I know what deprivation and discrimination

mean. They are not something abstract for me. These are my people! They have stood shoulder to shoulder with me through my long innings in politics,' she responded, looking all the while at the villagers.

Pointing to Chowdhury Ram Lal and the other members of the panchayat, she said, 'You are all upper caste. This killing must be your doing!'

Chowdhury Ram Lal, intimidated by the sight of the huge police contingent, trembled in fear. 'Behenji, it was the girl's uncle who committed this foul deed. We had nothing to do with it,' he said.

Leelawati snorted loudly and continued to walk at a brisk pace along the winding village path. Balram led her to Jano's house. He banged on the front door. A trembling Kapil opened the latch and was taken aback to find chief minister Leelawati standing outside his house. Had she come to arrest him?

'This is Kapil, Jano's brother. After having seen his brother being killed in cold blood, he is now in a state of shock and is incapable of attending college,' said Balram by way of introduction.

Leelawati put her arm around Kapil. The photographers clicked away.

'Where are your parents?'

'In Delhi. They are trying to meet some politicians in order to put pressure on the local police. We need to get an FIR registered,' Kapil mumbled.

'Don't worry! Your family will be given land and money in compensation for the loss of your brother. I will see to it!' She spoke loudly for the crowds to hear.

Kapil mustered up courage. 'No FIR has been lodged so far. Why are the killers being allowed to go scot-free?'

'The day I was sworn in as chief minister, I warned the police force – get cracking or else you all will end up in jail. Do not underestimate my intentions. I am one hundred per cent behind the Dalits. I am working to extend reservations of backwards and SCs in both educational and employment insititutions. Once that happens, all of you youngsters will get jobs.'

Tim Robertson, standing behind the Hindi journalists, raised his hand to ask a question. Leelawati smiled encouragingly, happy to be approached by a foreign journalist.

'Don't you think all these reservations are only serving to make your society more divisive? A once accepted form of social instrumentation need not necessarily prove effective in today's world?' he asked.

Chandanbhan Singh quickly translated Tim's question into Hindi. Leelawati snorted 'Reservations have proved effective. They allow people, exploited over centuries, a chance to enter the mainstream.'

Tim decided to prod her further.

'Your insistence on providing job reservations is creating resentment amongst the upper classes. Class antagonism seems to be on the rise,' Tim said.

'Where is it not on the rise? This trend is not specific to India alone. You have not grown up in a village in India. You have no idea how tortuous it can be to grow up in a society where one is deprived of basic conveniences. Our generation has suffered. Why should our children suffer like we did?'

Chandanbhan Singh and Balram Prakash were competing with one another to translate Leelawati's replies in their broken English for the English press. First Chandanbhan translated the reply, then Balram Prakash stepped forward insisting on translating it once again for Tim's benefit.

'Thanks mate!' Tim muttered.

Leelawati put her arm around Kapil and started walking from one Dalit hutment to another. The more broken-down the hut, the more time she spent there. The villagers, already surprised to find a chief minister in their midst, surged behind her in large numbers.

'Where is your husband?' she asked one old woman standing outside the doorway of her house.

'He is working in the fields.'

'How do the upper castes treat you?' Leelawati asked.

The woman did not understand her question.

'If you've come to distribute blankets, give one to this old woman also. It will protect me from the winter chill!' the old woman pleaded.

'Next time I come here, you will get two blankets, amma,' Leelawati promised.

'God bless you!' the old woman said with a happy smile.

In every Dalit home she stopped at, Leelawati asked the inmates how they were being treated by the upper castes. No one bothered to reply to this query. The womenfolk asked for saris, the menfolk wanted jobs.

'Chandanbhan – make a note of all these requests and act on them immediately.'

Dalip Jha and Pramod Tripathi walked closely behind her. While she stopped to interact with the villagers, Pramod gave Dalip a quick update on all the local developments.

'Chandanbhan is presently out of favour. The chief minister thinks he is goofing up too much,' Pramod whispered.

'Why is she making a special trip here?' asked Dalip.

'I'm positive it has something to do with the internal politics of the state. She has no love lost for Dalits. She behaves like a Brahmin queen,' Tripathi murmurred.

Oblivious of what was being said about her, Leelawati said, 'You see how much fear these people have to live under. My government is here to protect the Dalits. I will not allow them to be ill-treated. If anyone dares harass them, that person will be severely punished.'

Turning to the villagers she said in mock anger, 'The killing of this married couple is a blot on the fair name of Shamli. But I ask you menfolk – do you wear bangles on your wrists? What prevented you all from stepping forward and stopping those children from being persecuted? Were they not your children also?' she asked.

The villagers remained silent. No one replied. Kapil, walking by her side, could make no sense of these goings on. All he knew was that Behenji had helped instill a feeling of confidence in him. She was like a saviour.

Leelawati climbed up the steps of the temple to bid a final adieu. The public were eating out of her hands.

'Your Behenji may have come here for a short while but your concerns remain close to her heart. The days of Dalit oppression are over. We know how to fight back! Those who dare raise their fingers against us will be thrashed. I am willing to take the fight into the backyards of the upper castes. Why can't you?'

'We will! We will !' the crowd chanted.

'But Behenji, once you leave us, these people will start oppressing us again,' a villager shouted from amidst the crowd.

'I am leaving my phone number behind. If anyone dares to raise his voice against any of you, just dial this number. I will drop everything and come to your rescue,' she shouted.

The crowd cheered louder. It surged forward to receive her benediction. The NSG was finding it difficult to keep them under control. Leelawati waved to them and began walking to where the cars were parked. Her diamond jewellery sparkled in the sun. Her cropped hair rose and fell like a wave in the ocean. Her white dupatta flew in the breeze. The crowds followed her shouting 'Leelawati Zindabad ! BSP Zindabad!'

Flashing a triumphant smile, she stepped into her car. Its engine started with a roar and they rolled out in a smart flurry, leaving waves of dust behind. The large contingent of bureaucrats, police officials and journalists jumped into their respective vehicles. The villagers watched the cars roll away. Those in power knew how to cast a spell on the poor – a spell that would take a long time to lift.

**

Ajay Singh sat back on his chair and heard the Star TV news broadcast on Leelawati's padyatra for the umpteenth time.

'Garbage! Absolute garbage!' he muttered to himself.

The same headlines on Leelawati had been repeated in six successive telecasts. The same bleeding heart stories. 'What's happened to these guys? Aren't they capable of doing better than that?' he thought in exasperation.

His impulsive decision to submit his resignation to Vikram Aggarwal had begun to tell on his nerves. The last three days had been spent agonizing on the foolishness of his move. Apart from a few phone calls, none of his journalist colleagues had bothered to drop in and commiserate with him. He did not expect them to either. Journalists only revolved around people in power. They needed to survive. He understood their compulsions.

The country was facing an economic downslide. Very few jobs were going a-begging, especially in his own profession, where senior level jobs could only be got if one developed close contacts with the proprietor-publisher.

He had not spoken to Sheena from the day he had learnt of her abortion. Nor had she bothered to come to him and explain what she had done. Once she was able to walk about, she had got herself a separate phone extension and spent her time chatting with her friends from her bedroom. All her meals were served to her there and she seemed quite happy to spend her time lying on the bed exchanging gossip on the phone with one friend after another.

Five days after her abortion, she entered the living room where Ajay sat listening to the news, and with a shake of her shoulder-length hair informed him she was going to Hyderabad for a week.

Ajay made no reply.

'I'm talking to you – not to the walls in this house. I have been invited to hold a workshop on new Ikat techniques devised by NIFT. I will be away for a week. I'm leaving my contact phone numbers behind in case of any emergency,' she said.

Sheena placed a piece of paper on the centre table. Ajay made no attempt to pick it up.

Just then a car drew up outside their front gate accompanied by the blast of a shrill horn. Ajay recognized the horn. It was Meenakshi. She must be dropping Sheena to the airport or maybe the two of them had decided to travel together, in which case Meenakshi may have arranged with her office driver to have them dropped at the airport.

Ajay heard the front door shut with a loud bang. Did her abrupt departure mark the beginning of the end of his marriage? She had always been self-willed and opinionated. He had overlooked these shortcomings, confident that once they had children, things would change. This hope, like most other dreams, would be relegated to the dustbin. His marriage remained an empty façade.

He could not spend his time moping around the house. On an impulse, he picked up the phone and dialled Jayant Shah's number. Shah was the proprietor of the media conglomerate Vision Forever. They published several magazines and newspapers. Shah had often, in the past, expressed a keenness for Ajay to join his group but he always shrugged it off on one pretext or the other.

'Yes?' came Shah's booming voice on the other end.

'Sir, I'm Ajay speaking. I wanted to come over and meet you.'

'What d'you mean come and meet me? Now that you are a free bird, come and meet me at once. I need someone like you to give a push to this slumbering organization,' Jayant Shah growled from the other end.

This was all the encouragement Ajay needed. 'When should I come?'

'Come within the next one hour. I'm going to snap you up before someone else does.'

Chuckling with delight, he put down the phone. Thank god for saviours like Shah! With characters like him around, there was still hope for the rank and file.

An hour later, Ajay was sitting opposite Shah whose thick, bushy eyebrows and greying hairline gave him a dignified look, off-set by his twinkling, brown eyes. 'You've wasted yourself in that godforsaken Aggarwal organization for the last two years. You should have walked out a long time ago.'

Ajay kept quiet.

'My dear fellow, you have a flair for languages. I need an editor to manage all my regional editions. Why don't you join us from today?'

Ajay could scarcely believe his ears.

'From today – '

'It's not for nothing that I called my group "Vision Forever".'

'*Amar Prakash* has not yet given me a letter relieving me of my job.'

'Fuck them! You'll get it sooner or later. To give you a quick update – the Hindi and Tamil editions are doing well but the Gujarati and Marathi editions are bleeding. This must stop especially since I plan to get into television broadcasting very soon. I'm just waiting to get a clearance from the home ministry.'

'I've been hearing about this move for some time now. It's a great idea. Television is where all the ads have moved into – it's where you can make the mega bucks.'

Shah was staring intently at Ajay. 'A strange idea has just entered my mind. Let me take you across to the studios and give you a screen test. I've been on the lookout for an anchor – an identifiable face. You just might fill the bill! I want you to walk across to my studio and do a screen test.'

Shah's studio was located in the next building. It was typical of the man that rather than go there in his chauffeur-driven car, he decided to walk. Ajay found it difficult to keep up with his fast pace as they dashed past groups of foreigners and Indians. He was beginning to find this whole idea of doing a screen test a little bizarre.

As they stepped into the lift, to take them up to the fourth floor, Ajay protested feebly, 'I'm not television material – I'm a newspaper hack.'

'We'll soon know!'

Entering the studio Shah yelled, 'Come on! Lights!'

A crowd of technicians got onto the job of putting all the equipment in order. A script was thrust under his nose. Ajay read the first sentence out a little tentatively. It was smooth sailing after that and he finished reading the first page without any major hiccups.

'You're just the man I've been looking for! You've got the poise and the right amount of understatement! More important, you're a natural in the Hindi language. Ours is a Hindi channel and I think you'll work!'

Ajay looked around in a daze. The staffers were standing around giving nods of approval. Everything had happened so quickly. But Shah seemed to have taken over all the decision making and was not one to tolerate dissent.

'It's decided. You will start work from tomorrow!'

'I don't know anything about this medium.'

'An Australian team, led by the television director Kenneth Clark, is arriving here the following Monday. They will be holding a week-long workshop for the entire staff. They will teach you all the p's and q's. Stop worrying,' said Shah.

Ajay remained unconvinced. A writer at heart, he was not

comfortable with the idea of having to face the cameras and become a television anchor. 'What about editing those magazines …'

'That work will continue in the background. Let this channel settle down a bit, then you can move back to your first love. I've made a lot of investments in this new medium. It's an area of prime concern for me,' Shah countered.

As they walked back to the Vision Forever office, Shah looked excited. 'This new trend of hiring youngsters is all nonsense. I want grey-haired, mature-looking anchors who will inspire confidence amongst our viewers. You are well known amongst the Hindi-speaking world. My channel would be delighted to appropriate some of that popularity from you.'

fourteen

Amir Singh Yadav often wondered to himself if he would have been better off being a wrestler. He knew how to deal with male opponents, it was this clique of women in politics who were driving him nuts.

Watching a large TV screen placed bang opposite his bed for the last half an hour, the only figure who seemed to be popping out of the idiot box was his nemesis, the plump Leelawati with her shimmering gold chains and her redoubtable moustached upper lip. He always referred to her as 'She' or 'that woman', and never by name. When she started speaking, she reminded him of an AK 47 in action. Her words sliced the air with the strength of crackling shots.

Mukul Singh gave him a withering look. 'Each of us has carved out his own dominion. The practice is that no one trespasses in the other's territories. Leelawati has deliberately chosen to go to a Yadav-dominated village to raise the banner of rebellion against us. What can you make out from that?'

Mukul was Amir Singh's comrade-in-arms and chief fund raiser. A man of few words, he possessed a razor-sharp brain, used to keep track of how much wealth each industrialist possessed, both legally and illegally. It was their illegal wealth that he was interested in and which he had learned to extract with Mafioso-like ease to fund party work and other miscellaneous activities. Mukul rewarded these industrialists with special licences to set up factories. Prime land was distributed to them at throwaway prices. This distribution of favours was thrown off balance when Leelawati became chief minister. All their industrialist friends were blacklisted and made to eat humble pie, which in this case meant the revoking of licences and land deals. These were then given to her friends and wellwishers who were now being made to hustle up large sums of money to finance her party activities.

Mukul and Amir were sitting together in the large bedroom in Amir's bungalow on Mall Avenue in Lucknow.

It was a vast rectangular-shaped room whose walls were covered with mahogany wooden shelves. A large number of books, largely on law, politics and religion had been dumped in these shelves in a haphazard manner. Amir hated books. His only son, Avinash was an avid collector and had insisted on building up a large collection. Unfortunately, being an only son, he had been forced to shoulder some of the responsibility of running the party. This left him with no time to read. Some of the Samajwadi party MPs would help themselves to these books. They were never returned and the collection had begun to look frayed and worn out, almost like the Samajwadi leaders themselves.

Large grotesque cut-outs of the two leaders were stacked at one end of the room. The cut-outs made both these leaders appear as though they were a Laurel and Hardy team. Mukul, short and hunchbacked in real life, was made to look like a dwarf wearing what could best be described as a clown's outfit. In real life, there was little that was clownish about him.

From his childhood he had been particular about the way he dressed. Having come into big money, he now chose to wear Armani suits, which were altered for him by a special tailor he had tracked down in Hong Kong. The cut-out had distorted Amir

Singh's swarthy features and made him appear as a formidable, dictator-like individual. Why he had been given a bowler cap to wear was anybody's guess.

Loosening his crimson red tie, Mukul Singh scratched his cheek despairingly. Leelawati's visit to Shamli could do them a great deal of damage.

'We have to retaliate.'

Amir looked doubtful. 'How?'

'We can't send a Stinger missile to eliminate that woman. We have to think of something else.'

There was a long silence. Amir started tugging the lobe of his left ear. 'Should we hold a rally at the Red Fort? We can tear her policies to shreds. It will take the attention off her.'

'Our constituency does not extend to New Delhi. Holding a rally in Lucknow will not help either. Leelawati holds the reins of the city and does pretty much as she pleases. I think you need to go back to Shamli and demonstrate your sympathy for the entire Yadav clan.'

Amir was not happy with the suggestion.

'You need to galvanize your own community. The Yadav community in Lucknow and the surrounding areas has already spread the word that you will be holding a big rally in Shamli. You cannot let them down. You need to highlight how your clansman Pappu Yadav was being wrongly framed. He is a petty thief, not a murderer. Jano's father belongs to a powerful landowning lobby. He has connived to create problems for this fellow.'

The two exchanged uneasy glances. Amir looked downcast. Mukul was aware of the fact that Amir was in no mood to travel. His last few meetings had been poorly attended. The public were feeling slighted by his pro-rich policies and had dubbed him a neta of the rich. Now, his chief confidant and comrade-in-arms, was rubbing salt into his wounds and insisting he go to Shamli and hold a rally. It would be grotesque to imitate his rival in this fashion.

'I don't want to get into trouble with the courts. My support for the Yadav community should not be misconstrued.' Amir spoke slowly, determined to voice his unhappiness at this suggestion.

'My evidence is to the contrary. There has been no infringement of the law. No FIR has been filed so far. You don't have to make a big speech. Your presence will help to galvanize the Yadav community. She travelled by road, you should get there by air,' Mukul insisted.

'If I go by helicopter, I will not be able to take a press contingent with me,' Amir Singh protested.

'The press can reach there by road. We can arrange for them to reach there a couple of hours before you do. For those who can't make it, we can always distribute some handouts. I'll arm-twist the owners to make sure it is published,' said Mukul.

Mukul talks down to me as though he is giving a sermon, thought Amir Singh angrily. He seems to forget that I have established this party. The lines between their public and private personae had got blurred. They were spending far too much time together. I had hand-picked this political novice two years ago and now he has begun behaving as though he is my political mentor, Amir told himself.

Amir Singh decided not to voice his apprehensions and checked his growing sense of unease. On the whole, Mukul offered him worthwhile advice. He too was committed to the party. A resourceful and ingenuous operator, he could be depended upon to extract money from miserly industrialists who had shied away in the past from parting with a single paisa for a political cause. He'd follow his suggestion and make the trip early next morning.

Amir's eyes travelled the length of the room. Getting up, he walked to the end of the bed on which had been kept a black briefcase. It had been handed over to him a short while ago by an important industrialist. Opening it, he checked to see how much money it contained. Mukul Singh came and stood by his side. The eyes of both men bulged as they saw stacks of five hundred rupee notes arranged in neat bundles. Money bought strength and authority. Money bought solidity. It ensured there was no shortage of manpower willing to join their party.

The two men smiled at one another. For the time being they would remain loyal bedfellows and help boost each other's political prospects.

**

Pappu Yadav was sitting outside his hut when he heard the drone of a helicopter. He stared at the sky intently. The noise was getting louder. Could it be the police? Could it be Leelawati making a second quick trip? Pappu Yadav shook his head in frustration. All these bigwigs seemed to have lost a grip of their mental faculties. Otherwise why on earth would they be constantly making beelines to this nondescript village?

Satvir and Ramesh joined him outside. Their eyes were glued to the sky.

'Jai Kali ki,' Ramesh mumbled to himself.

'Leelawati is up to her old tricks,' Satvir muttered.

Putting his hand on his forehead, Kishan looked uncomfortably into the sky. 'The flying machine is almost touching the trees. It is looking for a place to land. It could be full of armed policemen. I think we need to move to a safer place for a couple of days. This place is getting too hot.'

Bhuja, lying on her charpai, followed their discussion. For the last few days, her body had been racked by fever. With no one to attend to her, the fever had kept rising.

Pappu's attitude to her was one of indifference. He had brought no medicines for her. Too frail to cook, she had been reduced to eating whatever leftovers were handed to her by these men.

'Pappu, you can't leave me and go,' she cried.

Pappu pretended not to hear.

'Pappu!' she yelled .

'Maaji, we'll be back in a couple of hours. A helicopter has just landed in our village. It could be carrying a police contingent,' Kishan told her.

'Give me a sip of water before you go,' she pleaded.

The men were keen to make good their escape. 'I'll send my wife to take care of you,' Ramesh cried over his shoulder as they crossed the threshold of the hut.

Bhuja's eyes opened briefly. They rested on the blue sky stretching all around her to infinity. The leaves of the neem tree cast their dark shadows over her face. She sobbed to herself remembering how as young children, Paro and Jagdamba would sit by her side as she cooked chapattis for them in the evening twilight.

The flickering flames of the wooden chullah created a feeling of mystery around them. The lengthening shadows of the summer evening intermixed with the flames helped create a chiaroscuro of rare and unusual beauty.

Paro always sat to the right of Bhuja. She would copy her grandmother's gestures, pretending to mix the flour with water and then knead it in order to make the mixture tight and hard. She would then pretend to roll out a series of thin chapattis. Bhuja would be busy baking thick, round chapattis, which would be turned and slapped on both sides, till they baked the right colour of brown. These would then be placed in a white aluminium box kept near the chullah.

Paro's game of make-believe continued right through the evening. Pretending to scoop some sabzi out of the pan, she would exclaim joyfully, 'It's so tasty! It's so tasty!'

Both her grandchildren had been so sweet and so innocent. The boy, strong and hot-tempered, had inherited a fair and handsome visage just like his father. The girl was slim and dark with perfect, almond-shaped eyes.

'It must all end,' Bhuja told herself.

She did not have the strength to pull herself from the charpai. The heat was intense. The sun was ready to scorch everything in sight. Bhuja was filled with a dark foreboding. Her end had come. There was no one around to offer her a few sips of water. She stared at the moving shadows being cast by the neem tree and drifted into a state of delirium.

All four men made their way to the bus stand from where they would board a bus to Hardwar. They would seek shelter with Bhuja's elder brother who ran his own grocery shop. They planned to stay there for a couple of days till all this noise and fury died down.

**

For the first time in many years Raveena woke up feeling cheerful. No more having to keep vigilance through the long, unending nights! No more conniving in order to persuade male friends for a quick midnight tryst! No more having to feel ashamed about her nakedness as strangers stared in horror at the gigantic contours of her bloated body.

Kala Muthu lay by her side snoring softly, his naked body covered by a white sheet.

The sheer fact of having a man lie comfortably by her side, not shrinking at her elephantine proportions or watching lewdly at the way her heavy breasts dangled against her chest or shivering as he touched her oversized buttocks, left her with a feeling of overwhelming relief.

She lit a cigarette and inhaled deeply. Kala Muthu must have heard her. He reached out and took the cigarette from her hand. He was doing what he enjoyed most in his life. Women were welcome to come in all sizes as long as they possessed tits and bums. Boy, was this one loaded. She reminded him of a she elephant on heat. When she had climaxed last night, he was scared the walls of the house might collapse.

Raveena snuggled against Kala Muthu. His body was compact and short. She could not grasp the mainspring of his emotions or comprehend what had led him to bed her so easily. He was obviously someone who hated being alone, and man, if the two of them could make merry, then why not?

Raveena wrapped a sheet around herself and went into the kitchen to make some tea.

'We've got to buy you some new clothes,' she announced, returning shortly with two mugs of tea. 'You can't go into the office looking like a Bollywood baddie.'

'Saar, you want to reinvent me!'

Raveena knew the two of them could make a formidable pair in the *Sentinel* office. She had a fair idea about why he had been hired. The office management wanted the unions destroyed. He must have been hired as their hitman.

'You mentioned you come from Chennai. What kind of work were you doing there?'

'Consultancy. Looking after sales. The usual! It was a mixture of work.'

'What do you plan to do after completing your apprenticeship here?'

'Mr Rajan told me he would absorb me in the organization.'

'Maybe he plans to hire you as a manager or something like that.'

'Yes, Raveenaji. You can help me. You are friendly with the big boss?'

'He dotes on me. He has given instructions that I be present at all his meetings. My heart melts when I see him. Such goodness! Such wisdom! He is a deva purush.'

'Why don't you introduce me to your devata?'

'By and by. We don't want to push our luck too far.'

Raveena insisted on escorting him to the Jainson showroom in Connaught Place so she could buy him a new set of clothes. The shop attendant, a young graduate, showed them a wide assortment of trousers and shirts. Raveena selected a black-and white checked shirt and black trousers for Kala Muthu.

Kala Muthu could scarcely recognize himself when he came out of the changing room. He looked like all those smooth arses who strutted around Connaught Place. His heart missed a beat when he saw the bill. Fifteen hundred down – he could have bought smarter clothes at half the price in Chandni Chowk. Or better still, he could have gone into one of the malls and done a little shop lifting ... Putting all these thoughts out of his mind, he slipped his arm into Raveena's and swaggered out of the shop. They hailed a taxi which drove them to the *Sentinel* office.

The receptionist at the paper did not recognize him and insisted on rechecking his newly made identity card. The security staff, perched on the landing created by the flight of steps, insisted on doing the same.

Eschewing the lift, Raveena and Kala Muthu climbed up five floors to enter the bureau office. Ajit Jolly's cabin was located at the far end of the room.

'Jolly! My dear friend! Look who I have brought to meet you!'

Jolly stood up immediately and greeted Kala Muthu with a warm handshake. 'Are you also joining the bureau? We already have a VIP amdist us,' he said pointing to Raveena.

Raveena patted Jolly on the shoulder. 'No yaar! He's a management type. Very soon, he'll be sitting on our heads and ordering us around.'

'No one can order Raveena around, not even the Big Boss,' Kala Muthu countered in his strong Madrasi accent.

'Who is becoming editor in place of Ajay Singh?' Raveena Bedi asked in a conspiratorial tone.

'Mark my words – you'll be appointed to the post,' Jolly countered.

'I'm not a Hindi journalist. Don't debase me to that lowly position.'

'I don't think they want to bring anyone from outside. They will opt for an inhouse promotion. Of one fact, I am certain. Now that you are in the good books of the big boss, he will ensure that you become the editor of the *Sentinel.* The whole office is talking about how you are the rising star in the establishment,' Jolly remarked with his strong American-Punjabi twang.

Raveena purred contentedly. It was still premature for her to comment on what Jolly had said.

She looked at her watch. 'Jolly, it's past one-thirty p.m. and you haven't even offered to take us out for lunch.'

Jolly shuffled uneasily on his chair. He hated having to spend money. 'You want to come to the Press Club?'

'Not again.'

Jolly shuffled through a pile of papers lying on his table. Pulling out an expensively embossed invite he said, 'Sony TV is launching a host of new serials today. They have called a few journalists for an exclusive press conference at the Taj Man Singh hotel. Why don't you both come along with me? We can all enjoy some five star khaana peena!' Winking at Kala Muthu, Jolly said, 'The Taj is known to have a team of very interesting escort girls!'

Kala Muthu grinned. He was always game for a free meal. 'I need to make a phone call before we leave,' he said.

'Our five bureau phones are all at your disposal.'

Kala Muthu walked out of the cabin and dialled from a phone located at the entrance of the room. The phone gave a static sound. 'It's giving a funny sound?' he asked.

'We do not have any direct dialling facility. You have to go through the operator. Press nine and ask the operator to connect you.'

The woman operator connected him instantly to Arati. She had been waiting for his call from the morning.

'Babu! You're ditching me!' she screamed in Tamil. She had hoped he would take her out for lunch.

'I'll come and see you after lunch.'

'No. Then I have an appointment with my hairdresser at three.'

'Should we meet in the evening? I promise I'll make amends.'

Arati giggled. 'Don't be a naughty boy. My husband is planning to return home early. Let us meet over lunch tomorrow at our favourite restaurant,' she said and put the phone down.

The Sony launch turned out to be a hectic affair with over a hundred journalists and an equally large contingent of PROs present at the meet.

Kala Muthu polished off six glasses of vodka and three glasses of beer. Some of the women invitees looked extremely interesting. Under Raveena's eagle-eyed gaze, he dared not speak to any of them.

Raveena tangoed between some wine and beer. After lunch, she insisted he accompany her to attend a press conference being addressed by the chairperson of the National Commission for Women at their Rouse Avenue office.

'Will they be serving us drinks?' Kala Muthu asked his self-appointed benefactress.

'Shut up! This is a serious government organization. You'll be lucky if you come away with a cup of tea.'

The press conference dealt with the increasing number of incidents of sexual harassment in the work place. Kala Muthu, despite the booze, listened to the chairperson, Malti Bhattacharjee with rapt attention.

As they came out of the National Commission for Women office, he said, 'Raveena, I'm feeling confused. I thought women wanted men to make a pass at them. Every woman enjoys the company of men. This battleaxe was saying something completely different.'

Raveena would not allow his remark to go unchallenged. 'No one is denying that. It's just that in a work place, you cannot use sex as a bait to get promotions and things like that.'

Kala Muthu kicked a stone. 'Women do that all the time. They love sex. They wouldn't worship the lingam if they did not want it between their legs.'

'Don't be cheap, man. You have failed to understand the fine distinction that exists between the work place and what one does outside it.'

'Tell me, if Big Boss wanted to make you CEO on condition that you had an affair with him, would you say no? Poor women marry rich men. No one creates a noise about such marriages.'

Raveena saw the logic of his argument. 'It all depends on what I can get out of a man.'

'Precisely. Why this hue and cry then?' he asked.

They continued to argue right up to the *Sentinel* office. Hurrying up to the bureau to file her story, she said, 'We'll continue the discussion at the Press Club this evening.'

Kala Muthu was not interested in going and spending time in wretched Cabin 65. He found the bureau a more salubrious place. It carried respectability and prestige.

Kala Muthu began to fantasize about joining the bureau as a special. Going through the schedules on the notice board, he found that both Ajit Jolly and Keith D'Souza were not filing any stories that evening. Walking across to Jolly's cabin, he spent the evening chatting with the two of them.

Realizing he had run out of cigarettes, he decided to go out and get a pack from Benarasi Lal's shop across the road.

Shankar Sen, the trade union leader, was also buying cigarettes.

'I haven't seen you around in the last couple of days?' Sen asked in his soft, cordial manner.

'Sir, I've been busy learning the ropes,' Kala Muthu replied, cursing his luck. He did not wish to be reminded about the real reason why he had joined this place. Life on the fifth floor, with all the reporters and specials, was more congenial.

Shankar Sen paid no attention to his obvious embarrassment. In his usual encouraging style, he continued, 'Good! I'm glad to learn you have turned out to be such an enterprising lad! This place can get a little intimidating!'

Kala Muthu decided he should steer himself back to doing what Rajan had hired him for.

'Er ... sir, I was hoping to come and visit you at your home this evening,' said Kala Muthu.

'You are most welcome. Come by seven o'clock. My wife and I have a dinner engagement at eight.' He gave Kala Muthu the address.

Disengaging himself from Raveena proved a difficult task. She insisted on knowing why he wanted to visit Shankar Sen alone at his residence. 'I can come along with you,' she said.

'No, yaar. I think I should go alone.'

Raveena gave him a suspicious look. 'Does Shankar live alone or does he have other family members living with him?' Raveena asked.

'How would I know?'

'Why can't you delay the meeting till tomorrow? I wanted to go and see a movie at Odeon theatre tonight.'

Kala Muthu hated possessive women. He found this kind of inquisition nauseous. If she continued in this vein, she was free to return to her old flame, Dalip Jha. He would be quite satisfied to go back to Arati. At least she did not harangue him with a host of questions every time they met.

Sen lived in a spacious three-bedroom flat in Green Park opposite the Evergreen Sweet shop. Kala Muthu was surprised to find the door being opened by a grey-haired distinguished-looking woman. Sen's wife, Ranjana welcomed him in fluent English. Their two teenage daughters dressed in shorts were sitting in the living room watching television. The minute he entered the room, they got up and left. The room was well furnished with velvet-lined sofas, a double-door fridge and a large-sized TV. Kala Muthu had expected Sen's house to be a run-down affair in a downmarket part of the city.

'I didn't see you saar, when Krishan Mohan Singh made a heroic stand against the management,' said Kala Muthu.

'Of course I was there. I was in my room till late in the evening. The response was quite overwhelming. We plan to keep up the pressure in a sustained manner. Who are you reporting to in the office?'

Kala Muthu fumbled. 'Mr Rajan saar.'

'Has he given you any specific parameters of work?'

'No sir. Not yet. He has been quite busy of late. Once I complete my training, let us see where I get deputed. I may try to go abroad,' he boasted. Kala Muthu was feeling out of depth. This man did not talk like the uncouth union types he had encountered in Chennai. He spoke like an Englishman with a perfect Oxbridge accent. His British influence seemed further accentuated by the long pipe he smoked. He gave the appearance of being a skilful negotiator leaving the workers with the crass job of sloganeering and sabre-rattling.

'Saar, I am still trying to understand why the workers turned so violent when I entered the office. What made them so hostile?'

Sen chose to give a roundabout reply. 'Young man, times have changed. People have become insecure. Old trusts have broken down. When this happens, people tend to behave in an irrational manner. You will learn all these things as you go along. It is good to see a young lad like you going out of your way to establish contact with us poor marginalized union leaders. People regard us as a dying species. No one wants to have anything to do with us any more. The management would be delighted if we were all sent into exile.'

'How long have you been a trade union leader, saar?'

'Ever since I can remember. I'm now forty-eight. Why do you ask?'

Before he could reply, Sen's daughter arrived with two cups of steaming tea and some chocolate cake. Her tight shorts exposed her slim buttocks and thighs. Kala Muthu kept staring at her legs. He could see a faint layer of hair growing on them.

Sen gave his daughter an indulgent look. 'Thank you, Supriya,' he beamed.

So that was the girl's name. He had begun to tire of both Arati and Raveena. Arati moved in an elevated sphere which had little place for country bumpkins like him. Raveena, on the other hand, behaved like an over possessive mistress – the kind who would question him for two hours if she so much as caught him talking to another woman. He saw no future for himself in either of these relationships. This Supriya girl seemed more interesting.

Putting his teeth into the soft creamy cake, he started plotting on how he could get close to Sen's daughter. Once he had her eating out of his hands, she could be relied upon to manipulate her old man.

The two men sipped their tea and chatted. When the time came for him to leave Kala Muthu touched Sen's feet and sought his blessings. Sen gave an embarrassed laugh. Kala Muthu walked out with a fresh spring in his feet. Seducing Supriya would lend some additional spice to his life.

fifteen

Simi raced back to the office to file her report. Pushing open the office door she stopped to drink a glass of water. Loud whispers emanated from the cubicle at the other end of the room.

'The whole world knows except that poor girl.' She recognized Rita Sawhney's voice.

Malvika retorted, 'The wife is always the last to know. He's sending her out of town almost every second day on one tour or another. Kiki is a smart operator, if you know what I mean. This younger generation is completely ruthless!'

Simi recoiled in shock. They were talking about her. She backed off abruptly, only to bump into Inder sahib.

'Are you all right?' His white hair fell artistically across his forehead. He was smelling of shampoo and a strong aftershave. It was obvious he was coming straight from the barber's.

'I think I ate something that didn't agree with me. For a moment I thought I was going to puke.'

Inder sahib handed her a small plastic strip containing some strange-looking green pills. 'Try one of these Pudinhara tablets.'

Simi, suspicious of all medicines, did not want to be seen to be refusing Inder sahib. Hesitatingly, she slipped the pill under her tongue and started coughing.

'I'm feeling better,' she spluttered.

'Good! I think you were deputed to attend a conference on how minorities should improve their educational achievements. Have you written out your story?'

'No.' Turning her back on Inder sahib, she spat out the pill. Taking out a packet of cigarettes from her bag, she lit one and offered the pack to him.

He gave her a stern look. 'I don't smoke.'

'I'll join you in a minute. I need to use the restroom.'

Her mind raced over the events of the last few days. Dalip had encouraged her to do out-of-town assignments. There was nothing new in this. Ever since they had struck up a friendship some six months ago, he had been telling her to travel.

Did her recent trip to Guwahati provide him with an opportunity to start a relationship with Kiki? Nothing could be ruled out, Simi told herself. There was never any smoke without fire. And here she had been imagining that something was cooking between Raveena Bedi and her husband.

Stubbing out her cigarette, she stepped back into the office. Her first reaction was to pack her bags and return to her parents' home in Noida. That would not help. Accosting Dalip with this information would not help either. He would simply dismiss her accusations as the ramblings of a jealous wife. She must keep her cool and try and catch the two of them red-handed.

The opportunity arrived sooner than she had expected. The following Tuesday, Dalip was asked to cover a protest rally being held by the All India Farmers' Manch in Saharanpur. It had something to do with the government's refusal to pay the cover price for sugarcane. On his way back, he could stop at Shamli and find out how the villagers there had responded to the visits of Leelawati and Amir Singh.

'Simi can go instead of me,' said Dalip tersely in response to

Inder sahib's suggestion. 'How can I leave office when I have so much rewriting to do?'

'Allow Kolkata to do the rewriting job for a change. You are being paid for your reporting skills. You broke the Shamli story. You did a big follow-up story about Leelawati's visit to Shamli. You are familiar with that area. It's only fair that you go there again.'

'Arre Inder sahib. I have broken so many stories in my career. Where has it got me? I have remained a struggling reporter in *The Chronicle* whereas my colleagues have become senior editors. There's no fairness or justice in our profession.'

'I'd love to go,' butted in Simi. She would use the opportunity to lay a trap for her husband.

'There you are. You have a willing slave,' said Dalip grinning broadly.

'Shame on you! Calling your wife a slave. You men are so disgustingly sexist,' Rita Sawhney butted in.

'Hardly! My wife enjoys complete freedom. I feel proud of her growing list of achievements.'

At any other time, Simi would have delighted to hear such praise. Today she realized Dalip's words were laced with irony. An idea had begun to take shape in her mind. A visit to Saharanpur need not be a time-bound affair. She could always reach the rally a couple of hours late or else collect the story from some local reporter. The Shamli story required her to collect reactions from villagers. That could be done at any hour of the day or night. She would pretend to set off for Saharanpur and then go and park herself outside Kiki's house. Knowing Dalip, if he had developed a fancy for Kiki, he would waste no time in trying to meet up with her.

Keeping a rein on her temper Simi played out her game. For the first time after her marriage, she forced herself, on returning home in the evening, to keep up some semblance of conversation with Aruna. The watery dal and insipid potato gruel served for dinner were praised. Papaji's inane remarks on journalism and the state of the nation were heard out with tolerance. Dalip did not say anything right through dinner. He kept raising his hand to look at his watch, forcing Aruna to ask him, 'Do you have to go somewhere, beta? You seem to be very agitated.'

Dalip mumbled an indifferent reply.

Next morning, a battered down white Ambassador arrived at the crack of dawn to pick up Simi. Dalip escorted her to the door, giving her a stream of tips for the story. Till the very last, he was pumping her with information.

'I'm sure you'll do an excellent job of ferreting information from the villagers. Do try and get a quote from both Pappu Yadav and that arch villain, the panchayat leader Chowdhury Ram Lal. They're both hand in glove. Quotes from both of them will help pep up your story,' Dalip told her as she got into the cab.

With a show of concern for her, Dalip added, 'If you have any problems, just ring me up. I don't think anything will go wrong. Saharanpur is a dirty little provincial town. Nothing much ever happens there.'

'Don't worry.'

'Make sure you're back in Delhi by five p.m. at the latest. It will take you at least two hours to file your story,' Dalip said taking down the number of the taxi.

It was a cool summer morning. A few bulbuls could be heard trilling away from the branches of the gulmohar tree that grew in front of their house.

Slamming the door of the cab, Simi slunk into the back seat and tried to get her bearings. In the last few months, she had journeyed many times to Khatauli and Roorkie and knew the journey by heart. The cabbie would drive her to the Dhaula Kuan roundabout from where he would get on to the Ring Road. He would then cross over the Nizamuddin bridge and head towards that faceless monstrosity of a satellite town called Ghaziabad. Simi generally dozed off by the time the taxi crossed the Yamuna river and woke up only when she had arrived at the place of her assignment. Since the drivers were all hired by the office, most of them knew their way around.

'I'm not going to Saharanpur right away. Get on to the outer Ring Road and drive me to Kalkaji Extension. I need to collect some papers from there,' she informed the taxi driver.

The driver looked surprised. He gave her a sharp look through his rear window.

'Kalkaji Extension?' he repeated.

'You understand English don't you?'

'Of course, madam. But sahib told me to drive you straight to Saharanpur.'

'Now memsahib is telling you to take her straight to Kalkaji. If you have any problem in going there, I'll ring up the stand and ask for another cab,' Simi said sharply.

The threat of hiring another cabbie decided the matter. At the Moolchand Hospital crossing, he turned right and headed south towards Kalkaji Extension.

The city appeared at its best in the morning. A lustrous yellow sun was rising in the sky. The trees on both sides of the road sparkled in the sunlight.

The taxi lumbered along at its indifferent pace, managing to steam past two morning cyclists and a jogger with some difficulty.

Finding the house was not particularly difficult. The address Kiki had written down in the office register was 62 Kalkaji Extension. It turned out to be a pink-coloured, double-storied corner house located opposite a large park. She asked the driver to park the cab in a bylane facing the house. He did so albeit reluctantly. Unfolding a greasy-looking newspaper, he began to read. Every few minutes, he would look over his shoulder, obviously surprised that she had not got down from the cab to collect the papers as she had said.

Fifteen minutes later, Dalip arrived in his ramshackle white Fiat and disappeared inside Kiki's house. Her colleagues had been right. She had married a cad.

What should she do now, she wondered. Should she send for the police? Or should she ring up her parents and ask them to come here and accost her husband? It was best not to get her father involved in this mess. A heart patient, the shock of learning about Dalip's behaviour might well result in his having a heart attack. Maybe she should ring up her mother-in-law and ask her to come here and witness her son's shenanigans.

Fighting back her tears, she slumped against the seat in despair. A million thoughts raced through her mind. She even thought of ringing up Inder sahib, then decided against it. He maybe a father figure but he was also a journalist. He could never hold onto a secret for long. By the afternoon, the entire Delhi press would be talking about the incident.

In a state of confusion she turned to the cabbie and insisted he go across to the first floor of the pink house, pompously titled 'Excalibur', and ring the front doorbell. 'A woman will open the door. She will give you the papers I need,' Simi told him.

But the Sardar had got more than an inkling of what was happening. 'I'm not going anywhere, madam. You go ahead and ring for another taxi if you want.'

'All you have to do is go to the first floor there and ring the bell. A girl will open the door. Give her my visiting card. She will hand over some papers to you,' she insisted.

The driver refused to budge.

'Do as I tell you!'

He continued to read the paper.

Gnashing her teeth, Simi crossed the road and climbed the steps to Kiki's apartment. Her heart was thudding loudly as she rang the doorbell.

Kiki opened the door. She was wearing a blue nightie. Simi

could see the outline of her breasts through the transparent material.

Pushing her way inside, Simi found Dalip sitting on a settee reading the morning papers. He stared at her with a mix of horror and rage.

'What on earth are you doing here? I thought you were on your way to Saharanpur,' he managed to stutter.

'I could ask you the same question. What are you doing here so early in the morning? Helping her out with a story?' Simi exploded.

Dalip's face turned from pink to scarlet. 'Yes, that's exactly why I came here – to help her out.'

'It's not enough that you help her in the office. You now need to help her in her own home Who are you trying to fool?' Simi looked around at the tastefully decorated house filled with an amazing array of gadgets. The plush surroundings only served to make her angrier.

Dalip got up and put his arm around Simi. 'Honey! Why are you getting so upset? Let's talk about this calmly.'

Simi pushed him away. 'What is there left to talk about now. You've been two-timing me for the sake of this bitch.'

Kiki was not the kind of person to take such a statement lying down. 'How dare you insult me in my own house,' she screamed.

'You haven't heard my insults yet. Let me get to the office. I'll show you that I mean business! I'm going to complain about both of you to Adhikari in Calcutta. He's already removed two people from their jobs for not knowing how to behave themselves. You two love birds had better watch out!'

Her threat worked. Dalip knew he could scarcely afford to have a fresh scandal on his hands considering his third marriage was just a few months old. The proprietor, Adhikari, despite his Anglicized façade was known to be a conservative man. He cursed himself for having got involved with Kiki.

Gripping Simi by the arm, he manoeuvered her to his car. 'Let's go home and talk this whole matter through in a more peaceful manner –'

'What home are you talking about? I'm never going back there again,' shouted Simi, trembling with anger.

Pushing her into his car, Dalip slammed the door shut. Running across to the cabbie, he slipped a one-hundred rupee note into his hand. 'The trip to Saharanpur has been postponed for the time being. I'll talk to you later in the day.'

Looking at the weeping Simi, Dalip wondered how he was going to extricate himself from this mess.

'Honey, I swear I had just come to help her with a story. There is nothing going on between the two of us. I swear it. Let's go to that restaurant you like at the Imperial and have a comfortable chat. I'll explain everything to you.'

Simi was not listening to him. Slumped on the front seat of the car, she stared distractedly at the traffic whizzing past her. The sun appeared a burning mass of molten light. She felt herself burning in its rays like a modern sati.

'Let's go on a special holiday. We could go to Spain or France or wherever you want, baby,' said Dalip in his most cajoling tone.

'Stuff it! I'm never going back! It's over! I don't care if I never see you or your family again. Take me home. I just want to go to my own home,' she said.

Without a word, Dalip turned the car at the roundabout and began driving towards Sector 14 in Noida. He would explain everything to her parents. Perhaps they would behave in a more rational and understanding manner. But knowing her parents, he found this a little difficult to believe.

sixteen

A nervous-looking Dalip Jha entered his office and shut himself in his little cubicle. Lighting a cigarette, he gave a quick look around the room. None of the other reporters had shown up yet. He would spend the next couple of hours trying to figure out how to get out of this mess.

His mind was not working. Switching on his computer, he distracted himself by playing a video game. Fortunately, Hare Krishna, the office peon, arrived a little later and made him a cup of tea.

Every time the front door opened, his heart gave a violent lurch. At two p.m. Kiki made a brief entry. Seeing him sitting in his cubicle, she flushed and turned her face away. She went across to Apu Antony, a young reporter who had joined recently, and started talking to him. Soon, the two of them burst into loud giggles.

'I need a smoke,' she said and walked out.

Dalip's eyes were glued on her as she walked out. He noticed how her bottom twitched from one side to another, encased as it was in a pair of tight, black jeans. Antony followed her, a sheepish expression on his face.

Kiki obviously did not want to have anything more to do with him. Damn woman, he told himself. Presumptuous and pretentious, imagining she was one hell of a poet.

Dalip's mind kept going back to the expression on Simi's face when she had caught him sitting in Kiki's room. Thank god he had been reading the morning papers and doing nothing else. Simi had looked devastated. For one moment he thought she might retrace her steps and leave the room without speaking a word. But she was always given to hysteria. Habit prompted her to scream and shout and that was what she had done. My God! She sounded like a virago, having spun out of control.

But Dalip realized then that he still loved her – his relationship with Kiki had been nothing more than an adventure born out of boredom.

He attributed his behaviour to the prevailing tension in his house. Simi was such an unpredictable person – always threatening to take some dramatic step against him and his family.

His home had transformed into a conflict zone.

Trapped in this existentialist dilemma, it helped to sit around with attractive women and allow his tension to be washed away in a swirl of smoke, booze and small talk. Energized by the conversation, however mindless, he would feel his spirits lift. The day-to-day emotional and financial problems melted away.

By nature, Dalip did not see himself as a possessive person. He doubted if he would go berserk if he had found Simi in a compromising position with another man. Simi, like all these smart Delhi girls, was a mixture of broad-mindedness for herself and conservatism for everyone else. These women were always climbing the moral high horse, while parroting socialist jargon, none of which was practised in their own lives. Her favourite one liner was the need to cultivate a sense of fair play towards others and especially the poor. And yet, most of her spare time was spent bitching about her colleagues and their boyfriends. She spent her entire salary buying fashionable clothes and expensive make-up.

Who would have tattled on Kiki and him? Hell! It must have been Rita Sawhney. She was a secretive sort who never told a soul about herself. Being unmarried, she had developed some kind of fetish about knowing what other people were up to and was always prying into the affairs of her colleagues. Who said what, who ate what, who wore what, who read what … peeping and prying and spreading one canard after another.

The other person who could have played dirty was Deepak Saran, their crime reporter. He had also developed the habit of listening in to other people's conversations. No wonder he had been given the CBI and police beat to cover.

A journalist had once mentioned to him at the Press Club that Deepak had recently returned from the USA with an assortment of sophisticated listening devices including a miniature microphone. During the last few days, he could have hidden the microphone in his shirt pocket, and then picked up all that stupid, flirtatious talk which he had indulged in with Kiki.

Dalip tried to put these negative emotions away. Simi would be all right in a day or two. If he stuck to his story of having gone to help Kiki with some editing work, she would begin to accept it. The only loophole in his explanation was that Kiki happened to be wearing a transparent nightie.

He must be ready with an alibi. He would tell Simi that Kiki had been about to go and change her clothes when she had landed up at her flat. He repeated the story so often to himself that he himself had begun to believe it.

He wasn't such a bad fellow after all. At least that was what his friends told him all the time.

**

A hysterical Simi, sobbing loudly, had got down from Dalip's car and run into her parents' home.

Her mother, watching a television serial in her bedroom, ran downstairs to find her daughter lying on the cold marble floor and crying at the top of her voice.

'What on earth has happened? Where is Dalip?'

'I refused to allow him to enter my house. I do not want to see that blackguard's face again for the rest of my life!'

'Calm down! What is the matter?'

Amidst sobs, Simi recounted the sorry saga of her marriage. 'I will never go back to that house, not over my dead body.'

Simi's mother had been brought up in a conservative middle-class family. From her point of view, no married woman could be allowed to live outside the ambit of a marriage.

'We showed you so many good boys from respectable families. You rejected them all,' Mother said tremulously.

'I wanted to marry a journalist, an intellectual, a somebody. I did not want to marry a businessman like Father,' Simi screamed, a fury rising from deep within her.

'Much good that did you.'

Her mother's words were like a slap in Simi's face. Even at fifty-six, her mother was incapable of showing any sympathy towards her. She had always been a cold-hearted woman. She thought with a sense of shame of how her mother had behaved when Dadi had died after a long battle with cancer. Simi had entered the room where her Dadi's dead body lay, to find her mother sitting on the bed, a gloating expression on her face.

Her mother had felt a consummate hatred for her mother-in-law. It was a hate that she must have passed on to Simi. For from the day she set had eyes on Dalip's mother, Simi found herself hating her.

Simi's mother had not waited for her husband to return from his factory to make all the arrangements for the cremation. Instead, she had picked up the phone and ordered the hearse to be sent to their address. Next, she rang up the chief pandit at Lal Mandir in Sector 10 of Noida and insisted he preside over the final puja. Late in the evening, after the cremation was over, Simi's mother enjoyed a long cool shower. Slipping into her finest chiffon sari, the green and red of the sari heightened by the loud red lipstick and rouge she had put on, she came down from her bedroom to sit amongst the mourners, primarily her three sisters-in-law, and show them how little she cared. The sisters-in-law did not say anything. Friction and discord were intrinsic to a nuclear family situation and they were used to it. Simi's mother was not one to forgive and forget.

Simi had always thought Mother's behaviour was particularly harsh when she had to deal with women. Following Dadi's death, her relationship with Simi's father also changed. She began to order him around. Engrossed in his work, her father obviously did not wish to rock the boat and meekly did as he was told.

Picking up the phone, mother rang up her husband, Rakesh Taneja, at his factory in Naraina and ordered him to drop everything and return home immediately.

Handing Simi a glass of cold Pepsi, she said, 'Drink it up. It will make you feel better. Every marriage has its ups and downs. Now look at your father. He has so many eccentricities. You know, when I had just got married – '

Simi cut her short. 'I do not wish to hear about Father and you! I don't want to talk to you! I hate coming home! I wish I could die!'

Simi's screams were so loud, her mother shuddered in horror. The whole colony would soon learn about the break up of her daughter's marriage. She closed the front door and then proceeded to shut every single window in the living room.

An hour later, a grim-looking Rakesh Taneja arrived home only to be told the sordid tale of his daughter's marriage. It did not take him long to work himself into a rage.

'I'll kill the bastard! I'll shoot him! How dare he misbehave with my daughter in this fashion!' Rakesh exclaimed. He rushed into his bedroom to take out a small revolver kept in the locker of his grey-coloured Godrej almirah.

Realizing what was on his mind, his wife followed him into the bedroom and snatched the revolver from Taneja's hand. 'Are you out of your mind? You want all of us to end up in jail?'

Pushing the revolver back into the cupboard, she slammed it shut and shoved the keys down her cleavage.

'We need to take some positive steps in order to bring the two of them together. They've just been married a few months. With some proper counselling, I am sure they can iron out their differences,' she said.

Hearing her parents argue only served to worsen Simi's condition. The family physician and neighbour, Lt Col Dr Ravinder Bedi, an elderly Sardar who had spent his life dispensing Disprins to army jawans, was sent for. Bedi arrived shortly, carrying his black medical bag as though it were a combat rifle.

'Why is Simi lying on the floor? Has she fainted due to the heat?' he asked.

'She's too weak to stand,' said her mother.

'Put her on the bed!'

The Tanejas, with Dr Bedi's assistance, half-dragged, half-carried their daughter to the divan in the living room. Bedi proceeded to feel her pulse.

'She's obviously suffering from shock. I will give her a sedative. She'll sleep it out for a couple of hours. By tomorrow morning she will be feeling better.'

Bedi gave her an injection and Simi fell into a slumber.

'Will she be all right?' Rakesh asked the doctor.

'Nothing to worry about! Journalists suffer from hypertension. I'll come and see her tomorrow morning,' Bedi reassured the anxious parents.

Neither Simi's mother nor her father slept that night. Mrs Taneja sat by her side the whole night, her mind tormented with all kinds of fears. Simi was an extremely headstrong child. There was the possibility, if she refused to go back to Dalip, that she may return home and start living with them again. The prospect was not heartening. A divorcee daughter would cause tongues to wag in their social circle.

Rakesh Taneja paced the floor trying to make sense of the situation.

Next morning, Simi woke up late. Feeling nauseous, she ran to the bathroom and threw up. Bedi was sent for again. He took her pulse and insisted her problems emanated from low BP.

'Too much tension,' Bedi repeated and gave her another shot.

The nausea refused to go.

Mother insisted Simi be shown to a trained gynaecologist. Another family friend, Dr Promilla Joshi whose clinic was located in Sector 15 in Noida, was sent for. Late that afternoon, Dr Joshi, overweight and bulldoggish in her features, arrived at their house. Taking out her stethoscope as though it were a continuation of her breast, Dr Joshi led her to her parents' bedroom where she proceeded to examine Simi's chest.

'Breathe in, breathe out,' she kept murmuring.

She then pressed Simi's stomach with both her hands.

'Oops,' gasped Simi.

The stethoscope was placed back on the table. 'I will have to examine your uterus.'

'Whatever for?' Simi protested.

The doctor ignored her protestations. Slipping a plastic glove onto her right hand, she pushed her forefinger into Simi's vagina.

'Congratulations! You are going to become a mother!' Dr Joshi informed Simi.

Mrs Taneja clapped her hands in joy. 'I can't believe it. This daughter of mine was getting worried without any rhyme or reason. I'll ring up Daddyji and give him the good news.'

Simi was horrified to learn about her pregnancy. 'I do not want to have a child. I hate babies!' she burst out.

Dr Joshi heard her pronouncement with interest. Her mother, on the other hand, pretended to have turned temporarily deaf.

Simi repeated what she had said.

Mrs Taneja looked at her with brown, piercing eyes. 'What do you mean?'

'I hate children. I don't want to be saddled with a child.'

'We all say that. I didn't want children but after getting pregnant, there is little we can do except bear them,' said Dr Joshi.

Mrs Taneja pursed her lips tightly. Simi's protests would now be repeated amongst her circle of friends. Motherhood was a subject in which she possessed more insight than was being shown by her stupid daughter. She had strong views on the subject. No one in this house was going to be allowed a contrary viewpoint.

'Who is asking you to be saddled with a child? I will look after the child for you. You can continue with your journalism,' she said reassuringly.

Dr Joshi nodded her head in encouragement. Richer by five hundred rupees, she waddled out to her waiting chauffeur-driven car. 'Our girls are all the same! They make a hue and cry about everything but deep down they are good children. They mean well,' she told Mrs Taneja as she clambered into the car.

Rather than continue to face her mother's bombast, Simi fell back on the divan and covered her face with a cushion.

There was little point in arguing with her mother especially since she had mastered the art of twisting and conniving every situation to suit herself. She did that all the time with her husband. A factory owner with fifty workers toiling under him, Rakesh Taneja had been reduced to soft putty before her. Now her mother planned to use these Machiavellian tactics against her.

Mrs Taneja seemed to have forgotten an obvious detail. Dalip had sired the child. As a father, he could lay claim to the child. She also seemed to overlook another fact. The child would be lodged inside Simi's womb for nine long months. Why should Simi put up with such a prolonged torture? If she decided to go ahead and have an abortion, there was precious little her mother or anyone else could do.

The next few hours were spent debating what course of action she should pursue. Since there was no likelihood of her returning to Dalip's house, she could not afford to enter into an open confrontation with her mother. Mrs Taneja was rigid in her views. She would not permit an abortion to take place under any circumstances. She must now endure nine months of agony while Dalip was free to enjoy himself.

The unfairness of the situation hit her. Cursing Dalip for having pushed her into a corner, Simi wondered how she could settle scores with both him and his mother. If she was going to be forced to bear a child against her wishes those two monsters must be made to face the guillotine.

A strange thought crossed her mind. Picking up the phone, she rang up DCP Protima Phukan who headed the Crime Against Women Cell. Phukan was known to nurse a soft corner for journalists and was generally compliant to their wishes. Some years ago, Simi had done a series of exposures on dowry deaths and other dowry-related problems. She had interacted closely with her and they had ended up becoming good friends. She had even invited Protima to her wedding.

'I need to come and see you, Protima.'

'You've outgrown the Crime Against Women Cell. You've become a VIP journalist. These days you cover no one other than the prime minister,' Phukan replied, happy to hear Simi's voice after a long break.

For the first time in two days, Simi allowed herself to smile. 'I need to speak to you urgently.'

'Come whenever you want. We can have a long chat. I'm going to be in office all day.'

After persuading her mother that she was well enough to go to work, a slightly flustered Simi caught a taxi which drove her to the Crime Against Women Cell office located near Dhaula Kuan.

Protima Phukan was small built, with fair features and a rosy complexion. She sat, almost hidden, behind a large table overflowing with files. A lady constable was sent for and asked to clear the table. The task performed, she was told to fetch some tea and biscuits.

After exchanging the usual pleasantries, Simi came straight to the point. 'I need to file an FIR.'

'Against whom?' Phukan asked. From Simi's washed-out face she had sensed that there was something amiss with her marriage.

'Dalip – my husband.'

Protima was taken aback. She did not want to get involved in filing charges against journalists. It would only create problems for her in her career.

'What is the matter?'

'They have been harassing me for dowry. I'm an only child. My parents have given me so much gold and jewellery but they keep demanding more.'

Protima looked at her sympathetically. 'You must show some patience.'

'I have shown a lot of patience. They refuse to mend their ways. Dalip hounded his first wife from the house because she did not bring a large enough dowry. She was bundled out of the house and thrown into the boondocks. Being a simple villager, she did not raise her voice against this injustice. Now he is trying the same tactics with me. Why should I stand for it?'

The police officer remained silent. 'I was a little surprised when you decided to marry him. He is not your type. Your family backgrounds are so different. Nevertheless, I would not advise you to do anything in a hurry. When one is agitated, one tends to do things without any proper planning. Have you taken any kind of legal advice?' Protima asked.

'My marriage is over.' Simi's voice was unbending. It was obvious she was not willing to change her mind.

Phukan took both her hands in hers and patted them gently. 'I've known both of you for several years now. Dalip is not a bad fellow. He's very impulsive and given to doing all kinds of foolish things. Give him time, he will settle down and make a good husband.'

'I don't believe that. I want to file the FIR just now.'

'Have you discussed matters with your parents?'

'Yes,' Simi lied.

Phukan realized Simi was not willing to change her stand. She asked the lady constable standing outside to fetch Chief Constable Som Pal.

'He'll assist you in writing down the details.'

Looking at her watch, she made a quick excuse. 'I need to step out of the office for a brief meeting. I'll meet you in a short while.' And with these words, Protima beat a hasty exit.

Som Pal entered the room carrying a red register. He looked like the typical Haryanavi cop – tall, loudmouthed and garrulous.

'You can write out all the particulars on this piece of paper and I will enter them into this register.'

'Will I be given a copy?'

'Of course,' he said.

Taking a ball point out of her purse, Simi wrote, 'List of items given to me in my dowry include one fridge, one TV, one sewing machine, one car, two beds, one dressing table, one motor cycle, six gold sets and Rs 25 lakh in cash. My in-laws including my mother-in-law Aruna Jha and her husband, Vishnu Jha, residents of 25 Anupam Vihar, New Delhi are now demanding an additional laptop computer, ten gold sets and Rs 20 lakh in cash. My husband beats me every day and has threatened to burn me if I do not produce these items within the next twenty-four hours.'

Som Pal looked astonished. 'You belong to such a high-class family and your husband's family is only asking you to give an additional Rs 20 lakh?'

'How much should they be asking for?'

'These days dowry demands run into crores of rupees.'

Simi tore out the sheet of paper on which she had written the details. 'I'll prepare a fresh list all over again.'

She once again wrote out the list of consumer items but increased the cash amount to one crore rupees.

Som Pal had mastered the art of executing arrest warrants based on dowry offences. But before such a warrant could be executed, every dowry victim was expected to give him ten per cent of the total worth of the dowry return being demanded by her.

Most dowry victims did not hesitate to inflate the cash amounts they were demanding. After all, not only did the men in khaki have to be kept satisfied, the astronomical amounts being demanded by lawyers, and often corrupt judges had to be paid for, and there was little harm in extracting the amount from the cruel husband and his family.

Paying Som Pal a sizeable bribe, Simi realized, was the only way she could ensure the arrest of both Dalip and Aruna Jha.

'Demanding dowry is a non-bailable offence,' Simi said.

Som Pal replied, 'There is no such thing as a non-bailable warrant. Those who assassinate prime ministers have also ended up being released on bail.'

Simi understood his hidden innuendo. 'I just want to teach my mother-in-law and husband a lesson. I want them to spend one night in jail. That is all.'

Som Pal smiled. 'All dowry victims want revenge. But you must not forget, when my team goes to their house, the other party will try and buy us out by offering us money.'

Simi did not want to pay him too much. 'You know who you

are talking to? I'm a senior journalist. If I report you, you can get into trouble.'

This cop was not going to be intimidated by empty threats. 'I can put you in touch with another cop who can handle your case,' he replied coolly.

'How soon can you have these people arrested?' Simi asked.

Som Pal did not give a reply.

Simi understood the reason for his silence. 'Between you and me, I am willing to pay a small sum towards executing these summons. I do not have very much money,' said Simi.

There was a distinct change in Som Pal's attitude. 'We can have them arrested today. As you know, demanding dowry is a non-bailable offence under Section 498A of the Indian Penal Code. This month alone, we have arrested over one hundred husbands and put them behind bars.'

'Good. They deserve that. I don't want you to go just now. My husband tends to reach home by ten p.m. or so. Go after that.'

Som Pal grinned. 'At that late hour, he will have a problem contacting his lawyer. Poor fellow! He will be forced to spend one night in jail.'

'Along with my mother-in-law.'

'Of course.'

Simi smiled. 'I live in Noida. You can come to my house right away and collect your advance.'

Picking up her bag, she walked out of the police station to the waiting taxi. Her hysteria and nausea were now things of the past. Being able to take revenge on Dalip and her mother-in-law had left her with a delicious feeling of contentment.

Late that night, a jeep load of policemen led by Som Pal, feeling richer with the Rs 25,000 he had received from Simi and which was now stacked away in a briefcase in his house, arrived at Dalip's house. He rang the front door bell a couple of times. The sound of the bell and the loud footsteps brought Aruna, wearing her grotesque maroon housecoat, marching to the front door.

Som Pal, armed with the arrest warrant, walked into the drawing room and informed her in his brusque style, 'Mataji, you are under arrest for harassing your daughter-in-law for dowry.'

Aruna collapsed on a chair unable to utter a word.

A bewildered Dalip, who had been lying in his bedroom listening to Bach, rushed into the living room.

'I don't believe it. Show me the arrest warrant,' cried Dalip.

Som Pal handed it to him.

Dalip was horror struck at its contents. 'We demanded one crore from her family? Has she gone insane?'

'You can explain all this to a court of law. This is a non-bailable warrant.'

'Hold on! I need to speak to my office!' Dalip shouted.

Som Pal realized journalists made slippery customers. Keeping up the pressure, he said, 'Sir-ji, I don't have time to waste. You can make all the phone calls you want from the thana.'

Aruna was sobbing. 'This can't be happening to me! I am the daughter of a retired judge. My husband Vishnu is a leading politician of Bihar. This list is false. I can swear on my father that I did not demand a single item from my daughter-in-law.'

'You can do all that explaining at the thana,' Som Pal countered.

Dalip picked up the phone and rang up his office. The bell kept ringing. It was past eleven p.m. Shit! Everyone had left the office.

He tried calling crime reporter, Deepak Saran, at his house. No one was picking up the phone there either. He must be boozing at the Press Club.

Dalip's mind was in a daze. He could not think of anyone who he could contact at this late hour.

'Let me speak to my lawyer!' he demanded.

'This is a non-bailable offence. You can contact your lawyer from the police station. I don't have all night to sit here while you make phone calls.'

Aruna's mind was a jumble of conflicting thoughts. If she were put behind bars, her reputation would be ruined. She had three daughters to marry off.

Turning to Som Pal she folded her hands and made a low bow. 'Wait for one day. My husband and my daughters have gone to Vaishno Devi. They will be returning tomorrow morning. My maid is new to the city. She does not know her way around. We will come ourselves to your thana tomorrow morning and court arrest.'

'Mataji, why are you getting so upset? Indira Gandhi spent one night in jail and then went on to become the prime minister. What is the big deal about spending a couple of hours inside a police station? I've spent my entire life there,' said the burly policeman.

Dalip was beside himself with anger. He was mortified by the way his mother had bowed in supplication before the constable. Som Pal's swagger only served to infuriate him further. Stepping forward, he raised his hand to slap Som Pal. Better sense prevailed. Slapping a constable in uniform would needlessly create more problems. He brought his hand down with a jerk.

Som Pal also fought back his urge to beat up this hulk of a journalist standing in front of him. He did not want to get into an unnecessary fracas with the press.

'Either you both come with us of your own choice or else we will have to take you away forcibly.'

A sobbing Aruna was led out by two policemen. 'This can't be happening to me,' Aruna kept mumbling to herself. She was followed by a grim-looking Dalip.

Sitting in the police van, Dalip realized that Simi had indeed succeeded in hitting back at them. He would not let her off that easily. Once he was let off, he would settle scores with her and her family.

The SHO at the Dhaula Kuan thana treated them with considerable respect. Tea was brought for them and Dalip was allowed the use of the phone. Protima Phukan refused to respond to his repeated phone calls. Dalip tried calling a few senior politicians. Not one politician was willing to take his call at this late hour. In despair, he tried calling Inder sahib.

A grumpy Inder sahib who had just returned home from a late night party picked up the phone reluctantly.

Dalip recounted what had happened.

'My God! My God! Tell Mataji to relax. I will be there in a couple of minutes!' Inder sahib said. He immediately rang up a Congress councillor who lived down the street in Pamposh Enclave. 'You've had my star reporter arrested. His poor diabetic mother has also been dragged to the police thana. I want you to come with me to the Dhaula Kuan police station and make sure he gets released right away.'

The councillor and Inder sahib reached the Dhaula Kuan thana to find Dalip sitting trying to persuade his distraught mother to drink a glass of water.

'She's fainted. I tried telling this beast not to arrest her. He refused to listen,' Dalip shouted.

'I was only following orders,' explained Som Pal.

'We'll take the matter right up to the prime minister,' thundered Inder sahib.

The councillor took the SHO aside. 'Have you all taken leave of your senses! Who dares arrest high profile journalists in this day and age?'

The SHO knew the councillor was well connected. 'Sir, these dowry cases have become the bane of our police force. If we implement the law we are abused; if we fail to do so, we face further abuse. You must try and understand our position.'

'Position my foot! Inder sahib has already rung up the PMO and by tomorrow morning, there will be hell to pay for all of you,' the councillor warned.

Som Pal heard the conversation with interest. The name of

the prime minister was invariably invoked every time there was a dispute in this country, more so when someone got arrested. These poor blighters did not understand that the prime minister had no say in any matter. No one, not even God Almighty, could remove a government servant from his post.

Knowing how devious the police tended to be, Inder sahib felt certain Som Pal must have tipped off a couple of local Hindi journalists about Dalip Jha's arrest. Andy Warhol's formula of five minutes of fame was being played out all the time by the civil service. Bureaucrats had become so publicity hungry that even a small-time constable wanted his name in the press.

A news item, however small, in the press only served to reinforce the individual's guilt.

He decided to contact Deepak Saran and ask him to ensure the story was not played up by his colleagues in the Hindi press. Saran's residential number kept ringing to no avail.

Turning to the SHO, Inder sahib shouted, 'This is your police force at its best. Instead of searching out criminals, you go after law-abiding citizens. You won't hear the last of this arrest. We'll put you in your place. Don't worry.'

The SHO tried his best to calm them down.

'The matter will be taken right up to the prime minister,' Dalip Jha shouted.

By now the SHO was also feeling intimidated. He had obviously taken on more than he could chew. 'As an exception, I will allow you to takc the old Mataji to spend the night at a nearby hospital. You can also spend the night there. I will keep a constable posted there for your protection.'

Inder sahib immediately agreed to this line of action.Catching hold of Aruna's arm, he led her to the door. 'I've always known the police were a corrupt body. I could never have imagined things could go so far,' he muttered.

Som Pal saw them walk out with an aggrieved air. Rules in this country were being bent all the time to suit the rich and the powerful. There was little point in blaming the police for not catching criminals. They were never given a free hand to do their job.

Next morning he rang up Simi and gave her the lowdown on all that had happened in the police thana. Simi heard him out with a mixture of pleasure and dismay – pleasure at having achieved vengeance against those who she believed had wronged her. Dismay because her marriage was over and this would destroy her parents' happiness forever.

seventeen

Attar Singh stared at the gibberish of numbers and sighed. Could these belong to a Swiss bank account?

The rich in India were known to siphon off their black money and deposit it in Swiss bank accounts abroad. These deposits were protected from police inspection by privacy laws and were attached to numbered accounts rather than people's names. This way their anonymity remained intact and no one came to know about just how much money had been stashed away in which account.

The chief accountant Purshottam Lal had once told him that opening these accounts was not difficult. The banks did not require the holder to supply either his signatures or photographs or fingerprints. All they required was the willingness to pay the bank depository charges in advance as also to stash away a large sum of money in order to justify those charges.

Vikram Aggarwal's family was rumoured to have siphoned off a large amount of money. It was not for nothing that his father had all kinds of FERA charges slapped against him.

He stared at the twenty account numbers written down on separate ledgers. Their distinctive feature was that they consisted of ten numerals unlike Indian bank account numbers which consisted of largely four to five digits.

Each of these accounts must open into a separate safe deposit box. The owners must be in possession of special keys to access these accounts. That made it twenty keys.

How could he be certain these were Swiss bank account numbers? He scratched his head. He had no way of confirming this fact. After the stabbing, he had gone across to have a chat with Purshottam Lal in his house. Lal told him that some of the details he had copied down had come from a top-secret file. The entries in this file had been made around the time large consignments of money was being siphoned off into foreign banks.

Flies and mosquitoes! What should he do next? Ramesh Tewari, secretary general of *Swadesh*'s trade union and popularly known as Ramesh Babu, was known to be close to the owner's daughter, Tania Mittal. Would they be interested in getting hold of these details? It could be a source of potential embarrassment for Vikram Aggarwal if these numbers were slipped into the hands of a rival organization.

Selling the account numbers to Tania Mittal was a gamble worth pursuing. He would walk across to the *Swadesh* office and sound out Ramesh Babu who in turn could speak to Tania. If he could earn a couple of lakhs through the transaction, Babu was free to take a commission from him.

Vikram would not allow him to survive this betrayal. The Aggarwals were not a family who could tolerate their employees passing on information to their enemies. As it was, every employee in *The Indian Sentinel* was treated like bonded labour, more so those of the rank of a peon.

Death was the ultimate price he would have to pay for this gamble. He was willing to pay the price, convinced as he was, that the stabbing had been an insider's job. Some senior manager in the *Sentinel* must have ordered it with Vikram's tacit consent. He could not frame his proprietor for being guilty but he could definitely ensure his being brought down a notch or two.

**

Attar Singh and Ramesh Babu entered the worker's canteen, a large, well-ventilated room with red plastic tables and white plastic chairs that lent it a strange, surreal touch. The canteen remained empty most of the time except during lunch and dinner recesses, or when a shift got over. The workers would troop in for tea and snacks and then empty the place within a few minutes. Attar Singh sat down in a corner while Ramesh Babu went to pick up some chai and samosas. Ramesh Babu had barely put the plate of samosas down on the table when a bell rang some distance away. One shift had ended and another had started. A few minutes later, several workers trooped into the canteen and began occupying the vacant tables. Kala Muthu came and sat down on a table next to the one at which Attar Singh and Ramesh Babu were seated. He had come to meet a friend from Chennai who was working in *Swadesh* as a sub-editor. His friend had suddenly been called up to the editor's room, so Kala Muthu decided to while his time by drinking a cup of coffee.

Ramesh Babu sat quietly on the chair and sipped his lukewarm tea as Attar Singh recounted the events of the last few weeks starting with the stabbing, the information conveyed to him by Gulabo Pathan and his realization that the coded numbers discovered in these registers might well be account numbers which belonged to a Swiss bank. These numbers seemed to have gained notoriety ever since the Directorate of Enforcement had filed a series of charges for violation of FERA against Papaji.

They were sitting face to face in the crowded office cafeteria overflowing with workers and other menial staff. The decibel levels were high and most of the workers were forced to shout at one another, in order to make themselves heard. Sometimes their tones became so aggressive, an onlooker would imagine the people conversing were going to come to blows.

Attar Singh found himself shouting for Ramesh Babu to hear him.

'Purshottam Lal had ordered me to make a back-up of some office files. Most of the work was routine in nature. Some of the files dealing with highly confidential matters were also lying in the basement. I made the mistake of seeing these half-empty files and taking them home. I thought I could use them to make records of my own moneylending business. I felt no one was going to miss them.'

'You've turned out to be a real Marwari, eh! Did those files contain some office secrets?' Ramesh Babu asked curiously. He was a tall, lanky man with sharp steel-like eyes that glittered with a strange intensity and had the habit of piercing into whatever they were observing.

'When I brought them home, I did not imagine they had any importance. I just thought I could save a few rupees by using office stationery. They had been lying in my house but I had never bothered to find out what rubbish lay scribbled inside. It was only after they stabbed me that I got curious. A couple of the ledgers had some strange notations, I showed them to Purshottam Lal. He believes those entries were made around the time a lot of money was being siphoned into foreign accounts. I suspect those notations are actually Swiss bank account numbers.'

Ramesh Babu raised his eyebrows. 'How can you be sure of this?'

'That can be checked out by any expert. Purshottam told me that Swiss bank account numbers come in ten digits and are accompanied by a key. I do not have the key but the numbers are with me.'

Ramesh Babu raised his eyebrows in amazement. 'Tell me from

the beginning. I cannot understand anything. Which proprietor will leave top-secret documents lying around in his office? He will obviously keep these numbers in a safe place.'

'Bhaiya, what you say is correct. Purshottam Lal is one of their most trusted accountants. Some years ago – he revealed this to me only after the stabbing – Purshottam was called up to Papaji's room and asked to make back-up copies of several crucial documents. There were two files with Top Secret written on their covers. I don't know what got into Purshottam, he made copies of those documents also. I don't think he had any ulterior motive in doing this. It was just done on a moment of impulse.'

'Then why should the owner go after you? He should have knocked off Purshottam Lal instead?'

'I asked that question of Purshottam. He sees the situation in a different light. When the whole FERA fracas started, Vikramji began to suspect that some of the unionwallahs may have gone and tattled about these transactions before the Directorate of Enforcement. Someone gave them my name and said that I was maintaining unofficial cash registers which kept a record of the company's licit and illicit transactions.'

Ramesh Babu looked baffled. 'My dear fellow! If that was the case, they could have simply raided your house and retrieved all their registers and other cash books.'

'I think they no longer trust me. They believe I must have kept another set of back-up registers in some hiding place. They suspect I may have given them for safekeeping to the union people. I think for them it would be easier to simply get rid of me,' explained Attar Singh.

'What do you expect me to do?' Ramesh asked in amazement.

'Ramesh Babu! When someone puts a knife into you, you begin to wonder where you have gone wrong. I have spent the last month lying on my charpai asking myself who I could have offended. I cannot think of a soul. Ever since I joined the *Sentinel*, my life has revolved around my work. I was there at the crack of dawn and never left till late in the night.'

Ramesh Babu looked bewildered. 'Why didn't you simply go and explain your position to Vikram Aggarwal? He would have understood.'

'I'm just a small insect crawling at the fringes of Vikramji's empire. Why would he hear out the complaint of a mere peon? If his father had been in charge, things would have been different.'

Ramesh Babu pressed further. 'Talk to someone else – talk to Rajan or some other senior guy.'

'No one is willing to listen. If they had just asked me to return the account books, I would have done so without a murmur. But instead, they thought it more appropriate to get me out of the way.'

Ramesh Babu sighed. 'Our days are numbered. We have no role left inside our organizations or even outside. No office wants to deal with people like us. Who wants a peon in these lean and mean times? How are we going to add to the profitability of a newspaper? If I owned some land, I would go back to Unnao and lead the life of a petty farmer.'

'I would do the same. You tell your madam that she is getting hold of this top secret information for a couple of lakhs. If she had hired a detective agency, she would have had to fork out a couple of crores to be privy to these details.'

Ramesh Babu's eyes went wide. 'You expect to be paid a couple of lakhs.'

'Arre bhai, you can take your commission.'

Ramesh Babu gave a soft whistle. 'I'll try my best.'

'The deal must come through in the next day or two. Tell your madam, I will give her the *Sentinel* ledgers which contain all the original notations. She can get this information checked by someone who knows about Swiss banking. If she is not interested, I can pass this information on to someone else.'

Kala Muthu's ears pricked up when he heard the words the *Sentinel* and Swiss bank acounts. He had heard enough to be able to put two and two together.

Kala Muthu mulled over what he had just heard. Vikram would be delighted with these nuggets of information. He felt certain he would be well rewarded for providing him these details. But before he spilled the beans, he must bargain for a management consultancy post and some hard cash. His future was looking bright. No one could stop him from racing to success.

**

Kala Muthu decided against seeking Raveena's help to reach Vikram Aggarwal. He must approach him alone. Fate had intervened to provide him with an opportunity to win the confidence of the proprietor. He would not share it with anyone else.

Kala Muthu hurried into the *Sentinel* office and decided to use the lift to go up to the top floor. Barging into Banerjee's office, he shouted, 'I need to see the big boss, saar.'

Banerjee looked exasperated. The older Aggarwal would never have tolerated such a devious looking character inside his organization. Nowadays, all they hired were filth. Before he could frame a proper reply, Kala Muthu had opened the door and marched into Vikram's room.

Vikram was sitting behind his large table staring gloomily at the peepal tree. Only two evenings ago he had expressed his displeasure with the way that cub reporter had covered the Shamli killing. 'I want someone experienced to go there. Let him go and stay in the Circuit House. Then the company will not have to pay hotel charges.'

Rajan had nodded his head in agreement. On leaving his room, he had sent for Ajit Jolly. A quaking Jolly arrived to meet him within seconds of the phone call convinced he was finally going to be given the sack. Instead, Rajan told him he wanted him to proceed to Shamli.

'You will be expected to stay in the Circuit House.'

Jolly looked at Rajan in surprise. Did he expect reporters to break sensational stories by sitting inside a government Circuit House? He did not contradict him however.

'When do you want me to leave?'

'Right away. I want you to do a better reporting job than that British journalist writing for some high falutin' London paper. Do you understand?'

'Of course sir.'

Jolly had been away two days and, to Vikram's chagrin, had not filed a single story. His campaign to put pressure on the government by sensationalizing the Shamli murders had been hijacked by other newspapers. The foreign press had also jumped into the arena and were pursuing the story with great zeal. That would not do. He needed to seize the initiative once again.

Just then, a black-skinned, greasy-looking character rushed into his room. Vikram stared at him in horror. Was this another attempt by the unions to kill him? Banerjee followed on his heels.

'Saar! I am privy to very secretive information regarding your foreign bank accounts,' shouted an excited Kala Muthu.

'I tried to stop him!' Banerjee interrupted.

Vikram ordered Banerjee out. 'Send Rajan here right away.'

'One of your peons, who was stabbed some weeks ago, claims to know your Swiss bank account numbers. I overheard his entire conversation. He is trying to sell them to a rival newspaper group.'

Vikram's face turned pale. Could this fellow be speaking the truth?

Just then Rajan hurried into the room. He was thunderstruck at seeing Kala Muthu in Vikram's room.

'Who gave you permission to enter this room? I'll have the security staff throw him out of here.'

Vikram signalled to him to be quiet. 'Tell me exactly what you heard and when.'

Kala Muthu did not open his mouth.

'You've been asked a question!' Rajan said angrily.

Kala Muthu kept mum.

Vikram understood immediately. He wanted money. He gave him a withering look. 'How much do you want?'

'A couple of lakhs and a good managerial job.'

'Agreed. I'll give you ten lakhs and appoint you as HRD in charge,' said Vikram and he indicated to Rajan to leave the room and bring the money. The owner had ordered a small safe to be kept in an adjacent room to which only three people enjoyed access. They were Vikram, Purshottam Lal and more recently, Rajan.

Kala Muthu was satisfied with Vikram's offer. The present HRD in charge had several good-looking chicks working under him. He had heard any number of stories about his being holed up with those girls whenever he had the opportunity.

Rajan returned carrying a small black leather suitcase.

Kala Muthu rushed across to open it. It was stacked with shimmering, new five hundred rupee notes. With so much money in his hands, he was willing to sing like a canary. He repeated the conversation he had overheard between Attar Singh and Ramesh Tewari.

'That man Attar Singh spoke to was a character called Ramesh Babu. He is a union leader and works in *Swadesh*,' Kala Muthu explained.

'Must be that trade union fellow called Ramesh Tewari,' said Rajan, disbelief written over his face. 'I don't believe a word of what he is saying. How can you accuse that doddering idiot Attar Singh of such deviousness? He's been with us for the last thirty years.'

'I swear it, saar. I'm speaking the truth! Attar Singh is selling all that information to your enemies. He said all your Swiss account numbers were ten digit numbers.'

Vikram drummed his fingers on the table. Looking at Kala Muthu he said, 'I will get back to you later. You can leave.'

Kala Muthu left the room, suitcase in hand. Snooping always paid excellent dividends. What a stroke of luck, to have been able to overhear such a vital piece of conversation, he told himself.

Rajan was unhappy with this turn of events. He did not like the idea of anyone else in this organization winning over Vikram's trust. It was for this reason that in the last few days, he had developed an acute dislike for Raveena Bedi.

Vikram looked out of his bay windows and said, 'He has given me an interesting tip off. Attar Singh, he claims, has learnt my Swiss account numbers and wants to sell them to the owners of *Swadesh*.'

'This is all a figment of Kala Muthu's imagination. He must have joined hands with these trade union characters who are responsible for the present government's focussing on these FERA violations cases.'

Vikram took a deep breath and stared outside at the luminous sky exuding so much strength and sanity. This wily Brahmin always talked sense. Those trade union monsters occupying valuable office space on the ground floor could be up to their tricks again. But then again, if the *Swadesh* group gained access to those numbers, they would not hesitate to publish them.

He must not allow the case to be re-opened and made public. They would arrest Papaji. His enemies would also be provided with additional proof of his wrongdoings. And this time it would come in black and white.

'I don't want those numbers going into the hands of the *Swadesh* people. That has to be stopped immediately.'

'I'll have Attar Singh dealt with right away. He is of no use to us.'

'What is the position of File 213?' Vikram asked in a low voice.

'I'm trying to get Hazarika transferred. The minister is not proving cooperative,' Rajan replied.

Vikram got up and started pacing the floor. He had always been particular about the kind of people who surrounded him. This low-down character who had rushed into his room was not his style at all. The smooth-talking Brahmin standing before him had done well under his guidance. He could guess what he was about to say and unravel the significance of many of his outlandish comments.

'Ministers can always be bought. We have to think of ways of cracking some of the tough nuts in the bureaucracy,' Vikram muttered.

His company had tried its best to bribe the concerned bureaucrat. Hazarika had refused to accept money. If there was one tribe he had learned to hate, it was the group of people who fell under the category of incorruptible bureaucrats. Anachronisms like them must be wiped out of the subcontinent.

Rajan hurried out of the room. He would have to contact Buddy, who worked out of a small basement in the Greater Kailash office. Nicknamed the Dirty Tricks Department, they would contact the appropriate people to get rid of Attar Singh. He did not want to be messing around in all this. Nor did he want his name to be tarnished unnecessarily.

Vikram stared icily at the sky stretching like a pearl. The roof tops of the surrounding building could be seen melting into the sky. He hoped in the near future to be able to buy out the owners of these complexes in order to expand his own empire.

**

Rajan walked back to his room deep in thought. There were too many loose canons floating around this organization. Bringing Kala Muthu into the *Sentinel* no longer seemed to have been such a good idea. He began to wonder just how Arati had got to know a skunk like him.

Opening the door of his cabin, he pressed the button to ask his peon for some tea. What kind of game was this man playing? Could he be a plant? It seemed too much of a coincidence that he happened to be present at the very moment that Attar Singh was confiding all these details to Ramesh Tewari. Now that the matter had been brought to the notice of Vikram Aggarwal, disposing of him was not going to prove an easy task.

There was a knock at the door.

'Ram Avatar! Dammit, you don't have to knock every time you enter my office!' Rajan shouted.

'Sir! It's me!' said Rameshwari Mathur entering the room. Rameshwari had been working in the *Sentinel* as a telephone operator for the last twelve years. Since the exchange was located at the far end of the building on the ground floor, Rajan had no idea who she was.

'What do you want?'

'Sir, I'm a telephone operator. I work downstairs at the exchange.'

Rajan was flabbergasted. What on earth was wrong with the employees in this organization? Vikram was right. There seemed to be no discipline left in the place. In the morning, one newcomer had had the gall to walk into the MD's room. Now another nobody did not think twice about sallying into his room.

'If you have any problems, kindly discuss them with your incharge. I hope I have made myself clear,' said Rajan.

His dismissive tone was not lost on Rameshwari. She was not the kind of person to take no for an answer. Opening her bag, she took out a cassette and handed it over to him.

'Sir, my work concerns only you. I do not want to go public in this matter. I have too much respect for you. I have personally brought this to your notice in order to avoid embarrassing you.'

'What do you expect me to do with this cassette?'

'Listen to it.'

My God! The impertinence!

'Sir, kindly do not jump to conclusions till you have heard it. I would like to remind you that I have kept the master copy. My contract in this organization has come to an end. My boss, Daryl Pinto Sir has told me it will not be extended. After you have heard it through, I am sure you will not hesitate to renew my contract for another three years.'

Rajan looked askance. This woman was actually trying to blackmail him!

'Are you trying to threaten me?'

'On the contrary. I am trying to help you. I could have gone straight to Vikramji but that would have served no purpose at all.' With these words, she stalked out of the room.

Rajan stared at her in disgust. Walking across to his side table, he placed the cassette on the tape recorder.

There were some loud, jarring sounds then suddenly a man could be heard pleading, 'Should we meet in the evening? I promise to make amends.'

A woman giggled and whispered. 'Don't be a naughty boy. My husband is planning to come home early. Let us meet over lunch at our favourite restaurant tomorrow.'

It was Arati's laugh. The man who was speaking to her sounded like Kala Muthu. He turned cold. Could this be true? He sank down on his chair in disbelief.

He heard the tape over and over again. He must have heard it at least ten times over before switching it off. There was no doubt that this was a conversation between Arati and this management flunkey.

He spent the next hour hitting his wrist on the office table. Arati had been the epicentre of his life. They had grown up together in the same village outside Mylapore. Sharp and aggressive, she had held him by his shoulders and lifted him out of his poverty-stricken childhood by insisting he complete his graduation and get an MBA degree. The early days of their marriage had been traumatic. They had seen so much poverty. There were days when they had little to eat except a few slices of bread dipped in a hideous solution of diluted tea. Lack of food and access to proper medical facilities had forced her to undergo two quick abortions that had left her Fallopian tubes damaged. The middle-aged doctor tending to her had informed her she would not be able to bear a child. On learning this, Arati had turned hysterical and wanted to kill herself. As she came out of her depression, she kept pleading with Rajan to allow her to adopt a child. He was too much of a villager at heart. It must be either his own child or no child at all. She had heard him out quietly. As he spoke, a dull, opaque look came into her eyes. It was as though the world around her had transformed into something vile and coarse.

For many months, she remained enveloped in a strange silence. She seldom spoke to him. Gradually, as she came out of her cocoon she began to spend all her time watching what the other women around her did. Since they seemed content to be attending kitty parties and playing cards at the Gymkhana club, she began doing the same. Soon she had picked up their mannerisms, their style of dressing and their behaviour. Her subdued style of dressing gave way to a coarser more ostentatious style. One day, she went to a beauty parlour and had her long, cascading hair cropped into a boyish style revealing her shapely head.

'What have you done to your hair?' Rajan rebuked her when he returned from work.

'I want to look like all these modern women. They look so smart. So chic!'

In retrospect, that had been the turning point of their relationship. Her decision to cut her hair had, in Rajan's eyes, left her spiritually naked. He felt hurt. He kept asking himself what had gone wrong. He could not understand it. Rajan had begun to do well in his career and was spending long hours away from home.

Somewhere along the line, like many other society women, Arati must have found herself a lover.

Rajan cursed himself for having neglected her. He could not have imagined the estrangement between them could have been so complete. Should he accost her with this tape? He felt hesitant. He had always looked upon her as his mentor and guide. He could not bear to demean their relationship. Nor could he bear the idea of losing her. Those abortions, he realized, had destroyed her soul.

He should have allowed her to adopt a child. Maybe it was not too late to undo this mistake. A child might help them recreate all they had lost. They possessed a large circle of friends who enjoyed visiting their beautiful home. He was not willing to give this all up.

And yet, despite his ability to make allowances for her, he could not forgive her for ending up in the arms of that guttersnipe. She had compromised him before the eyes of the world. His position in his company had become stronger but in his own home, the situation was completely disagreeable.

Kala Muthu was not going to be allowed to continue for another day in the *Sentinel* office. He may have managed to ingratiate himself with the owner.

But so many others had done so in the past only to find themselves dropped from the inner circle when they got too close to him. Vikram Aggarwal had experience enough in realpolitik to ensure that no one was allowed to remain a favourite for very long.

eighteen

Rajan did not have to wait long to get even with Kala Muthu.

The Sentinel School of Journalism was holding a one-day orientation course for college students gathered from Delhi's most prestigious colleges. The course was being held at the Oberoi Hotel. Five senior management executives from the sixth floor of Sentinel House had been asked to make high-power presentations to over 250 students, each of whom had paid Rs 2000 per head, to attend this one-day session.

Kala Muthu had learnt of the orientation course from Raveena Bedi. They had spent the previous evening boozing at the Press Club. With the advance of five lakh rupees he had received from Vikram Aggarwal now deposited in a Syndicate Bank account located on Bahadur Shah Zafar Marg, and with the realization that he was going to receive more money in the future and also be elevated to a good managerial post, he had metamorphosed into an overconfident, over-aggressive boor.

He had insisted on paying the bill for the drinks and the dinner. A grateful Raveena, arms wrapped tightly around him, walked out of the club telling herself she had never felt happier in her life. They had spent the night and early morning hours gratifying each other and while she lay curled up in a deep and satisfied slumber, Kala Muthu, under the pretext of meeting his sub-editor friend at the *Swadesh* office, had excused himself. Since *Swadesh* was *The Indian Sentinel*'s rival paper, Raveena did not insist on coming along with him. An hour later, he walked into the Oberoi hotel foyer.

Kala Muthu's reason for showing up at this venue was simple. Several college girls would be attending the course. He was confident he would be able to attract the attention of one or two of the more attractive ones. Under the pretext of offering them a job, he would be able to seduce them. Now that Vikram had agreed to make him HRD in charge, more than five thousand people would be working under him. Many of these college girls would go to any lengths to join the *Sentinel*. He could look forward to having some serious fun on the side.

Rajan was not present but one of his aides Sudarshan, was standing in the foyer, drinking coffee, and chatting with the delegates. Surprised to see Kala Muthu, he hurried forward to welcome him. Just then, Supriya Sen, daughter of the *Sentinel*'s trade union leader, Shankar Sen, along with two other college girls walked in. All three girls were students of Lady Shri Ram College.

Recognizing her, Kala Muthu hurried up to greet her. Supriya looked extremely stylish in a short white top and tight blue jeans. Her full lips were parted as she bent over the table to write down her particulars.

'Good morning! Do you remember me?' he asked with easy familiarity.

Supriya blushed. 'Of course, you came to our house to meet Dad a couple of days ago.'

'You've got a great memory! I didn't know you were interested in journalism.'

Supriya and her friends smiled at one another. 'We're all studing English Honours at LSR but it's good to keep one's options open.'

'Want to have a cup of coffee?'

'I think we should get over with the registration bit. We can join you for coffee during the tea break,' Supriya replied and walked into the large hall escorted by her two friends.

Kala Muthu could not keep his eyes off her. There was something so coquettish about her with her neat, short blouse and slim, graceful figure. Her voice had a strange, husky tone and he wanted to go up to her and snatch a half-kiss off those ruby red lips. He believed he was just the right sort of Prince Charming to lay his love down at her beautifully proportioned feet.

Following her into the hall, Kala Muthu sat down in one corner. He did not hear a word of what was spoken during the morning session. His eyes were riveted on Supriya and her friends. Then on an impulse, he walked outside to the foyer and peered into the register to see how Supriya had signed her name.

'What have you stuck your nose into, this time, you prying bastard?' a contemptuous voice asked him.

Kala Muthu spun around. Jodh Singh was standing behind him along with Krishna Mohan Singh.

'I think I need to ask you the same question? What are you both doing here?' Kala Muthu retorted.

'The management wants us to undergo a reorientation course,' Jodh Singh cackled.

'They want us to upgrade our skills so we can join the management cadre,' said Krishna Mohan Singh with a touch of sarcasm.

Kala Muthu grinned and stood his ground. These idiots would never succeed in joining the management. He was the lucky guy, getting a break to join this elite cadre, and that too within a couple of days of setting foot in the *Sentinel* office. He was confident the information he provided Vikram Aggarwal would ensure he ended up as his blue-eyed boy. Once that happened, there was no stopping him. Rajan would be one of the first guys to get the axe.

His wife, Arati could be hired as a receptionist. And the union would be drowned in the filthy Yamuna canal.

'I need to get some literature to distribute amongst the girls in the hall. Where will it be available?' he asked the girl manning the desk at the foyer.

She replied with a fixed smile on her face. 'The *Sentinel* has hired Room 336 on the third floor. A large amount of literature and pamphlets for dissemination have been kept there.'

These peons must have brought all that stuff here, Kala Muthu told himself. He walked out of the foyer to the central lift which would take him to the third floor. Knocking outside Room 336, he entered, to find the room practically deserted except for the presence of one emaciated-looking accountant who was making some entries in a register. He raised his head to see Kala Muthu enter the room. Recognizing him, he returned to making notations in the file.

'Nobody else in the room?' Kala Muthu asked.

'Nobody yet. I have made an entry of all the items that were brought from the office. I have to head back to Bahadur Shah Zafar Marg now. Why don't you wait here till someone comes to replace me.'

Kala Muthu looked at the spacious room and grinned. 'Did Jodh Singh and Krishna Mohan Singh bring all this stuff here?'

'Yes. They have to go back with me,' the accountant replied making an exit from the main door.

Kala Muthu grinned and breathed a sigh of relief. His two enemies were going to be leaving the hotel soon. He would have the field all to himself. Settling down on the blue velvet sofa, he peered down at the star-shaped aqua blue swimming pool. Wooden decks had been placed along its edges. Two foreign women in bikinis could be seen tanning themselves in the sun.

The small fridge in the corner contained a few bottles of booze. Kala Muthu pulled open the door and helped himself to a canned beer. His mind was filled with dreams of Supriya Sen. She had a ripe, full body waiting to be plucked.

Staring at the register left behind by the accountant, he let out a loud sigh. Office work was so boring! These unionwallahs were all scum! But he had seem that Vikram Aggarwal would never get rid of them. He needed to showcase to the rest of the world that he had a union in place. A few office-bearers would be allowed to retain their posts. They would be like fossils, to be displayed to foreign dignitaries and bureaucrats, with no inherent strength and dynamism to be able to take care of the workers' interests.

It had taken Kala Muthu a little while to understand this. For the first couple of days, he had literally gone around with his ear to the ground trying to overhear every whisper and nudge of the elbow that emanated from this dissolute lot. Rajan, he found, would listen to his tip-offs with interest but then he always made sure that developments within the union reached him through other conduits as well.

It was obvious Rajan did not want to put all his eggs in one basket. If Vikram indicated he was satisfied with an emasculated union, Rajan would immediately toe that line. If Vikram wanted the unions to be completely destroyed, Rajan would accept this. Rajan knew that no one in the organization could be allowed to become indispensable. He, nevertheless, hovered around Vikram to create the impression he could influence the course of action. The truth was no one except the owner was allowed to take key decisions.

Let Vikram worry about the state of the unions, Kala Muthu told himself. He had better things to occupy himself with. He looked at his watch. Gosh! It was time for the coffee break. Maybe, he could bring Supriya here for a couple of minutes. Shutting the door behind him, he hurried downstairs to find several young boys and girls, standing outside the main hall, drinking coffee. Kala Muthu hurried up to Supriya. She seemed pleased to see him.

'Join us,' she said, indicating he help himself to coffee being served by waiters dressed in spotless white uniforms.

'The *Sentinel* has hired a separate room stacked with all kind of literature on journalism and other related subjects. You could go and take a look there as well. Some of it is quite interesting.'

'I would love to do that,' said Supriya, finishing her coffee with a loud gulp.

They went up by the lift. Kala Muthu took out the key from his trouser pocket and opened the door with a quiet flourish.

Supriya was astonished to find the room empty. With a little sigh of pleasure, she sat down on the sofa. 'What a comfortable room. I wish I could always live here!'

'You're right, Miss Sen! Very luxurious!'

Just as suddenly, Supriya got up from the sofa and lay down on the bed. 'It's so funky! I wish I had brought a bikini. We could go down and have a swim.'

'Let's do that,' said Kala Muthu with a sense of bravado. He was watching her carefully. 'In a bikini, you would look like a mermaid surfing the ocean.'

'I've always wanted to be a mermaid! I love oceans and rivers. I come from Bengal.'

'We've got lots of rivers and oceans in Madras. Lots of storms also.'

Supriya looked at him with sudden interest.

'You have such a delicate complexion. Tamil girls are all dark,' said Kala Muthu.

'Bengali girls too. My grandmother comes from Kashmir. She's a Kashmiri Pandit.'

Supriya jumped off the bed and picked up some biscuits lying on the centre table next to the sofa. The surroundings seemed to fill her with a sense of wonderment.

'My grandmother wants me to study in Oxford. That sounds so boring. Let's do something exciting.'

Kala Muthu sat down by her side and proceeded to kiss her on her mouth. Her lips were warm and melting. He kissed her eyes, her ears, her neck, his hand hurriedly reaching for her breasts. She was in the mood to yield.

'Should we?' he murmured.

'Of course,' she said taking off her blouse. She then proceeded to unzip her trousers.

Kala Muthu could not believe his luck. 'You're too young for all this! Should we move to the bed?'

'This is like heaven,' she said and opened her mouth wider so that his tongue could caress her own. He stared in wonder at her sweet flower-like face. Her hand reached between his thighs. He could feel a hardening as he proceeded to mount her.

Just then, the door was unlocked and pushed open. Jodh Singh and Krishna Mohan Singh rushed in. They had seen Kala Muthu leave the main hall with Supriya Sen. Aware of Kala Muthu's reputation, they had hurried across to the main foyer and extracted a duplicate key from the administrative officer. 'How dare you?' Jodh Singh screamed, hurrying in to separate them.

Supriya screamed in horror and threw the bedcover over herself.

'Sen sahib's daughter!' cried a shocked Krishna Mohan Singh. 'He was trying to rape her.'

'Get out! Get out of the room! Leave us alone!' screamed Supriya in frustration.

The workers felt a tremendous sense of loyalty towards Shankar Sen. There was no way they would leave without taking his daughter along with them.

Jodh Singh took off his shoes and started thrashing Kala Muthu on his head and face.

'How dare you?' Supriya spluttered.

Kala Muthu tried to fight back but was outnumbered.

'Ring up the office! Tell Sen sahib this bastard was trying to rape his minor daughter. We will have to send for the police,' said Krishna.

'We can't do that. It will ruin her reputation,' Jodh Singh interceded.

'Leave us alone!' Supriya cried and tried to plead with them not to phone her father. They refused to hear her.

Kala Muthu, bruises on his face and arm, sat defiantly in one corner. The girl liked him. He would think of some way of establishing contact with her.

Sen sahib arrived an hour later looking pale and indignant. 'What is this?' he asked Supriya.

'I was just having a good time with this blackie when these two boors broke into the room. Why don't they just go away,' she replied.

'You will come home with me. Your mother will deal with this,' said Sen. He would give vent to his anger later. He did not want to make a public show of indignation.

'I'll deal with you later,' he told Kala Muthu.

Taking his daughter's arm, he forcibly led her out of the room.

Raveena Bedi was walking into the hotel when she learnt of what had taken place. The news upset her. Just when she had imagined she had found herself a steady and reliable boyfriend, he had gone and betrayed her. It would not be easy to find a replacement. Without a word, she turned on her heel and walked out. She required some time to think out a new strategy to deal with this situation. For the present, it was best to avoid Kala Muthu.

Kala Muthu's misdemeanour was the talk of the *Sentinel.* As soon as Rajan got wind of the news, he rushed upstairs to Vikram's room. Vikram Aggarwal had always been a prude at heart. Women frightened him. Their sexual escapades were something he did not wish to confront.

'It's nothing short of a scandal! This Kala Muthu tried to seduce Shankar Sen's daughter in the Oberoi Hotel. The college teachers on duty have threatened to file a PIL against us in the Supreme Court,' Rajan pointed out.

An agitated Vikram walked up to the bay window and stared out. He did not want to make a sweeping statement against Kala Muthu. Only yesterday, the man had provided him with a crucial tip-off.

'This Kala Muthu fellow was brought in to destroy the unions. He was not hired to seduce the daughter of a union leader. Doesn't he know the difference?' muttered Vikram.

'Sen has threatened to call the cops and sue us for a couple of crores!' Rajan said.

'He's trying to blackmail me! I'm being milked by the entire nation. I've become everyone's whipping boy!' said Vikram with a look of disgust. His newspaper was being dogged by scandal at every step.

'I realize that, sir. My suggestion to you is that you get rid of Kala Muthu immediately.'

'Not till I ensure those bank account numbers do not pass over to my rivals! Not only do my enemies want to put Papaji behind bars; they want to destroy me also,' said Vikram.

'I've already spoken to Ramesh Tewari of *Swadesh*. For ten lakh rupees, he is willing to ensure that no numbers reach Tania Mittal,' Rajan said with an ugly grimace on his face.

Vikam smiled. No one could outwit this Tamilian Brahmin.

'The money will be given. There is no problem on that score.'

'I thought as much, sir. We had a camera placed in the hotel room. We have managed to get some pictures of Shankar Sen's daughter in some rather compromising positions. Sen will have no choice but to keep his mouth shut when he comes to negotiate with us in the future,' Rajan added with a look of puckish delight.

Vikram was delighted. Sen had played right into their hands. No father would want photographs of his daughter, captured in a compromising position, to be in circulation. They had achieved a vital breakthrough. During the next round of talks with the union, Sen would be much more vulnerable. He could now speak to the Brand Manager HRD and push through a scheme to sack another four hundred redundant staffers. What incredible luck! This would ensure a salary savings of over three crore rupees per year.

Vikram did not want Rajan to receive undue credit for this breakthrough. He was the owner; his will must remain paramount in every situation. In this lay his power. Those around him must feel his strength at all times.

'I always knew we would find a stick with which to beat Sen. After all, no father wants to compromise his own daughter! Who gave permission to install the cameras in that hotel room?' Vikram questioned.

'Nobody, sir. The cameras had been installed there by some earlier client. The hotel staff discovered the presence of these tiny cameras when we were cleaning our stuff out of the room,' Rajan knew when to tell a half-truth. The cameras had been placed there as a precautionary measure by Sudershan and his team. Last year, when *The Indian Sentinel* had held a similar workshop, thousands of rupees worth of books and publicity material had disappeared from the hotel room. A cheap spycam camera costing just two thousand rupees helped keep trace of all those who entered and exited from this room.

Vikram once again seized the initiative. 'By trying to seduce a young girl in a hotel room, Kala Muthu has behaved in a completely depraved manner that is contrary to the values our newspaper espouses. His presence can no longer be tolerated here. Tell the HRD staff to pay him his dues. He must be shown the door.'

Rajan smiled inwardly. Vikram, as he was apt to, had once again somersaulted. Kala Muthu was no longer indispensable.

'Only yesterday, he was demanding I pay up a couple of lakhs. He didn't even have the patience to wait a few days for laying his hands on all the money. Get the information from that *Swadeshi* character and then proceed to disentangle yourself from this fellow.'

'Of course sir! Kala Muthu was hoping to blackmail you with the information he had collected.'

'No one can buy me out! I'm too big for them! Deal with him in whatever way you think is appropriate,' Vikram said coldly. He knew how to remain in control of a situation.

Dismissing him with a wave of his hand, Vikram returned to staring at the peepal tree doing its unending Bharat Natyam on his roof top. Maybe the tree had brought him luck after all.

nineteen

Attar Singh woke up in an exceptionally good mood. Completing his shave, he stepped into his grey office uniform. Shanti gave him a little hug before he stepped out.

'Bapu, don't forget to bring some rabri for me,' she told him with a smile.

'Of course, betiya,' he replied giving her a peck on her forehead. His little trick on Vikram Aggarwal had proved successful. Realizing that his phone in the house might be tapped, Attar Singh had asked Ramesh Babu to provide all the details of his transaction with Tania Mittal to Jodh Singh. Singh would then come personally to the house and convey the details to him.

Jodh Singh had dropped in late last night and informed him that Tania Mittal had agreed to pay him five lakhs. To be on the safe side, Ramesh Babu had suggested that the draft be made out in Shanti's name.

Attar Singh had immediately agreed with this suggestion.

The two men discussed the details of their strategy for the following day. Ramesh Babu wanted him to reach the *Swadesh* canteen by eleven o'clock the next morning. Attar must hand over the Swiss bank account numbers and the ledgers to him and Ramesh would hand him the draft. Attar had insisted Jodh Singh be present for the meeting. He would act as the decoy. On receipt of the draft, he must proceed to Bahadur Shah Zafar Marg and deposit it in Attar Singh's Canara Bank account. Attar would take a more circuitous route before returning home.

Jodh Singh was waiting at the bus stop near his house. The two of them boarded the bus headed for Connaught Place.

On the way, Jodh Singh recounted all that had transpired between Shankar Sen's daughter and Kala Muthu.

'She didn't want to leave that blackguard! She continued to cling to him even after her father arrived. God knows what magic he had wrought on her within a couple of minutes! He must have done some jadu tona on her!' said Jodh Singh.

Attar Singh was busy reading the imperious nameboards of the different shops in Connaught Place. Pearey Lal Motors, Paul & Sons, Bercos, British Motors. So many times he had read and reread these names haltingly in the past. He had never entered these shops, just as he had kept off so much else in this city. The poor never felt excluded from any situation. They simply went on to create an alternate niche for themselves.

'Thank God my Shanti is not like the Sen girl. I have found a good match for her. I have finalized her marriage with Ramu Shankar's son. He is working as a stenographer in the Ministry of External Affairs. They will be married soon,' Attar told Jodh Singh.

'None of our daughters is like that. If my daughter misbehaved in this fashion, I would strangle her with my bare hands.'

'Don't talk like that. There is enough violence in our lives. Shankar Dada is a respectable man. This Kala Muthu sounds like a strange kind of crook,' said Attar Singh.

He continued to stare out of the bus window. When he had first arrived in Delhi as a young lad, Connaught Place was ringed with a cover of green trees. Now it was ringed by tall skyscrapers that seemed to hug the sky.

'Of course he is a crook. Shankar Dada's face looked so

despondent when he walked out of the hotel. He could never have imagined this could happen to him,' said Jodh Singh.

'Once I give you the draft, you must go and deposit it right away in my account. I have a joint account with Shanti. She will face no problem in withdrawing the money,' said Attar Singh.

He added, 'I have to go to the State Bank at Parliament Street to find out about my Public Provident Fund. From there, I will catch a bus and return home.'

Ramesh Babu was already sitting in the canteen waiting for them. He immediately slipped an envelope into Attar Singh's hands. Attar Singh opened it and read the draft made out in the name of his daughter. He handed Ramesh Babu a sheet of paper on which was written twelve bank account numbers. He also handed him the original ledgers in which the notations had been made.

Ramesh Babu read all the notings carefully. With a satisfied smile, he folded the paper and placed it in his breast pocket. The ledgers were placed in a large red bag he had brought along.

Ramesh Babu leaned across the table and whispered, 'Some fellow from *The Indian Sentinel* office contacted me yesterday. They have learnt about this transaction. He offered me ten lakhs if I gave this slip of paper to him. But I had already discussed the matter with Taniaji. I cannot betray her now. Nor can I betray old friends like you.'

Attar Singh turned pale. Vikram Aggarwal had already got wind of this transaction. He did not have much time left.

He tried to quieten his sense of unease. Forcing a smile, he said, 'This morning, I dreamt I had returned home to my village. My mother was sitting outside the doorway cleaning wheat.'

'Islam says paradise lies at the feet of the mother. My mother never tired of cooking for us. We were eight brothers. She would wake up every morning at five o'clock and knead two kilos of atta from which she made chapattis. We ate her chapattis and gur for lunch and the same for dinner. The routine never changed. But

I've never eaten better roti than what she cooked with her own hands.'

Jodh Singh laughed. 'I used to sneak across to my neighbour's orchard to steal mangoes. All through summer, I stole mangoes from his house. In winter, I used to steal guavas and sugarcane. The neighbour had a huge stick. Each time he caught me stealing, he used to beat me up.'

Attar Singh gulped down some hot tea.

'I used to steal sugarcane from my uncle's fields. He was a miser. He never wanted to part with a single stalk,' said Ramesh Babu.

'Can't be a bigger miser than Vikram sahib. He's told the union that he does not want a single peon left in the office by the end of this year,' said Jodh Singh indignantly.

'They are all the same. My maalik too is like that. Yesterday, someone told me she has got gold knobs fitted in her bathrooms. One would think she wanted to perform puja there,' Ramesh Babu pointed out.

The conversation meandered from one subject to another. Ramesh Babu wanted to know the details about the incident in the hotel. Jodh Singh was delighted to tell the story all over again.

Ramesh Babu's face fell. 'Lady Shri Ram College is one of our best colleges. The girls attending the orientation course come from good backgrounds and yet Sen's daughter was willing to fall for such a cad. What is happening to our youngsters?'

Attar Singh turned sentimental. 'No one can make sense of what is going on.' Turning to Jodh Singh, he said, 'I want you to make sure Shanti is married off in a proper ceremony. Once that happens, take my wife to her sister's place in Unnao. She can live with her there.'

'Dada, don't talk like that. We are there to protect you. We have grown up together,' said Ramesh Babu. His heart was filled with a deep chill. His childhood friend was talking as though he had become a corpse.

Attar Singh gave a twisted smile. 'The rich have become too powerful. The poor have no one to turn to. Make sure my office pays all my dues to my wife. Get the union to put pressure on them in case they try and act funny.'

'What about the money Jodh Singh owes you? Don't you think it is high time he returns that to your family?' Ramesh Babu butted in.

'Each one of us is going to leave some bad debts behind. Let this be one of them. Billa, such a useless fellow, has not paid up either.'

Jodh Singh blushed. Embarrassment was written across his face. 'The money will be repaid, Ramesh Babu ! Don't worry!'

'I am not worried! Sen sahib is guarantor over my agreement with you. He will make sure the money reaches my family. The only person I am afraid of is Vikram Aggarwal. He is ruthless and will go to any lengths to achieve his ends. I do not want any harm to come to my wife and Shanti.'

'Why do you worry? Nothing will happen,' both men reassured him.

'That is what we grew up to believe. Throughout the late sixties and early seventies, we were so confident that no one could destroy the unions. And mind you, during their peak, the management would quake before them,' Attar Singh said with a sad, faraway look.

'The unions are still strong in our *Swadesh* office. We can bring the machines to a halt whenever we wish,' said Ramesh Babu.

Attar Singh shrugged. 'It is only a matter of time. Even if they do not destroy the unions, they will emasculate us. For them, we workers are little more than ants crawling the surface of the earth. Technology has rendered us redundant. If Shankar sahib calls a strike in Delhi, the paper will be printed in Chandigarh and brought here by taxi the next morning. What purpose will a strike, under these circumstances, serve?'

Ramesh Babu nodded. 'We grew up on a dose of liberalism which has lost its relevance. When I joined the *Swadesh*, I believed the paper would never change. It has. I believed Mother Earth would feed us all. Now, every time I return to my village, I find more and more starving mouths. They have no one to turn to. My father fought for the independence of India. He was in jail for thirteen years. In return, all we have received is a hard kick on our butts.'

The mood at the table had become increasingly dismal. 'Change has come so swiftly, no one has been able to cope. We are all being swept away by the cataclysm,' added Jodh Singh.

Attar Singh knew he did not have much time left. Vikram Aggarwal would not let him survive. The stakes for him were incalculable.

Clutching Ramesh Babu's hand he said, 'I am prepared for all eventualities. I just want my end to be peaceful.'

Ramesh Babu gave him a warm hug. Jodh Singh gripped his hand affectionately before taking his leave at the bus stop. Attar Singh stepped out of the office and walked towards Parliament Street.

**

Ram Bharose stood in one corner of Kasturba Gandhi Marg smoking one beedi after another. He had to wait two hours for Attar Singh to emerge from *Swadesh* office.

He had been promised a large sum of money to execute this killing. He knew the owner was a man of his word.

Ram Bharose followed Attar as he made his way to the State Bank office on Parliament Street. He stood outside the doorway while Attar went inside.

Attar Singh walked to the Public Provident Fund counter

on the ground floor and got his pass book updated. 'Come and collect it tomorrow,' the lady behind the counter told him.

Walking across to the manager's office, Attar Singh told him, 'I want my pass book couriered at this address.'

The manager recognized him. He was speaking on the phone but he still managed a smile. 'Leave it on my table. It will be done tomorrow, Attar Singh.'

It was only when he had stepped out of the bank and was walking towards the bus stop located in front of Park Hotel that he realized he was being followed.

The office's Dirty Tricks Department was already at work, he told himself. Who could it be? Was the executioner carrying a gun or would he again use a knife? Attar Singh had a strong desire to walk into the Parliament Street police station and hand himself over to the police. This would serve no purpose. His office would, in all probability, bribe the policemen and have him murdered in the cell. It was best to return home to Gautam Nagar, and remain there till he thought out an alternative survival strategy.

Ram Bharose was carrying his own ugly secret. Attar Singh regarded him as a friend. They had enjoyed a cordial relationship spanning two decades. Things had changed. Gulabo Pathan no longer gave him work. In these difficult times, he had a family to take care of.

It was best to get the job over and done with before Attar Singh recognized him. Best to keep some distance from him. Best to stay in the crowds and only get close to him when an opportunity arose.

It was a hot day. A cold sweat had broken over Attar Singh's forehead as he boarded the DTC bus. The bus was crowded. He forced his way to the front, and sat down next to the conductor. Human bodies milled around him making it difficult to see who was boarding the bus from the back.

Attar Singh got down at the Yusuf Serai bus stop. Ram Bharose had followed him in a three-wheeler scooter. His face was covered with a checked cloth.

Attar Singh walked quickly turning into the second lane which led to his house. The street was deserted. He could hear footsteps behind him. A man's shadow was closing up from behind.

Attar Singh turned around.

'Ram Bharose!' he cried. 'At whose behest are you working?'

'We all work for the same master. You have worked for him for many years,' Ram Bharose answered.

A sudden explosion of rage erupted behind Ram Bharose's eyes. He pulled out a knife from under his kurta and stabbed Attar Singh in the chest and stomach.

'I had warned you the last time. After this stabbing you will not get another chance. You should have heeded me and returned to Unnao instead of diddling around with your account books,' Ram Bharose muttered.

Attar Singh could feel the blood flow from his chest and stomach taking his life with it. For a moment, he felt he could smell the raw earth, a smell he had carried in his heart all these years. The face of his smiling daughter rose before his eyes and then he was caught in a web of darkness

Ram Bharose hurried away from the scene of the crime. He would go and spend the next couple of days with Gulabo Pathan in Daryaganj. His master would take care of the consequences. He was both wise and powerful. No one could touch him. Of that he was certain.

twenty

Tim Robertson cursed himself for not having pinned down Pappu Yadav in their earlier meeting. He should have used his guile and succeeded in getting a long and detailed interview out of him. Taking out his camera had been a bad move. Something like this would never have happened with him in England. It was like getting an interview with Jack the Ripper and then having no questions to ask him.

He explained away his bungling to the newness of the place and the fact that he did not know the language. Everything had happened so quickly. He had barely had time to unpack his suitcase when he was sent out in the boondocks in search of a story.

'We have to track that Pappu Yadav fellow again,' Tim informed Harpreet Singh, the taxi driver who was now playing several assorted roles for him, including translator, his Man Friday in general.

'Must be hiding in some forest place near Shamli,' said Harpreet in his broken English.

'I didn't see too many forests around there.'

'His family members will know where he is hiding,' Harpreet interjected.

'Yes indeed. His old mother should know. I suppose we will have to go back to his village once again,' said Tim.

The idea of returning to the heat and dust, the poverty and backwardness of Indian village life was hardly appealing. But within minutes, Harpreet had brought the taxi to the front porch of the hotel. Clambering into the back seat, Tim parked his laptop carefully by his side.

'Your car is much too big to serve as a taxi,' Tim remarked slipping a white golf cap over his head. He was not going to take any chances with the heat this time around.

'Money guzzler! Petrol guzzler,' said Harpreet. 'I need to sell this and buy a smaller car. When my father bought it, he thought the foreigners would enjoy sitting in a bigger car. I find they are much happier sitting in an Ambassador.'

In less than three hours they were winding their way down the narrow track that led up to Shamli. Getting down from the car, the duo made their way directly to Pappu Yadav's hut. Harpreet led the way. Tim followed, wiping the sweat from his brow after every few steps.

Pushing open the gate, Harpreet stepped gingerly inside. A gasp escaped his mouth as he saw Bhuja lying on the charpai with her eyes closed. He felt her pulse.

'Man, she's not breathing. She's dead,' he exclaimed with a shudder.

'How long do you think she's been dead?'

'I can't say. Her body has become cold. We better go and inform that fat old Chowdhury fellow otherwise the maggots will get to her,' said Harpreet stepping backwards and walking out of the gate.

'Where d'you think Pappu Yadav would be?' Tim asked worried his story might not fructify.

'We'll find him,' Harpreet said with bravado.

The two retraced their steps to the primary school from where they made their way to Chowdhury Ram Lal's house. Tim was not surprised to find Ram Lal lolling on a charpai with Balram Prakash by his side. Indian villagers seemed to have all the time in the world to loll around while their wives slaved for them.

'Sir, we did not expect you to return here so soon. It has been scarcely three days since Leelawati departed,' countered Balram Prakash with a look of surprise.

'We are coming from Pappu Yadav's hut – '

'There is no one there except his old mother,' interjected Ram Lal.

'She's dead.'

Prakash looked grave. Emptying a packet of paan masala into his mouth he said, 'Are you sure?'

'I felt her pulse. She's been dead for some time now,' Harpreet said.

'Who will cremate her now? There is no one in the village who will be willing to buy wood for her funeral pyre,' said the Chowdhury.

'You arc the panchayat leader. Surely you must be having funds at your disposal?' Tim countered.

'These are all figurehead titles. The funds never reach us,' Ram Lal countered back.

Harpreet decided there was no point in beating about the bush. 'Do you have any idea where Pappu Yadav might be?' he asked.

Ram Lal had still to get over Leelawati's whirlwind tour. Her warning against the Yadav community rang in his ears and he was determined to steer clear of all controversy. 'All this media publicity has forced him to go underground. I will ask my wife to get you some tea.'

Tim shook his head. 'No tea for me please. We have come in search of Pappu Yadav.'

Prakash scratched his head and spat out some red muck. 'Bhuja's brother lives in Hardwar. He runs a general merchant shop. He is known to have helped Pappu many times in the past.'

'Would you know the address?'

'It's in a colony called Ram Nagar. If I remember correctly it's House No. 17. Somewhere near Kankhal.'

'Are there any other relatives who Pappu could have sought shelter with?'

Prakash shrugged. 'Pappu is moving with a group of three men. They must all have relatives living around here. The gang could be hiding in any one of their homes. But my gut feeling is he's gone off to Hardwar. Otherwise we would have received some intimation or the other.'

Tim shrugged and wiped his sweat. 'I suppose I have to take a chance.' Turning to Harpreet he asked, 'What do you say?'

'Its past four p.m. We can easily reach Hardwar in less than two hours.'

Prakash got up from the charpai with a false show of concern. 'We will not allow you to go without sharing in our famed hospitality. You must partake in some refreshments and have some sweets.'

'Another time.'

'Hardwar is considered one of our most religious cities. It is an ancient town.'

Tim did not want to hear another historical account. 'Yes. I have read about it.'

'I will escort you to your car?'

'There is no need,' said Tim taking his leave and walking briskly towards the cab. Harpreet followed close at his heel.

'I hope my gamble will pay off?' Tim asked Harpreet.

'Sir, a lot of criminals disguise themselves as sadhus and end up in Hardwar. You will definitely find them there.' Harpreet gave him an intent look from the rear-view mirror.

Tim nodded, wondering how on earth they could recognize Pappu Yadav if he had decided to disguise himself.

He must have dozed off. When he opened his eyes, he found Harpreet driving through an ill lit street with crumbling, shadowy houses lining both sides.

'Why are the cities in India enveloped by darkness? You are blessed with such strong sunlight. During the daytime your cities appear robust and vibrant; at night they become dark and uneventful.'

Harpreet was busy looking at the numberings scribbled outside every house.

'We have almost reached,' he said.

'I hope my gamble pays off,' Tim mused again, wondering what approach to use to persuade Pappu to talk.

'Give them some money,' said Harpreet reading his mind.

'Yes, that is exactly what I am planning to do.'

Harpreet had to criss-cross several streets before he could find the house. All four men were sitting in a huddle playing cards under the light of a dim bulb. Tim opened the gate and strode inside.

'It's the same Englishman,' said Kishan, picking up his axe. The other men picked up their lathis. Pappu glowered in consternation.

'Put your weapons down!' shouted Harpreet rushing ahead of Tim. 'You already have the UP police after you. Do you now want the British police to come and arrest all of you? He has just come here to chat with all of you and will be paying you good money for your efforts.'

Tim took out a wad of one hundred rupee notes and handed it to Pappu Yadav. 'You'll require this in the coming months.'

Kishan looked at the money and grimaced.

Calling Pappu to one side he muttered, 'Don't touch it! It's a trap! He must be in league with the government.'

Pappu Yadav refused to heed him. They had run out of money and his uncle's wife, Vishnu, had hinted that she was not in a position to feed four sturdy fellows day in and day out. It was best they made alternate arrangements.

The faces of Ramesh and Satvir lit up when they saw the cash. Money was required to tide them over this crisis. 'Jai Kali ki!' Ramesh muttered.

Pappu found the money difficult to resist. Snatching the wad from Tim's hands, he stuffed it into his kurta pocket. 'With so much money in my pocket, I would be willing to recite the whole *Ramayana* for you.'

Tim grinned. 'I would love to listen to your recitation. How long do you expect to stay here?'

'A couple of days. This hue and cry is bound to die down soon. We then plan to return to Shamli.'

The other men listened intently to his replies. They were not comfortable with having a journalist in their midst. Experience had taught them journalists meant trouble. If it had not been for them, they would never have led to leave Shamli.

'Why is so much noise being created about this incident?' Tim asked.

Pappu glowered. He hated discussing the killing. 'You heard what our leader Amir Singh Yadav said the other day. The present chief minister is a Dalit. She wants to win the loyalties of the OBC and other backwards. She is behind all this drama baazi.'

'We Yadavs have a long history. Do you know that Lord Krishna was also a Yadav? He succeeded in destroying all his political enemies. Amir Singh is as astute as Krishna. He will destroy this Leelawati woman. She is fighting back because she wants to destroy our newly acquired political strength. The killing is being used as a pretext to fight their political battle.'

'You cannot underestimate Leelawati's strength. She has the whole government machinery behind her. Amir Singh Yadav, on the other hand, seems to enjoy little popular support,' Tim commented.

'Do not underestimate our leaders. They are very strong,' Pappu retorted.

Kishan lit a beedi. 'We are being used as political pawns in a much larger battle. Just yesterday, three Jatav girls were killed in Hardwar and their bodies were thrown in the Ganga. No one has made a noise about their killing. The local DM has not even bothered to find out why they were killed. Look at our fate. Our faces are staring up from newspapers all over the world.'

The beedi was passed around to his colleagues. 'We are all farmers. Our fathers and forefathers before us were also farmers. My family has lived in Shamli for eight generations. Now these Dalits want to destroy us and take over our lands,' Kishan added.

'Do you ever regret killing Paro?' Tim asked sharply.

Pappu's eyes turned blood red on hearing her name. 'Never. We are allowed to marry only within our caste.'

'Why are you bringing up this debate once again?' Kishan asked.

Tim did not reply. He took out his camera. 'A couple of photographs,' he said.

'No photographs!' Pappu screamed.

'Let him pay us some more money for them,' said Kishan.

'That's scandalous. I just wanted to take some shots of you playing cards,' Tim muttered and offered them another thousand rupees.

The men grinned and returned to their game. 'If we could earn this kind of money every day, I wouldn't mind giving interviews for the rest of my life,' laughed Satvir.

'What game are you playing?' Tim asked as he clicked the pictures.

'Teen paati! Who told you we were hiding in Hardwar? My mother?' Pappu asked.

'Bhuja is dead,' said Harpreet solemnly.

Pappu shrugged. Picking up the cards, he dealt a round to his friends. 'She'd been sick for some time. It's good her sufferings have ended.'

Harpreet Singh gave Pappu a disgusted look. This man obviously had no feelings even for his mother.

Tim took a couple of photographs, shook hands with the group and walked back to the car.

Driving out of the city proved much easier. Being late, there was less traffic on the road. As they got on to the main highway, Harpreet turned around to him and asked, 'Your owners must be very rich people. They do not seem to mind your spending 30-40,000 bucks on every story.'

Tim chuckled. 'Yes, they are quite rich.'

'Why don't you give me a job in your office. I will do all the work.'

'Then who will run your father's taxi?'

'Driving a taxi is no longer a paying job. There is too much competition. I consider myself lucky if I manage to get two-three customers in a day. If you can help me find some work in your organization, I will be able to earn a steady income.'

Tim grinned at the idea of this energetic Sardar joining his paper. He was an ambitious young fellow. It was obvious he would go places.

twenty one

Prime Minister Ananda Krishnan looked at *The London Times* with a growing sense of horror. The paper had published a series of photographs of the Yadav gang playing a game of cards in the city of Hardwar. One could think they had gone there to enjoy a vacation. The pilgrims who visited Hardwar went there to listen to religious discourses and attend meditation classes. The meditation of these pilgrims consisted of card games.

A revolution had taken place in this country and no one in his government had taken cognizance of it. The Americans liked to believe they were a free society. The Indians, he told himself, enjoyed more freedom than even the Americans. Everyone here did pretty much as he or she pleased. And everyone could do so by constantly passing the buck to the government.

It was the government that was expected to provide free education, free medical care, free drinking water, free electricity ... he raised his hands in exasperation. Tomorrow they would all want free food and free clothes. The list was endless. One billion people lolled around under these polluted skies doing precious nothing. Not once had they tried to seize the initiative in any substantive manner except to obfuscate and obstruct, and then they accused him of running a malfunctioning government. The public could have cleaned up the rivers, built roads, monitored health centres or at least ensured their schools ran properly. But no! All they could do was criticize and backbite! When a leader finally showed up at these miserable, poorly run places, all he was left to do was face their back-bending sycophancy.

The result of this inaction was there before everybody's eyes. Trapped in the ever-increasing spiral of poverty, the villagers had been divested of their traditional skills. The poor farmers needed help but these bloodsucking urbanites ensured no funds reached out to them.

He swore angrily as he looked again at the photograph published in *The London Times*. Their correspondent could not have found a more disreputable and dirty group to click. Filthy kurtas! Torn tehmats! An average foreigner would see this picture and never want to set foot in this country.

As an Indian, he felt ashamed that a foreign newspaper should have swooped down on these cattle thieves and then played up this story in such a sensational manner. It raised a question mark about the Indian media. Why were they always allowing foreigners to seize the initiative? *The Indian Sentinel* had been playing up the story with a vengeance. Then just as suddenly, it had fallen silent. Some of the regional newspapers continued making a few rearguard noises. No one took them seriously anyway. This was a nation of Duryodhanas. Everyone was having a siesta. No wonder these four cattle thieves had now begun to enjoy a cult status.

He decided this was not a matter to be discussed over the phone with home minister L.K. Puri. He would get him over to the office and give him an official dressing down.

An hour later, Puri was sitting across his large ebony table looking sprightly and dashing in his blue safari suit with a white rose adorning the lapel of his coat. Ananda Krishnan felt old and washed out in his white khadi shirt and dhoti.

This will not do at all. He's smartened up on the job; he cannot be allowed to outshine me, he told himself

Silently, he pushed the paper across the table. It was obvious he expected a studied reply. Puri rolled his eyes in an exaggerated manner. 'I had given DGP Rameshwar Prasad clear orders to have the gang arrested at the earliest.'

'Not only have they not been arrested, the paper highlights how no FIR has been lodged against them either,' said the prime minister in his slow, deliberate manner.

'This is terrible. I will have a word with Prasad right away. If required, I will travel down to Hardwar and ensure they get arrested.'

'The home minister travels down to ensure the arrest of some caste killers. I'm surprised you did not suggest that I should accompany you.'

Puri held his breath. The prime minister seemed livid with rage.

'We are creating a bunch of Veerappans in the north. We already have one monster performing a tandava in the south. Before entering the forests, all our para-military forces issue statements swearing they will arrest – Veerappan in no time at all. The minute they actually enter the forests, they begin singing another tune. I can understand the problems faced by the Karnataka and Tamil Nadu police – Veerappan is well armed. He knows his way around. But what excuse does the UP police force have for failing to file an FIR against this lot? This is ridiculous.'

Puri nodded in agreement. He understood the prime minister's compulsions. Both Leelawati and Amir Singh Yadav had jumped into the fray and were determined to make mincemeat of the prime minister. Both of them harboured prime ministerial ambitions. Krishnan's razor-thin majority in parliament required the support of one of these groups. Leelawati had sixteen MPs, Amir had thirteen MPs. The prime minister's position was precarious.

Puri did some quick thinking. Pappu Yadav belonged to the Yadav community. If something happened to him, Amir would create a ruckus. If on the other hand, something were to happen to his colleagues, Leelawati would use it as an excuse to launch a blitzkrieg against this government. At this juncture, the best policy was one of studied inaction.

'I think we should adopt a discreet approach and not rush into taking any untoward action,' Puri suggested.

Ananda Krishnan would have none of this cloak-and-dagger approach. 'Criminals are criminals. Anyone who breaks the law must be dealt with firmly.'

Puri tried not to look surprised. The prime minister seemed hellbent on committing political suicide. Trying to caution him he said, 'I agree. But we have reached a stage where no law enforcing agency can take action against any one powerful group because they invariably enjoy the support of a rival political formation.'

Krishnan was preoccupied with other thoughts. Getting up from his chair, the prime minister strode out of the room. Puri walked two steps behind him. Pointing to a clutch of newspapers lying on a side table, Puri said, '*The Indian Sentinel*'s editorial today says that battles in the future will be waged between the rich and the poor. The rich castes will gang up with the rich capitalists, the lower castes will turn to Naxalites and other fringe elements for support.'

Krishnan had not heard him. He looked at his watch. 'I have a meeting with the President at Rashtrapati Bhawan. I cannot afford to be late for it.'

Puri watched Krishnan make his way down the North Block corridor surrounded by a posse of security staff. His own NSG team followed him at a slight distance. Puri went over his earlier conversation with Police Commissioner Tandon. Tandon, a close confidant had verbatim repeated all that IGP Rameshwar Prasad had told him. Prasad was not the kind of man to disobey orders.

He must have issued orders to the local SSP Kataria to have those cattle thieves arrested in Shamli. Obviously that Kataria fellow must have disregarded the orders under some pretext or the other.

Kataria was known to be in touch with some RSS leaders. Presumptuous fellow! He must be shown his place. Long experience in the bureaucracy had taught him that a transfer to Bihar or the North-East ensured immediate compliance from even the most recalcitrant bureaucrat.

twenty two

SSP Kamal Seth of the Maharashtra cadre had built up a reputation as a tough cop adept at tracking down the most hardened criminal. Newcomers in the service who saw his stout body for the first time found it difficult to believe that this short, bullish man could slice down a criminal within seconds of his arrest.

An ace shot, he was known to have gunned down twelve militants during an earlier eighteen-month tenure in Mumbai. Most police officers avoided taking such extreme steps. Gunning down terrorists more often than not turned out to be a minefield with some officers spending their remaining service years bogged down in legal proceedings. Several NGOs and surviving family members of the deceased would needlessly drag the cop to court. It made much better sense to have gangsters gun down other gangsters; the majority of militants were nothing but hardened criminals saddled with ideological baggage.

Fortunately, Seth had managed, with a little tightrope walking, to steer clear of such controversies. He had his own justification for resorting to such extreme measures. 'You got to make these guys sing, and once they do, you got to make them croak,' he used tell his friends.

DIG Rameshwar Prasad from the UP cadre did not approve of such corrective action; the publicity surrounding the antics of trigger-happy officers invariably botched up the reputation of the police force. He had gone public with his disapproval. Some years ago, Seth had sought a posting at Lucknow. Prasad had had it shot down and the government had offered him a two-year tenure in Bihar instead. Seth did not have the stomach to face a posting in Bihar.

Seth had run into Ananda Krishnan when he had gone to attend a conference in Bangalore. Krishnan was then a newly elected member of parliament. Seth had made it a point to remain in touch with him and once he became prime minister, he had made a special trip to Delhi to personally congratulate both him and L.K. Puri.

Puri had assured him he would keep him in mind for any special assignments. His face must have remained stamped in their collective unconscious because he was the first officer they thought of to help them resolve the Shamli conundrum. Prasad's objections, if there were any, must have been overruled. The Home Ministry's advice to him was that he proceed directly to Muzzaffarnagar where he would receive all assistance.

Seth did as he was ordered. Packing his clothes into a small suitcase, he proceeded to catch the next Indian Airlines flight to Delhi from where he drove across to Muzzaffarnagar.

'What's happened to the bunch of nincompoops already there? Getting an officer over from Mumbai is stretching things a bit too far,' he told himself as he steered his Matador through the heavy traffic that criss-crossed the Dehradun-Delhi national highway. Such thoughts are not worthy of an IPS officer, he told himself. Being given a high profile assignment had many plus points. The home minister had specially singled him out to track down these murderers. This would send out a positive signal in his favour amongst both his colleagues and his senior officers. It would go a long way in silencing his critics, especially since a former IG of Police had castigated him over his aggressive tactics by making an adverse notation in his personal file.

Once inside the police headquarters in Muzzaffarnagar, Seth did not waste time. He got his adjutant to unroll a large map of Uttar Pradesh. Staring into the map, he noticed the huge Rajaji sanctuary that extended from Hardwar right up to the Himalayan foothills in Rishikesh. The forests surrounding Rishikesh were criss-crossed by rivulets and streams and were known to provide a refuge for criminal gangs on the run from the police. Since the newspaper reports on their hiding in Hardwar were only two days old, the chances were these Shamli killers had chosen to relocate themselves by hiding in these forests.

The adjutant stared at him with admiration. Seth, with his bull-like features, could easily pass off as someone who came from Madhya Pradesh, an area to which he himself belonged. Picking up the walkie-talkie, Seth spoke cryptically to SHO Jagdamba Rawat stationed at Hardwar.

'I want all the exit points of Rishikesh and Hardwar checked. These people could be taking refuge in the Rajaji Sanctuary. Or else, they may have moved north of Rishikesh where the dense teak forests are known to provide a sanctuary for thieves. Tracking and identifying them should not prove difficult. Their faces have been flashed in all the newspapers.'

'Sir, I'll alert all the chowkies and local thanas to keep a look out for this group,' Rawat assured him.

An unconvinced Seth slammed the walkie-talkie down and gave his adjutant a derisive look . These guys from Madhya Pradesh were all such sycophants, he thought in disgust.

'Pappu Yadav and Co were sitting around in their village for several days after that killing. Why weren't they arrested?' Seth asked the adjutant.

'Sir, you'll have to ask my predecessor this question. I just arrived here two days ago,' the adjutant replied by way of explanation.

Whose political support does this man enjoy, wondered Seth, giving him a sharp look. Then in a more ameliorative tone he said, 'That's all for now. I'll discuss the course of action with you later in the evening.'

The adjutant gave a surly salute and walked out.

Seth was in favour of a clean, surgical strike. Once that was over, he could move back to Mumbai. His wife and two sons would not be able to survive in this city, notorious for homosexuals and sugarcane growers, for more than one day. If this operation went off smoothly, he would put in a request for a posting to Washington or London.

Like most of his colleagues, Seth loved publicity. As a junior commissioned officer, it had not taken him long to realize that some deft media management went a long way in assuring quick promotions and key postings. During the last decade he had assiduously cultivated the press by providing easy access to crime reporters linked to all the major newspapers. Some key tips on criminal activities in the districts in which he was posted ensured that journalists kept coming back to him. They lapped up whatever information he gave them and kept returning to his fold for more. Most of the time he insisted these tip-offs were strictly off the record though in a few well publicized crackdowns, he was willing to go on record. In return, they kept him informed about all the latest political developments and also, what was happening in other government departments.

This case had already received so much publicity. It would suit him professionally if he ensured a large number of senior correspondents were present at the time of the arrest.

Since his journalistic contacts included several high profile editors in Delhi, he decided to personally get in touch with each one of them. They could make arrangements for the correspondents to reach Muzzaffarnagar after which he would arrange to have them transported to Rishikesh in police vehicles.

He was confident the publicity would propel him into acquiring a national celebrity status. Several police officers had used these tactics in the past – Kiran Bedi being the prime example.

The SHO Jagdamba Rawat stationed at Hardwar realized Seth meant business. He immediately sent two armed constables to Pappu Yadav's house. His uncle was not there but his wife, Vishnu, a tough, no-nonsense woman, opened the door for the police team.

'They're not here. They left the day the report was published in *Amar Ujala* and *Dainik Jagran,'* fifty-year old Vishnu informed them, standing at the front door, arms akimbo.

The two senior constables stared at her in disbelief.

'If you don't believe me, you can search my house.'

'Do you have any idea where they have gone?' one of them asked.

Vishnu shrugged, 'I can't say. One of them, Raman I think, is a devotee of Kali Ma. He wanted to go and get a special arati done at Mata ka Mandir located on the outskirts of Rishikesh.'

'Mata ka Mandir?'

Vishnu looked aggrieved. 'Why are you asking me? I've never stepped out of Hardwar in my life. I've been born and brought up here.'

The policemen eyed her with curiosity. 'Never been up to Laxman Jhula?' the older of the two asked.

'I'm saving all that for my next life. In my next birth I will not be stuck to a grocer who refuses to shut his shop for a single day.'

The two policemen reported their information to SHO Rawat who had spent his childhood in Tehri Garhwal. Pandit Joshi from his village had sometimes spoken about a Mata ka Mandir outside Rishikesh built two hundred years ago by one of the Maharajas of Tehri.

Picking up the phone he asked the operator to connect him to Pandit Joshi's house in Rudraprayag where he was presently living.

A few minutes later the phone bell rang. Picking up the receiver he said, 'Pranam, Joshiji!'

A long silence followed. Finally when Pandit Joshi was able to place him, he mumbled, 'Rawat beta, what can I do for you?'

'Do you know of a Kali Ma temple near Rishikesh?'

His question was once again followed by a long silence. Then once again he heard the old man mutter, 'The temple is located at Panchavati village which is 20 kilometres north of Rishikesh.'

'Do they have a motorable road to go there?'

The old man was taken aback by the question. 'I went there twenty years ago. At that time there was no road and I walked all the way from from Rishikesh to Panchavati. Maybe today there is a motorable road. You will have to go there and find out.'

Slamming the phone down, Rawat got the operator to connect him to the Muzzaffarnagar police exchange. He passed on the information he had gathered to SSP Seth.

'Should I proceed and have them arrested?' Rawat asked.

'I don't want any of you to move till you receive orders from me,' Seth directed.

Rawat's jaw dropped. 'But sir, I am just 25 miles away from that spot. I will arrest them and bring them with me to Muzzaffarnagar.'

'SHO Rawat, you will wait for me to arrive before taking any action. I have to get a clearance of this whole operation from DGP Prasad. That is an order.' Seth hung up.

Stunned, Rawat put down the phone with slow deliberation. It was obvious that Seth wanted to take the credit for the arrest before his superiors.

There was little he could do except wait for Seth to swing into action. This meant, he along with his entire team at Rishikesh were going to be bypassed completely.

**

And that was precisely what Seth was planning to do. He walked across to his residential quarters located in the sprawling police cantonment bordered with gulmohar, mango and eucalyptus trees. He spent the evening contacting his media friends in Delhi. A city police contact was used to phone the local Hindi and Urdu journalists working out of Muzzaffarnagar and Roorkee. They were informed that a police contingent was leaving early next morning to capture the dreaded Pappu Yadav gang. Those who wanted to cover the event must reach the police headquarters by six o'clock in the morning. The police would make arrangements to cart this entire jamboree of journalists in their own vehicles and return them to base camp by the afternoon after which they could proceed to file their reports.

To make doubly sure that the gang had arrived at Panchavati village, a local CID constable in plain clothes was deputed to make a quiet recce later that evening. He returned to Rishikesh late in the night and confirmed that four strangers, whose descriptions matched the Yadav gang's, were seen walking about in the village precincts.

Inder sahib was one of the first journalists to be contacted by Seth. He was sitting in the office going through the morning newspapers when the phone rang. Dalip sat across him engrossed in a computer game. Dejection was written across his face. He had still to recover from the humiliation Aruna and he had suffered, forced to spend several gruelling hours in a thana. In fact, the incident had proved such a blow to him that he had tendered in his resignation.

Inder sahib, who had visited his house the morning after his arrest, had torn the resignation letter and thrown it in the waste-paper basket.

'Are you out of your mind, giving up your job because of some family fracas? Learn to take adverse situations in your stride,' Inder sahib had ordered.

Feeling too broken in spirit to contradict him, Dalip did as he was told. No one in the office spoke about the arrest but an ominous undercurrent of tension seemed to follow him each time he entered the room. On seeing him, his colleagues would nod their heads in greeting and then, simply turn their faces away. Kiki refused to come anywhere near him and spent all her time in the corridor smoking cigarettes with her new-found confidant, Apu Antony. She was the new balm in his life. It was obvious Apu had recovered from his earlier wounds at losing out with Simi.

Looking at Dalip's gloomy face, Inder sahib thundered, 'You will have to go to Muzzaffarnagar tomorrow morning. The final countdown on the Shamli killing seems to have begun.'

'I'm not going anywhere.'

'You better snap out of it. Take your arrest on your chin and move on.'

'To be branded a criminal! To almost be forced to spend a night in a jail! I will never be able to get over this humiliation.' There were tears in Dalip's eyes. There was no one else in the office so they could speak freely.

Inder sahib patted him on his shoulder. 'It's part of the growing up process. We have all had to carry our crosses. When I first arrived from Ludhiana, I spent my first two weeks sleeping under Minto bridge before landing a job as a waiter in Embassy restaurant.'

'It's not the same as being arrested!'

'Hell hath no fury as a woman scorned! Simi has over-reacted but I have spoken to her parents and they are willing to withdraw the case against you.'

'I will have to carry this stigma for the rest of my life.' Dalip swore angrily. He would find a way to hit back at that woman. He also knew how to be vengeful. Those who committed injustices against him and his family would be dealt with in a similar manner.

Inder sahib must have read his mind. 'Don't allow your mind to get swallowed in all kinds of negativities! We all know the kind of person you are and what you have stood for all your life. I have spoken about you to Adhikari. He was extremely sympathetic. If the owner is willing to extend support to you, then you have no cause for worry. Now go home and start getting ready for tomorrow's story. We want a long and detailed report from you."

Dalip could see Inder sahib was in no mood to tolerate any dissent.

Seth had also contacted the *Sentinel* office. Since Ajit Jolly was not in town, the duty clerk for the evening duty had scribbled the message on a piece of paper and thrown it on Jolly's table.

Raveena Bedi, with her sharp eyes, read the message. Never one to miss an opportunity, she rushed to Rajan's cabin with the torn piece of paper. The message spoke about some police action from Muzzaffarnagar. It was obvious that those police fellows were not aware that Ajit Jolly was parked right under their noses. Considering that he had not filed a single story so far, she figured they were not to blame for this lapse.

She entered Rajan's office flashing her most obsequious smile. 'Rajan, I have some very exciting news to give you.'

A visibly off-colour Rajan did not bother to acknowledge her presence. Her dalliance with Kala Muthu had ensured she was no longer in his good books.

'The police are taking a press party to Rishikesh. They are trying to catch hold of those Shamli murderers.'

Rajan looked uninterested. 'We already have a person stationed in Muzzaffarnagar. Why should we send somebody else there?'

Raveena was not the kind of person to be deflected by an adverse reaction. 'Jolly has not filed a single story from there so far,' she said with a smile.

'Nothing much happened, probably.'

'*The Indian Sentinel* broke this story. We have has been going hammer and tongs about the need to curb caste killings and now when the curtains are coming down on this drama, we are not going to be anywhere in the picture? If you refuse to send me, you'll have Vikram Aggarwal coming down on you like a ton of bricks.'

Rajan squirmed uncomfortably in his seat. This fat chick had the guts to talk to a brand manager in this contemptuous manner.

'I'm quite preoccupied at the moment. The MD wants the organization to have a leaner, tighter look. I am in the process of trying to get rid of some dead wood. I'll get back to you in a day or two.'

'A press contingent is leaving for Muzzaffarnagar at four a.m. tomorrow morning. We don't have very much time. If you have a problem thinking this through, I'll go and speak to Vikramji directly,' Raveena said. The smile did not leave her face for a minute.

Rajan hated being forced into a corner. How on earth was he going to deflect this fat buffalo? If she had her way, she would ram her way into 7 Racecourse Road.

'Since you have set your heart and mind on going, I suppose no one can stop you.'

Raveena gave her most obsequious smile. 'I'm not dying to go. I'm here like everyone else trying to perform my duty.'

'It would be best if you went there using some mode of public transport. You could go there using a state transport bus or else you could go by train. I expect you would want to go there alone. The office will not accept your going there with any other individual associated with this organization,' said Rajan.

He was not going to give in so easily.

Raveena flinched. She knew he was referring to Kala Muthu. It was common knowledge that he was no longer part of the *Sentinel.*

But Rajan had not vetoed her going to Shamli.

Without uttering a word, she stalked out of the room and climbed down five flights of steps to reach the accountant's office on the ground floor. Determined to withdraw a hefty tour allowance, she would see how he dared not sanction her advance.

'All tour advances are being cleared by Mr Rajan,' the accountant informed her.

'Take it up to him,' she replied sitting down comfortably on a chair. The accountant returned a short while later. The slip was duly signed by Mr Rajan.

The PIB boss Nagendra personally contacted Tim Robertson to inform him about the police operation.

'Why does the police want journalists present during this encounter? Wouldn't it be easier to carry out these arrests without us?' Tim asked.

'The Himalayas are full of dreaded militants. The police obviously do not want to take a chance,' Nagendra replied.

'How would the presence of journalists act as a deterrent for the militants?' Tim asked in surprise.

'The press is being taken because the government wants to show how determined they are to keep all kinds of crime under control. Of course, the danger of militants has increased in the Terai following the rise of Maoistic violence in Nepal,' Nagendra added.

From the way Nagendra was invoking the dreaded word 'militant', he was hoping it would work as a mantra to decimate critics who believed there were alternate ways in which these arrests could have been handled.

Tim saw little point in arguing with the PIB boss. He had not spent enough time in India to know the extent and penetration of militancy in Uttar Pradesh.

He decided it was time to reverse the situation and fling a few accusations at Nagendra. 'During our first meeting, you had levelled all kinds of charges against foreign journalists. We were all branded under the same brush. I believe not all of us end up writing esoteric nonsense about your great nation?'

'Oh no! Your stories have been quite grounded in local reality,' Nagendra conceded.

'Are you also joining the press party tomorrow morning?'

'I haven't made up my mind. There is a lot of coordination work for me to do in Delhi. With Parliament in session, it is not possible for me to leave at such a short notice,' the PIB chief informed him.

Tim slammed the phone down. It was obvious the PIB chief did not want to be present in a hot spot.

Ajay Singh was another journalist to be contacted by Kamal Seth. Since the structural organization of their television wing was still to fall in place, Ajay felt it would be premature to cover this story at this stage.

'We haven't even started doing live telecasts. Most of our staffers have no experience in doing hard reporting. I think we should wait,' he told his boss, Jayant Shah.

Shah in his usual blustery style overruled his objections. 'We'll treat this as a soft launch. My hunch is that this is going to be a big story. We cannot afford to miss it. It will help us establish our presence on the national arena.'

SSP Kamal Seth was delighted to learn that sixteen English-speaking and twenty-five Hindi and Urdu journalists were willing to join his contingent. The presence of two television teams would provide an additional boost.

He sent for the adjutant. 'Make sure all the police constables coming with us are well armed. I want them to send out a positive signal on television.'

The adjutant hid his surprise. 'Armed? I don't think those cattle thieves will be carrying weapons.'

'I have just received intelligence reports that the whole area is teeming with militants. We need to be careful,' Seth said.

'I'll pass the orders,' he said.

The morning was dusty and hot. A storm was brewing. SSP Seth sat in the front verandah and glanced through the morning newspapers. His eyes kept straying towards the front gate. The journalists were trickling in slowly. He was afraid, many of those who had promised to come would not show up. A line of white Matador jeeps stood outside his front porch. These would be used to take the journalists to Rishikesh and then on to Panchavati. Six other jeeps carrying armed policemen were parked outside the main office complex awaiting the green signal in order to get cracking on the job.

Tim Robertson's white Contessa was one of the first to reach the police post. Seth hurried down the steps to welcome him.

'You must be working for BBC? Welcome to Muzzaffarnagar.'

'No. I'm with *The London Times.'*

'I stand corrected. Is this your first visit here?'

'Actually, no. I've been here twice in the last ten days.'

'Welcome anyway,' said Seth. Seeing that Robertson was wearing his dark glasses, he also slipped on his Ray Bans.

Pramod Tripathi had reached the police lines in a cycle rickshaw. Overhearing the conversation between the SSP and Tim Robertson, he gave Seth a disgusted look. 'Saala chamcha!' he muttered and walked across to chat with Ajay Singh and his crew who had just driven in.

Finding little likelihood of their providing work for him, Tripathi decided to try his luck with Tim Robertson. Tim was sitting in the Contessa jotting down a few notes on his laptop. Pramod concluded this was an excellent opportunity to try and extract some money from this firangi.

By way of introduction, Pramod told Tim, 'I'm the journalist who tipped off Dalip Jha of *The Morning Chronicle* about this caste killing. It was only later that the other papers picked up this story. If you need any background information, I would be happy to assist. I'm presently working with the *Amar Jagaran* newspaper. I am an expert on caste politics in rural India. It is another matter that by an accident of birth, I am a Brahmin and belong to the ruling elite.'

Tim gave him a quick appraisal. No Brahmin ever made any attempt to hide his ancestry. 'I think you have made an excellent suggestion. So far, my driver, Hardeep Singh has been helping me with the translation work. I would appreciate your help.'

'Can I travel in the same taxi as you?' Tripathi asked.

'Sure.'

'How much will you pay me as my translation fee? I won't settle for anything less than two thousand rupees.'

'We'll work that out.'

Hardeep Singh heard this conversation with discomfiture. He did not like the idea of usurper trying to occupy his place. Just then Dalip Jha arrived in a white Ambassador. Tripathi had heard about his recent arrest. He turned his face away. He did not want to be seen associating with a man who had been making dowry demands from his wife.

Dalip noticed Pramod Tripathi sitting with Tim. Since he had made no effort to speak to him, he too decided to ignore him. 'Greedy bastard! When he wanted to eat fancy food, he turned to me. Now he has found himself another bakra,' Dalip muttered to himself.

Dalip Jha lit a cigarette and walked up to Ajay Singh. They both belonged to Bihar and had worked for a short spell in *The Patriot* together.

Just then another white Ambassador drove up. Raveena Bedi got down and ran up towards Seth. 'SSP Seth! You bring with you a formidable reputation! You cleaned Mumbai of its dreaded underworld.'

Seth was visibly delighted. 'I only arrived in Muzzaffarnagar yesterday.'

'Your reputation follows you wherever you go. Can I travel in the same jeep as you?'

Seth looked nonplussed. 'Which paper do you represent?'

'The Indian Sentinel.'

'I've been reading that paper from the age of five. I'm addicted to it. You are most welcome to join me.'

The adjutant sitting on the side seat gave her a dirty look. Now he would have to sit on the back seat while Raveena settled in front. Taking out her tape recorder, Raveena said, 'I'm going to interview you while you drive. It's not often that one can get a chance to meet such a dashing police officer.'

Seth gave her a warm smile. This journalist certainly knew the ropes. He jumped into the jeep and indicated to Raveena to join him up in front.

The police constables and journalists standing around hurried into their vehicles. The convoy took off with a roar with Seth leading up in front. Driving at breakneck speed, the Matadors had sped past the Rishikesh bypass and were making their way towards the Panchavati village in less than two hours' time.

The metalled road made way for a small jungle track. On both sides, large sal and teak trees loomed against the horizon. The sound of the cicadas resounded through the forests. Seth, used to the scrubby terrain of Maharashtra, swore under his breath. It would be impossible to track down anyone in these thick jungles. If he failed to make these arrests, he would end up as a laughing stock amongst the media warlords.

**

SSP Seth was not the only person worried about his future.

Pappu Yadav stared at the pot-bellied pujari cleaning the large image of Kali, for conducting the special aarti and cursed under his breath.

From the beginning, he had found Ramesh's suggestion of visiting Panchavati hare-brained. The idea of landing up in a tiny village, visited by few outsiders, did not bode well for them. Strangers here would stick out like sore thumbs.

But Ramesh was an ardent believer. He had convinced Kishan and Satvir that a puja at Kali Ma's temple was the only way out of their present problems. The money received from Tim Robertson had only served to reinforce Ramesh's beliefs.

'The money is a boon! We've received this money for a special purpose,' Ramesh exclaimed after Pappu Yadav had handed him five hundred rupees.

'If you have so much faith, why don't you go there alone and get it over with? We'll wait for you in Rishikesh,' Pappu Yadav had interjected.

Kishan interrupted. 'Why should Ramesh go alone? We will all go together.'

'This is not the time to be getting special pujas done. Let us hop into a train and go to Gorakhpur. From there, we can cross over to Nepal where we can lie low for a couple of months. Once this hue and cry is over, we will return to Shamli and lead a peaceful life,' Pappu interceded.

The other three members of the gang did not agree. Pappu's last interview with the foreign journalist had not gone down well with them. It had brought them back to the limelight and had forced them, once again, to become fugitives from the police. They were weary of running around. At this juncture, to make their way to Nepal seemed an absurdity. All they wanted was that Kali Ma hear their prayers and allow them to make their way back safely to their families in Shamli.

'We have been needlessly roped into a family quarrel,' Kishan had whispered to Ramesh when they'd taken the bus to Rishikesh.

Pappu Yadav must have sensed their feelings. In an effort to mollify them, he gave each of them another five hundred rupees.

Disembarking at the Rishikesh bus stop, they had clambered into a tempo which had brought them to Panchavati village.

The drive through the forests turned out to be a frightening experience. The trees, with their tall shadows, seemed intimidating. Wild creatures were known to roam these parts. What if they were attacked by a tiger or wild boar? No one would know where they had disappeared.

Ramesh had wasted no time in getting hold of the temple priest who had agreed to perform a special puja for them the following morning. Meanwhile, he gave them a long list of items to buy for the puja.

'How will we find all these items in these jungles?' Ramesh wondered, scratching his hair.

They found a local baniya's shop. He provided them some of the items. 'For the rest, you will have to go back to Rishikesh,' he told them.

Some villagers were loitering outside his shop.

'Bhaiya, where have you come from?' one of them asked Kishan.

'We belong to Shamli,' said Kishan.

'That's a long distance from here,' the villager said.

'You're right. It is far. We have come here to get a special puja done.'

'All of you come from the same village?' the villager asked.

'No. We all come from different villages but we are friends,' said Pappu Yadav.

'Where can we have dinner?' Ramesh asked.

'There is a small dhabha right in the middle of the village. You can go there. He gives good dal fry,' the villager said.

After finishing their dinner, the foursome walked back to the temple and settled themselves on the temple verandah where they spent the night. It was a hot night. No one was in the mood to talk. Next morning, the priest arrived two hours behind the agreed time.

He had been called to do a mundan by a local Brahmin family. Opening the sanctum sanctorum, the priest began cleaning the Kali image, when they heard the muted roar of vehicles approaching in their direction.

Pappu nudged Ramesh. 'Something is wrong. Could this be the police?'

Kishan got up and peered towards the road. 'We better get out of here fast. It's the police!'

The four men picked up their lathis and began running in the eastern direction. 'If we can reach the river, we will be safe. The current will take us along,' Satvir shouted.

They ran past the foliage, their bodies brushing past the thick branches brimming with leaves. Pappu kept signalling with his right hand in an attempt to encourage them to run even faster.

'The river's close by. The current will carry us downwards.'

'I can't swim!' Ramesh cried.

'You can hide behind some boulders,' shouted Kishan.

The rumble grew louder.

The convoy came to a halt outside the temple located at the entrance of the village. Several villagers ran and gathered round the convoy. They had never seen such a large police force enter their village.

The frightened priest immediately blurted out, 'Don't blame me, sahib! All are equal before God. I perform special pujas for good and the bad alike.'

'Go after them,' Seth told the armed policemen carrying carbines.

'Why are these fellows carrying so many weapons?' Tim asked Seth.

'These are militant-infested forests. We cannot afford to take any risks. I've instructed them to use only as much force as is required. These guys will be given every opportunity to surrender.'

'There is nothing to worry about! I'm going to lead the operation to make sure that nothing goes amiss,' said Seth.

Raveena Bedi followed him as he hurriedly made his way along a narrow village path. Turning to Tim, she said, 'These fellows are not as innocent as you are making them out to be. They're killers. They killed a couple in cold blood before an entire village.'

Tim's attention was directed at the police constables who were making their way into the jungle. Her remark was heard by the SSP alone.

Seth had never met a journalist who agreed so completely with his own point of view. 'Nobody in the government wanted to deal with these guys. They are an eminently dispensable lot. No one is going to miss them,' he told Raveena.

Seth followed the sharpshooters through the dense vegetation. Stopping to catch his breath, he looked keenly around. The tall grass made visibility difficult. The heat was also beginning to get to him. Raveena, unused to walking, had already started panting heavily.

Dalip Jha and Ajay Singh were also cutting across the tall bushes in an attempt to keep pace with the police constables who had fanned out into the forests.

Hearing the noise and shouts coming from near the village, a group of village boys who had taken their cattle out to graze turned in the direction of the fleeing fugitives.

'Is there a problem there?' one of them shouted. His voice echoed through the valley.

His cry was followed by the cry of the other two boys. None of them was clear about what was happening. But their cries resonated loud and strong through the valley. Seth and the police contingent standing at the other end heard them.

'Be careful, men! They seem to have been joined by other criminals,' Seth shouted.

'Militants!' the adjutant shouted twice.

The constables, eyes alert, walked nervously ahead, fingers placed on their carbines.

Just then an explosion echoed through the forests. Two bullets tore into Ramesh's left thigh and kneecap. He crumpled on the ground, losing grip of his lathi.

'I'm dead! They have finished me!' he moaned.

A few seconds later, two rapid rounds of fire could be heard. One of the bullets riocheted through Ramesh's neck, killing him instantly.

A frightened Kishan and Satvir fell on their stomachs, looking around desperately for a place to hide. The guns crackled again and Kishan felt a bullet go past his ear. Another hit Kishan on the back. He gave a squeal of pain. Staggering forward in a frightened stupor, he struggled to gain hold of a bush.

A second bullet tore through his heart.

Satvir saw the bright red froth trickle through Kishan's back. Paralysed with fear, Satvir looked back to see who the attackers were. He must surrender. They were in no position to put up a fight.

'Help!' he squealed and tried getting to his feet. A bullet went through his forehead. A second entered his femur. Satvir spun backwards and fell to the ground.

Pappu Yadav had moved away from the others, trying desperately to find his way along a less travelled path. Hearing the bullets going off in all directions, a terrified Pappu desperately crawled forward on all fours in an effort to reach the river. Suddenly a 9-mm bullet crashed into him like a pile-driver hurtling him violently off his feet. A second bullet hit him on his side causing him to crumple on the ground. His hands and fingers twitched spasmodically as life ebbed from his body.

The three village boys stopped cold in their tracks. Petrified, they turned on their heels and ran for their lives. A foolhardy constable took a shot at them. Fortunately, none of them were hurt.

'They're firing at those cattle thieves! They're not even armed!' Pramod Tripathi shouted.

Ajay Singh's cameraman zeroed in from behind and rolled the camera on. Tim Robertson took out his Nikon to click a few pictures.

'No pictures,' a constable warned.

'Are you trying to threaten us?' Dalip Jha countered angrily.

'SSP sahib will come and speak to all of you,' the constable countered.

Seth arrived there a few seconds later. There was a victorious expression on his face. He had seen enough dead people in his career. Killing four more villagers was a matter of little concern to him.

'Each of these four men has been shot in the back,' Pramod Tripathi said.

'This is as good as a massacre,' Ajay Singh butted in.

Seth was not going to permit the press to put a spanner in his hour of triumph. The constables had already started picking up the dead bodies and carrying them back to the jeeps. Several villagers from Panchavati could be seen hovering in the distance.

'Of course they put up a fight. I'm sure they were armed,' said the adjutant.

Tripathi pointed towards their lathis. 'I've seen this lot hanging around Shamli. They were too poor to afford weapons.'

'Didn't you hear the screams and shouts of some villagers from across the river? For all you know, they could have been Maoists or terrorists,' Seth insisted.

'Maoists don't come shouting like that. They looked like village boys to us,' argued Ajay Singh.

Seth was not willing to brook any contradiction. 'Don't underestimate the strength and canniness of our average villager. If they knew how to behave themselves, we would have had a much easier country to govern. The heat here is killing. Let us go back to Muzzaffarnagar and have some lunch. That will be followed by a briefing. I will explain all events that have led to this denouement,' Seth said in his easy, comfortable manner.

Turning to the press party he said, 'This entire forest area is part of a restricted zone. There are some major defence installations around here. I do not think the army or senior police officials will be happy to know you have been taking photographs of this locale. I think it would be better if you all hand over your film rolls. Once I get permission from the authorities, I will return them to you once we reach Muzzaffarnagar.'

Ajay Singh heard him out with a feeling of outrage. Who did this man think he was? He had allowed four men to be shot in cold blood and now he did not want evidence of the killings to go public.

None of the other journalists present chose to speak out. The presence of so many armed men intimidated them. Most of them had heard any number of tales of the terror tactics employed by the police against dissenters in states like Kashmir and Punjab. They were not willing to put their lives at risk. Plus, there was always the chance that if they objected to these pressure tactics, the senior police brass would get in touch with their owners.

Some of the photographers removed their film rolls and handed over the blank rolls. Ajay Singh's cameraman, knowledgeable about police tactics, had hidden the film tape under a bulky cotton jacket. He too handed over a blank tape to the adjutant.

Tim Robertson refused to give his film roll to the police.

'I'm afraid I will not oblige you in this manner. I'm here to do a job. If you use any kind of force, my government will take up this matter at the highest level.'

Seth backed off immediately and strode back to his Matador with a menacing expression on his face. 'We will all proceed to Muzzaffarnagar where you will be briefed once again before we make a final dispersal.'

Raveena Bedi continued to gush before Seth. It was obvious to both Ajay and Dalip that she had some other plans up her sleeve.

'National security calls for quick decisions,' she said in a loud voice. 'Those villagers were running in this direction. They must have been in league with these killers and were coming to their rescue.'

'Nobody knows the extent to which militants have affected our body politic. We have borne the brunt of this violence. National security calls for dirty decisions. It's part of the game,' said Seth getting into his jeep. Raveena clambered back by his side.

A stunned convoy returned to the police grounds in Muzzaffarnagar. The journalists wondered what explanation Seth could possibly have to offer for the goings on of the morning.

**

SSP Seth was confident he could carry the press along with him. The journalists were not happy with the killings. He had decided to adopt the approach that an over display of strength was better than underestimation of the enemy's strength. He could not afford to take a chance; the government was in no mood to accept another goof up.

The journalists were all plied with beer and soft drinks. Raveena Bedi had helped herself to a large glass of vodka. Dalip Jha quickly downed two glasses of beer while Pramod Tripathi tossed down three gins and was picking up his fourth glass.

Seth looked around with a satisfied smile. The police briefing room was doubling as a temporary mess. Liveried waiters in white were serving large portions of food to everyone.

Seth walked to one side of the room. In his loud voice he said, 'Friends, I would like to use this opportunity to point out that our mission proved successful. My objective was to catch those murderers alive. Unfortunately, they proved to be far more dangerous than I had anticipated. They have all kinds of underworld connections which I do not think appropriate to rake up at this hour.'

'What kind of links are you talking about?' Pramod Tripathi asked, between digging his teeth into a leg of chicken.

'Friends, I must remind you that there is a blanket of secrecy over this operation. I am not in a position to divulge too many details,' said Seth.

'If that was the case, why did you think it appropriate to bring the press along?' asked Ajay Singh.

Seth gave Ajay a dirty look. 'This search has required a great deal of coordination at many levels. I have arrived here directly from Mumbai. As I just explained a minute ago, I am not in a position to divulge the details. The Terai is a tricky area. During the last few years, these thick jungles have provided a sanctuary for all kinds of disgruntled elements,' he replied.

Ajay looked around. Most of the other journalists were busy finishing their lunch. His voice was hardly heard above the din.

Dalip's mind was groggy with too much beer. The last few days had been tumultuous. His marriage was as good as broken. He was now a pariah in his own office and amongst his colleagues. The killings this morning had left him feeling nauseous.

There was one ray of cheer in this overall dismal scenario. He would soon become a father. His child was taking shape in Simi's womb. He may have been one hack of a journalist, he told himself, but he must try and become a good father. Someone his kid could look up to.

He decided to put his weight behind Ajay Singh. 'Why was no attempt made to arrest those cattle thieves alive?' Dalip Jha asked in his loud, challenging voice.

A sudden silence fell over the room.

'Precisely. Those fellows were given no chance at all. They were murdered in cold blood,' Ajay Singh repeated in his quiet, understated manner.

The cameras were on and Seth knew every word he spoke was going to be recorded. The transcripts would be later played out before his senior officers. He had better try and make this snappy.

'There are some fundamental safety measures which we in the police have learnt from the years of warfare conducted against us in Telangana, Chhattisgarh and other militant prone areas. We cannot afford to make mistakes.'

Raveena Bedi nodded her head in agreement.

'No one doubts what you are saying. But you could have done a much more effective cordoning operation and tried to arrest those guys,' Ajay continued.

'You haven't provided us with a plausible enough explanation. You could have employed some other tactics to try and capture those guys,' Dalip said with a loud burp.

'Are you trying to suggest the police orchestrated everything?' Raveena asked indignantly.

Dalip had been dying to hit back at Raveena for some time now. He spun around and shouted, 'Oh for God's sake! Don't act like his bloody chamchi!' Dalip shouted indignantly.

'Look how he spoke to me!' Raveena screamed.

'Since when have you become the police spokesperson!' Dalip's voice had become even louder.

'Look how this man is talking to me! A petty villain! He and his mother spent a day in the lock up only a few days ago. I know how to hit back at you! I can tell you a couple of hard truths about yourself,' Raveena retorted.

Dalip screamed back. Other journalists jumped into the fray and everyone was shouting at one another. Raveena's shrill voice could be heard the loudest of all. Complete pandemonium prevailed.

Seth was delighted. He had found the opportunity to extricate himself from a tight situation. 'I think you all understand our position very well,' he said and walked out of the room followed by the adjutant.

'Arre, he's forgotten to give us the film rolls,' a drunken Dalip shouted following him into the corridor.

Ajay Singh went after him and stopped him. Putting his hand on Dalip's shoulder, he said, 'He's got nothing but duds. Let's get back to Delhi and file our stories. Come along with me in my car.'

A grateful Dalip was only too happy to accept the offer.

Tim Robertson had chosen not to join the other journalists for the briefing in Muzzaffarnagar. Hardeep Singh drove him directly to the Claridges. He was up till late that night filing his report.

twenty three

Vikram Aggarwal could not believe his luck. The Vision Forever channel had been replaying the story of the four cattle thieves being killed in a police encounter for the last two days. Rajan, as his official informant, had told him that the Vision Forever cameraman had managed to smuggle the tape from under the nose of the police with considerable difficulty.

The channel was yet to have an official launch. This was their soft run. They were not doing too badly for someone in the process of cutting their milk teeth,

Vikram looked at Ajay Singh with a feeling of pride. He carried himself well on television, with his understated, convincing style.

The credit for Ajay's success should come to me, Vikram thought. It was his media conglomerate which had launched so many journalistic careers.

Timid Doordarshan was also telecasting clips of the killings on its prime time news bulletin. No one from the Information and Broadcasting Ministry had made an attempt to stop the telecast. It seemed obvious that Ananda Krishnan's writ no longer ran over the Information and Broadcasting Ministry. Well, if he could not control such a tiny ministry, he had no business trying to run the country.

He must be sure of his support base before he struck. He must remain calm and in control of every situation. The task of toppling the government was made easier since practically all the newspapers and TV channels were voicing outrage over these killings.

Rajan must have read his thoughts for he knocked and entered the room with a wary expression on his face. Vikram looked at the clock. It was eight a.m. and this fellow had already showed up for work.

'You've come in quite early!' Vikram remarked.

'My wife has chosen to go on a holiday for a week. There is no one else in the house,' Rajan replied.

'We are both in the same boat. My wife has gone abroad. She has taken the children with her. Sometimes I feel my relationship with my children has been reduced to signing cheques for them,' said Vikram.

Rajan knew Vikram's fertile brain was working overtime. He stood attentively waiting for a fresh set of directions. His observation proved correct.

'Well, what do you think? The time has come for us to strike.'

Rajan kept a discreet silence.

'Both Leelawati and Amir Singh Yadav must be upset over these killings. Both have been grievously wronged. The Central Government has committed a grave faux pas. Law and order is a state subject. The Centre has no right to intervene. They have created an intolerable situation. We need to contact both parties. They will help us pull the rug from under the feet of this stupid South Indian prime minister,' Vikram's hands were constantly moving as he spoke. Rajan watched him in fascination. It was as though he was trying to make sure all of nature would bend itself to suit his design for an ever-expanding empire.

Rajan refused to take cognizance of his anti-South Indian remark. Proprietors were a whimsical lot. One day, they cursed the Brahmin lobby, the next day they riled against the Dalits and on most occasions, they spat at the Punjabi go-getters, who, they insisted, had no scruples at all.

The long-awaited moment to extract a directorship from Vikram had arrived. But before he made mention of that subject, he needed to get one more rival out of the way.

'Our reporting has been quite good,' Rajan said pointing a finger at Raveena Bedi's byline splashed boldly across the front page.

Vikram frowned. He did not want to be seen concerning himself with petty details. Now that he had been asked a pointed question, he decided to briefly acknowledge her performance.

'The lady being mentioned has spoken on behalf of the company to the senior police official who handled this operation in Rishikesh. His younger brother is working in the Directorate of Enforcement and can help us with Papaji's case.'

Rajan was caught off guard. Raveena Bedi had already spoken to the boss. How did she manage that?

'SSP Seth's brother is working in the directorate?' Rajan asked.

'Yes. He is there in a senior capacity. To return to your question – her reporting is better than that of the other journalist you had sent a couple of days earlier. To my knowledge, he did not file a single story,' said Vikram.

'Jolly sent two small reports. He hardly possesses the calibre to become a chief of bureau. Maybe Raveena Bedi should be promoted to the post. We still do not have an editor for *The Indian Sentinel.*'

Vikram's patience had been stretched to its utmost. How dare an employee, even a favoured one, directly make a suggestion of this kind?

'We don't have an editor for *Amar Prakash* either. Tomorrow you will suggest this girl be shunted there ...' Vikram did not complete the sentence. It was not such a preposterous idea after all. Raveena appeared to be a fast learner. She was also the kind of person who could produce results without being unduly concerned with matters of conscience.

'I'll think about it. Meanwhile, I think you need to establish contact with the appropriate parties in Lucknow.'

'Leelawati will not agree to these suggestions all that easily,' Rajan remarked. Vikram should not be under the illusion this was going to be a cakewalk.

'She will be paid for her cooperation. I have assiduously cultivated politicians so that contacts such as these, will ensure the wheels of governance turn in my favour,' Vikram retorted.

Rajan gave him a sharp look. Behind those steel-rimmed spectacles was the face of a cold, imperious warrior.

'Of course, sir.'

'I don't see any possible movement taking place without the exchange of a couple of crores. The point to be noted is that both sides need to be played against each other. That is the only way we can bring down their prices. We will switch our allegiance over to whichever side agrees to meet our demands,' Vikram added in a derisory tone.

The virulent contempt in his voice had not been lost on Rajan. His attention had already turned to perusing the national dailies. Rajan returned to his cabin feeling slightly rattled. Leelawati was a difficult customer, more so since the illness of her mentor. Abhijit Nath understood political strategy and knew how to make a point without behaving in a crass and aggressive manner. Leelawati's unpredictable style of functioning invariably created a host of new problems for all those around her. Her party was already being made to pay a heavy price, having allowed her to gain an unchallenged grip on the reins of power.

Picking up the phone, Rajan dialled Leelawati's direct number in Lucknow. Chandanbhan Singh picked up the phone.

'Give the phone to Behenji,' Rajan ordered.

'Right away, bhaiyaji,' said Chandanbhan. Picking up the phone, he carried it to Leelawati who was sitting in her bedroom watching the latest round of television news.

'Get out!' she told Singh after he had placed the phone on the bed.

'Behenji, the present government is trying to destroy your political base,' said Rajan.

'They are busy digging their own grave,' Leelawati snapped.

'They have lost their mental balance. Instead of allowing the local police to act, the Central Government decides to take matters in its own hands. Law and order is a state subject. If the Centre begins intervening in this fashion, how will a chief minister be allowed to function?' Rajan remarked.

Leelawati was at her most sarcastic. 'This home minister handpicks a sharpshooter all the way from Mumbai and packs him off to Hardwar. Obviously, he will not come here to sit on the Lakshman Jhula and perform the Shiva Arati. He will do what he has done all his life. He will hire his goons to shoot down those villagers in cold blood,' she retorted.

By now, she had a good idea why Rajan had called but she wanted him to spell it out.

'Are they deliberately trying to destroy your constituency?'

'They can try as much as they want. Whether they succeed or not is a different matter. Leelawati knows how to hit back at her enemies,' came her loud reply.

'Of course. Amir Singh is also upset at the manner in which that Yadav fellow was killed.'

'Bhaiya, leave Amir Singh out of this discussion. He is a troublemaker. He will not remain idle as long as I sit on the takht of Lucknow,' retorted Leelawati.

Rajan smiled. A mere mention of her arch enemy was enough to turn this woman into a hysterical mess.

'He has contacted Vikramji and is swearing he will withdraw support to the Centre. He does not want to alienate the Yadav community,' Rajan whispered.

Leelawati was not amused. 'He is the most corrupt politician I have met in my life. He makes all kinds of noises because he enjoys the support of the moneybags in Mumbai. We all know that he and his trusted lieutenant, are dancing to the tune of a few rich industrialists. These same moneybags have tried to patronize me in the past. I can see through their snobbery and disdain. I am a Dalit's daughter. I do not want the support of the upper castes. My people will rally round me when the time comes. No one can erode my support base.'

Leelawati was not a person to beat around the bush. 'Politicians have become greedy. No one can blame them. They have their own constituencies to nurture. If you want my MPs to support a no confidence motion, then you must be willing to pay. Each MP will demand a minimum of five crore rupees before he agrees to cast his vote.'

Rajan did a quick calculation. At these rates, she was hoping to make a clean Rs 50 crore out of this transaction.

'Didi, we can thrash out these details at a later point. You know we are always there to support your every endeavour.'

Leelawati was not willing to walk into a trap. 'I will think about it,' she said and slammed the phone down.

She buzzed for an attendant. Chandanbhan Singh hurried into the room.

'Find out from some of Amir Singh's MPs when he is planning to catch the next flight to Delhi. I must reach Delhi before him.'

Leelawati knew she must speak to Abhijit Nath and inform him about these developments. Sitting in New Delhi, he must also be following the enfolding political drama. She needed to know who was in the running for prime ministership. How favourably inclined would such an individual be towards her and her party?

**

A few minutes later Rajan's phone rang again. It was Mukul Singh, Amir Singh Yadav's deputy. Despite his slow, hesitant style of speaking, there was no hiding the triumphant tone in his voice.

'What a pleasure to hear from you after so long!' Rajan sounded his sincerest.

Mukul Singh wanted to express a strong sense of outrage at the recent developments. 'We have been deeply hurt by the latest developments in UP. Our brethren have been shot in cold blood and no political leader has raised his voice in support,' he said.

It was obvious he was expecting a sympathetic response. Rajan was only too willing to oblige.

'It was a great tragedy. But our paper has been in the forefront of this whole campaign. We were the first to report what happened,' Rajan said.

'Your paper chose to support that young Jano-Paro couple. You did not launch the campaign in order to support us.'

Rajan sounded peeved. 'The media is the third pillar in a democracy. My owner, Vikramji treats his job with great seriousness. We are here to expose every kind of wrongdoing. We cannot support caste killing but then, nor can we support cold-blooded murder. A government indulging in atrocities has no right to remain in office.'

Mukul Singh was mollified, but he refused to show it. 'I have already got in touch with Delhi. A lot of politicking has started and I have been contacted by several leaders belonging to all the major parties. My own leader, Amirji, will be willing to give his support to anyone who is committed to the development of Uttar Pradesh. We cannot allow the present corrupt dispensation to remain in place. That woman has emptied out the state's treasury. The government money is being squandered in developing Dalit villages and parks. In a country where people do not have jobs, scarce resources are being showered exclusively on Dalits. As though no other castes exist in this country.'

Mukul more than matched his short stature with a rare

ingeniousness of character, thought Rajan. He possessed an amazing network of political connections. Those close to him boasted about how his political connections were more than outmatched by his close links with criminals. It was these criminal connections which helped provide him with a decisive edge in many a political battle. No wonder no corporate house wanted to be on his wrong side.

'I agree with what you are saying. We are willing to go all out to support you,' said Rajan.

'You have to choose who you want to support. Let me rephrase what you have said. If we go along with you, you must be willing to support our long-term political objectives,' Mukul added.

'Of course,' said Rajan. 'I will convey all that you have told me to Vikramji. This government is going to fall sooner than later and you must be aware of who is going to become the next prime minister.'

Mukul smiled. He knew the names of some of the prominent contenders. Lobbying for the numero uno post had started in full earnest. He also knew that Vikram Aggarwal was trying to ensure one of his distant relatives was elevated to the post.

'I'll come and meet you in your house later this evening,' said Mukul and put the phone down.

Mukul straightened out his crimson red tie and then turned his attention to putting in place the folds of his stylish silk kerchief placed in his right coat pocket. Rajan had begun talking like any other moneybag. He knew how to tackle him. Any politician who could handle the vicious politics of UP could handle this smart alec.

**

Ananda Krishnan was not willing to hear any more excuses regarding the general incompetency of the civil service. Home minister L.K. Puri sat before him dressed as always in an impeccably cut safari suit albeit with a pink scarf placed around his neck to hide the creases around his neck. Today he wore a particularly grim expression on his face. They were joined shortly by the industry minister, I.M. Guru, who also hailed from Karnataka.

'I do not want a post mortem done. I've had enough of all that. I am surprised that, despite using our best resources, we are so totally incapable of completing what should have been a relatively straightforward task.' Ananda Krishnan was trying desperately to keep his tremulous voice under control. He closed his tired eyes. It was as though he were desperately trying to shut out the world.

A nervous-looking L.K. Puri had his official reaction ready for the occasion. 'SSP Seth had been sent with very specific instructions to apprehend those cattle thieves. Unfortunately, since that area has been witnessing a great deal of militant activity, Seth claims he resorted to taking those extreme measures as a form of self defence. I believe a judicial enquiry must look into the whole issue.'

Guru jumped off his chair. 'I cannot even begin to explain the ineptitude of the entire operation. If I had been even slightly aware of yesterday's operation, I would have had it spiked immediately.'

Puri was upset by this accusation. He had tried to warn Ananda Krishnan against the whole exercise. 'The situation in Muzzaffarnagar was going from bad to worse. The government had to act,' Puri retorted.

Just before entering the prime minister's room, Puri had been in touch, over the phone, with DIG Rameshwar Prasad in Lucknow. He had asked Prasad point blank if it was still possible to salvage the situation with some last minute arrests. Some criminals or Naxalites could be gunned down in the Terai to show just how much pressure the security forces were under.

Prasad had deliberately chosen to sound aggrieved.

'Sir, I was not even consulted when the Centre decided to launch such an operation. What can I say now? It was a grave error of judgement to bring SSP Seth across to Hardwar. He had, some years ago, been up for a transfer to UP. Knowing his reputation, I had the transfer spiked.'

Being a garrulous person, Prasad had to restrain himself from giving the home minister a mouthful. The whole operation had been botched up. At this stage, there was little the state police could do to salvage the situation.

'Where are the dead bodies of those criminals?' Puri had asked Prasad.

'They have been cremated. The ashes have been cast into the Ganges at Hardwar. We did not want to bring the ashes back to Shamli. Leelawati and her opponents would have descended there and created more trouble,' Prasad replied.

'What is the situation like in Shamli and in the surrounding areas?'

'Sir, the sarpanch Chowdhury Ram Lal and other members of his team are sensible people. They have already warned the locals to behave themselves. I personally made a recce to Muzzaffarnagar and warned Ram Lal to bring everybody in line. You can be assured on that front,' said Prasad.

Puri put down the phone in a thoughtful mood. He was right. The government's Achilles heel now lay in New Delhi and not in Lucknow. Well, he had managed to push through his son's proposal for the shoe factory. Ananda Krishnan had also made sure both his sons grabbed a power project each in Karnataka. Rumours were rampant that Guru had helped push through several industrial projects at concessional rates for his three boys.

Puri quietly made his way back to Ananda Krishnan's room. The two men were discussing a matter loudly in Kannada.

Puri had barely entered the room when Guru jabbed his forefinger angrily at him. 'I am sure the home minister is aware of the situation on the ground. With both the major players in UP having gone on an offensive, one of them will surely move a no-confidence motion against our government. You must be aware – or do you imagine you are part of the bureaucracy and so your job will never be on the dock – that we required Leelawati's support to remain in governance.'

Puri was not going to be ticked off by a mere industry minister. Looking Krishnan straight in the eye he said, 'I am willing to give my resignation in right now. I accepted this job only because of my respect for you.'

Krishnan coughed discreetly. 'This is not the time to start fighting with one another. We need to present a united face.'

Puri decided to remain quiet. He still needed Guru's signature on one or two files. 'The JD(D) has more than twelve members. We can try and win them over to our side,' Puri said plaintively.

Ananda Krishnan cleared his throat. 'The numbers game has tilted against us. We do not possess enough economic clout to buy these people over.'

Puri stared at Guru. 'What about the bigger industrial houses?'

'This relentless attack that Vikram Aggarwal conducted against my government during the last few weeks has left them all feeling shaky. They claim they no longer have faith in us,' the prime minister explained.

'This Aggarwal fellow has been playing a very dangerous game. From when has he become a king maker?' Puri cried out indignantly.

'He is not a king maker yet but he will soon become one. He is in a position to throw a couple of hundred crores around. The Janata Dal (D) will be the key component in this government. His uncle, who is just one member in this ridiculous coalition, will become prime minister. As a reward for his anointment, the FERA cases against his father will be withdrawn. There must be many other skeletons in the *Sentinel* closet. They'll all be given a burial in the Arabian Sea. God help us,' Guru murmured.

'But his uncle has no political clout. He is not even a grass-roots man!' Puri cried, appalled.

'What does he have to lose? Especially since the largest opposition party, the Congress has informally indicated they are willing to support him,' broke in Guru.

'Why would Leelawati support someone like his uncle?' Puri asked indignantly.

'If she refuses to support him quid pro quo, he will get Amir Singh to give his support. Amir Singh will work out some arrangement. He will insist that Uttar Pradesh be placed under presidential rule for a couple of months. That will provide Amir Singh time to strengthen his presence and win over some independents. By whatever angle we choose to examine the present situation, we must understand, we have been checkmated,' said Krishnan in a voice of quiet despair.

There was a stunned silence in the room. Ananda Krishnan paced round the room. The trio sat and thrashed out the strategy they would work out in case the no-confidence motion was moved in the next twenty-four hours.

The meeting terminated an hour later. Word was sent out to the 65-member cabinet to assemble at 7 Race Course by five p.m.

Puri and the industry minister left separately. They did not exchange a word as they walked to their respective cars.

**

Professor Mangal Lal Gulati clad in a white safari suit, sat gracefully on a cuhioned bamboo chair and surveyed the vast expanse of garden that spread out before him in all its iridescent shades of emerald green. Large bougainvillea shrubs, ablaze with pinks and crimson reds, covered the front wall and gate.

The staggering gamble played out by his distant nephew with so much chutzpah was coming close to fruition. From the morning, several political leaders had come calling on him.

Initially, he had been taken aback. These developments had been unexpected. Politicians learn fast and the older the politician, the faster he learns.

Gulati spent the day in his front verandah, greeting all his visitors in his soft, courteous manner. Many of the visitors had gently questioned the suitability of his selection. But he was no novice. From being a small-time corporator, he had entered public life by winning an MLA election on a Congress ticket. The rise of the Sanjay Gandhi brigade and Indira Gandhi's decision to impose the Emergency had forced him to move to the Janata Dal. Unfortunately, the Janata Dal had proved to be a shaky alliance and, within, two years of his joining it, it had broken into four disparate parts. But today, he was determined to make all the correct moves.

He had got his Punjabi contractor friends to hurriedly put together a veritable circus outside his house. Groups of bhangra dancers and paid musicians had ensured that a long line of garland and bouquet-holding people continued to drift in all through the day.

The following day, both Leelawati and Amir Singh Yadav issued statements in favour of Gulati. Leelawati issued hers in the morning. Amir Singh Yadav's followed shortly afterwards.

Yadav's was a brief statement claiming that a consolidation of secular vote was required to out manipulate the communalist forces trying to gain power in the country.

Gulati showed no surprise at having received the support of two mutually antagonistic parties. A sea change had taken place in the mood of the nation. The public, led by the intelligentsia, was willing to lend its support to a Punjabi leader who had never fought an election in his life.

He had never courted Vikram Aggarwal who was related to him through his sister's husband. They held each other in affectionate esteem, meeting at family functions and, occasionally, over a high powered corporate lunch. If Vikram had decided he could help ensure a change in governance, he was hardly in a position to refuse such an offer.

Gulati's wife, Ratna, a Kashmiri Brahmin, who wrote novels and plays in her spare time, hovered around the guests, offering them tea and cake. Many of her friends had dropped in to get a firsthand confirmation on whether the rumours milling around the city were actually true. The crowds outside their home helped dispel their doubts.

The atmosphere inside the Gulati home was equally festive. A television was blaring the news from one of the bedrooms. Occasional shrieks and screams of excitement could be heard emanating from the other rooms. Gulati's sisters and their children had come in person to congratulate him.

Jayant Shah, Vision Forever's chairman, was one of the first media mughals to ring up and congratulate him. Gulati beamed with joy to hear his voice. Shah's father and he had been good friends.

'You did an excellent job of that coverage in Hardwar. You have the heart of a lion – just like your father,' Gulati gushed.

'Congratulations sir! Finally we will have a prime minister who is both educated and can speak for the middle class,' Shah said. What he did not say was that he was unhappy at the way other media companies were using his coverage of the Hardwar killings. Vikram Aggarwal nursed expansionist designs. He would now use his good offices with his kindly uncle to ensure he was given a licence to launch a slew of channels thereby hitting out at him.

'Thank you. You will have my complete cooperation. When will you come to see me?' Gulati replied.

'Sir, I will come whenever you choose to have me over. You can start by giving an exclusive interview to my star editor, Ajay Singh.'

'No problem. The details can be coordinated with Vinayak, my secretary.'

Just then Dalip Jha rang up Gulati. Dalip had been a cub reporter when Indira Gandhi had declared the state of Emergency. Dalip had reached his house early in the morning and wanted a detailed interview with him.

'You can come any time in the afternoon,' Gulati told Dalip.

Tim Robertson called soon after.

'My goodness! I think I should hold a press conference,' Gulati told himself. He must see this bloke. A London paper would help him put across his views on foreign policy. He had called all the press journalists to meet him at five p.m.

The phone rang yet again. Tania Mittal of *Swadesh* had also phoned to congratulate him. She and her father were not oblivious to Vikram Aggarwal's proximity to Gulati. She was now in possession of a weapon that could turn this proximity around. The Swiss bank account numbers given to her by Ramesh Tewari had been forwarded to two of her most reliable bankers. They had got these numbers cross-checked by their contacts abroad and certified that they did indeed pertain to a leading bank with branches in all the key cities of Europe. She would wait for this political hue and cry to die down before she went public with the numbers. Vikram would be forced to duck for cover and the newly installed prime minister would perforce have to distance himself from at least this particular friend.

Gulati sat down for a leisurely lunch with his family.

Post lunch, he was planning to take a brief nap when Vikram Aggarwal, escorted by Rajan and Sudershan, arrived unannounced.

Vikram's mouth tightened in disapproval when he saw Gulati's nieces and nephews sitting around him cracking jokes. He did not approve of any display of familial affection.

Seeing him, a smiling Gulati immediately got up and walked

into the study. Vikram followed him in. Rajan and Sudershan waited in the front verandah. Not one of them had the courage to ask Ratna Gulati if they could be allowed to wait inside the air-conditioned living room.

The meeting between the two men was brief. Gulati knew Vikram was spending a great deal of money to ensure he get elected. His desperation for this changeover had been a matter of surprise for him.

Rich men went to any length to buy what they required. Politicians in turn had learnt to rely on their generosity. But the hallmark of a statesman lay in never showing his cards to anyone. So, Gulati refused to show even an iota of gratitude towards Vikram Aggarwal. He merely enquired about Papaji's health. After that, he allowed Vikram to do all the talking.

'I have only come here to pay my respects. How is Auntyji?' Vikram asked, his cool, measuring eyes trying to gauge just how indebted this old man would be towards him.

Ratna, eyes flashing, had entered the room followed by a bearer carrying a tray of cold drinks.

Gulati looked boldly at Vikram. He was sitting before a man who had no moral scruples. He too had learnt that moral scruples were not required in politics. Without pretending to possess them, it was impossible to rule such a large nation. He hoped this dichotomy could be bridged in the near future.

In a stern tone Gulati said, 'A huge responsibility has been placed most unexpectedly on my shoulders. I hope they can bear up to the weight.'

Vikram decided to keep the talk general. 'Uncleji, you have been in politics for the last fifty years – '

'Fifty-five to be precise.'

'You have seen India partitioned and then come together again as a nation. We now need to update its history and bring it in sync with the modern times,' said Vikram.

Gulati pretended to be surprised. 'What are you referring to?'

'All these outdated laws. The lack of freedom given to industrialists to expand.'

'Of course. Antiquated laws must be changed. We will treat this matter with priority.'

'To give you an example of antiquated laws – our Telegraph Act has not been changed for over a hundred years.'

Gulati smiled. 'When the British left India, only a handful of our cities had roads and electricity. You cannot say that we have made no progress.'

Ratna hated all these unnecessary shenanigans. She put her arms around Vikram, 'My dearest boy!' she cooed.

Vikram recoiled as though he had been hit by a hammer.

But Ratna insisted on holding onto his hand and saying, 'Mera pyara beta! Mera pyara beta!'

Getting up from the chair, Vikram said, 'Uncleji, I will be in touch with you. I am leaving my direct numbers with Vinayak. He should be in touch with Rajan and Sudershan.'

Gulati gave him an affectionate handshake and sent him off.

Vikram stepped out of the room and almost bumped into Ajay Singh standing near the door with his cameraman and sound technician. A look of recognition passed over his face. For a minute it seemed as though he was about to say something. He changed his mind and strode away without a word.

Dalip Jha was standing at the other end of the room. He lit a cigarette.

'When he needs us, he talks to us; when he doesn't need us, he pretends we do not exist. Our owners are the masters of our destinies and we do not even exist for them,' said Dalip.

'It's all the same,' said Ajay philosophically.

'He's ensured his uncle gets the top job. He doesn't have to worry about anything else,' said Dalip bitterly.

'That's all right. If it is not his uncle then it would have been somebody else's uncle,' Ajay Singh said with a sigh.

'We do so much for these guys. We sweat and die for them. Your shots created such a storm!' exclaimed Dalip.

Ajay said nothing. In his long career as a journalist, he had broken several outstanding stories. People knew about him. This did not mean he was immune to being sacked or pushed around like any other bloke. Each pathbreaking story had carried its own inner momentum. It created a sensation and then, in the coming weeks, was overtaken by another earth-shattering event. Little changed on the ground. The country continued to amble along in its elephantine fashion; the public remained indifferent to the morass they were surrounded by.

Gulati walked into the room and shook hands with both Ajay and Dalip. 'I'm sure both of you do not mind doing the interview together?' he asked.

Just then Tim Robertson walked in looking extremely confident. Robertson had now begun to believe that he could take credit for having helped topple a Third World government. This was no mean achievement. It would look great on his resumé.

'You are also welcome to join us,' said Gulati cordially.

Tim was not happy with the arrangement but decided not to protest. Although they had all travelled together to Panchavati, Tim had not bothered to acknowledge the presence of either Ajay or Dalip.

The interview turned out to be a fluff job. Gulati refused to be pinned down to saying anything specific. He talked sweet generalities about all the influences in his life including his widowed mother who had been a freedom fighter from Jammu.

When the cameras stopped, he turned to the three journalists with an apologetic air. 'The no-confidence motion has not even been moved in the house. There is no point in making a premature statement. I agreed to meet you only because you are such good friends of mine,' he said, sounding cautious.

Ratna hurried into the room carrying some chocolate cake. She seemed a more decisive person than Gulati.

All three journalists walked out feeling disappointed. One of the main reasons why the country remained in this lackadaisical state was because puny men were made to occupy chairs of enormous power. Instead of making this land a place of infinite hope and possibility, they had ensured it remained a dungeon, devoid of all hope.

Turning to Tim Robertson, Dalip said, 'I broke the Shamli killing story. I was the first journalist to go there.'

Robertson ignored the remark. Indian journalists were in the habit of making tall claims, he told himself.

'Damn foreigner!' Dalip said loud enough for Tim to hear. 'Doesn't know a word of Hindi and then imagines he can teach the monkey how to dance. We know how to waltz and foxtrot! We also know how to do Kathakali!'

For a moment Tim Robertson looked embarrassed. His embarrassment soon gave way to anger. This fellow had no business being insulting because Tim was getting all the credit for breaking the story.

The three men were walking towards their cars parked outside Gulati's Willingdon Crescent house when a young Jawaharlal Nehru University activist walked up to them and handed them a protest note.

Ajay Singh read the note carefully.

> After forty-eight years of independence, 27 per cent of MPs have become crorepatis; 50 per cent have fify lakh rupees assets per person; 10 per cent have assets worth less than ten lakh rupees;
>
> One in four MPs has criminal records;

One in two MPs is reported to have outstanding debts to public financial institutions amounting to Rs 41.3 crore;

The per minute expenditure of the Lok Sabha is Rs 15,700 – This works out to a cost of nearly seventy-five lakhs a day.

By contrast, 26 per cent of the country lives below the poverty line and 35 per cent of the people are living on less than one dollar a day. India's position has slipped from 124 to 127 in the Human Development Report (HDR) in 1997 out of 188 countries.

Is this a matter of concern or not? Whose interest is our elected representative pursuing? Have we become complacent? If not, we need to join hands and implement the preamble of the constitution.

Ajay read the piece of paper and decided to file it away carefully once he returned to his office.

Dalip Jha gave it one quick look and chucked it on the road. 'These jholawallahs go on and on with the same old rubbish! Better to move with the happening crowd,' he told himself.

He stared enviously at Ajay getting into the new Ambassador car given to him by his office. He needed to act fast otherwise he would be stuck with a Fiat for the rest of his life.

'Hey Ajay! Hold on a sec!' Dalip cried running after him.

Ajay saw Dalip waving desperately at him. He asked the driver to halt the car.

'What is it?' he said rolling down the window.

'I just want to have a word is private with you. Do you want to join me for a drink at the Press Club in the evening?'

'No. By the time, I wind up at office, it's past eleven p.m.'

Getting down from the car, he walked up to Dalip. 'What's on your mind?'

'I'm fed up of newspaper journalism. It stinks. I want to move into TV. I think there is much more scope there.'

'I'm still learning the ropes,' Ajay said staring at Dalip's large beer belly.

Dalip rubbed his stomach apologetically. 'I need to get rid of that. Television does not want fat correspondents.'

Ajay grinned. 'You'll have to get rid of a lot of other things as well.'

Dalip's mind raced over the recent events of his life. His three attempts at marriage had ended in failure. When he married for the first time, he had imagined his wife would symbolize the highest ideals of womanhood. She would be the fulcrum around which his happiness would turn. She had turned out to be a sullen marionette, unable to voice an opinion on any subject under the sun. His second wife married him and then found everything about him down market. Their marriage lasted six weeks. Simi, he had imagined, would combine the best in terms of the Indian and western traditions of womanhood. The fact that she hadn't hesitated to have him and his mother arrested had shattered his trust in women. After such an experience he could only believe the worst.

Simi had arrived at work earlier that day. An ironic smile flickered on Inder sahib's face as she returned his greeting. She arched an eyebrow contemptuously at Dalip. They had not found happiness together, though they had expected so much. Dalip tried to remember the best moments he had spent with her. He could not think of any: he could remember only the pain she had inflicted upon him.

Simi too remembered only the pain. She had lain awake the night before, preparing for the moment she would be face to face with Dalip. She too had married expecting a great deal. A husband and a wife should be a source of joy for each other. It had not worked out like that. He had taken everything from her; her reputation, her family's reputation and had left her with a child growing inside her womb. Rita Sawhney had already told her on the phone that Dalip and Kiki were not speaking to each other. It didn't matter; Simi no longer wanted to work in this office where she would be running into him all the time. Dalip had also decided to move on.

'I promise to turn over a new leaf.'

Ajay was not sure whether Dalip would fit into Vision Forever. Maybe he was being too cautious. He could not boast of having had a formal training in television either.

'Come over to my office tomorrow with your bio-data. I'll introduce you to the boss.'

Dalip could not believe his good fortune. His life was about to change all over again.

Journalists had the gift of the gab. Every one of them possessed nine lives. No, not really. Maybe they possessed many more than just nine lives. The Hindu theory of reincarnation claimed every individual had to constantly reinvent himself in order to achieve nirvana. He did not want another lifetime to taste success. He was going to do well in this lifetime, or so he would like to believe.